FATHER FIGURE

A thought-provoking novel of modern fatherhood...

Jason Kirk believes he is happily married until he returns home one day to find that his wife has left him, taking their two young children with her. Suddenly Jason finds the role of father denied him. The law is weighted against him and his wife produces a series of excuses to withhold contact with Jake and Leah. Jason not only has to face the pain of loss but also has to endure the misery of persecution by the Child Support Agency – and he discovers that among friends and colleagues are others in the same situation.

FATHER FIGURE

FATHER FIGURE

by

Ann Widdecombe

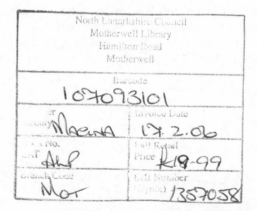
Magna Large Print Books
Long Preston, North Yorkshire,
BD23 4ND, England.

British Library Cataloguing in Publication Data.

Widdecombe, Ann
    Father figure.

    A catalogue record of this book is
    available from the British Library

    ISBN   0-7505-2443-X

First published in Great Britain 2005 by Weidenfeld & Nicolson

Published in Large Print 2005 by arrangement with
Orion Publishing Group

Magna Large Print is an imprint of Library Magna Books Ltd.

Printed and bound in Great Britain by
T.J. (International) Ltd., Cornwall, PL28 8RW

For my brother, Malcolm, a devoted father

AUTHOR'S NOTE

Although the events in this book take place in Somerset, the schools, teachers, children, representatives of the Education Authority, officials of the Child Support Agency, and all other characters are entirely fictitious. They are not based, even loosely, on real people and should there be any similarity of name between someone in this book and someone in a similar occupation in Somerset that is purely coincidental.

1

Kat walked out between the Roman and Norman conquests. Jason knew this because she had rung him on his mobile as he was making his way to the staffroom having spent the last period before break explaining straight roads, mosaics, central heating and *veni, vidi, vici* to a Year Seven class which would never have any acquaintance with the Latin language nor read the works of Julius Caesar. As usual Nick Bright asked too many difficult questions and Terry Pepper daydreamed, spending the last five minutes of the lesson carefully colouring a toga in his workbook despite Jason's clear statement that togas were mainly white.

Kat's call had surprised Jason. She too taught and rarely rang him at school, being deeply critical of the use of mobile phones for what she described as idle chatter and wary of the possible effects on the brain. The second reason for his surprise was that the number on his screen was that of their home not her school or her own mobile. He was about to ask if she was all right when she forestalled him with an enquiry about the whereabouts of Jake's Harry Potter, which he had confiscated at midnight after his eight-year-old son had started reading in the forlorn hope that his light would not be noticed once his parents had gone to bed.

Jason might have wondered what had prompted such a query in the middle of the working day if he had not been so preoccupied with the need to locate one of his colleagues in the short time allowed for break. He replied that he could not remember but that he would look for it after school, sensing that Kat found this frustrating. Any puzzlement he might have felt was immediately forgotten as he glimpsed his fellow teacher and hurriedly set off in pursuit.

He did not think about this conversation with his wife until just after lunch when he was in the middle of describing the Bayeux Tapestry. The girls winced as King Harold received an arrow in the eye but some of the boys looked mildly interested for the first time during the lesson. For some reason he suddenly recalled where he had put the Harry Potter and rang Kat between classes. When she answered her mobile it was obvious she was using the hands-free kit in her car. This time he did ask what was going on. Why wasn't she at school and was that the kids he could hear in the background? She said, 'Tell you later' and rang off.

On Tuesdays he returned home late because the history club met after school and today it took longer than usual because the pupils were practising an archaeological dig in a nearby field which was being excavated for development. The finds were minimal, had no historical significance and caused a great deal of merriment.

Nick Bright was studying a halfpenny. 'It says 45 BC, sir. Do you think Julius Caesar dropped it?'

'I am more interested in who made it. He must have been a clairvoyant if he knew when Christ was going to be born.'

Amid the laughter Jason noticed one or two disappointed faces. Surely they hadn't fallen for so obvious a joke? He looked at his watch and decided it was time they went home.

Collecting a set of Year Twelve essays from the classroom, he made his way to the car park, vaguely noticing the few remaining vehicles: a Fiat belonging to a young drama teacher, the sports coach's Ford Focus, a battered Vauxhall Estate in which Ed Deacon, head of geography, used to bring his older children to school. Ed's wife had left him a year ago, taking the children with her, and now the geography teacher delayed his return home for as long as possible each evening.

The car of Angus Gaskill, the deputy head, stood in front of the school under the sign saying 'Reception'. Jason did not need to look at the space beside it to know it was empty. The head, Ralph Hillier, only stayed late for meetings of the governors, leaving parents' evenings and other functions to his deputy. Ten years ago pupils went to Oxford from Morton's, now applications were falling year on year and the arrival of children such as Nick Bright was greeted with sarcastic speculation as to whether anyone had told their parents that there were other schools in the area. The police came to the school several times a week. Hillier was focused on his retirement, now less than eighteen months away, and the rest of the staff were waiting for it to happen before deciding what to do next.

Not everyone had given in to the malaise and those who still had hope and energy left tried to stimulate and inspire, drawing closer to each other as they pooled their efforts. No one contradicted them or made any overt attempt to cool their enthusiasm, simply meeting their ideas with shrugs rather than argument. Their numbers dwindled each term as some left for other schools or, in two cases, other professions. Kat had nagged Jason to follow their example and he had talked, without originality but with much conviction, about rats and sinking ships. Kat too had shrugged but with impatience rather than resignation.

Jason put the pile of essays and his jacket on the back seat of the Astra and his boots, muddy from the archaeological exercise, on the floor behind the driver's seat. As he was about to get in the front he heard his name called and looked up to see Angus Gaskill approaching from the main entrance. He stood by the open car door and watched warily as the deputy head walked towards him. He was conscious suddenly of fatigue and was unwilling to be further delayed.

'Just had Social Services on the phone. They're taking the Beggs children into care.'

Jason's heart sank. Chrissy Beggs was in his form and already disruptive to the point of having been twice suspended. He had tried to persuade Hillier to exclude her and believed that the head was close to agreeing but now he knew that he would decide to wait and see how the new domestic arrangements worked.

'Why?'

'Mister is in prison and Missus injecting heroin.'

'So what's new?'

'The disappearance of the three-year-old for an entire afternoon. Mother was too spaced out to notice and it only came to light when said child wandered into the path of a car.'

Jason shuddered. 'My God!'

'It's OK. The driver managed to stop but he was pretty shaken.'

'I suppose they'll want reports?'

Gaskill gave a sympathetic grin. 'Yes, sorry. The good news is that the nearest relation lives in Blackburn so it may become Lancashire's problem rather than Somerset's. I wouldn't shed any tears.'

'No, but I wouldn't uncork the Champagne either. The relative may not take them.'

'Not if he or she has any sense.'

The callous, careless words lingered on the air. Even Gaskill was becoming disillusioned, thought Jason sadly. They all were. The Beggs children were merely nuisances, not small beings to be pitied and helped. If Chrissy and her brothers got through the day without misbehaving it was as much as their teachers asked; whether they were also happy or had absorbed even the most minimal information were not questions which would actively preoccupy those who saw to their education.

Gaskill read his thoughts. 'I'm getting too old for it all.'

'So am I and I'll be thirty-two next month.' Jason climbed into his car and looked up at the deputy head. 'Don't let it get to you.'

'Ghastly American expression.'

'Is it?'

'Totally ghastly and also illiterate, but you teach history not English so I don't suppose it matters.'

'I meant, is it American? Anyway Matt Johnson tells me he doesn't teach much grammar any more. Not enough time for it in the curriculum.'

'That doesn't stop me. Not that they let me do much teaching now. It's all paper, paper, paper, targets, statistics and meetings. Not for much longer though.'

Jason, who had been wondering how to cut the conversation short and who had inserted the ignition key as a hint, now looked up sharply. 'Not for much longer?'

'No. I'm not applying for Ralph's job next year and I'm not staying in this one either. I'm going early.'

'Will they let you?'

'I shan't be giving them a choice in the matter.'

'What about your pension?'

'It will do. My parents left me money and Elizabeth will have a pension too. Anyway I can always try to teach in the private sector for a couple of years. I haven't told anybody else so keep it under your hat for a while.'

Gaskill gave the roof of the car a pat of farewell and stood back to let Jason drive away, leaving him unsure as to whether he should actually do so. He wondered if Gaskill wanted to be argued out of his proposed course of action, if he wanted to talk, if the fate of the Beggs children were not the real reason the deputy head had stopped him leaving, but when he looked in the mirror Gaskill was already walking back into the school.

Relieved, Jason let his thoughts turn to home.

16

He would still arrive in time to read to Leah and have supper with Kat and Jake. The essays on which he had already made a start would only take a couple of hours after that. On the way he stopped at Oddbins and bought a bottle of Jacob's Creek. It had not been an easy day and Kat had sounded fraught when she had rung him earlier.

It was not the absence of Kat's car from the side of the house or the unlit windows which told him what had happened: it was the silence. The stillness he felt as soon as he entered his home, *their* home, was not that of temporary absence but of emptiness, taking Jason back twenty years when he had walked into his great grandmother's house after her funeral. Twelve years ago he had returned to the flat he shared with his student girlfriend and had known she was not coming back even before he saw the note on the kitchen table, carefully placed between his knife and fork as if she had measured the distance and straightened the envelope with a plumb line. It might have been a statement of finality, of careful thought, of an orderly departure, or maybe she had stood there, uncertain, her hand still on the letter while she pushed it into place, adjusting it, lining it up because she did not want to let go.

Now he stood in the hall and switched on the light, uncomforted by its yellow beam, untouched by the warmth of the central heating, cold with shock, numb with fear, seeing everywhere the evidence of desertion even as he mentally denied it. There was no pushchair in the hall, no schoolbag carelessly dropped, no boots by the back door, which he could see through the kitchen. In the hall cupboard were no coats or jackets or waterproofs but his own.

Foolishly he still hoped as he entered the other rooms, searching in each for some contrary sign, some flood of reassurance, some wakening from the nightmare. Instead he found, as he had known he would, only the misery of confirmation, the chill of certainty. Kat had not found the time or the space in the car to take everything from the children's rooms yet they already looked empty, dusty, abandoned, as if their occupants had left long ago. In the room he had shared with Kat a screwed-up tissue with lipstick stains lay on the otherwise bare dressing table. Lipstick stains, not tear stains, thought Jason. Kat had been thinking about her appearance as she left him.

What had she told the children? Had she said they were going away for a little while, a big adventure in the middle of the school term, or had she told them the truth? We are leaving Daddy. You won't be able to see him every day any more. He won't be living with us.

There should be a law against it. That sentiment up till now had been a family joke, a superior distancing of the small unit of Kirks from those who could use the statement and mean it. Even Jake had taken to uttering the words with smug amusement especially when commenting on Leah's three-year-old antics. Now Jason found himself at a loss to understand why what had happened to him was allowed to happen, though he was scarcely aware of the question forming in his mind beneath the turmoil of shock and denial.

The telephone shrilled and he sprang to it. 'Kat?'

There was a brief but discernible pause on the other end of the line. 'No, it's me. Is anything wrong?'

'No,' he lied as he wondered what to tell his mother. Eileen Kirk was a worrier who doted on her grandchildren and he would need to work out how and when to tell her that full-time parenthood had suddenly been snatched from him, without explanation, without a quarrel. Despair made him want to be cruel, to devastate as he had been devastated, to say, 'Kat has walked out' and to listen to her reaction, but he did not do so because her response would inevitably be, 'Why?' and he had no answer.

The momentary anger was succeeded by deep misery as he realised he could not protect his mother for much longer, that she must know. Three months a widow, she must now face a son's broken marriage. He could no more shield her from life's spears than she had been able to shield him as he passed from childhood to adulthood. Although relations between her and Kat had always been perfectly cordial they had never progressed to warmth in the way his friendship with Kat's parents had and he knew that she would hate her access to Jake and Leah resting on the goodwill of her daughter-in-law.

For now he must be content to deceive. 'Kat is out somewhere and I was wondering if she wanted me to do anything about supper.'

'Oh. It sounded more urgent. Is my little Jakey there?'

Jason's teeth automatically prepared to grit at the diminutive but tonight pity replaced irritation. 'Sorry, no. They're both with Kat.'

'Well, ask him to ring me when he gets back.'

'I'll do that.' He knew he was playing for time, to find some way of minimising the pain. When his mother did not receive Jake's call she would ring back and by then he would have had time to think. Some dim recognition flitted across his mind that he was postponing not her misery but his own, that he was refusing to confront what had happened, that he wanted urgently to end the conversation not so that he could order his thoughts but to avoid them altogether.

'Dear, you do sound a bit distracted. Are you sure there's nothing wrong? Anything I can do?'

'No. Look, I've got something I must do right now but I'll get Jake to phone as soon as I see him.'

As soon as I see him. Would his mother notice the odd phraseology, that he had not said 'as soon as he gets in'. Would it in some ill-defined way give her an inkling of the truth, some vague preparation for what he would soon say?

After he had replaced the receiver on its rest, which lay on top of a small pile of books on the bedside table, Jason lay back on the bed, waiting for the despair and disbelief to subside, knowing they would not. Somewhere, deep within his stomach, his heart, his soul, a small cold knot waited to explode.

He knew of no unhappiness on Kat's part. They had been married for ten years and he still loved her. Until just under an hour ago he had thought the feeling fully reciprocated. Fruitlessly he

20

searched for clues to what had happened and found none. They rarely rowed and when they did the storm passed fairly quickly. It occurred to him now that perhaps he had been too complacent, had taken his marriage too much for granted, but if so then there had been no warning signals that he could recall.

He was surprised to find himself prowling the room in circles, having no recollection of rising from the bed or of what he had been thinking. He glanced at the clock. Two hours ago he had been turning into his drive, his mind on Angus Gaskill. Two hours ago desertion was something that happened only to other people, to the Ed Deacons of this world not to the Jason Kirks. Two hours ago he could pity from afar.

The two hours became three and Jason had twice thought he was hearing Kat's car turn into the drive when the telephone rang again. He picked it up reluctantly, preparing to tell his mother the truth, to absorb her distress and her questions, to prevent her making any precipitate journey from Dorset.

'Jason? I'm sorry. I know it must have been a shock but I didn't want a scene, especially with Jake and Leah there.'

He found he was shaking though now it was with anger not grief.

'Why? What have I done to you or the children that I deserve this?'

'Nothing. It's just not the same any more.'

'Is there someone else?' He heard the fear in his own voice as he suddenly grasped at the only explanation which might make any sense.

'No, no one at all. It's just not the same.'

'Where are you?'

'I can't tell you yet. I don't want you coming here until the children are settled.'

'For God's sake, Kat, they're mine too. You can't just take them and not tell me where they are.'

'I will tell you, but not now. If you need me I'm still on the same mobile. I'm sorry, Jason, really sorry. The last thing I wanted to do was hurt you.'

Alice in Wonderland, thought Jason, Alice in bloody Wonderland. He listened to the dialling tone for some seconds before accepting that Kat had cut the connection. Almost immediately the phone rang again and he answered its summons to explain why his son would not be able to talk to his grandmother that evening.

Much later he found himself back in the bedroom, swaying towards the bed, unsolaced by the concentration he had forced from himself to address the Year Twelve essays, by the routine of preparing and clearing up a meal he did not eat, by the overindulgence in red wine for which, never having been able to hold an excess of drink, he knew he would pay in the morning.

In the bathroom he had looked around at the emptiness, at the space where Leah's huge cat-shaped sponge used to sit, at the slightly dirty shelf where Kat had kept her make-up, at the bare corner where the bath met the wall and which used to be occupied by Jake's plastic battleship. Once in bed he pulled the duvet over his head to shut out the silence.

The same silence woke him before the alarm clock had a chance to do so and he sat up abruptly, sure that he had overslept, that everyone else had already left for school. As his memory suddenly supplied the true explanation he sank back, not wanting to get up at all, eager only to shirk the day ahead and to withdraw from the complexities thrust upon him from a new and unwelcome routine. He pushed back the duvet and placed his unwilling feet on the carpet. A warm, furry body began to weave around his ankles and he looked down in surprise.

If he had thought about the cat at all he would have assumed Kat to have taken it, reasoning that Jake would never have agreed to leave it behind. It came to him now that Objubjub's presence must mean that Kat had found only a temporary base, that she must be postponing the removal of her son's pet until settled somewhere permanently. There was of course another explanation but this did not occur to him.

'So where were you last night?' Jason bent down to stroke the animal's head. 'Come on; breakfast.'

His own breakfast would be Alka Seltzer, he thought ruefully as he went downstairs, trying not to fall over Objubjub, aware that normally he ran down lightly and today walked with all the reluctance of Jake when called from his computer to accompany his mother to the shops.

In the kitchen he opened the cupboard where the cat food was kept and was surprised to see so low a supply, but it was only when he hunted in vain for a bowl that he realised that Kat had not intended to leave the animal after all. She had packed feeding bowls and a sufficient supply of food. Presumably when the moment of departure arrived Objubjub could not be found or had resisted being put in the pet carrier and had escaped.

Jason went out into the hall and looked in the cupboard under the stairs, the one Kat always referred to as 'the glory hole'. The pet carrier was missing. His brain worked slowly towards the only explanation. Objubjub had been taken with the children and had made his way back to the only home he knew, which in turn meant that Kat was nearby, that the time which had elapsed before she rang him the previous night had been calculated to mislead him into thinking she had just completed a long journey, or perhaps she had delayed calling out of cowardice or until the children were in bed and he had subconsciously arrived at the wrong conclusion.

When his shaving was interrupted by the telephone Jason went to answer it not in the bedroom but in the hall where the screen showed the caller's number. He wrote it down as Jake's words came tumbling out.

'Dad, is Objubjub there? He got out of the bathroom window last night.'

'It's OK. He's here. Where are you?'

'At Mrs Mackenzie's. Dad, I don't want to leave–'

A click on the line announced the lifting of an extension.

'Jake, I told you not to bother Daddy. Objubjub will be all right. Now hurry up and get dressed. Say goodbye to Daddy and put the phone down.'

'Mum, Objubjub's gone home. I want to go home–'

There was a sob from Jake before the line went dead and, for the first time since realising his family had left him, Jason felt tears in his own eyes. The children would have been as unprepared and bewildered as he. He must stop this folly for their sake and he must stop it now.

He raced upstairs and made a cursory finish to his shave, pulled on his clothes and ran outside to the car. Mrs Mackenzie was Leah's childminder. She lived three miles away and Jake was not yet dressed. After half a mile he joined a traffic jam and cursed impotently, beating the steering wheel with his fist. He glanced at his watch. In half an hour Kat would have to leave for the primary school which Jake attended and where she taught but she might guess his intentions and leave sooner rather than later, relying on the unlikelihood of his creating a scene at the school. Afterwards he wondered at his simplicity in basing his plans on Kat's following a normal routine.

He felt a small tremor of relief as he saw Kat's Vectra outside Mrs Mackenzie's house. He was in time.

'I'm sorry, Mr Kirk, they've gone.' Alice Mackenzie looked not only embarrassed but regretful. She followed Jason's bewildered glance towards the Vectra and added, 'In the van.'

Jason could only nod dully when she asked him in. He sat at the kitchen table with his head in his hands while she made tea, her eyes full of anxious sympathy.

'Where have they gone?'

'I don't know – no, truly, I don't – but it can't be that far because Leah is coming back to me next week.'

Jason looked at her, trying to absorb what he was being told. Mrs Mackenzie was sixty-something, forty years older than most of the childminders they knew, and had also looked after Jake in his pre-school years. She herself was bringing up a twelve-year-old granddaughter whose father had walked out when she was two and whose mother had died four years later. Jason had always pitied the child, comparing her lot with the security enjoyed by his own children. Now their world too was being brutally shattered.

'I can't believe it's happening.'

'I'm so sorry.'

That was what everyone would say, thought Jason. It was what he had said over and over again the previous evening as he listened to his mother's heartbroken sobs before the end of their conversation left each in a pool of loneliness. It was what Kat had said when consigning ten years of marriage to the scrap heap; it was almost certainly what she had said to the children as she stole them from their father.

Horrified, Jason heard himself swear violently as a fresh tide of misery and bewilderment flowed into his heart.

'I'm so sorry,' he apologised to Mrs Mackenzie but she seemed perturbed less by the profanity than by the helpless, bitter laugh which followed his words. He got up from the table and thanked her for the tea, knowing that she wanted to say more but was constrained by awkwardness.

As he drove to Morton's he watched the parents taking their children to school, looking at everyday scenes with new eyes, envying, protesting, grieving. A young woman who looked scarcely out of her teens pushed a small girl of Leah's age in a buggy while two boys scampered beside her. A child of about eleven walked along with a large bag on one shoulder, holding a much younger child by the hand. A healthy-looking redhead in jeans and trainers urged on a group of five youngsters of assorted ages. Jason wondered if they all belonged to her or if she were helping out a neighbour. Then he saw the man.

He was tall with a shaven head and arms covered by tattoos. He wore jeans, a T-shirt and very dirty boots. Jason guessed that he was taking the children to school because he was unemployed and his wife was working or perhaps not yet up: the boy and girl looked none too clean. He watched the man say something to the boy and the lad respond with a huge grin, running jauntily alongside his father, happy, carefree, loved. The girl in the pushchair dropped a soft toy she had been clutching, a purple creation of indeterminate species, and the man stopped to retrieve it, ruffling her hair as he handed it back to her. Long after he had passed them Jason kept glancing back in the mirror.

He was often to think of them in the coming weeks, his mind showing him again a scruffy, tattooed man, a small mischievous boy and the infant girl in the pushchair with her earrings and too adult hairstyle. They had so little and so much.

He sought out a parking space in the school

grounds and found himself looking for Ed Deacon. Instead he saw Gaskill talking to two boys from Year Nine. Jason was reaching for the pile of essays in the back of the car when he began to focus on the deputy head's words.

'Ignorant ... basic grammar. It is not "like I do". It is "as I do".'

Jason paused in the act of retrieving the papers, listening incredulously. The pupils being berated were of an ability level just above special needs. He withdrew his head from the car and stared at the pair who were just then being dismissed. Gaskill greeted him briefly and walked after the boys towards the assembly hall.

'What on earth was all that about?'

Jason turned to see Carol Marsh, the newest recruit to the staff at Morton's. She taught food technology and resolutely refused to call it anything but cooking. 'Mum taught it too and called it domestic science and I learned it as home economics but Gran calls it cooking and Gran's right,' she had said. Even Hillier had looked amused.

'That,' said Jason, not sparing her, 'was the sound of our deputy head cracking up.'

Carol looked back at him, uncertain if he was serious. He could read her thoughts. *A time-serving head, the deputy having the next best thing to a nervous breakdown, an Ofsted inspection on the horizon, the doziest school in Somerset: what am I doing here?*

'Are you OK?'

It was not the response he had expected but he answered immediately, deriving satisfaction from the words.

'No, I am not. Yesterday I had a wife and two children and today I don't know where they are.'

Somewhere in the distance a car door slammed and the high voice of a young boy called out, 'Bye, Dad!'

The words hung in the air, a reminder of his loss, an eloquent description of his future. Jason turned towards the school and other people's children. Goodbye, Dad.

2

'Sir, I've found out how the Romans dated their coins.' Nick Bright joined Jason as he walked along the corridor to the staffroom and gave him an excited explanation.

Looking down at him, trying to take an interest in the child's recently acquired knowledge, Jason felt some of his tension dissolve. He wondered if Kat was able to concentrate today, whether Jake would settle to lessons, if Leah was crying.

'Where did you find out all that?'

'My dad's got this book on the antique world but I beat him to it on the net.'

'I suspect it's called the ancient world, but that's very good, Nick. Next time you really will be able to fool us that you've found a coin from Caesar's time or better still you might find a real one and be able to tell us the date.'

'Wow. Of course, they didn't put years on their

coins like we do but they did have years, sir. They added them all up from the beginning of Rome. Do you think we might find a coin, sir?'

Nick was clearly savouring the prospect and Jason pictured the scene in the Bright household with father and son racing each other for historical information. When Nick was discussed in the staffroom, often with nervous anticipation that his parents might move him to a school with a better position in the league tables, the standard joke was that he lived up to his surname but Jason thought not. Nick was not especially clever, sometimes struggling with maths and making banal points in class discussion, but he mopped up knowledge at a formidable rate.

His father was a lorry driver and his mother a dinner lady. The whole family was hugely enthusiastic about quizzes and rarely missed any of the large number of general knowledge contests which appeared on television: *Who Wants to Be a Millionaire?*, *The Weakest Link*, *University Challenge*, *The National Lottery*, anything. Jason had once taken Nick and his father home after history club when their car had broken down and had found a semi-detached house lined with floor-to-ceiling shelving, where bookclub editions of works of history, geography, science and nature fought for space with encyclopaedias and paperback quiz books. It was the sort of family which produced *Mastermind* contestants of whom viewers would exclaim, 'I don't believe he only drives lorries,' as if information were the exclusive preserve of the professions and City whizz kids.

Nick Bright would never become a doctor or a

lawyer, but if he persevered with subjects that relied largely on the accumulation of knowledge he would achieve the success which his enthusiasm deserved, despite having no more than average academic ability. Jason wished he could be as hopeful about many of the other pupils he taught.

In the staffroom he found Ed Deacon peering moodily into a cup of coffee.

'Ed, can you spare a moment later on? I need some advice.' His urgency caused several heads to turn in expectation of a drama but as the same heads turned away again Jason knew his colleagues had already guessed the nature of the counsel he was seeking.

Then every head suddenly faced the same direction as a torrent of profane abuse cascaded down the corridor. Jason, the nearest to the door, hurried outside to see Chrissy Beggs pinning Terry Pepper to the wall and screaming within an inch of his face.

'That's enough,' he called, less in the hope of persuading Chrissy to desist than in warning to other children who might be tempted to intervene. He advanced on the pair, surprised to see that Terry's eyes were full of puzzlement rather than fear, and tried to attract the girl's attention, preparing to intervene with force, the guidelines against doing so knocking insistently at his mind.

Chrissy turned on Jason, clawing, spitting, swearing, before his colleagues came to his aid. Jason let go as soon as he saw the other children had moved away and were in no danger. Then Gaskill arrived at the scene and Chrissy began to scream loudly, hysterically, maniacally.

Just another day at Morton's, thought Jason. They would have to exclude Chrissy now but it was Terry Pepper on whom his thoughts lingered. The child had shown no fear at all, seemingly unaware of any physical peril despite his being trapped against a wall by a screaming, violent virago. It was as if he did not regard the world about him as real.

Jason's misery nagged dully in the background as he discussed the Second World War with a GCSE class later that morning. One child gave a convincing rendering of an air raid warning, generating helpless mirth among the rest. At any other time Jason would have been amused but today he was irritated and the class looked surprised. He was glad when break arrived but Ed Deacon was nowhere to be seen and he had to contain his impatience until lunchtime when they sat together in Hillier's office, the head being at a conference for the afternoon.

'Try to agree on everything first, before the lawyers get their hands on it,' Ed was advising him. Jason looked out over the car park and freedom. 'Even then they'll try to persuade one or other of you that you could get a better deal. Their trade is greed.'

'I'm not at that stage yet, Ed. I want them back. Kat must get in touch some time.'

'That's when the trouble will start.' Ed's grief made him insensitive. 'She'll tell you the future as she sees it and it had better be how you see it too. She'll want the children and their keep and because she's a lawfully wedded wife she'll want you to maintain her too. If you agree to all of that she might very kindly agree to let you see your own children once a fortnight, so long as they're not ill or visiting her mother or on a school trip somewhere. You would be surprised how often there's a good reason not to let them see Dad.'

Jason absorbed Ed's bitterness while he wondered how to explain that it would not be like that between him and Kat, that they still loved each other, that even if they did break up permanently they would be civilised, that the children would not become pawns in a game of adult hatred. But a small, cold worm of doubt wriggled even as he resigned himself to comforting Ed instead of relying on the older man's counsel. He escaped as soon as he could to be alone, to plan.

Mrs Mackenzie had talked about Leah's returning to her care the following week, which presumably meant Kat was looking after her now, but it did not follow that Jake was off school. The following day he would go and see if he was there at lunchtime. The manoeuvre was just possible, given that Jason had a free period at the beginning of the afternoon. At least the idea offered some prospect of action, of regaining some small element of control over his madly tilting world. Meanwhile he must live in the uncertain present and leave his worries at the school gate, if he was not to add another failing teacher to Morton's dissolution.

Yet when he found himself once more at home that night he longed to be back at the school with its familiarity, predictability and order. Home had become an alien place, a land where all the green growth had dried up and withered into brown desolation, where an unnerving silence had replaced a reassuring hum, where he was not quite sure what to do because he suddenly had a series of choices where before he had followed, unquestioning, a comfortable, set routine. Tonight he would not be keeping an eye on Leah while Kat collected Jake from Cubs, would not be making sure that a dish was placed on the top shelf of the oven at two hundred and twenty degrees a quarter of an hour before his wife and son reappeared, would not be visiting his children's rooms to say goodnight before collapsing on a sofa with Kat and talking over their days.

Jason noticed immediately that someone had been in the house while he had been at work. In some indefinable way his home bore a different appearance, which he gradually identified as an increase in cleanliness and tidiness. The sink and surfaces in the kitchen gleamed more eagerly than when he had left that morning. The coffee tin, which he had left on the small pine table, was back in the row of matching tins lining the wall on the left of the sink.

Disconcerted, he recognised the evidence of the cleaning lady's twice-weekly visit and wondered what she had made of the changes in the house. Had Kat told her what she was going to do, had confided to Mrs Mansfield that which she was keeping from her husband? Or was the domestic helper as baffled as he had been by the sudden disappearance of nearly everything belonging to Kat and the children? Perhaps, he thought with bitter mirth, she had wondered at the absence of a note.

On reflection it was more likely that she worried about her job and he tried to work out the answer in his own mind to the question he must inevitably be asked. Certainly a bachelor would not require the same degree of support as a married man with a working wife and two young children so he supposed a single, separated male should take the same view. Separated. His mind rebelled against the very word. Separated. It was an admission of defeat. He at once decided to keep Mrs Mansfield on the same terms as before because it gave him some hope of a return to normalcy, of the return of his family.

It was an irrational decision, one that would have caused him to raise disbelieving eyebrows had it been made by somebody else, and he suspected it might be the first of many. Lonely, he switched on the news and tried to take his mind off his own woes by concentrating on the much greater catastrophes which now played before his eyes. At the end of the programme he could not have said what he had just seen and heard.

His mother rang at seven and told him she proposed to join him for the weekend. He responded with forced enthusiasm, knowing that he would have preferred the solitude he must learn to deal with, that her visit would postpone acceptance of his situation, that after she left he would have to begin the process of acclimatisation all over again. He thought of Kat's parents and wondered what they were making of it all and how much awkwardness would attend his next contact with them. It did not seem a question that required any immediate answer and he was disconcerted when he heard his father-in-law's voice on the telephone.

'Jason? It's Alex. This is a bad business. Sheila's devastated.'

'Do you know where she is?' The aggression in his own voice shocked him.

There was a pause. 'She'll get in touch soon. She told us she would but she wants to settle the children down first. It's been hard on them too.'

'That was entirely her own doing. There must be better ways to manage a split. Did she say why she's done it or is that something else which she promises to tell me in due course?'

Once more a few seconds passed before Alex Johnson responded. 'I can guess how you're feeling. We're just so sorry.'

You have no idea how I feel. You and Sheila have been married for nearly forty years. You raised your children together. The words were unsaid but they pulsated in Jason's head and, he suspected, also in Alex's.

'I know things are different these days,' began Alex cautiously, 'but–'

The cliché played on Jason's nerves, causing the simmering despair to boil over into a hot flood of angry words. 'Different? Do men love their children less *these days?* Do children not mind their parents splitting up *these days?* Is marriage as disposable as a Sainsbury's carrier bag *these days?* Is it no longer a big deal when a man comes home from work and finds his wife and children gone God knows where *these days?*'

This time he knew that Alex was using the silence to wonder how to end the call on a tactful note which left the door open for future contact. He knew he was being unfair and was mentally assembling words of apology when his mother-in-law began to speak.

'Jason, please don't be cross with us. You've no idea how upset we are about it all.'

'I know, but I can't believe it's happening. I just can't think what was going wrong. Kat always seemed happy enough.'

It was the question to which over the next few days he returned again and again, driven by his anguished, mental sob 'Why?' He searched wretchedly for clues he had missed and found them in unlikely recollections. When they had first met she had been Kath Johnson but friends from schooldays called her Kate. As she progressed from training college to her first job she began to call herself Katharine and none of her colleagues used a diminutive for fear of giving offence. When a few years earlier she had taken to Kat, her parents had observed that they never knew what to call their daughter. Jason had never accorded these changes, nor the insistence with which she introduced them, any significance but now he wondered if they were symptoms of restlessness, of a search for novelty, perhaps even for a new identity.

Jason had taught at Morton's for ten years, settling into professional life with the same steadiness he had brought to marriage. So long as his career progressed at a reasonable rate he was content to remain and, as the school declined, this intention was reinforced by the claims of moral obligation towards the children in his charge. Kat, by contrast, had twice changed school in that period and on neither occasion for reasons of promotion. She had talked a great deal about broadening her experience and until now Jason had never queried her motivation.

It would appear the marriage that he had thought founded on solid rock had foundered on the shifting sands of boredom, that he had been discarded as easily as a variation of a name, that he was as expendable as a past job, that what he now suffered was the price of Kat's restlessness.

It's not the same, Kat had told him. He was no longer new and exciting. It was the only explanation he could find.

'It's mad,' he told Objubjub as the cat sprang into his lap and his words sounded like pistol cracks in the silence.

'It's mad,' he said aloud to himself as he pulled up outside Jake's school the day after his conversation with his in-laws and realised that he felt as furtive as a criminal just because he was determined to see his own son.

'Hello, Mr Kirk,' called a boy who often came to the house to play with Jake.

'Hello, David. Have you seen Jake?' His eyes roamed the playground and he made his way through the gate in the direction of the school office. A teacher turned from helping a small girl who had fallen over and walked towards him.

'Jason!' she greeted him. 'What brings you here?'

Simultaneously David said, 'Jake doesn't come to this school any more, does he, Miss Cotterill?'

38

Jason came to a full stop, staring at the child without comprehension, not believing the words he had heard, trying to take in their meaning.

'Thank you, David. I'll take Mr Kirk in to see Mrs Acton. Come on, Jason, you look as if you could do with a cup of tea.' Daisy Cotterill looked anxious, although whether this was on his behalf or because she feared a scene Jason could not be sure.

Jason followed, feeling as bewildered as a small lost child, empty, adrift. His confusion gave way to anger as he heard the head's explanation. Kat had given in her notice at the end of the previous term and was, so far as Janet Acton now knew, a supply teacher near Frome. Normally the head would not have let her go until the end of this term but her replacement was an enthusiastic young teacher from the North who had moved to Trowbridge with her husband's job. She was available immediately and there seemed little point in forcing Kat to remain.

'And Jake?'

'She did not tell me till the last minute that she was taking him away. Although I knew she was leaving the school I did not know she was moving house as well and had no reason to believe that Jake would not continue here as before. Kat had said she would be doing supply but not where she would be doing it. I just assumed she was finding the demands of a full-time job and two small children too much to manage.'

'But you must know where Jake has gone. The receiving school would have asked for his record.'

Janet Acton looked embarrassed. 'I'm sure you

will understand that I cannot answer that question.'

Jason kept his voice level. 'No, I'm sorry, I don't understand. I am Jake's father and I have an absolute right to know where he is.'

'Mrs Kirk specifically said that I should not reveal Jake's whereabouts to anyone.'

Mrs Kirk, not Kat. The head was signalling that formality was about to replace sympathy as she prepared to take refuge behind the rule book.

'I am not anyone. I am his father. Anyway you have already told me it is somewhere near Frome.'

'I'm sorry, Mr Kirk. Your wife is the parent with care.'

Jason's control broke and he heard his voice rise. 'The parent with care? We aren't exactly divorced.'

The head responded sympathetically but without yielding, muttering about the best course being to consult a solicitor. *We are not at that stage yet.* Those words, which he had uttered to Ed Deacon as he mentally dismissed his plight as different from his own, now rang hollowly in Jason's brain. He rose to go.

Janet Acton saw him to the gate, doubtless grateful for his failure to persist, for his resigned, somewhat graceless farewell. On the way back to his own school he drove the car into a side road and sat staring through the windscreen as he faced the stark facts of his betrayal.

Kat had not acted on the spur of the moment. She had been planning her desertion for months. When they had chosen their next holiday, spreading out the brochures between them, debating destinations, she had known they would not be going together. When, only last week, she had booked Jake into another course of swimming lessons, she had known that he would not be taking it up. On Sunday evening she had peered into the freezer and announced that the children's favourite ice cream was about to run out when she knew they would not be there to enjoy any replacement. She had made love to him while planning the change of job and the removal van.

Betrayal, desertion, but above all finality. A woman who planned the break-up of her marriage as a general might plan a military campaign would not be coming back. He wondered if she was ashamed of her shamelessness, if the sheer magnitude of her deceit unnerved her, if that was why she would not yet face him. He imagined himself visiting every primary school within a ten-mile radius of Frome, searching for his son, before remembering that Leah was due to return to Mrs Mackenzie the following week.

That too could have been a deceit, designed to lure him into a false sense of security. Kat might already have rung the childminder to say that Leah was not coming back to her care but he could find out. He would let Monday pass without attempting to see Leah and then report sick on Tuesday morning. Mrs Mackenzie would not expect him to call in school hours. So he too was now planning lies and subterfuge. Disgusted but still resolute he began the drive back to school.

'Whatever have you been teaching young Bright?' asked one of the maths teachers as he walked into the staffroom. 'I came across him in break trying to explain the Roman dating system to Terry Pepper of all people.'

'I didn't teach him. He learned it all at home. If the truth be told I had half forgotten how it was done. What did poor Terry make of it?'

'Presumably not much but he was making a good job of looking interested.'

Jason smiled sadly and was aware of several members of staff looking at him covertly. He had not the energy to resent it.

The last period of the afternoon saw him once more teaching the Year Seven class which contained Nick Bright and Terry Pepper. He watched faces light up as he announced a trip to Bath to look at the Roman Baths.

'Just think, in two thousand and three we can still—'

'Two thousand, seven hundred and fifty-six, *ab urbe condita.*'

Jason broke off and stared at Terry Pepper who looked imperturbably back at him.

Nick Bright began a frantic sum on a piece of lined paper. 'Wow! He's right, sir.'

As the rest of the class turned to look admiringly at Terry, a cold flutter moved in Jason's stomach.

'Well done, Terry.' He studiously avoided mentioning any other year for the rest of the lesson but afterwards he took Terry aside.

'That was very clever of you to work out two thousand and three in Roman dating. Can you do any other years?'

The boy nodded matter-of-factly, showing no emotion, no pleasure at being praised. He looked up trustingly at Jason, who in turn looked round to make sure nobody was listening.

'Nineteen forty-five?'

'Two thousand, six hundred and ninety-eight, *ab urbe condita.*'

'Fifteen fifteen?'

'Two thousand, two hundred and sixty-eight, *ab urbe condita.*'

Jason committed the answers to memory, intending to check their accuracy as soon as he could, knowing that they would be right, that Terry could carry out complicated calculations in his head at lightning speed and that he had learned the principles only hours ago. He looked pityingly at the child, wondering if he could persuade him to keep the ability a secret, if he could spare him from admiration turning to unease and unease to ridicule as his peer group realised his oddness, if he could save him from the fate of a performing clown as kinder mortals tried to persuade him to amaze the world with his unexpected skill.

'It's very unusual to be able to do that. Some of the other children might be jealous. Shall we keep it a secret for a little while?'

Terry looked at him from dreamy eyes and nodded, leaving Jason unsure whether he had done so because his tone had invited the answer yes or because he had understood the warning. He had no pastoral responsibility for Terry Pepper but he had for Chrissy Beggs and decided to use the earlier incident as an excuse for contacting Terry's parents, aware that Terry's own year head, Sarah Myatt, was too crushed by Morton's to initiate action unless serious disruption was in evidence.

'Autism?' Sarah said sceptically. 'I shouldn't think so. If you feel you ought to see the Peppers by all means do but don't alarm them. They're pretty simple souls.'

Jason drove the memory of a younger, enthusiastic Sarah from his mind and prayed that the Ofsted inspection might be miraculously brought forward. He would rather work for a school branded as failing than struggle on in a school whose patent inadequacy went unacknowledged and unaddressed, where the best of each year's crop straggled in untended soil and the rest never raised its head above the empty earth.

As he drove out through the school gates he saw an older teenager with a small knot of Morton's pupils round him. Jason braked sharply and the group scattered, the pupils at speed, the young man slowly and with an insolent shrug. He looked back twice and Jason watched him until he was out of sight. One of those pupils was barely twelve, thought Jason angrily, twelve years old and buying drugs. He reported the incident to the police on his mobile, knowing there was nothing they could now do, that the dealer would have got rid of any evidence even if they did catch up with him. He could only hope that he had arrived at the scene in time to prevent transactions.

On Friday nights he or Kat had gone to the supermarket for the weekly shop while the other stayed at home and gave Jake and Leah their supper. Jason hated taking his turn with the shopping and was always glad when Kat offered to go

44

instead. Once when she was ill he had taken the children along as well and had returned frazzled and exhausted much to Kat's amusement.

He would not have gone this Friday but for his mother's expected visit. As he cruised slowly through the car park looking for a space, someone rapped on the window and he turned to see a neighbour smiling through it. Jason let down the window and smiled back.

'Your turn this week? It's real bedlam in there. Full of Christmas already. How's Kat?'

'She's fine, thanks. And Bob?'

'Fine too but Jasmine's got flu.'

Jason expressed sympathy. The driver behind him hooted furiously and the neighbour hurried off. Jason glanced in his mirror, raised his hand in apology to the irate motorist and spotted a gap in a row of cars. It had hardly been the time or place to tell the neighbours, he reflected, and a harsh laugh briefly filled the car. It was a moment before he realised it was his own.

As he steered his trolley between a stray child and two cabbages which had fallen on the floor, Jason mentally made a list. One joint of lamb or beef, potatoes, three veg, bread, milk, fruit, red wine, cheese, biscuits, one of those frozen dessert thingies. That was Sunday taken care of. What about Saturday? Pasta. His mother liked pasta. He did not know what household goods were in short supply at home nor did he care. He wanted merely to escape from everybody else's cheerful bustle as soon as possible.

A young woman appeared at the corner of the aisle and called the child sharply. The toddler responded by running in the opposite direction and Jason stood still while the mother gave chase, uttering threats. An older woman tut-tutted and glared after them. Pushing his trolley towards the pasta, he found himself beside a couple debating whether to try a new brand.

'Why not?' asked the man and the girl giggled as he threw it on their heaped trolley.

A cold, dark, cloak floated down on to Jason's head. Misery flooded through him. To his horror he felt tears well up into his eyes and he hastily bent over his shopping as if adjusting the position of the goods in his trolley. He found himself staring at the couple's retreating backs. Self-pity engulfed him. He watched their togetherness, the man touching the woman's arm to draw her attention to something on the shelves.

Later he found himself behind them in the check-out queue. He stood staring in wonder at his own trolley, which seemed to have accumulated so much more than he had intended to buy. He was vaguely relieved to find the total was within their weekly budget before the knowledge came to him that now it was only his budget and that he did not even know what it might be in his changed circumstances. Adrift, he thought, uncharted waters, long journey and hadn't worked out the rations. He would still have responsibility for the shore rations too, for the feeding of the three who had cast him adrift.

It would cost more to keep two houses supplied with food and household goods because they would need two lots of what his mother called larder stocks: sugar, coffee, tea, flour. He became immersed in the detail of it, responding to some mental challenge to list everything he and Kat would need in their separate kitchens, occasionally thinking of an item and then discarding it because only one of them liked that particular food. The game lasted until he had stowed all his purchases in the boot of his car, its only purpose to keep his concentration away from other people and their families.

At home he found light, warmth, fresh flowers and the smell of cooking. *Lived in.* He pondered the words as they came into his mind. He lived here as did Objubjub but since Tuesday – was it only Tuesday? – he had thought of the house as empty, waiting to be reoccupied, to be rewarmed, relit, once more to resound with childish delight and quarrels.

His mother embraced him before surveying the carrier bags he was depositing in the hall. 'Darling, there's enough there for the army. I hope you don't mind my coming today instead of tomorrow. Mrs Bishop gave me the spare key. Is there any news?'

Jason thought about Mrs Bishop, the next-door neighbour. She and her husband were retired and might well have seen Kat packing the van or the car or have noticed that no one but he had been living there for the last few days. Perhaps his mother had mentioned the situation when calling for the key or perhaps they were still in ignorance and he would tell them casually one day as they talked over the privet hedge.

'No. Alex and Sheila have been in touch but they won't tell me where she is. She has taken

47

Jake out of school and changed jobs. It must have been planned over quite some time. According to Mrs Mackenzie, Leah is due back with her next week and I'm going to try to see her but I'm not sure she'll be there.'

He watched his mother absorb the implications, realising as he had that Kat had left permanently, that she was not waiting for him to be sorry so that they could carry on as before, that next time Jake and Leah played in his house it would be as visitors.

It was of the children he expected her to speak first. Instead Eileen Kirk picked up one of the carrier bags, turned towards the kitchen and said to him over her shoulder, 'You must get a good solicitor. First thing, Monday morning.'

'I know. I still can't believe things have got this far so soon. I keep thinking we can somehow sort it all out.'

'Darling, have you thought what would be happening now if *you* had taken the children away? Kat would have told the police on day one, there would have been a hue and cry in all the newspapers about a man who had mysteriously disappeared with his children leaving his wife distraught and everyone concerned for their welfare. The strong implication would have been that they might be in some sort of danger from a man who could behave so unpredictably and with such cunning. A woman can walk out with her children and everyone protects her. If you were to go to the police they would dismiss the whole thing as 'a domestic' and tell you to see a solicitor.

'The law is not on your side. A woman's right to

her children is sacrosanct. A man's is not. Last Monday you faced the world and whatever it threw at you together. Now you are facing each other and Kat is doing the throwing and her missiles are big, serious ones, not toys out of a pram.'

She was afraid for herself as well as him, yearning for her grandchildren, wondering when she might see them again. As Jason watched the urgent, angry exhortations dissolve in tears, he knew that somewhere Jake and Leah also sobbed and raged on the wasteland of battle and that he was a powerless warrior in a lost cause. They would not be coming back.

3

Eileen Kirk stayed till Tuesday and was a willing party to his deception, phoning the school herself to report him sick. They had decided upon a stomach upset as the most satisfactory ailment for the purpose as, unlike a cold, it was an invisible complaint from which speedy recoveries were normal. Jason could not repress a miserable feeling of guilt as he listened to his mother's lies. Not only was he naturally truthful but he knew that he was causing his colleagues extra work and inconvenience. Indeed when he had told Eileen what he proposed she had looked surprised and wondered why he could not just warn Gaskill that he could not be in until break.

'I just don't want anyone to know. I'm sure no

one would tell Kat, or even could tell because no one has any idea where she is, but I still want a surprise attack.'

'But Mrs Mackenzie must realise she told you that Leah was coming back to her this week.'

'Yes, but she may not have confessed that to Kat and if she did they will have been expecting me yesterday, the very first morning.'

His mother shook her head but argued no further. Jason knew he was acting childishly, perhaps irrationally, but he was set on his course and he guessed that she had stayed on an extra day in some vague hope of seeing Leah. He was not surprised when she said she would drive him to Mrs Mackenzie's, forestalling any objections by promising to wait outside.

'It will look better if anyone from Morton's should happen to see you. You were obviously too ill to drive.'

It was Jason's turn to shake his head, wondering if either of them was capable of thinking straight, if such behaviour was an isolated occurrence, borne of misery and the unfamiliarity of the situation, or if it was just the first of many such incidents of subterfuge and hope. The thought surprised him with its assumption of helplessness, its belief that he had no control, that he must be carried along by Kat's tide, but as he sat in the passenger seat of his own car his main concern was that he would not be able to use illness as an excuse too often and that he might have wasted the stratagem by deploying it now for so uncertain a result.

Leah was usually delivered to Mrs Mackenzie

at eight-fifteen so Jason planned his visit for ten. His mother asked at the last moment to come in with him but he told her with regret that he thought it might look mob-handed and that diplomacy was his best hope.

There was no response to the bell. He rang again without result. He looked towards the car and shrugged, then turned his attention back to the house. Perhaps Mrs Mackenzie had seen him approaching and was now trying to avoid a scene. Jason bent down and put his ear to the letterbox, his heart leaping with hope and triumph as he detected faint sounds of childish tones. Leah was there. He tried the doorbell once more before deciding to go round to the back of the house but he found his way barred by a locked side gate. He might have climbed it and was tempted to try but sense reasserted itself. He broke no law by attempting to see his own daughter but if he resorted to trespass then Kat could later cite his conduct as proof of unreasonableness.

He returned to the front door, pushed open the letterbox and called as loudly as he could manage, 'Leah, Leeeahhh!'

Elation at her excited response was swiftly replaced by distress as he heard an altercation between his tiny daughter and a gentle but firm Mrs Mackenzie. He was content to await the outcome, sure now that he would see his daughter, knowing Mrs Mackenzie would not be so heartless as to deprive a child. Presently the door opened and his daughter threw herself into his arms, while the childminder looked uncertainly at the car. After a moment or two Leah also looked in that direction and shouted, 'Granny! Granny!'

'Can we come in?' asked Jason. He saw the relief in the other's eyes and knew that she had decoded the request correctly. *I am not about to snatch Leah and carry her off in the car. I just want to see her.*

He voiced the intention more directly while his mother distracted Leah.

'You can relax. I am not here to take her away although there is no lawful reason why I should not take her home. Leah is as much my child as Kat's. When I leave without her it will be to avoid any further distress and confusion for her and Jake, not because I accept for one millisecond what all the rest of you believe so unquestioningly – that somehow Kat has a God-given right to our children and I have none.'

Mrs Mackenzie accepted the situation with good grace until Jason announced his intention to visit every day. It was not practical as a return journey could scarcely be squeezed into his lunchbreak, much less any meaningful time with Leah, but the statement of intent offered some illusion of control, some restoration of the initiative with him.

'Leah won't be here after this week. Mrs Kirk has made other arrangements nearer to where she is now.'

He had expected as much and knew it must happen some time, but the words pierced his defences and he felt a fresh access of misery. Kat was in control as she had been, ruthlessly, throughout.

Leah looked up from where she played with his mother. 'Are we going home now?'

Jason knelt down in front of his daughter. 'Daddy has to go to school. Mummy will come at teatime to take you home.'

'I want to go home with you.'

'I have to go to school.'

'Granny take me.' Leah looked up hopefully into her grandmother's face.

Eileen blinked back tears. 'Darling, of course I want to take you home but I have to go back to my own home and there won't be anyone there to look after you.'

Leah's face puckered. 'See Objubjub.'

'Objubjub can't wait to see you,' put in Jason. 'He'll come and live with you soon and he's looking forward to it.'

'See him now.'

'Soon. He'll be coming with you soon. He's just got a few things to pack in his bag.'

'Don't want him to pack. Want to come home. Daddy take me home.' Leah's voice crescendoed into a wail. She stood up and clung on to Jason, screaming. He too rose and tried to pick her up but she began to beat his legs with puny, frustrated blows. 'Daddy take me home. Daddy take me home.'

Into the noisy scene the doorbell chimed a summons. Mrs Mackenzie went to answer it and suddenly Kat erupted into the room with blazing eyes and a voice of righteous indignation. 'What is the matter with my child?'

'Our child,' said Jason quietly. 'And why aren't you teaching?'

'That is my business. Honestly, Jason, surely you don't need to take it out on the children. You mustn't see them until they are settled. For that matter why aren't *you* teaching? I suppose you thought you could take Leah.'

'I see no law to prevent me.'

'Well, you will soon. I have instructed solicitors and I suggest you do the same.'

Jason continued looking at his wife, knowing that her words spoke not of boredom but of hatred. 'What did I ever do to you?'

'Nothing. That was the problem.'

Leah, who had briefly stopped screaming when Kat appeared, half reassured by the sight of both parents together, sensed the hostility and began to cry noisily, tears running down her cheeks. Jason moved to comfort her but was immediately pre-empted by Kat who swooped her kicking, struggling daughter up in her arms and carried her into the hall, one hand already stretched out to open the front door.

Jason tried to stop her but she eluded him and instead he ran in front of her, barring her way to her car which was parked in front of his.

Kat faced him angrily. 'Jason, please. Leah is already upset enough.'

'And whose fault is that?'

'Probably both our faults. Now please let us go. I'll be in touch.'

'Tell me when.'

'Next week, probably. I must settle the children first.'

'If I promise not to contact them before next week, will you give me your address now?'

'Frome.'

'And the rest?'

'Later.'

'No. Now.'

Kat set Leah down, holding her firmly by the hand. The child howled again, clutching Kat's skirt, as the two adults stared at each other and Jason knew looming defeat. There was no method, short of actual violence, by which he could force the information from Kat. Any further insistence on his part could achieve nothing but increased distress for Leah. It was time to bring the scene to an end. He bent down to kiss Leah goodbye but her screams grew louder and he was forced to abandon the attempt. Without a backward glance he returned to the house where both his mother and Mrs Mackenzie were fighting back tears.

'Why?' said Jason and Eileen simultaneously, each knowing the question could not be answered.

'See a solicitor, right away,' his mother urged him and repeated the advice when he dropped her off at the station.

'Seen a solicitor, yet?' asked Ed Deacon when Jason arrived at school with tales of a swift recovery.

Jason had consulted Alan Parnell only once, when he and Kat were making wills leaving all their worldly goods to each other with a few small, token bequests to their parents and Kat's siblings. He knew the solicitor as a friend of a friend but also because he advised Ed Deacon and occasionally called at the school when Ed found it difficult to make time in his day for a visit to Parnell's office.

He supposed that Parnell's office would now

become as familiar to him as the staffroom at school, that he would call here often, that the post which fell on his doormat would now contain, amongst the bills and the junk mail, regular communications from Parnell and Janner or Lane and Webb.

'...automatic entitlement to fifty per cent of the matrimonial home ... access arrangements ... maintenance ... mutual agreement...'

Jason became aware that Parnell had been talking for some time and that he had absorbed hardly a word. He roused himself to a dull protest. 'It's my family we are talking about.'

The solicitor looked regretful. 'Well, let's talk about the children, Jacob and, er, um...'

'Leah. Jake and Leah.'

'Yes, of course. Sorry. Jake is eight and Leah three?'

'Yes.'

Jason knew what was coming next.

'In such circumstances the court would be likely to take the view that the children should reside with Mrs Kirk, unless of course it considers she would be an unfit mother or there are very unusual circumstances.'

Jason shook his head.

'So we will need to consider access arrangements. It helps, of course, if the parents have a joint view. You say you have not been able to discuss this with your wife?'

'No. I don't know where she is, she won't talk on the phone for more than a couple of minutes and I haven't seen Jake since she left and that was two weeks ago. I saw Leah for five minutes last

56

week before Kat came and took her away. She wouldn't talk then or tell me where she was living and all the time she shelters behind the children's so-called welfare. Says it would unsettle them, that they have to get used to the situation before seeing me again, but she won't put any time limit on it. She just keeps on saying that it's over and she wants a clean break.'

'Clean breaks are rarely possible if there are small children involved, Mr Kirk, but you do not have to put up with being denied access to them. I shall tell Lane and Webb that you wish to see them within seven days and that proper visiting arrangements must be agreed. In reality it may take somewhat longer. These things tend to rely on goodwill until legally binding arrangements are in place.'

'Visiting arrangements? I'm their *father*, damn it, not a bloody visitor.'

Parnell did not reply and Jason listened to the echo of his futile words ringing in his brain. Their *father*. The words had become meaningless, his fatherhood reduced to a biological fact of life, his relationship with his children to that of a benign uncle. Only his love for them remained the same, a love unacknowledged by the law, which took no account of a man's need to see, hear, smell, hold his children, except at strictly regulated intervals.

Visiting arrangements. It was a term he associated with prisons, hospitals and old folks homes, but especially prisons. One could visit hospitals and residential homes every day – all that was needed was the wish to do so – but prisons were different. To visit a prison one needed an order, valid only for a particular day at a particular time. His children had been taken prisoner by adult lunacy.

'Don't they have any say in it? Supposing they want to be free to see their father as often as they like?'

Parnell looked at Jason sorrowfully then cleared his throat. 'If they were older their wishes would have considerable force but the court will acknowledge the importance of an orderly and predictable routine. Whatever is agreed will be a minimum, not a maximum. It will not preclude additional informal arrangements.'

'So long as Kat agrees. If she doesn't then the minimum is also the maximum and if the way she is behaving at the moment is anything to go by then that is exactly what will happen.'

'Things may get easier.'

'Or they may not. I want open-ended access.'

'The court will take into account only what is best for the children.'

'Good. Then it will allow them to see both parents on a daily basis. Those are my instructions and if Kat doesn't agree then I'll fight her for it.'

Kirk versus Kirk. What would that do to Jake and Leah? He knew it was impossible and Parnell, recognising that, did not bother even to argue but instead began to take him through the law on legal separation and divorce, on the defin- ition of a marriage which had irretrievably broken down, on the various stages and the intervals of time which must elapse between them. Jason forced himself to concentrate and at the end of the interview had sufficient grip on his galloping thoughts to call in at the estate agent on his way back to school and put what the solicitor persisted in describing as the 'matrimonial home' on the market. A young woman of about twenty-six in a sharply-cut, mustard-coloured suit said she would call to do a valuation and Jason agreed to drop off his spare keys. He wondered where he would live next and realised that he had little interest in the answer.

As he drove to school, glancing uneasily at his watch which told him he might be late for his Year Eleven class, he found his mind wandering away from his own misery and focusing once more on Terry Pepper. He had called on the family the previous week and found Mrs Pepper cooking the evening meal of steak pie and boiled potatoes. She told him he had just missed her husband who had gone off to his night shift but that Terry's older brother would soon be home from work. A sister was present and visible but her attention was wholly engrossed by a magazine whose cover proclaimed the possibility of losing a stone in a fortnight.

Jason had accepted a cup of tea while he tried to engage Mrs Pepper's interest in her youngest child. An hour later he left defeated. Terry, she told him, had always been a dreamy little boy but he was no trouble to anyone, never had been and she was sure nothing was wrong with him. He always did as he was told, ate well and hadn't needed the doctor since he was eight. Yes, he was a bit quiet but there was nothing wrong with that, was there? When she had got up to check something on the stove Jason had looked around the room as unobtrusively as he could. The only reading material was the girl's magazine. There were no books or music but stacked against the far wall was a large collection of videos. *The Blair Witch Project* sat on top of *A Hundred and One Dalmatians*. Jason thought of the images which must be played before Terry's eyes and wondered what he made of them.

Returning, Mrs Pepper had tried to enlist the support of her daughter.

'What do you think, Em? There's nothing wrong with our Terry, is there, love?'

'He's OK,' the girl grunted without taking her eyes from the magazine.

Mrs Pepper looked pleased with this endorsement and Jason gave up. On the landing outside he had almost collided with Terry's eldest brother who had asked, 'You all right then?'

'Yes, my fault. I'm from Terry's school. My name is Jason Kirk.'

'Oh, right. Rob Pepper. So what's the kid been up to? He's not one for trouble, like.'

'No trouble. He's a bit too quiet.'

'Yeah. Good kid. Bye, then.'

Dispiritedly, Jason made his way along the landing and down the stairs of the block. As he was driving away from the estate, a voice had called, 'Hello, sir!' and he had waved to a girl he vaguely recognised from school.

Recollecting that evening now, Jason knew it was hopeless. Terry Pepper came to school clean, physically healthy and fed. His parents were stable and hardworking, ran an orderly household and produced nutritious food. They would probably do anything for their children but could not be convinced that in Terry's case there was anything to do. The school would have to take the lead and persuade an overstretched County Education Authority that it might have yet another child with very acute special needs.

Jason knew Terry would just be too far down the queue of Hillier's priorities. There were disruptive children he wanted dealt with first. It would be necessary to persuade Gaskill of the urgency and Gaskill was increasingly erratic and unpredictable. He still talked about leaving for the private sector but Jason could not see him teaching anywhere for much longer. Once he might have set out to lighten the deputy head's load but now he needed time for his own worries, time to plan, to suffer, to brood.

He was just in time for the lesson with Year Eleven. As his pupils began to look at the old, curled, faded black-and-white photographs of the war years, taken by their grandparents or great-grandparents, Jason tried to repel the images of the brightly-coloured contemporary photographs which had adorned his own house in the days when it had been a home and not an empty shell. Kat had taken most of them. Leah's gap-toothed smile no longer greeted him from the top of the television set, there was no lopsided, ill-hung picture of Jake in his pedal car, taken four years ago and positioned too high on the landing to be adjusted without difficulty. There was emptiness on the mantelpiece where their christening photographs had stood. She had left one picture of the children sitting beside each other, informally posed by the photographer at number three, the High Street.

'Sir, my gran was evacuated. She used to live in London and she had to go off all by herself and live in Essex.'

'Sir, my granddad fought in the desert with Mounty.'

'Monty,' chorused a dozen voices.

'My nan's brother was a prisoner-of-war. His wife died in the Bath Blitz and she had to look after his children until he came back. They didn't know him and my nan says they screamed when he took them away.'

At least Jake and Leah would see him regularly, no longer daily but at least regularly. They would not be sent to Essex to live with a strange family for an indeterminate period or be brought up by an aunt for so long that they forgot what he looked like. But he could find little comfort in the comparison. A man who has lost a foot will know that he is vastly better off than a man who has lost a leg but such knowledge will not reconcile him to his own pain and loss. Jason wanted his children emotionally whole not comparatively less pitiable. It did not matter to him that others suffered more and he felt no shame that it should be so.

At four o'clock he was pouring coffee into his usual mug in the staffroom. All the crockery was communal but most members sought out a particular mug just as they tended always to sit in the same chair if it was vacant. His own preferred receptacle had been obtained on a school trip to the Roman Villa at Cirencester and was decorated with a mosaic pattern, now fading as were the letters which proclaimed its provenance. Beside him Ben Fuller, who had a first in maths from Oxford, inspected a carton of semi-skimmed milk with suspicion.

'It was OK earlier,' Jason assured him. 'Ben, how fast can you add one thousand, five hundred and fifteen to seven hundred and fifty-three?'

The maths teacher raised his eyebrows but performed the calculation with what Jason would normally have considered impressive speed.

'Eat your heart out, Carol Vorderman,' conceded Jason. 'But Terry Pepper can do it about three times as fast as that.'

'Who is Terry Pepper?'

'A new kid in Year Seven.'

'Must be destined for great things.'

'No. He's special needs and if the world were a fair place he would have a Statement by now.'

'You want me to talk to him?'

'Please. But, Ben, I've told him not to tell the other children. It could make him quite vulnerable.'

'Leave it with me. I'll be discreet and if there is something Morton's should be doing, then we can join forces. Year Seven, you say? Which form?'

Jason gave the details, relieved to have an ally. Ben Fuller had not been teaching long enough to have been ground down by the hopelessness of Morton's and if he believed Terry Pepper needed help he would probably battle his way through even Hillier's indifference and Gaskill's increasing oddness.

At the end of the day the October air seemed lighter and he felt a reluctance to go home where it would be heavy with desolation and dark with anxiety. In the car park he paused, wondering whether to stroll into town instead of driving home. He inhaled deeply.

'That's what Mole did to spring.'

Jason turned round and smiled into the teasing eyes of Carol Marsh. 'Sorry?'

'Mole in *The Wind in the Willows*. He stuck his head out of his underground house and sniffed the air of spring.'

'And, if I remember correctly, abandoned his decorating, flung aside his tools and went dancing off across the fields.'

'You remember correctly. You looked as if you might do the same.'

'Mole did it in hope. I want to do it out of sheer bloody despair.'

'Bad luck. Why not come home with me and have a bite of supper instead? I have a great pie in the fridge. New recipe which I invented at the weekend.'

'Isn't cooking at the weekend something of a busman's holiday?'

'No. I love it, especially when I can just get on with it without having to instruct twenty-odd youngsters at the same time.'

Jason smiled. 'How far away do you live?'

Carol gave him directions and he said he would follow in his own vehicle but as he did so, keeping his eye on the bright red, rather old car, an absurd thought came to him that Kat might be having him trailed by private detectives in the hope of hurrying up the divorce by proving adultery. Somewhere in the back of his mind was a crumb of knowledge informing him that if he spent twenty minutes with a woman alone in her house, intimacy was deemed to have occurred. In 2003? Surely not.

Would he mind if the divorce were speeded up? Perhaps it might even be less expensive that way. Angrily he slowed his galloping thoughts to an orderly walk. Fear of Kat and her spite must not be allowed to dictate his every action. He wanted to have dinner with Carol Marsh and he would do so.

At first he saw no reason to regret his decision. Carol waited for him to join her before letting them in to a big Victorian house which had been divided to make three flats. Carol's was on the first floor and as he followed her up the stairs he noticed the way her camel, demurely-pleated skirt swung against her legs. He averted his eyes, afraid Kat's watchers might be concealed in the shadows of the staircase.

The flat was small but cosy and he was not surprised when she suggested eating in the kitchen. Jason offered to help but Carol said she coped better alone and he sat at the small pine table with a glass of red wine while she, seemingly effortlessly, produced soup, pie and vegetables.

'A real winter meal,' Carol commented. 'More wine?'

'No, thanks. Driving.'

Jason thought of his own house, cold, unwelcoming, deserted. It had not seemed like that for the few days his mother had been staying and he had assumed, subconsciously, that the reason his home now seemed but a shell was because of the absence of people, of their noise, their smell, their demands, their being. The short time he had been in Carol's flat caused him to revise this vague assessment. The moment he had entered it he had sensed a lived-in atmosphere, a home waiting to welcome its owner back. It was his own presence which was dampening the charm of his residence not the absence of Kat and the children.

'Do you believe that people can leave their feelings in the atmosphere of the places they live in?'

Carol looked surprised. 'You mean those stories where someone goes to stay in a house or hotel and becomes very frightened for no reason and then in the morning he finds out a murder was once committed in his room?'

Jason grinned. 'Perhaps nothing quite that dramatic. I mean, can you tell, just by entering a place, if the people there are happy or not?'

'I doubt if it's as simple as that but I did once have a rather odd experience. It was when I was flat-hunting as a student. Three of us were looking for somewhere to rent. You know what it's like – you can never quite find the perfect place for the price you can pay. Well, I did. It had the right number of rooms, no garden to look after and was only two miles from college. I could not fault it but I just hated the atmosphere. It was a very bare place – hardly any ornaments or pictures and sparsely furnished – but somehow I just could not fill it with warmth and fun in my imagination.

'I told the others and they went along and felt

just the same. We thought we were quite mad – the perfect flat and we were going to refuse it on grounds which none of us could name. I was so frustrated I went to see it again and this time I commented to the landlord on the bareness. He told me the current occupant was going blind and had to have clear, uncluttered space in order to move around in safety and comfort. That was when I realised that the problem was not the absence of goods and chattels – it was the bitterness. The atmosphere was full of bitterness, of a man not reconciled to a cruel fate.

'I told the others and they didn't laugh at me. We turned down that flat and got another further out.'

There was a short silence. 'Why are you asking?'

'I came tonight not just because I like your company and was ready to demolish a fantastic meal but also because I didn't want to go home. It just doesn't feel like home any more. Even Objubjub seems to hate it. He wanders from room to room mewing.'

'What did you say his name was?'

'Objubjub. We got him for Jake when Leah was about eight months and used to lie in her cot making noises to herself. We were debating names and Jake asked Leah her opinion. She was sitting on Kat's knee and made a sound like Objubjub.'

Carol laughed. 'Going back to your house, have you made any changes since the others left? Turned one of the kids' bedrooms into a study? Moved the lounge furniture about? Hung up some different pictures?'

'No. I suppose I've kept it all the same because I wanted them to come back.'

'In other words your home has become a giant waiting room? Have you ever sat in a waiting room that wasn't impersonal? Make it *your* house, *your* haven, *your* blessed retreat from the world.'

'I suppose you're right. Anyway, I'm selling it so it all becomes a bit academic.'

'Not if you're right about people absorbing atmospheres. You should get it as cosy as possible. Resolve to do it next weekend. Have you really heard absolutely nothing?'

'Pretty well nothing. There was a dreadful scene with Leah.' Jason described the episode at Mrs Mackenzie's house. 'What I can't get out of my mind is the way Kat looked at me. I had decided that she had walked out because she was bored, and indeed something she said in the course of that argument seems to prove that, but as she was taking Leah away she stared at me in black hatred.'

'She was probably terrified you had come to reclaim Leah.'

'If taking a child away is a cause of hate then I have cause twice over.'

Carol reached across the table to cover his hand with hers. 'Don't be bitter, Jason. That will only destroy you and in the end it might affect Jake and Leah.'

He did not reply.

'Sorry,' said Carol after a few seconds. 'That wasn't very clever of me.'

'No. You're quite right and I know you're right but that can't change what I feel. If only she would just sit down and talk to me face to face.'

'She will in time. She must.'

Jason was not convinced but he turned the

conversation to neutral topics and when he had judged they had talked long enough to satisfy the laws of social intercourse he said he must leave. Carol refused his offer to help with the washing-up and he did not insist. Entering his own home, he recalled her words: *the atmosphere was full of bitterness, of a man not reconciled to a cruel fate.*

Jason closed his eyes and felt his way to the kitchen where he nearly tripped over Objubjub. Would he rather be deprived of sight than of fatherhood? Would he prefer to lose his eyes rather than his children? Both, he thought, were cruel fates and he was no more reconciled to his than had been the blind man of Carol's story.

4

Jason knew he was dreaming and wanted to stay immersed in the trance, dreading the loss of the illusion, of Leah's voice, which would fade on his wakening, of the comforting sight of the small vision walking hand in hand with him through sleep. Other voices, childish, playful, were tugging him back to a world he did not want to face.

It was Saturday and, forced into wakefulness, Jason lay listening to the sounds of other people's children playing in the street and neighbouring gardens. Once he would have been woken an hour ago by Jake hurling himself on the bed, or he might have woken to find Leah already there, lying between her parents. In the day facing him he would have been taking both children to the swimming baths, or pottering in the garden while they and their friends played around him, sorting out arguments, admiring achievements.

The weekend yawned ahead of him, empty. In the past he had yearned for 'a couple of days' peace', believing that some small space in the crowded routine of his life would allow him miraculously to catch up on every neglected task, to write every outstanding letter, fulfil long-ago promises to contact old friends, tidy the garage, deal with the hairline crack which had spoiled his decorating efforts in Leah's bedroom, clamber into the loft to search out some items Kat had deposited there and then wanted. Now he had two days' peace each week and had no idea what use to make of them. The silence deepened around him. He was tempted to slide back under the duvet and try to recapture the dream. As he resisted he noticed that he was still lying on one side of the bed, the one nearer the door, the one the children leaped on first when they ran into their parents' room. The other side was cold with Kat's absence, preserved uninvaded for her return. Jason moved into the middle of the bed, wondering why he found the small manoeuvre so difficult, assailed suddenly by longing for Kat, mourning his loss.

He pictured Kat beside him, her light-brown hair trailing on the pillow, her face innocent in sleep or awake and provocative. He had thought she would always be there, her face growing older, the worry lines deepening as the voices in the background also grew older and fretted about exams and careers and the opposite sex. She would be there when those voices had disappeared to be replaced with the infant wails of grandchildren.

Around him friends and acquaintances married and divorced, cohabited and split up, and he watched them as he watched sick friends – with sympathy but without premonition. Once he had been at a party where a man – a stranger to him, young, married, cheerful – had dropped dead with a heart attack. For days afterwards Jason and Kat had been aware of their own mortality, checking insurance arrangements, thinking of the children. Then they had forgotten and once more made plans for old age. Yet the matrimonial disasters he encountered had scarcely given him pause, so sure had he always been of Kat.

Carol Marsh had advised him to spend his weekend rearranging his house but instead he spent the day away from home, walking in the countryside, taking lunch at a pub where he sat by the fire and spoke to nobody. On Sunday he drove to the coast and walked the cliff paths and shores till it was dark, his collar pulled up against the biting autumn wind. He had told himself he needed time to think but instead his mind was blank, his walking mechanical. He felt no exhilaration when he climbed a steep path in the wind and rain, no triumph when he calculated the miles walked. The principal benefit of his exercise was two nights' sound, deep, sleep, uninterrupted by visions of his wife and children.

On Monday he resolved to take his mind off his

own woes by finding a keener interest in those of others, seeking out Ed Deacon at break.

As he was preparing to leave for home, Ben Fuller came into the staffroom and told him he had talked to Terry Pepper, Sarah Myatt and finally Angus Gaskill.

'You were right, although interestingly he seems able to do these sorts of calculations only if you present it in the form of Roman Dating. When I asked him to add seven hundred and fifty-three to one thousand, three hundred and one he couldn't do it. Just disappeared into a dream before shrugging, but as soon as I said, 'What's thirteen oh one in Roman years?' back came the answer before I had even finished the question. Odd.'

'What did Sarah say?'

'She said she would talk to him herself and take the view of his form tutor so I said thanks very much and went to see Gaskill.' Ben paused, a bemused expression on his face. 'It was a pretty unreal conversation. Angus spent about five minutes telling me it was the wrong method of dating, that the Romans did not start their years in January, that I had confused the year nought with the year one, that some Pope had messed around with the calendar and that if we took all that into account the figures were quite different. What on earth is the matter with him?'

'He's fantasising about tutoring a sixth form group at Eton.'

'What? Anyway, when I got him to concentrate on the main issue he was quite helpful. I don't think young Pepper will be lost in the system much longer, at least not so far as Morton's is concerned. County will be another matter, although it's a very, very unusual case and I don't think they'll take it lightly.'

Jason thanked him, stowed some books and the props for the following night's history club in his locker, turned the key and put it in his pocket while feeling for his car keys. His mobile, which was lying on a table beside his coffee mug, suddenly vibrated wildly, startling Jason with the noise of its movement on the wood. Some of his colleagues turned their heads in the direction of the sound and Jason grabbed the instrument with the haste of embarrassment.

'Hello, it's me.'

'Kat!' Jason stood stock still in the middle of the staffroom. One or two of the teachers now looked at him with covert curiosity, knowing his situation and the name of his wife. He began to move towards the door.

'I think we should talk. The children are a bit more settled and there's a lot to be sorted out. The more we can agree between us the less work for our expensive lawyers.'

'I won't agree to anything until I know where you are and I have seen the children properly.'

'There's no need to be so aggressive and you didn't need to get Alan Parnell to write that stupid letter either. I had always said you could see the children as soon as they were settled.'

So Parnell had delivered the goods. Jason felt a rush of gratitude.

'So when can we meet?' Kat's voice was insistent.

'Whenever you tell me your address and I can see the children.'

'I'll give you the address now but I think we should talk before you see the children.'

'No. The other way round.'

Kat sighed in exasperation. 'Very well, but I hope you're not going to be like this all the time.'

He made no reply to that, committing to memory the address and telephone number she now gave him, arranging to see the children at the weekend, to take them out by himself on the Saturday and to see them with Kat on the Sunday. He walked to his car with a lighter step than he had come from it that morning, feeling the darkening afternoon dissolve into morning sunlight, conscious of birdsong, of hope. Reality asserted itself even before he had left the school gates. He would have to wait till the weekend to see his children and that would be his future. Jason Kirk, weekend Dad.

'Dad!' Jake ran to meet him as Jason parked outside Kat's new home, a small run-down cottage on the outskirts of Frome. How long, Jason wondered, before she became disenchanted with such an abode? His son began chatting, eagerly describing his new school, new friends, new life. Inside Leah allowed him to pick her up and at once began to cry.

'Want Daddy, want Daddy.'

'Daddy's here,' said Kat and Jason together, their tones identically bright with false reassurance.

Leah was not fooled. 'Want more Daddy.'

'You will have lots more Daddy,' soothed Kat.

'He's come to take you and Jake out.'

'Want to go home.'

'This is home.'

'Home Daddy.'

'I wish you and Parnell had been a bit less selfish. It's too early for Leah. A couple more weeks would have made all the difference.' Kat looked at Jason with angry eyes.

He would not argue with her in front of Jake who was looking at his sister with an expression of grown-up concern. Instead he told his son to find his jacket and asked Kat the whereabouts of Leah's outdoor clothes and shoes. As his wife went sulkily to find the items she called over her shoulder, 'Where are you taking them?'

'To the museum. They have a special dinosaur exhibition. Jake will love it.'

'What about Leah? She might get tired and grizzle if there's too much walking in crowds.'

'I'll cope. I'll have them both back by five. They'll have had a big lunch so you needn't worry too much about the evening meal.'

'What about you? Are you staying for supper?'

Surprised at the invitation, Jason hesitated. If he stayed he could bath Leah and read to her, play games with Jake. 'OK. Thanks.' His reward was Jake's whoop of delight, which was repeated when his son saw the dinosaurs painstakingly reconstructed for the purposes of the local museum's attempt to capitalise on the continuing popularity of *Walking with Dinosaurs*. There was not the space for the kind of startling exhibits displayed by the Natural History Museum but it was nevertheless a fairly spectacular parade, which greeted what felt like half the population of Frome under the age of ten. Jake ran around happily exclaiming while Leah, from the vantage of her father's arms, stared about her with large, wondering eyes. When Jason set her down she held stubbornly to his hand.

'Want to go home,' announced Leah when Jake called his father over to decipher something on a large drawing of an assortment of dinosaurs. He walked over slowly to accommodate Leah's pace. 'Want to go home,' she repeated as Jason let go of her hand temporarily to point to something in the drawing.

'So do I, Dad,' whispered Jake and, looking at him, Jason was horrified to see tears in the child's eyes. 'It's horrible,' he protested. His father put an arm round his shoulder. 'Why can't it be like it used to be?'

'I wish it could too but nothing stays the same for ever and you will get used to it, Jake. It won't always feel like this. Promise.'

Jake shook his head, miserably unconvinced.

'Look, come with me a moment.' Jason took both children by the hand and led them right up to a scaled-down version of a Tyrannosaurus Rex. He positioned Jake a couple of inches in front of it.

'What can you see?'

'Just grey scale.'

'Quite. So start backing away. What do you see now? More of a body? Legs? Now you know you are looking at an animal.' Jason looked behind him to make sure they were not about to bump into anyone as they slowly backed away from the beast, with Jason asking at regular intervals, 'And now?'

At length they stood at a sufficient distance from the recreation of a long-extinct being to identify it, to see its shape clearly, to appreciate its proportions. Jake looked up at his father, expectant, puzzled, his expression saying more eloquently than words that what had just been demonstrated was so obvious he could see no purpose to the exercise.

'It's the same with life's problems. At first they just confuse you, then you learn to stand back a bit and get them in perspective and they look different.'

'Dad, we got the T. Rex in perspective by walking away from it. I can't walk away from what's happened to you and Mum.'

Jason stared down at him in admiration. 'That's a pretty good answer, Jake, but try to think of the walk we made as time. As time passes it will all look different, more manageable.'

He saw that he had not convinced Jake, that nothing but time itself would do so. He took them to McDonald's, letting them eat their fill of burgers, chips and ice cream. It had long been a tradition that on Saturday they could eat what they liked instead of the carefully balanced meals which Kat provided throughout the week, but he felt uneasy, hearing in his imagination a solicitor from Lane and Webb saying, 'My client tells me that when your client has care of the children they are fed on junk food.'

Paranoia, thought Jason. He was succumbing to paranoia, as uncertain about taking his children to McDonald's as he had been about having an innocent dinner with Carol Marsh. The thought made him reckless so when Leah said yet again, 'Want to go home,' he replied, 'Why not?'

It was perfectly feasible. There was time to drive them to his house and back by the five o'clock he had promised Kat. They could play in the garden and see Objubjub. Kat had not specifically forbidden it and it did not contravene any agreement between them as to how the day was to be spent. His only fear was the effect on Leah, that seeing home again might augment her distress when it was time to leave for the cottage.

Jake, however, received the idea enthusiastically and before Jason could find time to retreat from the plan they were all in the car and heading in the direction for which the children had clamoured. Leah began to chatter for the first time that day and Jake became voluble with excitement. Jason alone felt disquiet. Perhaps they were expecting to find home as they had left it, not realising that the removal of their own possessions and Kat's had rendered it so different; perhaps they thought they could persuade him to let them stay, that they could ring up Mummy and she would come back.

His misgivings gave way to joy as they arrived and both children raced enthusiastically around the house calling to each other, to Objubjub and to him. They played noisily in the garden and after a while some neighbouring children came to join them. The return to normalcy was so beguiling that it was a shock to realise the time had come to return them to Kat. To his relief neither child argued but their spirits were so visibly subdued that his misery turned to anger on their behalf. He briefly hated his wife.

When they were but half a mile from the cottage Leah began to scream, long drawn-out cries which seemed to split the very air, to fill the car with din, to suggest madness. Jason pulled up at the side of the road and tried to calm her, imagining Kat's reaction, hearing again in his imagination a lawyer speaking but this time addressing some unspecified judge: 'And when Mr Kirk takes the children out the younger child returns visibly distressed.'

Paranoia or prophecy? Assisted by Jake's clumsy efforts, Jason tried to calm his daughter, whose screams eventually subsided to grizzles, but as they arrived at the cottage she began once more to howl loudly and Kat erupted from the doorway with a look of horror on her face.

'What on earth is happening? What's wrong with Leah?'

'Nothing. She's just a bit tired and upset.'

'Why is she upset?'

'You know why. Let's get her inside.'

'Want Daddy,' sobbed Leah.

'Daddy's not going yet,' said Kat. 'But he won't stay here with all this noise, so be a good girl.'

Jason despised the implied threat but it worked sufficiently to reassure his daughter who giggled in the bath, ate a good supper and demanded her favourite story. He tucked her up in the unfamiliar bed in the tiny room and when he saw her asleep made his way downstairs. Kat was waiting for him with accusation in her eyes.

'Jake says you took them to the old house.'

'To my house, yes. What of it?'

'It's far too soon. No wonder Leah was so distraught.'

'You, not I, have upset Leah. Now I suggest you let me concentrate on Jake until he goes to bed. We can talk tomorrow as planned.'

'If you're to take the children out I have to be able to trust you. You didn't say anything about taking them to the old house.'

'It is where I live and they are going to have to get used to visiting me there. You did not say I wasn't to take them.'

'No, because you talked about museums.'

'Which is where I took them this morning but at lunch they both said they wanted to come back home with me and I saw no reason to deny them.'

'Mum, Dad, don't argue, please don't argue. Mum, I loved it. I saw Objubjub and Gavin came round to play. I haven't seen him since we left. What's wrong with going home, Mum?'

'This is your home now.' Kat was tight-lipped but Jason saw signs that she was relenting and he tried to end the conversation by suggesting a game to Jake.

'Scrabble?'

'OK.' There was no enthusiasm in Jake's voice and the adults glanced at each other guiltily before sitting down to play with a determinedly cheerful air.

It was not a successful game. Jason scored fifty extra points in only the second round for using all seven letters and his opponents effectively gave up. Jake spelled 'yot' instead of 'yacht', provoking sarcastic comments from Kat. There was an argu-

80

ment between the grown-ups about the validity of 'ai', with Jason insisting it really was a three-toed sloth and Kat eventually giving in on appeal to the dictionary. Then Jake yelled that he had a 'great word' which would earn him triple points and proceeded to put 'cemist' rather than 'chemist' on the board. Kat reacted with irritation rather than sympathy and their son refused to play further.

'Don't be such a spoil sport, Jake. You can't win every time,' remonstrated Kat.

'Shut up,' retorted Jake.

'Bed,' said Kat and Jason in unison.

As Jake trudged mutinously up the stairs, refusing to say goodnight, his parents looked at each other in misery.

'My fault,' acknowledged Kat. 'It's just that I'm so tired. So dog-tired. I've had all the moving and packing and unpacking, settling the kids has been hell and the supply jobs are pretty rotten.'

Jason refrained from observing that all the sources of her fatigue were of her own making. He attached no special significance to the last complaint, assuming that she intended to offer supply teaching as a temporary measure and would apply for a permanent job in the not too distant future. He wondered if he should still stay for a meal now that Jake would not be with them but Kat was setting two places and he began to help.

They ate spinach and nutmeg soup in silence and talked determinedly about the children over the chicken casserole. It was not until Kat put the coffee pot on the table that Jason asked simply: 'Why?'

'I told you. It's just not the same. I really don't want to hurt you, Jason, and if we keep talking about it we'll both say things we might regret. It's happened and we ought to look forward not back.'

'Did you say if we *keep* talking about it? Dammit, we've never talked about it at all. You've walked out on our marriage, stolen the children, spent weeks refusing to see me or let me see them and you don't even see the need for some explanation. It's cloud cuckoo land. This is a marriage you're throwing away not a used tissue.'

'I'm not going to argue. I understand why you're upset and I'm sorry but all the talking in the world won't alter the facts.'

'Just tell me what those facts are. Did I hit you or the kids? Neglect you? Fail to provide?'

'There's more to marriage than being a good father and a good provider.'

'Yes, and when did we ever have a problem?'

'I wasn't talking about sex.'

'Just tell me what you *are* talking about. Tell me one thing, anything, that might make sense of all this.'

'Jason, this is pointless. Please stop now. Surely we can be civilised about it and act like grown-ups? We can work it all out and save ourselves a lot of hassle and expense.'

'Do Jake and Leah come under the heading of hassle and expense?'

'Jason, if you are going to go on like this we had better stop talking about it.'

'As I said just now, we cannot stop what we haven't yet started. I ask you again: why?'

'All right, because I needed a new life, breathing

space, a chance to be me, not just Mrs Kirk. I was tired of merely existing; I wanted to rediscover my life force, to take charge, to find Kat Kirk as she really is and not be just the other half of Jason Kirk. I wanted the flowers to look brighter, the birds to sing louder–'

'And the sun to shine yellower? Spare me the psychobabble and come back to where the rest of us live – in the real world. Jake and Leah deserve better than to be made the guinea pigs of your experiment in self-discovery. How loudly do *their* birds sing?' Jason's voice began to rise as he grappled incredulously with what Kat had said.

'They will get used to it if you let them.'

'I'm not in the least sure that I should let them. If you believe that rot you've just churned out and believe it's worth taking two children from their father to try to achieve it, then you're certifiable. I loved you, for heaven's sake, and I thought you loved me.'

'I did and I still do in a way but it's not the same.'

They looked at each other with anger and hurt on his side and self-righteousness tinged with embarrassment on hers. Jason knew it was time he left, that he should go before his rage exploded and the children heard him shouting that their mother was mad, that he did not understand her and that he no longer wanted to, that Jake and Leah should be protected from such lunatic instability, that he would contest custody, that he hated her, that he wanted her damned birds to be silent for ever. He got up and strode to the door, then suddenly turned to find Kat behind him.

Jason grasped his wife's shoulders and hissed through his teeth. 'I'll fight you for them, even if there is not a penny left at the end of it. I'll fight you every inch of the way. You are quite mad, absolutely barking, bloody mad.'

Kat stood calmly, waiting for his anger to abate, for him to relax his hold or perhaps she wanted him to hurt her, to strike her, to put himself in the wrong. On the instant of the revelation he dropped his hands and stood back. He thought he glimpsed a brief shadow of disappointment in her eyes. Then a more substantial shadow moved and he saw Jake watching from the stairs.

Alerted by the movement of Jason's head and the change in his expression, Kat turned and together they watched their son slowly descend the staircase. Jake came miserably, his head hanging, taking one stair at a time, as the grown-ups tried to drive the confrontational fury from their faces. He tugged at Kat's arm and she bent down to listen to his embarrassed whisper but Jason knew what his son said, had already seen the state of his pyjamas. Kat took the child's hand and turned him towards the stairs.

'Say goodnight to Daddy,' said Kat. 'He's just going.'

'Night, Dad.' The tone was dutiful, mechanically obedient, listless. It was a tone which did not vary when Jake added, as an afterthought, 'Thanks for a great day.'

Jason watched his wife and son climb the stairs, then walked to his car. A beam of light fell across his path. Kat was switching on the bedroom light, changing the bedlinen, finding fresh pyjamas.

Jake had wet the bed for the first time in four years and in his shame and discomfort had turned to his mother for help, scarcely aware of his father's presence except as a dim addition to the awkwardness of his circumstances.

Jason shivered with the ice of exclusion.

5

Even before he drew the curtains Jason knew it was snowing. When he had woken, the world had that muffled sound which followed upon a heavy fall of snow, the light streaming into his window was brighter than usual and among the sounds of neighbouring children there was suppressed excitement. He looked out and a neighbour who was scraping ice from his windscreen glanced up, waved and mouthed, 'Could be a white one this year.'

Jason stared bleakly at the white landscape. Barren, he thought, icy, cold, desolate: any of those words summed up the prospect of his Christmas. He imagined Jake rushing outside to play in the snow before school, eagerly making snowballs, searching for a victim for the missiles, but especially he thought of Leah who would be seeing the phenomenon for the first time, walking gingerly through the white, crunchy powder, entranced, excited, uncertain. Kat would be watching her expression as they had both watched her first steps, heard her first words, felt the wonder of her small discoveries as she began to explore the world about her.

It was Jason who, while planting carrots in the small vegetable patch they then maintained, had looked up and caught the very moment of Jake's suddenly understanding how to steer his pedal car and who had watched as ten minutes later his son transferred the knowledge to the tricycle he had been unable to guide earlier that morning. It was Jason who had seen Jake swim his first width unaided. He and Kat had been together, watching cricket on television, when Leah at last mastered the art of crawling and made them laugh with her surprised expression.

The future offered little chance of such moments, moments to take him by surprise, producing small events, minor triumphs, great milestones which never seemed to come when he watched, alert, for them. Leah would be able to appreciate Christmas this year, would feel the thrill of anticipation, stare in wonder at the tree, hear the tale of Father Christmas, strain to stay awake listening for the tinkle of reindeer bells and the sounds of descent through the chimney. He would share none of this with her. Of course, when he took her to spend New Year with his mother they would celebrate Christmas afresh, but it would not be the same; the newness, the wonder, would have gone, the experience of Christmas now a part of his daughter's knowledge, filed away for annual retrieval.

In the ten weeks since Kat had left, Jason had been riding a giddy roundabout of despair, grief and anger, but now he fell, in slow motion, conscious of the descent and its dangers, into an abyss of self-pity and black depression. No, he thought then, not an abyss: verdant pastures could lie either side of an abyss. Instead he was in a crevasse whence there was nothing to climb up and out to except icy wasteland. He stood still, experiencing the darkness, the will to cry, the loneliness, the desire to stay there in his bedroom, in bed all day, to hand his life over to someone else to run while he gave in, gave up.

Objubjub, who had never been transferred to the cottage because the children had decided he wanted to stay at home and see them when they came, called him from the other side of the bedroom door. The task of opening it, admitting the cat which would immediately begin a suppliant entwining of Jason's legs, of going downstairs and feeding the animal fresh food in a clean bowl, seemed too great. He sank onto the bed, seeking the relief of tears only to find them elusive. Above Objubjub's protesting cries he heard the clatter of the letterbox and the thud of post landing on the mat. He knew what was there, what waited for him.

For the last week the solicitors' letters had arrived along with the Christmas cards and the increasingly difficult bills. For the first time in his life he had come to dread the daily post, looking at it from the top of the stairs, a small knot of fear in his stomach as he tried to brace himself for the worst, while the innocent Objubjub ran ahead of him, turning his head and mewing for breakfast.

In the far-off past he had awaited the mail with eagerness, sometimes with anxiety, as he looked for letters from girlfriends, for examination results and those of job applications. Some of his contemporaries had been less fortunate, getting into debt, filling in social security forms and dreading the frequent reassessments, awaiting confirmation of unwanted pregnancies, in one case enduring the agony of a well-merited prosecution.

Jason's maturity and well-ordered life had spared him these miseries and the established routine of his subsequent years had reduced the arrival of the post to an event of which he was scarcely aware. Occasionally there would be a jolt when a letter from a friend told of the death of a mutual acquaintance or of some other catastrophe but he experienced such pain at a distance. The post was predictable: quarterly utility bills, the income tax return, postcards from friends, advertisements for catalogues, notifications that he had yet again been selected for a chance to win a quarter of a million pounds in the latest Readers' Digest Grand Draw. From time to time there would be a pleasant surprise – a minor win on the Premium Bonds, an invitation to a wedding from a long-unmarried friend, a present for Jake or Leah.

Now facing the post was a daily ordeal and his principal pleasure in a Saturday night was the knowledge that there would be no long cream envelopes on his mat the next morning, that fear was leashed for twenty-four hours.

The cold misery still gnawed at his stomach as he forced himself to embark on the day. He postponed collecting the large assortment of envelopes which lay beneath the letterbox. The last had become stuck in the flap but he left it there despite the draught until he had fed Objubjub and made toast and coffee for himself. Then he steeled himself. There were two letters from Alan Parnell enclosing three from Lane and Webb and Alan's interim bill. Mrs Kirk did not believe it reasonable to allow Jason access each weekend and one day during the week. She was sticking to her suggestion of a weekend once a fortnight with one evening's access during the other week. Mrs Kirk did not find the proposed financial arrangements adequate to the maintenance of herself and two young children.

Mrs Kirk did not consider the current argument necessary, found Mr Kirk's demands profoundly unreasonable and therefore believed he should fund the cost of any further prolongation of the dispute. Lane and Webb's bill was already £2,000. Jason glanced at the bill from his own solicitor totalling £906 plus VAT. He refused to add the two sums together, turning away from the unthinkable, the unpayable. Jason Kirk, debtor. He knew he was not yet out of control. He had savings and could raise a loan or apply to his mother for help. However, the pace of escalation frightened him. It could not be in Kat's interest to beggar him but her response to his regular pleas was invariably that if he would agree to her terms then there would be no need for the intervention of solicitors. Alan Parnell said much the same in gentler tones: 'Once a fortnight is reasonable if you are to have them for the whole weekend. Your wife knows she will win this one and Lane and Webb will be advising her to that effect.'

Desperate, Jason had asked if he could

represent himself. Alan had taken him through the various stages and was only a quarter of the way into his explanation before Jason became aware of the futility of the suggestion.

'Before Kat took the children from me I saw them fourteen days a fortnight. Now you're telling me that I should accept three days out of fourteen and be grateful. What right has she to steal my children for the other eleven? What is the law of nature which says a woman should see her children over three times more often than a man? We had our children together in order to raise them together. Why else would I have had them?'

Parnell was sympathetic but his advice did not vary: Give in over the access. The money was a different matter.

Jason turned his attention listlessly to the rest of the post. Two of the cards contained circular letters giving news of the sender's past year. He consigned them to the bin unread. A third bore the inscription 'wishing you all you could wish yourself in 2004'. The fourth simply read 'love, Angela'. Jason's brow puckered. Who was Angela? He looked at the envelope again and realised it was for Kat. Viciously he threw the card in with the discarded envelopes and neglected circulars. To hell with Angela, whoever she was: he would not act as Kat's postman.

He arrived late at school and did not care, snapped at innocent levity in the Year Eight class on the Tudors, bawled at two older boys who were lounging against a wall when they should have been hurrying into class and refused to help a colleague who had to leave a lesson early because she felt unwell. He repelled Carol Marsh's tentative enquiries as to what was wrong and brought tears to Nick Bright's eyes by pouring scorn on an uncharacteristically silly question. He was not surprised when Angus Gaskill asked to see him after his last class.

Had Jason any energy left he might have defied the deputy head but instead he complied wearily, his attitude implying that his behaving like a bully all day did not really merit comment. He was surprised to find it was the old Angus who confronted him rather than the frustrated pedagogue he had come to know during the current term.

'Just as well it's the last day of term,' observed Angus. 'You need a break.'

'I'm getting a break – from my children – and I need it like a hole in the head.'

He half expected Angus to correct his grammar. Instead Gaskill remonstrated with him, gently, but in unmistakable terms of reprimand. Everybody was sorry for what he was suffering and would do anything that might help, but he must keep his personal life separate from his professional one. Of course, that was easier said than done but no other course of conduct was acceptable. Morton's relied on teachers of Jason's calibre. The school needed him and that was why it was imperative that he had a proper break.

Jason briskly agreed, with neither apology nor meekness, before cutting short the interview. Angus sighed and looked worried but made no attempt to prolong matters, perhaps unwilling to precipitate a real confrontation, perhaps having faith in the therapeutic effect of the holiday ahead.

Back in the staffroom Ben Fuller was pulling on a Barbour. He cycled to school every day, regardless of the weather.

'Go carefully,' advised Jason, watching his colleague fix clips to his trousers. It was the first time that day he had considered anyone other than himself.

'I will. What are you doing over Christmas?'

'Going to my mother's. The children are joining us for New Year. What about you?'

'My parents for Christmas. Debbie's family for New Year. She has six younger siblings so it should be quite a party.'

Ben's eyes were happy and, as he picked up a pair of fur-lined gloves, he gave a small smile as though hugging himself with a pleasing secret. He is going to ask Debbie to marry him, thought Jason.

'Don't,' said Jason.

'What?' Ben looked startled.

'Don't skid on the ice.'

Ben stared at him. 'You weren't talking about the weather, were you?'

'Don't take any notice of me. I wasn't thinking.'

'Yes, you were. You were thinking out loud. You meant to warn me off Debbie. I'm sorry, Jason, sorry about you and Kat and about you and the kids, but it doesn't always end like that. I know you can't even imagine it now, but one day you'll probably find someone else and next time it will work.'

Jason grimaced. 'No way. Absolutely not. I have spent the last ten years in a fool's paradise and I still don't know how I could have got it so wrong.

92

I thought Kat was a good woman and now I find she's just a scheming little toad and that's putting it mildly.'

Ben put his gloves down on a table and began to unfasten his Barbour. He looked at Jason.

'I once had to deal with a scheming little toad. It was five years ago when I was all of nineteen and I had my first car. It was only an old banger but I was over the moon at having it and, of course, I wanted to show it off, especially to girls. Then one night I was driving back from Reading, where I had been visiting an old schoolmate, and I passed a girl hitch-hiking. It was raining and it was a pretty lonely stretch of road so I stopped.

'She said she was going to Exeter so I offered to take her as far as Swindon. She looked great and we chatted away as if we had known each other all our lives. By the time we were approaching Swindon I was determined to see her again but when we stopped everything changed. She asked me to drive her on to Exeter and then stay the night and, believe me, I wanted to. Now I shudder to think what might have happened if I had.

'I told her I couldn't. My folks were expecting me and I had to start my holiday job the next morning. Then she told me, very quietly, quite matter-of-factly, that if I didn't drive her on to Exeter she would go to the police and say I had tried to rape her.'

Appalled, Jason waited for Ben to continue.

'As it happened I knew Swindon well. Half a minute later I pulled up outside the police station and said, "Let's go in and tell them together, shall we?" Of course she vanished but not before she had uttered some of the most obscene filth you could imagine. I went in and reported the incident anyway, partly because I was afraid she might have taken the car number and then made up a story just to get revenge on me but partly also because I thought she might try it on some other poor chap.

'Afterwards I shook just thinking about it. In my worst nightmares I thought of myself on trial for rape, named in all the papers while she remained anonymous. My parents were horrified, of course, but my mother gave me some very sound advice. It would have been easy enough for her to say that I should never give a strange girl a lift again but she told me the exact opposite.

'She said I must not let one bad woman colour my view of the world, that most girls were kind and that I was right not to ignore one on a lonely stretch of road at night. I could see my father had his doubts but he backed her up. A fortnight later I stopped to help a young woman whose car had broken down. We pushed it off the road and I lent her my mobile to ring her boyfriend. She couldn't get through so I gave her a lift to her office. She couldn't thank me enough and although I didn't say so I couldn't thank her enough either because she had restored my faith in women.'

Jason smiled. There was little similarity between their situations but Ben had meant to be kind and he did not want to seem ungrateful.

Ben smiled back. 'I can see you're not convinced, but the reason I've told you all this is that the woman in the broken-down car was Debbie. I met her again in the local library and took her for coffee. We exchanged telephone numbers and a month later she rang, feeling low because she had just broken up with the boyfriend. We got to know each other quite well but that was all. Indeed she came up to Oxford for a commem and promptly fell in love with my best friend. That came apart as I was doing finals and it was that summer we fell in love. If I had predicated my view of women on that ghastly girl I drove to Swindon I would not have risked stopping to help Debbie.'

This time Jason's smile was genuine. 'That's quite a story. I wish you both every happiness.'

'But you're still not convinced.'

'That there are plenty of Debbies about? I know you're right, but I'm not yet ready to believe they won't turn into Kats at midnight.'

Ben picked up his gloves again. 'Well, have a good Christmas anyway.'

That, thought Jason, as he arrived home and scooped the second post from the mat, was unlikely. He switched on the kettle and began extracting Christmas cards from their envelopes as he waited for it to boil. He glanced at the signatures without interest and left the cards on the table. In the sitting room was another pile and there was yet a third on the hall table. In previous years the cards would have been hung round the walls on string, a tree would have stood, decorated and festooned with winking lights in the corner of the living room, holly would have trailed from the mantelpiece.

This year Jason had seen no reason to bother, had not the energy to get out the stepladder or to fetch the Christmas tree and the boxes of decorations from the loft. There were no small voices to exclaim in delight, no childish eyes to light up with wonder. Even packing the car, locating and capturing Objubjub, pulling electric plugs from their sockets and locking up the house before leaving for Dorset to see his mother seemed quite disproportionately onerous tasks the next morning. Gaskill, he realised, was right: he needed a break.

As he put his bags in the car his neighbour, Alan Bishop, hailed him from the other side of the privet hedge, wishing him a Merry Christmas. Jason, conscious that they had not spoken for some time, wandered over to him and they asked after each other's families and what they were doing for Christmas. After a few minutes Janice Bishop emerged from the house and joined her husband by the fence.

At once she began to ask about Jake and Leah, saying she missed their voices in the garden and asking Jason to wait because she had presents for them indoors which he should take with him. Alan looked embarrassed and Jason realised that he thought the children were too delicate a subject to mention, that it would be more tactful to leave it to their father to introduce their names into the conversation. Alan could hardly have been more cautious if they had died.

Jason smiled and tried to set his mind at ease by talking determinedly about his children. He did not, however, mention Kat. He rarely spoke of Kat socially at all now and when he did it was never as his wife but always in the context of the children. He had taken to referring to her as 'their mother'.

'It will be hard on them, this year,' commented Janice with unapologetic frankness when she returned with the presents. 'Christmas is such a family time.'

Alan Bishop shifted his weight from one foot to the other and Jason realised that his neighbour's discomfort with his wife's bluntness stemmed from her disapproval of the situation and that he feared she might challenge Jason outright.

He met the challenge before it was uttered. 'Yes, very hard and it's not what I wanted but I could hardly compel their mother to remain. She is very convinced that she has taken the right decision and we must just try to make it as easy for Jake and Leah as possible.'

Janice Bishop softened. 'It must be hard for you too.'

'Yes, I miss them every minute of the day.'

He had the satisfaction of knowing this discomfited her, made her feel that she had been wrong to blame him. When they returned indoors she would vent her fury in disapproval of Kat, saying that she did not understand the modern generation and that it was no wonder so many kids went off the rails these days.

Jason took the presents she offered with thanks and half an hour later began the drive to Dorset. Glancing in his rear mirror, he saw his neighbours' Christmas tree lights shimmering in the window.

Objubjub protested volubly before falling soundly asleep. Jason drove through rain which hurled itself against the windscreen, forcing him to drive slowly and with the kind of concentration he had applied when he was a learner and regarded other drivers with anxiety. He was almost relieved when the traffic slowed to a snail's pace but then irritated as he saw ahead of him a long queue of red tail lights. When Objubjub woke and mewed piteously, he decided they both needed a break and pulled into a petrol station.

He spoke soothingly to the cat, waggling his fingers through the front of the pet carrier as reassurance. Presently the mewing ceased, to be replaced by a tentative purr. Jason grinned and turned away towards the pump. In the shop, as he waited his turn to pay, he listened to the conversation between the assistant and the woman at the head of the queue.

'Nasty accident near Sherborne. Been like this for a couple of hours. They say it's a motorcyclist, poor lad. There's a couple of cars involved. Your best bet is to turn off next right then go on to the next roundabout then...'

In front of Jason a man told his daughter of about ten to get a map from those displayed on the other side of the shop. Jason, knowing the area well, decided on a different route. He thought of the motorcyclist's mother and pictured Eileen Kirk answering the doorbell to find a policeman on the doorstep instead of the son she had been expecting. The same scene played across his imagination twenty minutes later when he braked sharply, narrowly missing a car which had stopped on a blind corner.

Once he would have wanted to stay alive for his children's sake, have thought of them in moments when he was reminded of his own mortality.

98

Perhaps it was because he assumed the motor-cyclist was young that he felt for the mother rather than for any children, or perhaps he had begun to adjust his perceptions of those who needed him, was already subconsciously believing that he had become dispensable as a father but was his widowed mother's all.

'Nonsense,' said Eileen with brisk scorn when he shared the thought with her over lunch. 'Just because they don't see you every day doesn't mean they need you less. Think of all those children who go to boarding schools or whose parents are abroad for months on end.'

Unconvinced, Jason turned the subject and they began to plan for the arrival of the children at New Year.

'We'll make New Year's Eve Christmas Eve for them and New Year's Day Christmas Day. So if you're happy with a standard roast for the real Christmas Day…'

Jason listened to his mother's happy babble with affection, ran errands to the off licence and helped to decorate the tree, watched by the baleful eyes of Objubjub who had taken refuge behind the television and was monitoring the activity in the unfamiliar surroundings with alarm. The afternoon was darkening into evening and he was setting out a crib on the dining-room sideboard when chimes rang through the hallway. Calling out, 'I'll go,' he opened the door to find four carol singers who immediately burst into the notes of 'Good King Wenceslas'.

At once his eyes were fixed on the two smaller children who stood in the middle of the group, a boy and a girl of about eight and five who sang eagerly until, disconcerted by his stare, they hesitated and fell silent. The older children, seeing nothing amiss, sang lustily on until the strains of the last verse died away.

Jason went on looking at the two smaller ones before becoming conscious that the older pair now looked at him uneasily. He smiled and drew change from his pocket. A girl with a woolly hat held out a collection tin and Jason inserted two £1 coins, aware that there was now a tangible atmosphere of relief. As he closed the door behind him he heard them running along the short drive and thought he discerned the word 'weirdo'.

'Carol singers,' he told Eileen.

'I could hear. We'll have carols round the piano when Jake and Leah come.'

'So long as you play. All I can do is "Silent Night" with my right hand.'

His mother smiled. 'It's a pity you haven't managed to interest the children.'

'Leah is still too young and Jake thinks it's boring.'

'So did you. Except I think you said sissy.'

'Now, of course, I wish I had learned an instrument just as I wish I'd paid more attention to languages at school and really mastered one. I wonder which wasted opportunities Jake will regret when it's too late.'

'It's never too late.'

It was too late to rescue his children, thought Jason, as it was too late to rescue his marriage or the love he once felt for Kat. Jake and Leah's future of rotation between two households, of a daily mother and a fortnightly father, of being piggies in the middle between two hostile adults was cruelly certain. He supposed that in time the hostility would subside into indifference but it would not turn to warmth. For that it was certainly too late.

Eileen Kirk's house was full of reminders of a time when it had not been too late, when there might have been something he could have said or done to avert the catastrophe yet to happen. On the mantelpiece was his mother's favourite photograph of his wedding to Kat. On the piano was an assortment of portraits of Jake and Leah at different ages. Over the fireplace he and Kat stared down at a newborn Leah propped on Jake's lap.

When? he wondered bitterly. When had Kat decided this was not enough for her? This year? Last year? Or three years ago when she was looking after a new baby?

He finished the crib and glanced at his watch. 'Tea?' he called to Eileen.

His mother peered through the hatch from the kitchen. 'You've done that well. Leah will love the snow effect. I can put the kettle on now if you like or would you prefer something stronger?'

Jason shook his head and wondered if his mother normally drank so early, if she was lonely and had not liked to tell him so. Everyone said how wonderfully she had coped following his father's death six months ago and until now he had taken her strength at face value. He had been so preoccupied by this being his first Christmas without his children that he had virtually forgotten this was her first without her husband.

He, who had always been impatient with Ed Deacon's introspection, had apparently been following on the same path.

Eileen handed a mug through the hatch, telling him to be careful how he took it because it was hot. Jason grinned, wondering if he would still nag Jake and Leah about the small hazards of life even when they had children of their own.

'It's my turn to take Teddy out,' went on Eileen. 'I'll have my tea when I come back.'

'I'll do it, if you like. I could use the exercise.'

Teddy was a small West Highland terrier belonging to an elderly friend, John Phillips, who had been a golfing companion of Jason's father and lived alone. Having recently suffered a stroke, he was now out of hospital and being helped by friends and members of the local Baptist Church. He let the dog out in the garden each day but was far from well enough to take it for walks. Eileen obliged twice a week.

Jason decided to leave the car and walk the mile and a half to the old man's house. Phillips greeted him warmly, recognising him at once, thereby causing Jason to hope that he would make a full recovery from the stroke despite his advanced age. Teddy began to bark wildly and run about the hall, jumping up against both his owner and Jason as soon as his lead was produced.

Jason walked the dog towards the local park, dawdling as the terrier sniffed trees and gateposts, reeling in the lead when it seemed willing to challenge an Alsatian, tugging it gently away from the kerb, remaining still when a small boy let go his mother's hand and bent down to admire it.

The park was an open one, usable round the clock. In an hour or so lovers would wander through it but for now it was full of people hurrying home from work and children snatching the last chance at outdoor play before their suppers. The early evening was dry but cold and Jason wondered that they did not prefer to be indoors. He too had once played in this park but he had done so unsupervised, a risk no responsible parent would allow today.

He released Teddy from the lead and smiled as the small creature, barking with excitement, ran across the grass. From a nearby bench a slurred voice bade him good evening and asked if he had change to spare.

'Sorry,' muttered Jason and quickened his pace in the direction Teddy had taken. He whistled and the dog barked but did not come to him. To his right a girl and a boy practised handstands. Jason watched them briefly then set off in pursuit of Teddy, calling the animal by name, surprised and disconcerted when it burst out of a bush with a red tennis ball in its mouth. Teddy waited for Jason to attempt to take it, letting him approach until he could almost touch it and then immediately running out of reach where he stopped, letting the ball fall from his mouth, challenging Jason to try again.

The children of the handstands rushed to help and were shortly joined by others who cried that it was their ball. The resulting bedlam drew several amused adults to the scene and Jason retreated to the sidelines to watch the outcome. One child, the only one not wearing jeans, kept falling down, showing her knickers and rolling over giggling. When the ball was finally retrieved, Teddy once more on the leash and the grown-ups taking their reluctant children home, she alone was left unclaimed and unaccompanied. None of the other adults threw a backward glance.

'Time for home,' observed Jason. 'Where's Mummy? Is she with you?'

The girl shook her head.

'Does she know you're in the park?'

This time it was a nod.

'Were they your friends?'

A shake.

'Well, it's a bit dark to be here alone. I'll walk you to the road.'

The child fell in beside Teddy and they turned to go. As they passed the huddled form on the bench, the child drew closer to Jason and he had to repress an urge to put a reassuring arm round her. Had a grown-up done it to him in his childhood it would have been called kindness but now it was assault, inappropriate touching. Jason would have defied such lunacy had he not been a teacher with a job to protect. The figure on the bench was a derelict, part of the flotsam and jetsam of society, which once had been loved and now lay unregarded, but many others sat on benches and watched the children play: kindly, elderly, lonely, harmless, they had become objects of suspicion in an age of wild licence and obsessive taboos.

They emerged from the park and the child ran off. She must have been about seven, thought Jason. Seven and playing alone, exposing her

104

underwear in a park full of strangers. Her mother must be excessively trusting or profoundly indifferent or maybe she had been deceived and thought her daughter was playing in a friend's house. Perhaps there had been a childish quarrel and the girl had flounced out; maybe she had come to the park with someone else and that child had gone off in a huff.

'You can't protect them from everything,' observed Eileen when Jason recounted the episode. 'Children quarrel every day and storm off alone. Thousands are doing it at any given time and it just doesn't matter until that one occasion when the child does not return and amidst all the hue and cry come the blame and the recriminations and the self-torment. Once you were missing for two hours and I knew I would never forgive myself if you didn't come back, but you did, perfectly safely and not in the least able to understand all the fuss.'

Later Jason woke from a dream in which Leah wandered alone in a park of hostile bushes and malignly whispering trees. A drunken form menaced her from a distant bench and she turned to face Jason, screaming, tears running down her face, but he was too far away. He sat upright, sweating, even as the dream faded and he absorbed its terrible message.

6

On Christmas Day the void, which was the absence of childish delight and chatter and which had seemed somehow greater when Jason returned from a long telephone conversation with his children and in-laws and a much shorter one with his wife, was suddenly filled by a single bleep. Jason picked up his mobile, wondering idly who might be texting him amidst the festivities and was deciding it was almost certainly Carol or Ben when he saw the words and his heart jumped:

'UR GR8 Dad. CU Weds. Jake.'

A second bleep announced another message in which Jake explained that the mobile was a Christmas present but he was not allowed to use it except in emergencies other than for texting.

'He must have mounted a serious charm offensive to get it,' Jason said to his mother. 'Kat absolutely hates the things. She is terrified about effects on the brain.'

'Hence the rule about sticking to text, I suppose. It means Jake can contact you, though, whenever he likes,' Eileen replied.

Kat must also realise that, thought Jason, and wondered if the purchase of Jake's mobile heralded a weakening in her resistance to his claims to his own children. His son had not mentioned the present in the conversation he had just had and must have been longing to surprise him with the message. Had Jake crept away to his room to send it, hugging himself on his secret, or had the whole family been watching as he punched out the words, laughing, encouraging, happy?

He began to send a message back.

Jake bombarded him with text messages for a week and on the day that he and Leah were due to be dropped off for New Year he sent regular reports of the progress of the journey.

'Look out of your window now,' commanded the last one and Jason opened the door as the car swung into the drive. To his surprise it was not Kat but Alex who had brought the children. They tumbled out enthusiastically, greeting Jason and Eileen noisily and then running indoors to find Objubjub.

Alex grinned. 'They've had a whale of a time and have been telling everyone that they are having two Christmases this year. Sheila sends her love.'

Sheila but not Kat. There was a short silence.

Jason decided it was time to mention his wife. 'Did Kat say anything about the arrangements for picking them up?'

'I think the assumption is that you'll take them when you return to Somerset. There isn't much point in Kat coming down here when you have to drive back anyway.'

In that case he would delay their return by two days, decided Jason, and if Kat didn't like it she would just have to put up with it. He did not, however, communicate this to Alex but instead went in search of his children.

'Can I stay up for New Year, Dad?' asked Jake.

'Yes,' said Jason at once but when the carriage clock on Eileen's mantelpiece chimed midnight his son had already been fast asleep for three hours.

'Let's hope two thousand and four is a better one for all of us,' said Eileen as she kissed Jason. The year which had just slipped away into the past had seen his mother robbed of the husband she adored and him of his children. The next twelve months could hardly be worse.

'Any resolutions?' asked Eileen in a mischievous tone.

'Sell the house. Change jobs. See my own kids as often as I like.'

The first two might just be possible but neither he nor his mother was willing to spoil the occasion by voicing any thoughts on the likelihood of the third.

'Take it step by step,' advised Eileen. 'First sell the house.'

'I'm sorry – you don't mind if we bring the children in as well, do you?'

Jason looked at the latest prospective buyer, a woman of thirty-something in a dark-green trouser suit and polo-necked red jersey, and forced himself to smile. She was the third such caller that Saturday and he suspected that moving house had featured in a number of New Year resolutions. The first enquirers had been a couple about to start a family who had exclaimed joyfully over the size of the garden but had looked at the kitchen with politely concealed dismay and the second had been a single woman who had inexplicably wanted a second garage. Jason wondered why they had come at all when the estate agent's details had so accurately described their sources of disappointment.

'No, of course not.' He stood aside to admit the couple and their two young children, catching sight of the small bulge beneath the woman's trousers. If they were looking for more space to accommodate an expanding family then his house was an odd choice, thought Jason, with its small third bedroom. In the lounge a log fire crackled comfortably and the aroma of freshly brewed coffee drifted from the kitchen through the hall. 'Make it welcoming,' Carol Marsh had advised, causing Jason to wonder if she would have offered Kat the same counsel or if there was something particular about the circumstances of a deserted male which suggested his home might lack the warmth to charm a stranger.

The visitors introduced themselves as Dan and Sandra and seemed content to let the children run unsupervised through the house while they concentrated on the loft. With some surprise Jason agreed to open it up and pull down the loft ladder. Dan climbed up with a tape measure. After calling a cursory exhortation to the elder child to look after the younger and keep her out of mischief, Sandra followed and Jason, deciding that the adults were unlikely to rob his loft but that the children might well cause damage elsewhere, went in search of the youngsters whom he estimated to be about seven and three. He found them in Jake's room.

'This will be my room,' the boy was telling his

younger sister confidently. 'You'll have that little one.'

'No, I won't. I'll have this one. It's a girl's room – look.'

Jason followed her gaze to an abandoned rag doll lying in the wicker chair where he used to sit to read to Jake. His attention was reclaimed by the boy demanding to know who was right.

'Well, this is my son's room but it could be a girl's if that is what your parents want. It would be up to them.'

The boy pulled a face but continued looking round the room. 'This isn't a boy's room, anyway. It's empty. I don't like it. It's horrible.'

The words were thoughtless, ignorant, innocent and they pierced Jason's armour more effectively than any cruel utterance of Kat's. The room, with its furniture and residual toys, was not empty in any literal sense of the word but even a child knew that it was unoccupied, spare, reserved for visitors. His own children did not live here: they merely visited. When they came they brought toys, games, books and clothes as adults brought toiletries, flowers and clothes. Clean linen and towels were provided, enquiries made as to whether they had all they needed, thanks exchanged on departure. The normal routine of the house was suspended for Jake and Leah when they were guests here because they no longer formed part of that routine, their needs demanding attention on an occasional rather than daily basis.

Jason felt tears in his eyes and turned so that he would not alarm the children. Urgently needing to distract his thoughts, he wandered over to the

110

window and asked the boy over his shoulder why his mum wanted a new house.

'We're having a little sister and we haven't got room and we can't afford a big house so Dad wants a loft because my uncle's a builder and he can make us a loft room for a sing.'

'A song.' Jason turned and smiled as the boy stopped for breath. 'Haven't you got a loft in your own house?'

'No. It's a mantelpiece.'

Jason blinked. He was used to interpreting childish malapropisms but it was a few seconds before he converted mantelpiece into mansard and a surge of amusement dulled some of the ache within. He heard the parents descending from the loft and went out on to the landing where they stood, still staring up into the roof as a saint might stare with wonder and expectation at the heavens. Their inspection of the rest of the house was perfunctory, leading Jason to wonder if the loft had failed the test or if it was so satisfactory that nothing else mattered. When they left, Objubjub uncurled himself on the fireside mat and looked at him balefully.

On Tuesday evening Jason returned from history club to find a message on his answering machine from the estate agent to say Mr and Mrs Holder would like to see the house again and when they arrived two evenings later they were accompanied by the woman's brother. This, thought Jason, must be the uncle who could convert a loft for a song. After they had gone he began to consider the consequences of a success-ful sale. He would have to decide where to live and what kind of accommodation he needed. For the first time it occurred to him that if he moved to Frome he would be sufficiently close to the children to see them without all the complexity of advance arrangements and, as the thought came to him, he stood still to contemplate it further, conscious of excitement and malice.

'Why not?' he asked Objubjub, who had just materialised through the cat flap.

'Why not?' he asked Carol Marsh when she had said surely he would not commute that distance every day.

'Why not?' he asked Kat and enjoyed her outraged expostulations.

'Why not?' he asked the estate agent when Mr and Mrs Holder decided they did not want his property.

The refusal caused him disappointment but also relief as he realised how few plans he had made for his future. He began to spend his evenings immersed in financial calculations based on Alan Parnell's advice as to what he was likely to have to pay Kat, his anger steadily rising. Teachers on his point on the pay spine did not normally budget for second homes, for two mortgages or for two lots of gas and electricity, water and council tax. It would be no good his moving back to a bachelor-sized flat when he wanted regular visits from Jake and Leah.

'It's not easy,' replied Ed Deacon when Jason asked him how he managed. 'In our case she stayed in the house and I moved out. I'd always paid the mortgage but suddenly found I had to pay rent as well and then another mortgage when

I found something to buy and I'll have to wait until the kids are grown up before I can force a sale and take my half. That's the reality unless of course she remarries and moves. It gives me nightmares just thinking about it, imagining some other man becoming Dad to my children.'

The same fear had flitted shapelessly across Jason's mind but had never been immediate enough to occupy him for long. Now he tried to focus on the unthinkable, looking out of the staff-room window and counting the children he knew who had stepfathers. Sometimes the mothers came to parents' evenings with the former husbands or partners and sometimes with the replacements. One father came alone, having three children in the school whom he brought up as best he could on income support; his wife had not left even a forwarding address and the children had not heard from her since she walked away from their lives and their love. Jason had regularly pitied him but now experienced an irrational envy.

Ben Fuller's angry voice brought him abruptly from his self-absorption. 'Of course they're right but it's the final nail in the coffin of Morton's.'

Jason looked across at him while Carol supplied the explanation. 'County have finally decided to close the sixth form. Ralph told Angus this morning. I think he's going to tell the rest of us at a formal meeting later, but it seems the cat is already out of the bag.'

Around them was a collective shrug of resignation. Anger required energy, indignation, enthusiasm, a belief that a course of events need not happen and could be changed. Ben was one of only a handful with the necessary hope and belief to be angry.

'Where's Angus?' demanded Ben loudly. Nobody would have thought of asking for the head himself.

'Gone home,' whispered Carol to Jason. He looked at her with concern.

'Is he all right?' he asked, trying to keep his voice inaudible to all but her.

'I don't think so. It's probably the last straw.'

Jason rose and went in search of the head but had not found him by the time the bell rang for afternoon classes. He headed for his Year Seven lesson with no very great sense of loss so far as the sixth form was concerned. Once he might have felt it keenly but his private woes had blunted his professional ones and there could not be a teacher in the entire school who considered the decision unjust. Seventy per cent of Somerset's children who continued their education beyond GCSE did so in sixth form colleges and the exceptions were those taught in the further flung rural schools. Morton's had escaped on the basis of its past glories when it had some of the most glittering A level results in all Britain let alone the county. Now it offered but a limited syllabus and produced an indifferent collection of GNVQs enlivened by the occasional grade B at A level.

Nevertheless the existence of a sixth form had been an attraction for those parents who had dim notions of continuity from eleven to eighteen or who thought it conferred greater choice and offered opportunities their children might one day wish to take up. Ben was right that its abolition would damage the school still further and that was what would anger those still capable of caring, whereas ten years ago staff would have resented the loss of engaging with bright, enquiring minds. These days bright, enquiring minds sought engagement elsewhere.

Jason's principal source of alarm was the withdrawal of Angus Gaskill who, before Christmas, had seemed so much more like his old self. He could not be feeling the loss of the sixth form from any teaching point of view but he must see it as final confirmation of failure, of the nadir of Morton's decline, which he, as deputy head, had been powerless to reverse. Jason became impatient for the day to be over, resolving to visit his colleague after school, wanting to offer him some ill-defined solace but wanting also to know that Gaskill had the strength to continue, that he would still be the rock that anchored Morton's.

So immersed was he in thoughts of Gaskill that Jason almost missed the suppressed activity taking place in the class he was teaching. Almost. As he sought to identify the source of whatever was happening, he became aware that the children were more voluble than usual and that there was something odd about their contributions, which he eventually recognised as the unusual high frequency with which dates were mentioned and their random nature.

When Nick Bright managed to refer to 1066 in response to another child's mentioning that his great-gran had been born in 1910, with both observations occurring in the middle of a discussion about the Tower of London, Jason realised what game was being played and wondered that it had taken him so long to work it out. Chilled, he glanced at Terry Pepper and saw the list of figures in front of him. Nervous giggles broke out as the class followed his gaze.

Jason walked over to Terry's desk and removed the calculations. The boy watched him in a detached fashion, registering neither anxiety nor disappointment, seemingly oblivious of the muted reaction around him. Jason sensed rather than saw enlightenment begin to dawn among Terry's classmates, as if there had been a collective intake of breath, a soft but audible clatter as scales fell from eyes. In a few seconds the image of Terry Pepper changed from that of a quiet, placid participant in the class to that of an outsider, a benign alien, a wanderer.

Jason continued the lesson, mentally dividing the class between those who would be kind to the outsider and those who would react as if he were not among them. He did not think there would be any active cruelty from this group but there was no shortage of bullies in the wider school. He wondered to whom he would turn if Gaskill lost interest in the child's plight.

He considered asking Carol to accompany him to the deputy head's home but she was too new to the school to know Gaskill well and Jason thought his older colleague might be inhibited by her presence and refuse to confide in him. Ben Fuller was still too angry and Ed Deacon indifferent so he went alone.

Gaskill greeted him irascibly while his wife, Elizabeth, hovered, worried and embarrassed, in the hall. He appeared disinclined to invite Jason inside, snapping that of course he was all right and that he could not see what there was to talk about, demanding to be left alone and for any discussions to be postponed till the morning. Jason persevered only briefly before bidding them both goodnight and retreating. As he walked down the short drive he could hear Gaskill shouting and guiltily wondered if his coming there had sparked a row. Elizabeth was a quiet, kindly woman and he hated to think of her distressed.

Gaskill did not appear at Morton's in the morning nor did he telephone with any message. Hillier grumbled that it was unacceptable and that the school was falling apart to which Ben retorted, sotto voce, that he was glad the head had finally noticed what half the parents in Somerset could have told him long ago. Hillier could not hear what had been said but he suspected it to be both insubordinate and unflattering and he glared at the maths teacher with a resentment which had roots in his recognition of his own inadequacy.

'That was right out of order, Ben.'

Jason gave Ed Deacon a surprised stare. The words had been uttered with a quiet authority as soon as Hillier had left the room.

'We may well have to manage without Angus for a bit and we may each have an opinion as to what is wrong with Morton's but Ralph is still the head and we must support him and each other. Otherwise the only ones who will suffer will be the children. Now let's get on with it.'

There were approving murmurs in which Jason heard his own surprise reflected. He thought Ed's

117

last sentence referred to more than Morton's. His colleague was saying that he was dispensing with his own bad-tempered preoccupation, was putting his marriage behind him at last and wished to get on with his life. Jason felt a lightening of his own mood: Ed Deacon had returned to Morton's, to normality, to fellowship with his neglected associates in the staffroom. Jason could only hope that such resolution would be sustained and not crumble when confronted with the wiles of the woman who was so determined that Ed should be kept at a distance from their children.

The staff began to leave for their various classes and the teaching began. Distant shouts drifted towards the school from the sports pitches, a muted throb of music came from the assembly hall where a drama class was in session, an aroma of fresh baking made its way enticingly along the corridor outside Carol's Food Technology room, adult voices rose and fell in explanation, childish ones called out answers to questions. High in the bare branches of the winter trees which lined one side of the school's perimeter birds flapped and sang, oblivious of the child who hid behind one of the trunks and wept.

The child took no heed of the bitter wind which tore mockingly at his green jersey and thin school shirt. He had fled immediately after morning register, not stopping to retrieve his coat from the cloakroom, wanting no comfort but that of solitude.

Another child in a house a long way off was whiling away the convalescent stages of a nasty episode of influenza by playing with the telescope his grandfather had given him at Christmas. With pride he adjusted the focus, minutely, to find that he could now see even a blackbird in a black-branched tree. He moved the instrument so that the scene panning before him was the ground under the trees and he saw the child.

From such a distance he imagined rather than saw the shake of the boy's shoulders as he sobbed. Half an hour later he was surprised to see the same child by the same tree. He frowned and called his sister who was in an earlier stage of the same illness.

'Hey, Zo-Zo, what's the longest you ever cried for?'

'Oh, shut up,' said Zoë crossly. Her throat ached and she resented the energy of her younger brother who had disobeyed parental instructions not to visit her room in case he should become re-infected. 'If Mum finds you here there'll be hell to pay.'

'You're not allowed to say hell. It's swearing.'

'Only at your age. At mine you can say it.'

'There's a boy in those trees who's been crying for ages. Ever since I came here.'

'You'll be crying if Mum catches you.'

'Really, Zo. He's been crying all that time. Come and see.'

'Why on earth should I get out of a warm bed to watch some kid bawling in the bushes?'

'Not bushes, trees. He must be freezing cold without a coat.'

Zoë frowned. 'No coat? How old is he?'

Reluctantly she pushed back the duvet and joined her younger brother at the window, but she required a different focus from him and they began to quarrel as she adjusted the telescope with limited success. When she did succeed she stared through the glass for a few seconds and then called her mother, who came up the stairs wearily to see what was the matter. A few moments later she ran down to the hall and called Morton's.

'Jason.' Ed Deacon caught up with him as he made his way along the corridor to the staffroom. 'We've just had a call from a woman who says one of our pupils has been crying in the grounds for more than an hour. Apparently he has no coat and she says it's disgusting no one has noticed his absence.'

'Where is he?'

'Under one of the trees opposite the science block. Ralph was going to ask Joanna to go out to him but she's not well so I said I'd go.'

Jason thought of the pleasant, calm, school secretary and knew that he and Ed would probably make poor substitutes. It took them a while to find the boy, whom Jason recognised with horror as one of his own form, Harry Jackson. He had been present that morning. Surely someone had noticed he was no longer with his classmates.

The priority was to get the child inside, away from the wind and cold. Jason put his own jacket round him while he and Ed led him back. They took over Joanna's small but organised office, which was warmed by an electric heater attached to a wall. Harry shivered, his sobs turning to great gasps for breath and sending shudders through his small frame.

'What is it?' asked Ed gently.

Jason switched on the kettle.

'Mum's gone.'

Jason paused in the act of putting coffee in a mug, meeting Ed's eyes over the child's head.

'She's gone with Kate and Sue because she doesn't want to live with my dad any more. She says she loves us but it didn't work out and she'll be happier with Tim.'

'Who are Kate and Sue?' asked Ed. 'Your sisters?'

Harry clasped his hands round the mug, seeking its warmth, and Jason hoped it was not too hot. He began to cry again.

'My stepsisters. They're Mum's but me and Jake are Dad's so she can't take us. She can't take Lisa either.'

'Who's Lisa?'

'My first mum's. She didn't take her when she went even though she was hers and not Dad's.'

Jason's head whirled with names. 'Who's Tim?' he asked reluctantly.

'Mum's boyfriend.'

'I think we had better ring up your dad,' said Ed gently. 'You're not really well enough to be in school today. We'll have the number somewhere unless you know it off by heart.'

Harry gabbled a collection of digits and Jason asked if it was for his home or his father's place of work. Harry said his father was a lorry driver and could be contacted on his mobile. Mr Jackson answered from the M1 and said they would have to keep Harry until Lisa got home from school and could look after him.

'How old is Lisa?' asked Ed when Jason had

121

relayed this information.

'Fifteen,' sniffed Harry miserably. 'But she won't want to look after me. When Dad's away she goes to Mike's. I'll be all right at home, Mr Deacon. Mum was often out all night.'

At that moment Joanna appeared with a pale face and it was with relief the two men handed Harry into her care, confident that she would track down a grandmother or aunt or neighbour with her usual ingenuity.

'What a crazy tangle.' Ed sounded weary rather than surprised as they made their way to the staffroom. He glanced at his watch. 'I've got a class in five minutes but it sounds like one for Social Services. We can't have thirteen-year-olds abandoned to their own devices. Sometimes I think the whole world has gone mad, although if one of my pupils said that I would make sarcastic remarks about clichés.'

'It has gone mad. You, me, Harry Jackson, half my form. I suppose somewhere there are some normal, happy families.'

'Indeed there are. Thousands of them, damn them. You can see them everywhere you go, out shopping on Saturdays, at the leisure centre in the evenings, sitting in pizza houses when you walk past, queuing for the cinema, smiling at us on parents' evenings and I hate every one of them.'

Ed turned in the direction of his class and Jason listened to the bell clanging its announcement of a change in lessons, his heart sinking. Ed had seemed to be rallying but was now mired once more in bitterness. He thought of Harry Jackson and wondered if Jake had wept like that when

122

Kat had uprooted him from home and father. The image haunted him throughout the day's lessons and the lonely evening which followed. He began to focus on the weekend when Jake and Leah would come to stay.

On Thursday Carol stopped him on the way to his car and presented him with a large cake.

'They'll love it,' she told him as he opened the tin and stared at the layers of chocolate smothering the top of the cake. A delicious smell teased his taste buds.

'So will I,' grinned Jason.

At home he put the cake away and went to check that Mrs Mansfield had put clean sheets on the children's beds. He turned up the heat from the radiators in both rooms to dispel the chilly air of disuse and replace it with the warmth necessary for two small children to play in. He planned to take them out only on Saturday morning and for them to pass the rest of the weekend as they would have done before they had been taken from him. He had already alerted their friends that Jake and Leah would be around for a couple of days and he was looking forward to the house once more being alive with the sound of children.

Jason went down to the kitchen to make sure that the necessary supplies of food and drink were in place. Mrs Mansfield had filled the fridge with fresh food and added six cans of Coca-cola. He must remember to check with Kat if Jake had already seen the Disney video he intended buying the next day. Excited, he found himself talking to Objubjub, telling him that the children were coming.

Kat rang at nine and Jason returned her greeting and routine enquiries as to how he was with good humour and something approaching warmth. A more detached part of his brain told him he was a fool to be ready to forgive Kat anything so long as his children were coming to see him. He recognised that he was adjusting to the change, that the sharp pain had become a dull ache, that he was accepting he must be content to see his children on three days out of every fourteen. He postponed confronting his meekness, wanting instead to concentrate on the detail of the imminent weekend.

'Jason, I'm sorry, I won't be able to bring the children over after all. I really am sorry but it's Mummy's birthday and I've promised to take them to see her and stay the weekend.'

'But you've always known it was Sheila's birthday this weekend. Why the sudden decision?'

'Daddy rang up to say they are having a party on the spur of the moment and invited me to help and spend the weekend at the same time. I could hardly say no.'

'Did you tell him it was my turn this weekend?'

'Oh, Jason, don't be so childish. Your turn, my turn. You make the children sound like a game of Ludo. You can have them next weekend instead. Damn it, Jason, they *want* to go to see their grandparents. They're excited about it.'

'I was excited about having them.'

'I'm sorry, but they must go to their granny's birthday party. Surely you can see that?'

Ice moved inside him but he tried to believe her, to accept that it really was a sudden decision on Alex's part to throw a party for Sheila, that the disappointment now engulfing him would not become a regular occurrence, but Ed Deacon's words rang in his brain: *It's surprising how many excuses they can think up for keeping your own children from you.*

'Definitely next weekend?'

'Actually I've just realised that's not a good idea after all. Jake has a sleepover on Saturday at the house of a new friend. Sorry, but the weekend after would be better. Let's say definitely that weekend.'

'No. This is impossible, Kat. I haven't seen them for a fortnight and now you're suggesting I wait another two weeks.'

'Well, call in and spend an evening with them in between.'

'When?'

'Wednesday. They don't have any activities on Wednesdays.'

'Fine. Wednesday and also Friday. They can come here on Friday evening and you can collect them on Saturday in time for Jake's sleepover or maybe you should just collect Jake and I'll bring Leah back on Sunday.'

'I'll have to think about it all. We can talk about it on Wednesday. I must fly now. Sorry, really sorry.'

Kat put down her receiver and Jason turned to face his suddenly empty home from which all the expectation had been so abruptly drained. For a few hours it had felt occupied by the children who had yet to arrive, now it was once more lifeless, just a place where he could be dry, warm, clean and fed.

His mind became filled with fantasies he knew he would never enact. He pictured himself arriving at Sheila's birthday party with a large bunch of flowers for his mother-in-law. No one could reasonably complain if he then played with his children or talked to them or watched them for the rest of the day. While the adults enjoyed the party he could take them up to bed, bath them, read to them.

He knew he would not do this, would not spoil the celebrations, would not create an atmosphere which might dimly communicate itself to the children. He made a mental note to ask Alan Parnell what redress he would have if Kat did this when they were legally separated or divorced. Could he then insist on his fortnightly access?

When he put the same question to Ed Deacon next day his colleague shook his head.

'Not if there's good reason for you to miss a weekend. Anyway, after a while the kids settle down in their new life and start making their own arrangements and commitments. They don't put their life on hold waiting for the fortnightly access weekend with Dad, even though they love it when it happens. So you get the school sports matches, the birthday parties and sleepovers, the godparents taking them to London and heaven knows what else. I've even had Ros pleading Sunday school as an excuse. Of course, they can feel guilty if there is something they would rather be doing when you want to see them so it's not easy on them either but don't get the idea that a nice legal agreement, all tied up in red tape and stamped by some court, is the answer to your problems. The only answer is a civilised break-up, with goodwill oozing from both sides and neither you nor I have that.'

Yet he and Kat had enjoyed a civilised marriage. Why then must the ending of it be characterised by cruelty? Why was the woman who was still legally his wife and who would always be the mother of his children so determined to steal his fatherhood, to deprive him of all that was most precious? Surely he must know her well enough to be able to work out the answer and, armed with the knowledge, persuade her to a different course?

'Forget it,' advised Ed when Jason voiced the thought. 'You don't know her at all. The one thing you're going to realise over the next few months, or however long it takes to sort out your life, is that for the last ten years you've been loving and making love to a stranger. Talking of strangers, has anyone any idea what is happening to Angus?'

Jason shook his head and turned away, trying not to let Ed see the damage caused by his brutality, too absorbed by his own misery to think of Angus's. He saw Ben Fuller watching him and recognised concern in the younger man's eyes. He made a brief gesture of reassurance in Ben's direction before gathering up his jacket and making for the door.

Ahead of him yawned the childless weekend and beyond that the years of battle as Kat played her conscienceless game. Two Year Eight girls ran past him towards the gate. He caught a snatch of their conversation.

'Dad's coming this weekend. That means steak and chips. He hates salads as much as I do. Mum says we'll die of early heart attacks...'

Mentally Jason heard a twelve-year-old Leah talking to her friend: 'I was supposed to be seeing Dad tomorrow but Mum's put it off again...'

'No,' said Jason aloud and a passing pupil stared at him curiously. *I'll fight you all the way, Kat, even if I beggar both of us in the process. Jake and Leah need both parents. Their father is not an optional extra.*

An hour later he found himself shouting the same words in reality, drowning out Kat's voice on the telephone as she tried to explain that Wednesday would not after all be convenient.

7

'I haven't seen them for six weeks.'

Jason kept his foot resolutely on the doorstep so that Kat could not shut the door without risk of doing him a serious injury.

'I know and I'm sorry but I have explained. You really can't see them now. They're at a party and won't be back for ages.'

'I'll wait.'

'I've got to go out myself otherwise you would be very welcome to come in and wait. Anyway, I don't want you getting them even more excited. I need to settle them down and get Leah to bed as soon as they come in.'

'I'll wait in the car then and I won't get them excited but I will not leave without seeing them.'

Kat sighed wearily. 'Have it your way but I do have to go out and it will get cold in the car. Why not find something to do and be back here about seven?'

It was a sensible suggestion and Jason pretended to agree but he drove only a short distance before turning into a nearby road and parking. He got out of the car and walked back to a point from which he could see the cottage. Twenty minutes later all the lights in the cottage were turned off and Kat came out of the front door. Before returning to lock it, she put a bag in the back of her car. As Jason took in its size he knew that he would not be seeing his children that night.

A fury of frustration and anger tempted him to follow the car but he forced himself to think rationally. He knew where his family lived and where Jake went to school and it was quite impossible for Kat to deny him access indefinitely. He must surely make her understand that. Perhaps Alex and Sheila could be prevailed upon to persuade her to a more reasonable course of action.

At eight o'clock his telephone rang and Kat's aggrieved voice demanded to know where he was. The children had been looking forward to seeing him and it was not fair to raise their expectations only to have them dashed on his every whim. He had made such a fuss that she had taken the children from the party early and got Leah into her pyjamas so that he could have maximum time with her when he arrived but they had waited and waited and Leah was crying and Jake in a mood and it was a monstrously selfish way for him to behave.

Jason heard her in disbelief, knowing that he had been comprehensively fooled. Realising that he did not trust her, she had been expecting him to keep watch, so she let him think she had plans to spend the night away and he had fallen into her heartless trap, as easily gulled as Malvolio. How she must be laughing at him, at the ease with which she had put him in the wrong, made him seem irresponsible, untrustworthy, uncaring.

Yet he could hardly believe that she would willingly cause pain to Jake and Leah, would play with their hopes and watch in satisfaction as those hopes crumbled in tears and recriminations. Perhaps after all the bag had been for a quite innocent purpose and Kat was merely transporting goods to a friend. His instincts told him this was not so but for now his principal concern must be to put matters right between himself and his children. He asked to speak to Jake.

'You must be joking. He's been upset enough for one night.'

'Kat, you are going to have to let me see them. No matter how many tricks and stratagems you employ, I will see them because I know where you all are and where Jake is at school every day. What you are doing is hurting no one but them so why don't we act like grown-ups and why won't you just accept that I am still their father and that I am going to go on seeing them until they in turn are grown up?'

'Anyone would think you were perched on some moral high ground! It's you who is hurting them. You arrive on the doorstep, refuse to leave, then say you will be back to see them, then disappear as if seeing them was too boring to hang around for and then you dare to lecture *me*. I think you are quite mad.'

Kat's voice had risen and in the background Leah began to wail loudly. Jason, who had no answer to Kat's repeated demands to know why he had not waited which would not have gravely worsened the situation, brought the conversation to a bitter and unsatisfactory end.

'Sounds par for the course,' observed Ed when Jason described the scene next day. His tone was one of disgust, of sympathy for another wronged father, but Jason thought he could detect some underlying, perhaps subconscious, satisfaction that he did not suffer alone or that he had been proved right when Jason had sought to dismiss his earlier advice, believing that he and Kat were different and would sort everything out in an amicable way.

'Go for a legal separation. Otherwise she may fool around like this until the divorce and then claim that you haven't taken an interest in them as a means of limiting access. It won't guarantee much apart from a large lawyer's bill but at least it will put some pressure on her.' Ed bent down to retrieve a fallen pencil.

Jason took it with a grunt of thanks. Deliberately he turned the conversation. 'Any news of Angus, yet?'

'No. He's being assessed for long-term sickness and I expect it will turn into early retirement on medical grounds. Ralph is going to have to get round to appointing an acting deputy soon.'

There should have been hope in that observation, thought Jason. Ed was sufficiently experienced and senior to have been considered for the post and would once have been eager for the promotion not only for its own sake but because it would have put him in a better position to influence the running of the school, to change much of what was wrong, but now the energy of hope had been replaced by the inertia of private misery and Ed might well not even apply for the vacancy. Jason wondered if he was looking at his own future, if in a year's time all the colour would have drained from the canvas of his life. As if to prevent such a fate he taught his classes with extra vigour, joked with other members of staff at lunchtime and pushed Kat resolutely to the back of his mind. At four o'clock he began to persuade himself that he had an interesting evening ahead when he expected no more than a cursory meal, some form-filling and an early night with only Objubjub for company.

He and Carol Marsh arrived at the school doors together. As he stood aside to let her go first Jason heard himself asking, 'Have you tried that new restaurant yet? What's it called? O Sole Mio?'

'No. Some friends went last week and came back raving about it.'

'I was thinking of going there tonight. How about coming along? My treat.'

Carol smiled. 'I'd love to but I've got my sister coming round. How about tomorrow?'

'Tomorrow it is.'

Jason felt his spirit lighten and knew that it was not the thought of pasta and Chianti which caused the small, long-forgotten, fluttery sensation that briefly entered him only to be replaced by an equally small and fleeting chill. The chill told him that even now he had not given up hope of regaining his old life, of Kat and the children returning, of the past few months passing from sharp, unhappy reality into nightmare – a disturbing nightmare indeed but one from which he had fully awoken.

He wondered if Kat sensed his desperate clinging to the past, if it made her wary and if her unreasonableness sprang from that uncertainty. Perhaps she would relax and let him see the children if only she could believe that he had accepted the future as she wanted it, was looking with resigned eyes at the scene upon which she gazed with eagerness and hope.

He could turn right towards his own home or left to try once more to see Jake and Leah, unannounced, defiant, pleading. Behind him a car horn sounded, sending its clang of impatience into the midst of pedestrians and traffic, startling people who hurried along clutching briefcases, sports bags and small purchases, and irritating drivers. Jason turned left.

The cottage was in darkness and remained so while he waited. At eight he gave up, knowing that Kat would protest it was too late and already well past Leah's bedtime. At home he found a note from Mrs Mansfield asking him to ring her and when he did so she told him she was taking a job as a care assistant and would not be able to clean for him any longer. Jason wished her well and promised a glowing reference, unable to decide if he were relieved at the diminution of the demands on his increasingly strained budget or depressed at the thought of taking on her tasks himself. Her withdrawal from his life was just another sign that it was changing irretrievably.

Objubjub wandered in and began to weave between Jason's legs. He bent down to smooth the tabby creature, suddenly grateful to it for its permanence, for its symbol of stability, suggesting that all was not lost. He mocked himself for the thought, laughing aloud, wanting instead to cry as he opened a tin of Whiskas for Objubjub and of baked beans for himself.

When he had eaten he found himself unable to concentrate on the SATS forms he had brought home to fill in and, choosing television instead, flicked irritably from channel to channel, attending to none of the output for more than a few minutes, unable to recall what he had seen. At ten o'clock he yawned noisily and went to bed where he found he was not tired enough to sleep. Objubjub leapt onto his feet and he lay still until the creature's contented, loud purring lulled him into fitful, dream-laden slumber.

Between snatches of sleep he saw himself from afar and knew he must take control or his life would become weary and purposeless. Take up a sport. Join an evening class. Find a new hobby. Learn a language. Get out and meet people. The advice, so often heard in the background as it issued tritely from radio programmes where experts purported to solve the problems of the lonely, or read in the agony columns of the magazines Kat had brought into the house, haunted the night hours of his rejection, laughing at him as he had once laughed at it with its simplicity, its assumption that the loss of his fatherhood could be salved by an hour's squash, a lesson in carpentry or conversational French. Awake, such banality would not even have occurred to him but, half asleep, he was powerless to resist its disorderly, sporadic invasion.

He woke unrefreshed and knew that the false energy of the previous day would dissolve into irritation and fatigue. He knew also that the present situation was beyond his own solving, that he must enlist whatever help the law offered, however slender its hope, however uncertain its outcome and however great its expense. He would telephone Alan Parnell during morning break and demand that he institute immediate proceedings to re-establish contact between Jason and his children. Immediate, repeated Jason to himself, not after giving Kat time to respond to yet another letter written to Lane and Webb by Alan Parnell and passed by them in due course to their client, Katharine Mary Kirk, who would claim its delivery had been delayed and that she needed time to reflect fully on its contents.

At break Jason found an empty classroom and sat on a table to make his call. He was scrolling through the numbers on his mobile when it rang unexpectedly and Alan Parnell's voice came on the line.

'Jason, glad I've caught you. Is this a good moment to talk?'

'Yes, I was going to phone you.'

'Can you look in after school?'

'I can tomorrow. Tonight it's history club and

then I'm taking a lady to dinner.' Jason kept his tone light to quell the shaft of unease which had suddenly entered him as he wondered why Parnell wanted him to call in person. Surely if he had good news to impart he would have given it to him there and then on the telephone, taking pleasure in his client's relief, in his grateful thanks?

'I think we need to talk a bit sooner if it's at all possible.'

The unease swelled and burst, filling Jason with cold waves of premonition. Mentally he began to re-arrange his day and was soon doing so in reality, grateful to the younger colleague who said of course he would take history club and to Carol who wished him good luck. He saw the shadow of anxiety in her eyes and a fresh set of doubts battered his tired mind: he was not yet ready for the demands of a new emotional relationship. He wanted Carol as a friend with her practicality, serenity and unsmothering sympathy. He wanted her easy, humorous, undemanding company but he did not want her love, did not want her or anyone else depending on him for happiness.

Jason found his stomach shaking as he swiftly passed through the niceties required by the conventions of good manners. Parnell replied that he was quite well, thank you, and he hoped Jason was too despite all the worry. It was very cold, wasn't it, and two of the partners in the firm were down with flu which he trusted Jason had escaped.

Jason confirmed his good health and waited. Parnell cleared his throat and looked embarrassed.

'I have received a rather difficult letter from

Lane and Webb which I would like you to read as soon as possible. I am afraid your wife claims that you have been threatening and harassing her and the children.'

'She says *what?* That's absurd.'

'Specifically she accuses you of having said that you know where she and the children live and that you know where Jake goes to school. Your tone was such that she took this to be a threat of abduction. She further claims that you have waited for long periods outside her house, just watching, and that you have gravely upset the children by promising to visit and then failing to do so even though you must have known that they would have to be withdrawn from a children's party in order to meet your impromptu demand for access. You are said to have shouted at her on the telephone, to have called at her house unannounced and to have wedged your foot in the doorway, leaving her so frightened that she fled the house when you left. She says she had overlooked a previous incident in which you tried to snatch Leah from her child-minder because she believed you were distraught and not responsible for your actions but that she cannot go on making allowances for behaviour which upsets not only her but the children. If we do not give Lane and Webb undertakings in writing that such conduct will cease immediately, then she will seek an injunction.'

Jason stared at the solicitor in disbelief. Parnell looked sympathetic but kept his mind on his job.

'I think we had better look at the facts first. Did you say that you knew where she and the children live and where your son goes to school?'

'Yes, but not in the context she has invented.'

He felt the fury rising within him and knew that he must not let the other see it, must not give Parnell even a scintilla of cause to think Kat might be right when she called him unreasonable.

'I hadn't seen them for six weeks and I still haven't seen them. Kat made a whole series of excuses and I simply said it was a quite pointless exercise because I knew where to find them and would eventually do so. Eventually I lost patience and turned up unannounced.'

Parnell's expression did not change as Jason described his subsequent actions before finishing with the lame, miserable observation that he could not understand why Kat was behaving in such a fashion.

'That gives me enough to reply to Lane and Webb and to threaten some action of our own but I think it would be better if you came to me in future rather than engaging in a course of action which may be innocent but which can all too easily be misconstrued.'

'All I want to do is see my children. I don't want it going on like this until the divorce. I want a legal separation.'

'That will be costly.'

'What price would you attach to *your* fatherhood?'

'I will do what I can, Jason, but meanwhile do not make any attempt to see them except by prior agreement. I'm sorry – I know it's all too easy for me to say, "Don't see them", but my hand will be stronger with Lane and Webb and you will not give your wife any more ammunition.'

138

Jason was silent, trying to force the images of a small boy and girl from his mind.

'I'm sorry,' repeated Parnell as his client rose to leave.

'Two weeks.' Jason forgot his vow of reasonableness. 'If Kat doesn't agree to let me see them in the next two weeks, I'll turn up at her door with a battering ram.'

'I think you'll find the law more effective on this occasion. Mrs Kirk will not want to prejudice her own position and I am sure Lane and Webb will advise her accordingly.'

Five days later Jason's faith in the law was partially restored when Kat rang to say he could have the children from Friday to Sunday the following weekend. She was cheerful and seemingly oblivious of the last two months' stratagems and arguments, of having accused him of threatening and alarming conduct. As they made arrangements and exchanged news of each other's parents, Jason grew increasingly doubtful that his wife would honour the agreement they were now making, certain instead that she would find some emergency at the last moment. He could not bring himself to trust that her present mood would last, briefly wondering if she were becoming mentally unstable even as some deeper instinct bade him beware. *Timeo Danaos et dona ferentis.*

'I fear the Greeks, and I fear them bearing gifts,' Jason translated when he used the same phrase to Ed Deacon next day. 'It's what some Trojan said when his countrymen let the wooden horse into the city or maybe it was Cassandra herself. Can't remember. I'm only a history teacher.'

He knew Ed was not deceived by his apparent light-heartedness, that he understood Jason genuinely did fear Kat as any victim fears, however unwillingly, his tormentor, knew that for the rest of the week Jason would alternate between hope and misery, between certainty and dread, between gratitude and hatred.

As the week drew to a close, he began to fear the sound of the telephone, convinced that at any moment Kat would ring with some excuse to put off the children's visit. When he picked up the phone and heard her voice on Thursday evening, his anger was almost blunted by resignation, by the grim satisfaction of being vindicated but she rang merely to confirm some detail and the next evening Jake and Leah were delivered to his door.

His offer of a drink was more polite than warm but Kat declined airily and departed after only a few minutes' conversation, which took place as they stood by her car. Jason watched his wife's retreat with disbelief, half expecting to see the car return and Kat lean from its window to say sorry, she must take the children back now. The sound of loud protests from Objubjub reclaimed his attention and he hurried indoors to find the tabby cowering behind the sofa.

'Why doesn't he love me any more?' demanded Leah tearfully. 'I want to stroke him.'

'He hasn't seen you for a while so he needs time to get used to you again. If you leave him alone for a bit he'll come out and then you can stroke him.'

Leah turned away pouting sulkily.

'Where's Jake?'

Leah rubbed her eyes with her fists and did not answer so Jason went in search of his son in whom he had sensed a subdued spirit. He found him sitting on his bed trying not to look mutinous.

'What is it?' asked Jason gently.

'Nothing.' The response seemed designed both to repel and encourage further enquiry. Jason had only to persist a moment or so before the dam of Jake's resentment burst.

'I was going to France with the rest of the class on a boat. Mum promised and I wanted to go. I was going to see the Eiffel Tower and tomorrow they're all going to Disney...' Jake struggled with tears.

'Jake, you should have gone. You know I wouldn't have minded. Why didn't you go?'

'Mum said I had to come here. She said you would think I liked France more than you.'

Appalled, Jason stared at his son in helpless sympathy, his indignation swelling. Not even the last two months had prepared him for ruthlessness on such a scale. He wanted to telephone Kat immediately, to confront her with the heartless choice she had offered their son, to give relief to his feelings by shouting at her in an attempt to blast his way through whatever she had become to find what he had once known and loved. He refrained, because he believed that was what she wanted him to do, so she might complain to her lackeys at Lane and Webb that he frightened the children with his rages.

'OK, Jake. We'll go to Disney in the summer. You, me and Leah. It will be more fun than going with the school.'

How was he to afford Disney? He might just be able to manage Weston-super-Mare if Parnell's next account was less than he feared. It was odd that Kat had not asked him for a contribution towards the school trip. Chilled, he thought it would be not at all odd if she had never intended Jake to go.

The knowledge that Kat hated him had turned from a sharp, stabbing pain that sometimes caught him unaware to a dull ache somewhere in the background of his consciousness, which hurt enough if he confronted it, if he concentrated on it, but made little protest if he preferred to ignore it. Until now it had not occurred to him that the hatred was strong enough to involve direct cruelty to Jake or Leah.

Of course, it was a monstrous cruelty to deprive them of their father but their suffering was not Kat's aim: to her it was merely the regrettable but unavoidable consequence of the split. By comparison, perhaps, the petty cruelty now exposed was insignificant but it seemed to Jason incomparably horrible. Surely Kat would not raise Jake's happy, childish expectations of a treat in the full knowledge that it was to be snatched away at the last moment just to spite her abandoned husband, just to punish him for his wish to remain a father to his children?

He sought for other explanations. Perhaps her solicitors had warned her about the consequences of denying access any longer and she had over-reacted, afraid to plead another, this time genuine, cause for delay. Perhaps there was some other reason why she had decided that she did not want Jake to go with his class to France and a visit to his father had provided a timely excuse. He prayed for any reason except the one on which he had at first fastened.

Jake, only partially mollified by the promise of Disney in the summer, accompanied Jason reluctantly when he said they should go and find Leah, who was sitting in an armchair with the edge of a cushion in her mouth. Her eyes were full of tears and she began to grizzle.

'I've got some chocolate cake.' Jason could hear the forced enthusiasm in his tone. 'Want some?'

Leah shook her head and bawled. Jake headed for the kitchen with dutiful rather than eager anticipation. Jason scooped his daughter off the sofa and held her in his arms. She let him press her head into his shoulder and her wails subsided to small moans. After a while Jason set her down, searching for a tissue to mop up the tears. As he commenced the task he felt her skin burning through the paper and, in alarm, laid his hand on her forehead.

'She's got a dreadful temperature. Did Mum say she was ill?'

Jake swallowed an uncomfortably large piece of cake. 'Nope.'

'Well, was she crying like this before you arrived here?'

Jake, his mouth full again, shook his head.

Jason mentally debated the merits of ringing Kat. If he did not do so and Leah were really ill over the weekend then she would berate him for not letting her know, for leaving it until the last minute when she would have to make arrangements for appropriate care to enable her to carry out her teaching commitments. She would call him irresponsible and might use the incident against him in the future. If he did ring she might decide to come and take Leah back with her or even interpret the call as a tacit request to do so.

He decided to put Leah to bed and postpone the decision until he saw how she was the following day. First he took the rest of the cake away from Jake and was about to ask him what games he had brought when the doorbell rang and two of Jake's old playmates stood on the step. Jake's mood swung dramatically and soon the sound of children's laughter filled the house.

Leah began to bawl again as Jason changed her into her nightdress. He felt thick, warm pyjamas would have been better suited to her state of health but Kat had not packed any. He tucked her into bed and said he would bring her a hot drink. However, when he returned with a steaming cup and a story book it was to find his daughter sound asleep.

In the night Leah was sick and Jason wearily changed the bedding. Two hours later she was sick again and clung to him wailing. There was no further spare bedding and he did not want to put her in with Jake in case she passed on the infection. He could see little option but to take her into his own bed where he laid her on the side Kat used to sleep and waited till she drifted into feverish slumber. Once her breathing had become regular he quietly switched out the light and began to drag the bedding downstairs, having some notion that the quicker it was washed the quicker he would have a spare supply. He had just put soap powder in the machine when Leah, waking in an empty parental bed, feeling unwell and wanting Kat, began to cry loudly, this time waking Jake, who protested irritably.

Jason glanced at the clock. Three a.m. He called out a reassurance to Leah and began to climb the stairs to calm his sobbing daughter, wondering if he was to get any sleep that night. Jake appeared on the landing, asking for a drink.

It was nearly five o'clock before Leah fell into a sound sleep. An hour later Jake was wide awake and pottering noisily round his room. Jason telephoned Kat as soon as it was decent.

'Can you cope?'

'Yes, if I can get the bedding dry. I'm really just warning you that she will need looking after on Monday. She won't be fit to be taken outside to a minder and indeed I'm not at all sure she is well enough even to leave here. Are you teaching on Monday?'

'Yes, but she can't stay with you if she is ill. She needs me. I'll come over now and put blankets and a hot water bottle in the car.'

Kat rang off before Jason could protest. He was not even sure he should protest. Leah had several times asked for Kat and he could not reasonably object to her being looked after by her mother when she was ill.

'Where's Jake?' demanded Kat when she arrived shortly before ten.

'Gone off to play with Gavin. He and Tom came round last night.'

'I would have thought that after all the fuss you made about wanting to see your son you would have been entertaining him yourself.'

'I will be later. Why didn't you tell me he was supposed to be on a school trip to France? It was a rotten thing to do to him.'

'Tell that to your solicitors.'

'Kat, we mustn't make pawns of our children. There was no need to make Jake suffer. Isn't it bad enough that we've split up, that Mummy and Daddy aren't together any more, without making them feel part of an unending battle?'

Jason watched her draw in her breath for the luxury of shouting at him just as Leah, waking and sensing Kat's presence in the house, began a distressed calling. Kat turned and sped upstairs and an hour later both she and Leah were gone.

Jake came back at lunchtime, his face glowing from play in the cold air, his trainers caked in mud. Jason looked at them in dismay.

'Mum says I need new ones anyway. We're going to get some next Saturday. Mum says my feet grow while she just watches them. Dad, why can't we see things grow? Things like grass? You never see it move upwards, do you, but it must move, mustn't it? Mum says it's because it's so slow but if you watched it always and never blinked you still wouldn't see it move, would you?'

Jason grinned, rejoicing in his son's conversation, realising how much he had missed it, trying not to think about the silence to which he would wake on Monday morning. He wondered if Kat would consider it helpful or hostile if he offered to buy Jake the new trainers he had been promised. Would she be grateful to be spared the expense or resentful to be deprived of Jake's pleasure in the treat? If he telephoned to ask her Jake would hear and would be upset if she said no.

'We could get them today.'

Jake gave a yell of triumph. 'Can we get some like Gavin's?'

'I expect so.'

'Cool.' Jake spread tomato sauce on his sausage, his expression one of happy expectation. Sausages, mash, tomato sauce and new trainers seemed to have replaced France and Disney with remarkable ease.

Two hours later Jake sulked and protested as Jason gently but unwaveringly refused to buy the most expensive designer trainers the shop had to offer.

'You said I could have a pair like Gavin's. You promised.'

'No. I said, "I expect so". You didn't tell me Gavin had these. I really would love you to have them, Jake, but I just can't afford it. I'm sorry.'

'Mum would let me have them.'

'OK. Then buy them next Saturday with Mum as you were going to do.'

'Gavin's dad can afford them.'

'He's richer than I am. Sorry, Jake.'

Jason knew the answer would not make much sense to his son. Gavin's father was a bus conductor with four children and a small, two-bedroomed house. Jake had often been invited to join Gavin on family outings and Kat had always lectured him on asking for the least expensive food or drink. He had never been encouraged to consider the material wealth of his friends but some vague notion must by now have occurred to him that his family was more affluent than Gavin's. He would have no understanding of the strains imposed by legal bills and the necessity to keep two houses instead of one, nor would it be right to burden him with such information.

Jason noticed one or two disapproving glances cast at his sulky son. It did not help that a girl of about the same age as Jake was excitedly trying on the shoes he coveted.

He had been about to tell Jake that because his feet were growing so fast it would not make sense for even a millionaire to buy them but now that would be a tactless remark. He was alarmed to find that he wanted very much to give in to his son, to let him have what he yearned for regardless of the cost and he knew he was trying to compensate for his absence from Jake's life. He knew it even as he compromised and, while still denying Jake his first choice, bought trainers more expensive than he would normally have contemplated.

Jake trudged dispiritedly beside him as they returned to the car.

'How do you fancy Longleat tomorrow? I could see if Tom and Gavin can come and we could take a picnic. It would mean getting up pretty early.'

'OK,' Jake shrugged. He wanted to imply that he was indifferent, that he was not in the least excited but would go if it pleased his father. Jason was not deceived but despised himself for trying to bribe happiness from his son.

On the way home he called at Gavin's house to

issue the invitation and then at Tom's, feeling a chill of envy as he always did when in the midst of family togetherness. He supposed this reaction would fade over time but occasionally it was as painful as in the early days of Kat's departure.

When he spoke to his wife on the telephone that evening to enquire after Leah he told her about both the trainers and Longleat and was assailed by her scorn. He was quite mad to buy such expensive shoes when Jake's feet were growing so fast, it would look ostentatious and worse still it would mean that she would have to restrict Jake's use of them. She could hardly have shoes like that ruined in the first five minutes and it would be a lot of hassle. Perhaps he should leave the purchase of clothes and shoes to her in the future.

As for Longleat, it would mean Jake returning very late and she would have to give him supper and get him off to bed in an excited state and she already had her hands full with Leah being so ill. Jason listened with both resignation and surprise. In the ten years of their marriage Kat had hardly ever nagged. He wondered if her nerves were breaking and if the split was proving more complicated than she had imagined.

'Kat, are you sure you're happy?' He had uttered the words without time for thought and endured the resulting explosion of anger in silence.

Later, as he and Jake put together the ingredients for the next day's picnic, talking excitedly about lions and seals, he wondered how Kat could begrudge any child the fun of such an outing and was fired by a momentary flash of renewed anger about the cancelled trip to France.

149

He thought of some of his divorced friends but, other than Ed, he knew of no case where the animosity of the parents was deliberately visited on the children.

He wondered if even Ed's wife could be behaving as badly as Kat, little knowing that on Monday morning Kat's current meanness would pale into insignificance as a new, terrifying trap yawned under his feet.

8

The morning had been tranquil enough, if teaching at Morton's could ever be described in such terms, and when a message reached Jason halfway through the lunch break that Ralph Hillier wanted to see him in his office immediately he had no cause for alarm. As he made his way along the corridor he glanced through a window and saw Ed Deacon getting into his car. Jason frowned and looked at his watch. Ed would be due in class for the first of the afternoon lessons soon and it seemed a strange time for him to be leaving the school grounds.

'Ah, Jason. I'm glad you could spare me a few minutes. It's all very awkward but I think you're as close to Ed as anybody and I'm hoping you might help.'

Jason looked at the head, puzzled, unease beginning to stir inside him.

'I am afraid I have had to suspend Ed Deacon.

In these sorts of circumstances there is really no choice.'

Jason gaped. While he struggled to make sense of what he had just heard, Hillier was reluctantly continuing, his tone embarrassed rather than sorrowful, his demeanour stiff rather than distressed.

'Ros Deacon has complained to the police. She says Ed has been abusing the youngest child.'

'But that's outrageous. I can't think of a more unlikely paedophile. Ed adores his children.' Jason found himself stumbling over the words, unable to marshal them in the right order. He was shaking with fury.

'I agree but neither of us can be really sure, can we? People who are engaged in serious evil don't wear a badge proclaiming it. The Moors murderers were junior clerks in an office and their colleagues worked alongside them for years without any inkling as to how they were spending their spare time. Nobody suspected the Yorkshire Ripper or Harold Shipman. We may think we know someone well but we could be utterly wrong and I have to play it by the book. I'm sorry, Jason.'

'What do you want me to do?'

'Keep in touch with him, keep his spirits up, make sure he gets the right sort of help.'

'I'll try – of course I will – but we're not that close.'

'Ed isn't close to anyone here except Angus and he won't be much use at the moment. At least you understand Ed's situation so far as separation from his kids is concerned. I would be grateful if you would call him tonight.'

'I suppose everyone is going to have to know?'

'I can hardly conceal the suspension even if there is no charge at the end of it all. Of course, if that happens he can come back.'

Come back to what? To the whispers of his colleagues, the curious glances of the pupils? Ed Deacon was destroyed. Beneath his indignation was some vague fear, which suddenly took shape and pierced him so sharply that he caught his breath. Kat could do this to him, could speak falsely and ensure that he had no access to the children as a result. He arrested his thoughts in mid-gallop. Such a notion was preposterous.

Hillier was looking at him curiously and he forced his thoughts back to Ed and reality, saying that yes, of course he would call. As he left the head's office he found the other geography teacher waiting outside. His face was bright with the prospect of increased importance and Jason realised that the news was spreading already. In the course of the afternoon he discussed the Industrial Revolution, the nature of trench warfare and the Peasants' Revolt, his mind preoccupied instead with the twenty-first century and the men who struggled as flies in its web.

He decided to call on Ed in person rather than telephone, half expecting that he might refuse to see him as Angus Gaskill had done. He was relieved when Ed opened the door, unweeping and sober and apparently glad to see him.

'The police are coming to see me tomorrow. I suppose I might find out more then. Can I get you some tea? Something stronger?'

'Can you do coffee?'

Jason followed Ed into the kitchen and sat down at a small pine table. On the fridge was a magnetic photo frame from which smiled two boys and a much younger girl. On a small notice-board a child's drawing of a snail flapped on its pin as the steam from the kettle lifted it. On the shelf to his left were mugs with motifs from children's stories and films. It was a kitchen such as one might find in any family home up and down the country, thought Jason, but this was no longer a family home.

As if reading Jason's thoughts his colleague murmured, 'They have only come here twice in the last three months and after this I suppose they won't be allowed to come at all and the law may take a long time to decide I'm innocent. Meanwhile I can't work but as I'm on full pay that won't affect Ros. She'll go on getting the maintenance as usual.'

'What about the big ones? The ones that used to go to Morton's? They must be teenagers by now. What do they make of it all?'

'Chris is fourteen and Luke nearly fifteen. I do not know what Ros will have told them but I suppose Social Services are bound to interview them in the circumstances and maybe the police as well. Given their ages, I don't suppose the ban on seeing them will last for long but God knows when I'll next see Chloe.'

Jason was silent, unable to ask the only question which might have made sense of what was going on, because Ed himself did not know the nature of the allegations.

Ed, as if reading his thoughts, began to talk

153

about the practicalities of his absence from Morton's, giving Jason messages for the other geography teacher, asking him to locate some small personal item in his locker, sending his regards to Hillier. Neither of them mentioned Angus as though the subject of breakdown had suddenly become taboo.

'You'll get through this, Ed,' was Jason's prediction as he left, his mind briefly reverting to Angus. 'Chloe is nine and old enough to be believed when she denies it all. Ros will back off.'

'Not Ros. She wouldn't go this far just to back off, believe me. Whatever it is she is saying she will try to make stick.'

'Let me know how it goes with the police.'

'I'll tell you everything. Good luck with Kat.'

Good luck with Kat. Jason felt the familiar ice move inside him. Was that apparent politeness a belated recognition that his host had been too self-absorbed to enquire after Jason's own situation or was it more sinister, a concealed warning that Kat could do to him what Ros Deacon had done to Ed?

Even as he dismissed the possibility as too fantastic to contemplate, Jason began to seek in his mind for incidents which Kat might misinterpret or distort. He remembered Leah crying when she was ill and he was changing her into her nightdress while Jake played downstairs with his friends. He dismissed the incident angrily. The others had seen Leah crying and knew she was distressed so why should they think differently when they heard her screaming upstairs? But later that night he had moved her into the parental bed

154

– his bed – while he changed the sheets on hers. That was where Kat had found her next day.

Kat, of course, had seen nothing odd because she had not been expecting to but supposing she had come to the house actively seeking evidence for a purely vindictive allegation? Surely then she would find it in half a dozen innocent episodes? How long before she realised that it was in her power to deprive him of Jake and Leah permanently? To get rid of him by sending him to prison?

He found reassurance not in any belief that Kat's malice would not stretch so far but in thinking of Alex and Sheila who would surely fight such nonsense. In the morning he recognised the nonsense as stemming from his own mind. What was happening to Ed was of a major order of magnitude and was the exception not the rule. Most ex-wives would be horrified by the very thought of such a manoeuvre, would not dream of subjecting their children to such an ordeal.

Most ex-wives would not have built up a child's hope of a trip to France only to snatch it away at the last moment to spite the father. The thought reminded him that he had promised Jake Disney in the summer and it was already April. It now occurred to him that he would need Kat's permission to take Jake out of the country and hoped she would see no need to disappoint her son a second time.

'Disney? I'd clean forgotten you had promised him,' cried Kat when he broached the subject as he collected his son and daughter for an access weekend. 'Oh, dear. His godfather is taking him at half-term.'

'Henry is taking Jake on holiday? To Disney? Since when?' Jason tried to keep his voice even, to suppress the rising tide of fury.

'He and Frances have had it planned a long time. They are going with friends and five children between them but they've got some special deal and could take another child free. Jake has always got on with Henry's boys and it seemed too good an opportunity to miss and I just said yes. Jake is wildly excited so I hope you are not going to be difficult.'

Jason turned to look at his son in disbelief and found him very red in the face, staring studiously at his toes. He tried to be reasonable and failed. The summer would seem unbearably far off to Jake and the temptations of a trip in a few weeks together with other children must have been irresistible, especially as Kat, in whose supposed lapse of memory Jason did not believe, would have been enthusiastically urging him to go. He still felt betrayed and bit his lip lest he should say so and add to the burden of Jake's guilt.

'Sorry, Dad,' muttered Jake unhappily as they drove to Jason's house. 'I won't go with Uncle Henry.'

'You must. It's all arranged. We'll do something else in the summer.'

There was an uncomfortable silence before Jake suddenly said, 'Dad, you and Mum don't like each other, do you?'

Startled, Jason looked at his son through the car mirror. 'Of course we do. It's just that Mum doesn't want to be with me all the time.'

Jake shook his head and tears poured down his cheeks. 'You hate each other. That's why Mum wanted me to go to Disney with Uncle Henry ... you hate each other.'

He began to sob, his small frame shuddering with the effort to stem the tide of grief. Jason glanced in the mirror again, this time at Leah and was relieved to see her asleep. He pulled the car to a halt beside a grass verge and got out, opening the back door to put his arm round his son.

'Mum and Dad do not hate each other. Promise. You and Leah quarrel sometimes but you don't hate her, do you? Mum just forgot I was supposed to be taking you to Disney, that's all. It doesn't matter. As I say, we'll find somewhere else to go in the summer holidays. Anyway it's ages away. You have all this term first.'

'I wish it was like it used to be, when we all lived together.'

'So do I but this can also be fun.'

Jake took the tissue Jason proffered and blew his nose miserably. He handed the dirty handkerchief back to his father who pocketed it with a grin. But his son still looked unhappy and, knowing that this time he really must confront Kat, Jason resolved that if necessary he would appeal to Alex and Sheila. The children must not be used as counters in his wife's mad game any longer.

He was not surprised when Kat was dismissive.

'If you hadn't let him see you were upset it wouldn't have happened. You could have said how brilliant it was that Jake would be going with other children instead of just you and how you would think up something even better for the summer. Instead of which you acted like a spoilt child.'

'Granted I could have handled it better, but you could have warned me instead of letting me find out when Jake was there. He thinks we hate each other and he's not far wrong. At the moment we appear to be doing our best to produce a well and truly screwed-up kid. I can't believe you want that any more than I do. We have to have some ground rules.'

Kat shrugged. 'It seems to me those rules work pretty well in your favour as things stand. I'm the one who copes with all the work and washing, who gets them to school each day, who imposes the discipline and looks after them when they're ill, while you just waltz along every other week-end, taking them out, spoiling them, giving them a good time. If I tell Jake off what does he do? Disappears to his bedroom and sends text messages to Daddy. He's always pestering to ring you up and doesn't believe me when I say we can't afford it. Meanwhile you just ring up at your convenience regardless of what I might be trying to get them to do at the time.'

'All of which is entirely of your own making. I was quite happy to share all that with you when we were together but you, and you alone, decided to walk out, so don't expect me to shed any tears if now you find it is not as easy as you thought.'

'I left because I wasn't happy.'

'Why not? What had I done?'

'You've asked that many times before and I'm not going through it all again. The answer does not change. What matters is now.'

158

'What matters is our children. You have to stop using Jake.'

'Oh, don't be so ridiculous. I don't use Jake. What a drama about absolutely nothing.'

Jason gave up, hoping the warning was enough, that in private, away from him, Kat would review her conduct and find it wanting. She loved the children as much as he and must surely see the harm in what she was doing. For the time being he must be content to rely on that.

He gave little thought to her lengthy complaint about the difficulties of bringing up two small children single-handed, believing he had answered her when he had pointed out that it was her choice. He read no danger to himself in her lament, sensed no premonition of consequences yet to flow. Kat had been in a temper and had vented her disgust with her lot and that was all the significance he saw in their exchange.

Indeed he scarcely thought of Kat at all as events at Morton's claimed all his attention over the next few days. Ed Deacon rang to say the police visit had been postponed and would now take place towards the end of the week, Ben announced the date of his wedding to Debbie, and Hillier that the Ofsted inspection would now take place in May.

'Just as we're gearing up for exams,' grumbled one of the science teachers.

'About time, too,' muttered Ben, sotto voce.

Hillier followed that announcement with the news that Matt Johnson was to be acting deputy head until Angus's future became clearer.

'It's taken them long enough,' said Carol.

'God help the English results,' said Ben. 'He's the best we've got in that department.'

It was not the fortunes of the staff which preoccupied Jason as the week unfolded but those of the children. On Tuesday Social Services decided to take Harry Jackson into care, having given up all hope of his father making satisfactory arrangements for him to be looked after in his absence. Harry screamed when they came for him and was abducted by his father from outside Morton's the following morning. No one saw it happen and it was lunchtime before the school rang Social Services to check that Harry was being kept away. The hue and cry which followed was on regional television that evening and in the national newspapers the next day.

The lorry Jackson had been driving was found in a service station near Dover instead of Newcastle. Harry's sister confirmed that, yes, Harry had a passport. Jackson's bank account had been emptied. The police swarmed into Morton's and the press massed outside the gate. Two girls from Year Ten turned the waistbands of their skirts over several times to shorten the length and found more than one occasion to be standing about in the vicinity of the entrance.

'I seem to recall another child from that tangled tale,' Jason told Hillier. 'I remember because he had the same name as my son, Jake. What's happened to him?'

'He and the sister are in care while Social Services try to track down relatives. The mother of Jake and Harry is dead but the sister's mother is still alive somewhere, they think. It's a hideous

160

mess. Apparently Jackson asked Jake if he wanted to run away too but the lad said no. His father appears to have taken that in his stride and left him behind.'

Jason groped for words. 'But didn't they take him into care with Harry?'

'No. He's just sixteen and so of course can be left alone when his father is away overnight.'

'Couldn't he have looked after Harry?'

'Social Services tried that but he was no more reliable than the sister. They also tracked down the stepmother who left not long ago and she wouldn't have him.'

'They could hardly have done more, I suppose, but I can't help observing that Harry now appears to be with the one person who loves him enough to fight for him.'

'Perhaps, but he didn't bother too much with the boy's care, did he? Leaving him alone all night? That's what is alarming everyone. He hasn't a clue and is just as likely to leave Harry alone wherever he is now as he did before. Only they're abroad and Harry will be even less likely to cope. Damn it, Jason, the child is barely thirteen and a very young thirteen at that. He is far away from every-one he knows and he isn't streetwise. If his father just leaves him while he goes off in search of work anything could happen. Jackson needs shooting.'

'He may not be shot but they will probably send him to prison and for what? For loving his own child enough not to want to see him in care.'

'For neglecting that child, Jason. Don't be too influenced by your own situation. This one is different.'

'Hundreds of kids are left alone all night, some by parents who should be horsewhipped, but many by parents who just don't know any better. Jackson wasn't feckless or he wouldn't have worked all hours of the day and night and he appears to have been willing enough to look after – in his own way – whatever children were foisted on him by deserting women. It's just that his norms aren't our norms. That doesn't make him bad.'

'He is bad for Harry.'

'He loves Harry.'

'Jason, it's not as if Social Services didn't make every last attempt to sort something out. They tried with both brother and sister who each said they would look after Harry and then went off all night when Jackson wasn't there. They tried with neighbours and they tried finding relatives. Jackson knew all that, knew there was a problem, knew they could take Harry away, but still did nothing about it. He could have given up the night driving but he didn't. He has only himself to blame.'

Jason could not argue, knowing that Hillier was right, that it would be better for Harry if he and his father were to be found. Perhaps he would have sympathised less with Jackson had he not often imagined a scenario in which he took Jake and Leah away, far away, to a place where they could be together and unthreatened by Kat's malice. He had always known the dream was a fantasy but Jackson had somehow crossed the line which divides reality and whimsy, had confused what he would like to do with what he must do, had taken no thought for consequences in his urgent need to outwit the authority which denied him his own son.

He must at least have known that he could not return untouched, that he was giving up house, job and the other children for a long time even if he evaded detection. He must have realised that he would be embarking on the life of a fugitive, that, if caught, he would face retribution and would still lose Harry. Perhaps he saw no risks beyond that, took no cognisance of the possibility of prison, which would cut him off from his son far more comprehensively than Social Services had in mind. Did he wonder how he would educate a fugitive child on foreign soil? Or was it all intended as a cry for help, a cry which would echo across the continent as he and Harry stayed one step ahead of their pursuers? Had he intended it as nothing more than a piece of giant blackmail?

The details of Harry's life became public property and the subject of a leader, in one of the broadsheets, which lamented the travesty of family values embodied in the kaleidoscope of shifting relationships to which Harry had been subjected in his short life. At Morton's staff and pupils talked of little except the abduction for days until the trail went cold and the Jacksons ceased to feature, first prominently and then at all, in the news. The press contingent at the school gate petered out and normality returned.

Normality for Terry Pepper was to be teased. Jason knew this and kept a careful watch lest the jesting turn to taunting or bullying. Terry himself seemed oblivious to the others' amusement,

163

thereby protecting himself for longer than might otherwise have been the case. Nick Bright appeared kindly disposed towards him and sometimes fended off the more insistent tormentors, so when Jason saw Nick and Terry at the centre of a group of voluble Year Seven pupils on the following Monday morning he wandered over to see if Terry needed help.

Even before he reached them he knew this was not so because their noise was that of excitement not quarrel.

'What's all the racket about?' Jason asked amiably.

'Sir, Nick's father is going to be on *Who Wants to Be a Millionaire?*'

Jason looked round the group, at the happy expectation on some faces and the barely concealed jealousy on one or two others. Even Terry looked momentarily interested.

'We just kept ringing the number, sir, and took it in turns to hold on. We do it every week, sir, but this time it worked. Of course, you don't get to play unless you're the fastest finger. Do you know how it works, sir? Have you seen it? My dad says he doesn't know who to have for phone a friend...'

Mr Bright's potential millionairedom dominated conversation in the staffroom at break.

'He'll probably send Nick to Eton,' was Ben's contribution.

More surprising was Carol's: 'Lucky devil! I've been trying to get on for two years.'

Jason could only reflect on the different fates of Nick Bright and Harry Jackson, both of whose fathers drove lorries. One child was the centre of a loving, stable family whose days were organised and whose fun was shared, the other a casualty of multiple fractured relationships, chaos and neglect. Yet both were loved. Jason wondered where the Jacksons were now. What was Harry doing? Was he indoors, afraid to go out, afraid to be recognised? Or was he having a good time on some foreign beach, playing innocently, blissfully unaware of the Interpol hunt?

Perhaps Jackson had been cleverer than they thought. He had committed no crime other than wanting his son. There was no tug-of-love mother at home trying to keep the interest alive and no suggestion that he might actually harm Harry through any physical abuse. The aggrieved party was the Social Services Department which had only limited sympathy among the public. It was possible that Jackson believed that the interest would fade and the forces of law and order have more important quarries to pursue but it was still not credible to think that he could have formed a proper plan for a new life.

The thought kept recurring to him as he tackled the subject of exile with Year Nine. He read them Macaulay's *The Jacobite's Epitaph* and was pleased to see he had the class's full attention. The worst fate of all, he told them, must have been if the exile's family was left behind. He asked his pupils to imagine how they would feel.

'I'd be worried about their safety, sir.'

'I'd worry who was going to earn the money and would they starve.'

'I'd worry that the landlord would turn them out of their cabin.'

'So your family is left behind in Ireland, Robin. Good. Anyone else?'

'I'd just miss them, sir.'

Jason looked at the girl who had just spoken, a quiet pupil of average ability, good behaviour and tidy appearance, one of hundreds who would pass through Morton's to be immediately forgotten because her leaving would cause neither relief nor regret. He would now remember her because she had seen a simple truth. He wanted to say, *Yes, that's right, Amy, and they wouldn't even have to be on another continent, you would miss them if they were no further away than Frome.*

Instead he confined his appreciation to the word 'good' before moving from exile to transportation.

The last lesson of the day saw him trying to interest a class of Year Sevens in Britain before the Norman Conquest when all its members wanted to talk about was what Nick's father would do if he won a million, or rather what they would do in the same fortunate position. Jason, asking himself the same question, thought that he would never again have to worry about a lawyer's bill and found himself stopping on the way home to buy a lottery ticket.

'Good luck!' laughed a voice behind him. He turned to see Carol Marsh with a litre of semi-skimmed milk in her hand and an evening paper under her arm.

Jason grinned. 'This is my first for ages. It must be all this talk of millionaires. Nick Bright is fairly crazy with excitement.'

'Have you time for a bite to eat? I was just going

to the Pizza Hut because my sister visited at the weekend and ate me right out of everything. She's expecting twins and says she must eat for three. I haven't the energy to shop tonight.'

Jason agreed because there was very little in his own fridge, because he had more or less completed his marking and because Leah's birthday was looming and he wanted Carol's opinion on a suitable present. Kat had brushed off the question with an irritable 'whatever you want to give her' and Leah had demanded a bicycle to rival Jake's. When Jason had pointed out that such a bike was too big for her and that her tricycle was new only six months ago she had sulked and refused to offer a second choice.

'What about a doll? One that cries and sleeps and needs changing?'

'She has one and never looks at it. Ditto the doll's house and all the furniture that Kat spent hours choosing. All she wants to do is copy Jake.'

'OK. A wigwam.'

'What?'

'A wigwam. She and Jake can play tents on the lawn even if Cowboys and Indians is too old-fashioned. Perfect for the coming weather.'

Jason smiled, appreciating the possibilities. Carol smiled back, pleased to have helped, contented, intimate, happy. It was a smile which haunted him as he bought the wigwam.

9

Jason looked wonderingly at Leah. The mass of light-brown curls which had once framed her face had been cut into a short, boyish style that did not even reach her ears, but the dungarees she habitually wore had been abandoned in favour of a light-green skirt with matching bolero top.

'I'm four now and Mummy says I'm too grown up for baby curls.'

Jason smiled. 'You certainly look different.'

'She looks awful,' said Jake crossly.

Jason was about to protest when it came to him that his son was uncertain about the change because it might threaten him. Until now Leah had been his baby sister who could not win an argument with him, who did not understand the things he did at school, who had to go to bed before him. Perhaps he feared all of this would change with his sister's altered appearance, with the shock of realisation that Leah would not always be an infant, that she was growing into a person in her own right.

'Jason! How nice that you could come!' Kat's mother came from the kitchen into the tiny hall. Leah ran off back to the party in the sitting room and Jake reluctantly followed, looking back over his shoulder at his father. 'There are ten small guests, would you believe, in this dinky cottage and of course it had to rain.'

'Hello, Sheila. Jake looks ready to start a mutiny.'

'He wanted to go to the cinema with William but Katharine quite rightly insisted he should attend his sister's birthday party instead.'

'Who's William?'

'His friend who lives along the road. Goes to the same school but I don't think he's in the same class.'

It was an innocent arrow Sheila had let fly but Jason felt its small barb. He had never heard of William who was part of Jake's new life, of a daily and separate existence which excluded his father. When Jake came to visit him he played with Gavin and Tom, who were known to Kat because they were figures from her son's past as well as his present, but Jason knew nothing of Jake's new friends, could not picture them in his mind, could not assess their suitability or their effect on his son, could not warn or encourage. That was now Kat's province, in effect solely Kat's province.

Even Sheila knew William. Kat had talked about him to her mother but not to Jason. She no longer wanted to share information about their children with her husband any more than she wanted to share the children themselves. A clean break.

'What's the matter?'

Jason, aware that Sheila was looking at him with a puzzled face, tried to look cheerful, then opted for truth.

'I've never heard of William.'

The statement appeared to have no significance for his mother-in-law, who muttered a vague,

169

'oh.' A few moments later he found himself in the living room in the middle of a game of musical chairs, recognising some of Leah's friends, knowing that the others would be familiar to her, to Jake and to Kat, and that his ignorance set him apart, proclaiming him a guest not family.

Kat acknowledged his arrival with a perfunctory wave from the other side of the musical chairs. They had yet to exchange any further greeting when Leah was blowing out the four pink candles on the cake. By then Jason had talked again to his son, to Sheila and to Alex, who appeared towards the end of Pass the Parcel, but not to his wife. As parents began to arrive to take their offspring home he decided to wait till the last guest was gone, relying on his in-laws' presence to prevent a scene.

Leah seemed to take his being there for granted and, distracted by presents and the excitement of the celebrations, paid him little attention but Jake, as if sensing that the time for his father's departure was drawing near, began to cling. Jason found himself thinking of Leah's last birthday party and wondering at his innocence in being so blind to the fate that waited for him. Perhaps even then Kat had been planning to leave him. Perhaps, as he had helped her clear up the debris of balloons and party poppers, of paper plates and napkins, she had been secretly rejoicing in the knowledge that next year he would join his daughter's birthday party by invitation rather than by right.

Eventually Kat could ignore him no longer. There were no more guests to whom to bid goodnight, no more parents to detain her on the doorstep, no more cars to wave on to the road. Sheila began to tidy up and Alex to pour drinks. Jake looked anxiously at Jason, willing him to stay.

'It was good of you to come, Jason.'

Jason, recognising dismissal, smiled at his wife. 'I wouldn't have missed it for the world.'

He sank down into one of the armchairs and, when Alex offered him a glass of wine, he accepted the drink immediately, even though he knew he was driving and was unlikely to finish it. Jake perched on the arm of the chair and produced his Gameboy. Jason was not looking at Kat but he knew that if he did meet her eyes they would be angry and he felt obscurely gratified.

'Why don't we play something everyone can join in?' Jason spoke to his son but looked at Alex. 'What about cards? Beggar my neighbour?'

His father-in-law received the notion enthusiastically. Only as Jake ran to find the cards did Alex look at Kat and Jason saw uncertainty enter his eyes. He looked from his daughter to her husband and back again, aware now of tension, aware that he had inadvertently taken sides in the unspoken battle. Embarrassed, he cleared his throat, possibly as a prelude to something he then decided not to say, possibly just for the sake of making a sound in the sudden silence.

Jason played with determined hilarity, which Alex and Sheila tried unsuccessfully to emulate. Kat said she had too much to do and retreated to the kitchen. Leah continued to potter among her presents, occasionally interrupting the game to show them to one or other of the grown-ups, causing irritation to Jake. Sheila was eliminated first and, with ill-disguised relief, went to join Kat. Their conversation, punctuated by the clatter of dishes and cutlery, drifted into the living room where Jake was gleefully eyeing Alex's diminishing pile of cards. Alex played a king and took three cards from Jason. His pile began to grow again.

Twenty minutes later Alex lost his last card to Jake, who turned to Jason with nervous competitiveness. Alex disappeared in the direction of the kitchen and Kat called out, 'Ten more minutes, Jake.'

Jake did not protest but when the allotted time had passed and Jason was tantalisingly near losing he pleaded for five more minutes.

'Only five,' said Kat. 'Your father wants to put Leah to bed.'

Jason looked up angrily, trying vainly to convert his expression to a neutral one as he realised Jake was watching. He was being offered a choice between disappointing his son or seeming not to want the opportunity to spend time with his daughter.

Fortunately Leah, far from being enthusiastic at the prospect, set up a howl of protest, wanting the excitement of the day to continue and not be curtailed by bed.

Sheila came to the rescue. 'I'll take Leah up and Jason can come when they've finished their game.'

Kat shrugged and Sheila, picking up both Leah and a present to distract her, was turning towards the stairs when her granddaughter, conscious that her day was about to be ended, shrieked and kicked so violently that she struggled out of

Sheila's arms and landed feet first amidst the cards, which were abruptly and chaotically scattered across the carpet. Jake gave a roar of chagrin and pushed Leah furiously out of the way. His sister retaliated with screams, tears and blows.

Kat yanked her son to his feet and pulled him unceremoniously towards the stairs.

'For shame on your sister's birthday! Only bullies push little girls. You can go to bed *now*.'

Jake yelled in protest and clung on to the banister to prevent further progress towards his bedroom. Leah, aware of bad temper and of somehow being the cause of it, sank down on the carpet, threw a corduroy cat at an armchair and started to sob. Sheila bent down to comfort her and the men looked at each other in comradely disbelief.

Jason picked up Leah and joined the scene at the foot of the stairs. 'Come on,' he said to Jake. 'I'll read you some Harry Potter.'

'You will not.' Kat was uncompromising. 'He doesn't deserve it. And as for Leah, please put her down. She is far too old to be carried up to bed.'

There was a short, dangerous silence. Jason could sense Alex and Sheila holding their breath as they listened in the living room. Jake slowly released his hold on the banister and Leah's screams subsided into snuffles. For a moment Jason and Kat looked at each other, then, without taking his eyes from his wife's, Jason lowered his daughter to the floor. He made a vague gesture in the direction of the upstairs landing and after only a momentary hesitation both children began to climb towards it.

173

'Goodnight, Dad.'

'Goodnight, son. Night-night, Leah.'

Leah, still snuffling, ignored him but at the top of the stairs Jake turned.

'When will I see you again, Dad?'

'In two weeks.'

Jason was aware how far off that must seem to an eight-year-old. Adults talked about this time next year and the imminence of Christmas in August but to a child an hour was a long time, a week an eternity. Two weeks. In that time Jake would acquire new knowledge at school, progress with his skills, find out how to do things he could not do a month ago. He would laugh and cry and make friends and fall out with them. He would whisper secrets and plans to Kat. He would alternately help and quarrel with Leah. He would take infinitesimal, barely discernible steps towards being the man he would eventually become. His father would know none of it, would not be part of the same world.

Jason began a miserable, resentful calculation. Fifty-two days a year plus a fortnight in the summer, five days at Christmas, five at Easter and alternate half-terms. He was missing out on three-quarters of his children's lives. A surge of hatred for his wife washed through him, alarming and satisfying. A few minutes ago he had been finding reasons to stay, to be with his children, to talk to his in-laws; now he had to force himself to take his leave politely and not merely turn his back on those who still cosily took for granted all that he had lost.

Hours later he stood looking down at what had once been Kat's side of the bed, consciously trying to miss her, to mourn the passing of love, to feel sorrow not hatred. He failed and knew that such feelings were dead not dormant and that there would be no miraculous resurrection. If he could regain Jake and Leah he would be content never to see Kat again.

Soon he would be as bitter as Ed Deacon, morose, preoccupied by injustice, hating publicly as well as privately. The reflection startled rather than depressed him, sending him in search of a pen and notepad. Lying with his head against the wall above his bed he began a list: Mike and Christine Taylor; Jen and Rob Appleby; Sara and Mark Gilchrist. Friends who had divorced amicably, whose children rotated cheerfully between their parents. Well, perhaps not cheerfully, amended Jason. Resignedly, maybe, acceptantly. Family break-up did not have to follow the mode of Deacon and Kirk.

He began another list: divorce Kat; sell house; change jobs. Jason paused, looking at what he had written, at the triumph of his subconscious resolution as it broke through the fog with which he had so determinedly obscured it and challenged him in his own handwriting. Leave Morton's, desert the sinking ship, let Nick Bright and Terry Pepper grow up without his kindly tuition, let others rescue the Harry Jacksons when they wept in the playground, let Carol Marsh secretly mourn his departure. He could not really be needed; it would only be a matter of months before Ofsted would ensure the school was subject to special measures, a temporary head would replace Hillier and everyone would live happily ever after with a finally buried reputation and no sixth form. Meanwhile he, Jason Kirk, would be embracing fresh challenges in a high-achieving school with a demanding head and no time to brood on the poor hand fate had dealt him.

In the morning he told Objubjub of his plans and forked Whiskas into a bowl. He collected the post from the doormat with a whistle and was relieved it contained neither bills nor solicitors' letters. The day was fine, the traffic was light and his optimism received a fresh boost when he saw Terry Pepper laughing with a classmate. His mind told him that his mood would not last, its cold little voice suggesting that the resulting fall to earth might leave him angrier and more miserable than before. He repelled its message and felt a small thrill of vindication when the estate agent rang him at lunchtime to say Mr and Mrs Holder wanted to offer him the asking price for the house.

'Holder? The loft people? What happened?'

'The loft they wanted has dry rot or at any rate the house beneath it has.'

Jason laughed. A small piece of clear path had just appeared in the jungle.

Kat angrily dragged the brambles back over it.

'My client,' wrote Lane and Webb a week later, 'is not satisfied that Mr Kirk is obtaining the best possible price for their house. This sum was first suggested some months ago and my client has not been properly consulted...'

'House prices have fallen, for pity's sake. Even an idiot would know that. We're lucky to get an offer at that price now,' Jason raged in vain.

'I think we must find out what price Mrs Kirk has in mind,' reasoned Alan Parnell. 'Then I can better advise you how to respond.'

'I'm selling, anyway.'

'To do so without at least some attempt at agreement might prejudice your share of the proceeds.'

'You said she was entitled to half.'

Parnell formed his fingers into a steeple and spoke in the low tone with which Jason had come to associate bad news.

'Half the *value*. If Mrs Kirk can show you to have sold at an unreasonably low rate without due cause and without her agreement, she may apply for a sum equivalent to half of what you could have realised if you had acted reasonably.'

'I'm selling.'

'The house is in your joint names. You cannot, in any event, act unilaterally.'

Jason looked down at his hands and was startled to see flecks of blood where his nails had penetrated the flesh of his clenched fists. He relaxed his wrists slowly.

'I cannot maintain both the house I now live in and Kat's cottage and pay maintenance. It's as simple as that. If Kat believes she can get a higher price in a falling market then let her try. Let her move back into our house and try and I'll go somewhere else. Otherwise if she wants another five grand then agree it can come off my share but I must sell the house. Damn it, Alan, if she ruins me she'll lose too. Lane and Webb must be pointing that out, surely?'

'I'll see what I can do,' prevaricated Parnell.

'Begin the process of exchanging contracts,' insisted Jason.

The solicitor did not answer and Jason stared at him in disbelief.

'Alan, can she really stop me? Can't we go to court?'

'Yes, but no judge wants to determine these sorts of issues piecemeal. We need a full settlement and that will take time to negotiate.'

'It's preposterous.' Outrage fought with misery for possession of Jason's mind, a mind which suddenly seemed to find the contest unbearable. He thought of Angus Gaskill and briefly glimpsed the abyss of the truly maddened.

'Yes,' agreed Parnell sadly.

'What on earth can I tell the Holders? I can't let them incur the costs of surveyors and solicitors if I'm not going to be able to sell.'

'No. It would be fairer to explain.'

'And lose the sale altogether?'

'That is indeed a risk,' observed Parnell unhelpfully.

Jason sank his head in his hands and the solicitor added, 'Sleep on it.'

The words mocked Jason as he woke for the third time from a dream-laden, child-haunted sleep and, glancing at the luminous digits of his alarm clock, saw it was just before three. The clock had been a present from Jake, two birthdays ago. He had found it hilarious because it made the sound of a cock crowing. Jason and Kat both found it irritating and had frequently speculated whether they could pretend it was broken and replace it with a device which buzzed or rang. It

178

came to him now that he need use it in future only when Jake visited and was surprised that such a ruse had not occurred to him before.

A fleeting satisfaction suffused him, as if he had solved a problem of great magnitude, before dissolving into irritation as he wakened to the triviality of his thoughts. He turned over and felt the form of Objubjub curled up on the bed. Jason ran his fingers along the cat's fur and was rewarded with a loud purr.

'Lucky old you,' he muttered. 'You neither spin nor reap but not even Solomon had half as much Whiskas.'

Talking to a cat. At least it was easier than talking to a Kat. The inane joke produced a giggle as he fell back into slumber. When he next woke the rejected clock told him it was still only three-nineteen.

'The still watches of the night,' he rambled to Objubjub but the cat had gone, preferring the outdoor excitements and dangers of a cold night to the comfort of a warm bed.

Jason wondered if he could find comfort in danger. Perhaps he should simply leave it all to Parnell and go to Africa and spend a year surrounded by crocodiles and lions while he performed some unspecified good works for the natives. He struggled to repel the whirl of illogical thought and again slept to dream of Leah and Jake being chased by an angry elephant, then of himself alone, stranded in the desert beneath an African sun.

Three forty-seven, indicated the clock as he emerged into consciousness but when he next woke a weak dawn was preparing to banish the shadows and Objubjub had returned. Jason knew he would face the day still tired and mentally tormented but, instead of looking forward to its close and an early night, decided to visit either Gaskill or Deacon, telling himself it was time he thought of others, knowing that in reality he wanted the comfort of seeing others suffering more than he.

He was ashamed of himself when Elizabeth Gaskill, smart, dignified but with sad eyes, greeted him enthusiastically. Although she made no reference to the desertion, Jason was keenly aware that the staff of Morton's had simply stopped visiting their colleague. Ben had been the first to call when Elizabeth had rung Hillier to say that the doctor thought Angus should see people and that her husband had reluctantly agreed.

The maths teacher was shown upstairs to the bedroom which Angus refused to leave and was greeted with a querulous demand for the proof of Pythagoras. The deputy head sat unshaven in his pyjamas and surrounded by scores of discarded sheets of paper on which he had vainly endeavoured to reconstruct the theorem. Ben accepted the pencil his colleague pointed at him and gave a speedy demonstration.

'That's not the way I was taught,' was Angus's aggrieved response.

Ben obligingly went through the longer, schoolboy version.

'Why couldn't I remember that?' demanded Angus irritably, peering at the proof as if it personally offended him.

'I can only just remember it myself,' soothed Ben, sitting on the side of the bed and wondering how to make conversation with a madman.

'I don't suppose you teach it now,' accused Angus. 'I often wonder what you do teach. All that binary nonsense probably and Venn diagrams?'

'He went on like that for half an hour,' Ben told the staffroom the following day. 'It was pitiful. I had to explain Venn diagrams and then suddenly he started on about log tables. Why didn't we use them? Of course, I had the prize folly to mention calculators and you would think I had blasphemed his gods.'

'I think we need an older colleague to visit,' Hillier had confided to Jason in indulgent tones.

Matt Johnson, the English teacher, had complied three days later.

'I should never have warned Elizabeth I was intending to go round,' he lamented next morning. 'He was ready for me, demanding I translate Chaucer and wanting to know why we didn't teach it before the sixth form. I said we could, and indeed did, if we had the right children. He said that was all rot and there was a time when every child had to know Chaucer.'

'He smells,' said a female science teacher, with a reminiscent sniff. 'Given up washing on top of everything else.'

'God knows how Elizabeth copes,' sighed Hillier when he at last followed his subordinates' example and called on his deputy one Saturday morning.

Jason recalled those words and echoed them in his mind as he looked at Elizabeth now. Beneath the carefully applied make-up he could see the worry lines, the concealed haggardness, the ravages less of age than of torment. He was angry on her behalf not with Angus but with Morton's and Hillier, mourning a good man brought low, a well-earned retirement ruined. He repressed an expletive and, as if reading his thoughts, Elizabeth smiled at him.

'I think you'll find him quite quiet today. He's much less angry and frustrated.'

'Is he still in the bedroom?'

'Yes.'

'Elizabeth, what are they doing for him? This is way beyond any normal nervous breakdown. He needs all the help they have to offer.'

At once Jason regretted the words, fearing them to be not merely tactless but also alarmist. He wished he had thought out what he was going to say before he came and asked himself why he had not done so. Her reply surprised him.

'He needs admitting and treating but he's not a danger to himself or others and so they can't do it. Dr Hobbs assures me that is the law and he is powerless in the face of it.'

'Get another doctor.'

'I have. Dr Hobbs is the third I've tried. Before him two doctors from the practice we have used for the last twenty years said exactly the same.'

Five minutes later Jason looked at his superior and thought that he had never seen a clearer case of danger to oneself. Angus was emaciated, unwashed and looked at him through listless eyes. In the hour that Jason sat with him he uttered scarcely more than ten sentences and none was rational.

Of course he was eating. Elizabeth fed him enough to keep an army going. Medication? The doctor did not think he needed it. He was a good doctor, not a fusser. Elizabeth fussed all day and now Jason was flapping about like a mother hen too. Why couldn't he be left alone? There was nothing wrong with him. Missing him at Morton's? After all those years? It must be nearly a decade since he left.

'He's all over the place,' admitted Elizabeth as she said goodbye. 'But he's also cunning. Oh, so cunning! He won't take his pills. I have to keep them down here to stop him hiding them and if I crush them up in his food that's the bit he always leaves.'

'But surely he wants to get better?'

'He doesn't believe he is ill.'

Jason kissed her, holding her a little longer than a social farewell would have called for, wanting to comfort, to share her helplessness, her lack of comprehension, her yearning for a miracle.

'Poor Angus,' said Carol when Jason described his visit over Sunday roast in her flat. 'What an ass the law is. It kids itself it's giving protection to the vulnerable and instead is comprehensively betraying them.'

'The law doesn't do any of that. It's the lawmakers and their damn political correctness. Apparently it is a mark of greater respect to let someone starve to death than to force treatment on him against his will. Angus would have years of normal, healthy life ahead of him if only someone would take control now. He is not in his

183

right mind, his wife is and she is the one the law should be respecting not the half-wit she is looking after.'

'You're angry, Jason.'

'Do you blame me?'

'No, but it can't help Elizabeth. It must be devastating watching that happen to someone you love.'

Love. Jason did not tell her that his greatest shock had been realising that Elizabeth still slept in that bedroom. Immaculate and dignified, she still shared a bed with the stinking, shrunken skeleton that was her husband. He hated himself for the thought and could share it with no one.

He hated himself also for deciding that he would not yet visit Ed Deacon but for the moment he wanted no more reminders of mortality. It served him right, he thought grimly. He had visited Angus to reassure himself that his own burden was light by comparison with that of others and instead had come away feeling his load increased. Angus had once been as capable as he was of going to school each day and coping with what-ever the demands of his post threw at him and, unlike Jason, he had returned each night to a loving, stable marriage and the comforting know-ledge of children well and safely brought up. Now he was degraded, anguished and probably also secretly despised. Why should Jason assume his own fate was bound to be different? If a slide into irrationality could be resisted merely by previous soundness of mind then Angus would be suffering less.

He gave voice to the thought. 'Do you think it

possible to prevent breakdown, to baulk madness? I mean, is there always a point at which you just let go? A point at which you say, "I can't cope any more and I am not even going to try. I am just going to curl up in bed and leave my life to others to sort out?" Because sometimes that's how I feel.'

'Can you walk with a broken leg? Not until someone has set it and supplied some crutches. So you can't think straight with a broken mind either until someone has given you something to get it functioning at least a little bit. From what you say that is Angus's problem. He is like a man with a broken leg who wants to walk without having the bone set. Somehow someone has got to persuade him to take the tablets. What you have described is something quite different. If someone says, "I can't cope", that person is halfway to a cure.'

'People do cope, though, don't they? I mean, with really devastating things that you think nobody could deal with? Like all their family being wiped out in a single accident? Or losing both legs? Or going blind suddenly? Or being taken hostage for a year by a terrorist?'

'Yes, and we look at them and say that they put all our problems in perspective and then five minutes later we go half insane because we can't find the car keys.'

Jason smiled, grateful to her for lightening his mood, pleased and not resentful when she began asking about his children.

'Jake has just discovered stars and planets. He thinks the universe is wildly exciting and speculates about what will happen when we discover

185

life in some distant world. He never says if, always when. He seems utterly convinced it will happen soon. He finds his telescope a mere plaything and wants something more along the lines of Jodrell Bank for his next birthday.'

Carol laughed. 'When I was about three my mother showed me the moon and the stars from the landing window and said the stars were cracks in the floor of heaven and we could see its light. My father had died when I was one and every night that we could see stars I used to wave and hope that he could see me through the crack in the floor. Of course, I didn't believe that for very long but even when I was older I kept up the fantasy until, when I was about eleven, I realised why.

'It was because space was cold and empty so it comforted me to think it was just a gap between my warm security at home and all the bustle, light and happiness of heaven. It was as though it were a corridor between two cosy rooms in the days before central heating. That was why I liked to pretend that old, childish nonsense about cracks in the floor might be true. It was to avoid accepting that space was an infinity of coldness, emptiness without end.'

It was not until much later that Jason realised she had not merely been recounting an anecdote. She was trying to tell him that the cold, empty void in which he now floated would not last for ever, that there was a star ahead which offered warmth, companionship and security. Uneasily he thought she meant to be that star and he knew he was not yet ready to place his trust in another woman, to feel the gravitational pull of love.

10

Jason told Ed about Angus Gaskill when he visited because he wanted to offer him the obscure comfort of fellow suffering, but Ed, absorbed by his own misery, showed little interest, other than a formal, distant enquiry about Elizabeth's health. Duty over, he turned at once to the allegations he faced.

'It looks as if the police think it's all rubbish but that didn't stop them giving me the third degree twice over.'

'Don't answer this if you don't want to but can you give me any idea what Ros is saying?'

'Oh, yes. Why not? She appears to be busy telling everyone that when Chloe comes to stay I go into the bathroom with her and that is not natural now that she is nine and more than capable of bathing herself. What is more I have stared at her and told her to turn over in the bath so that I can look at her.'

'But surely Chloe denies it?'

'She is the innocent cause of it. When she was last here she and a friend were fooling about on the top of the stairs and Chloe fell down the whole flight. The next day she complained of back pain and, naturally, I wanted to see if there was any bruising or whether it might be something more serious. Of course I don't normally go into the bathroom.'

187

'But the police can't possibly take that seriously.'

'No, but that's not all. Ros is also saying that Chloe is far more sexually aware than she should be and that her knowledge seems to increase when she comes here. I couldn't understand it at first because they seem to know more at six these days than we knew at sixteen and nobody would tell me what it was that Chloe supposedly knew. Then I realised it was probably Alice.'

'Alice?'

'The friend she was playing with when she fell downstairs. Ros was never keen on her. Her mother is on boyfriend number five and I'm not sure there has ever been a husband. There is however an older brother who has been in trouble with the police. We used to disagree over allowing Alice here to play but she was Chloe's best friend at school and I saw no reason to visit the sins of the rest of them on Alice.

'Then, when Ros left and Chloe was at a different school, she wanted me to discourage the friendship. I didn't and it would seem I am now paying the price. Alice would see and hear all sorts of things in that household and has probably passed some of it on to Chloe.'

'Do you let Chloe go there?'

'Not often. I want her largely to myself when she comes.'

'Anything else?'

'Yes. Apparently I take an interest in Chloe's knickers.'

'What?'

'I was looking for something in her case once

188

and saw Ros had put in a set of brand-new underwear. I said it looked pretty.'

'Ed, none of this is worth a row of beans.'

'I've kept the best till last. When Chloe went home last time Ros found a pornographic picture in her bag. Alice, of course. She must have found it at home and sneaked it out to show Chloe and then left it behind, causing Chloe to panic and hide it in her bag. I hate to admit it but Ros is right to say I should never have let the friendship continue.'

Jason felt a cold fog settling in the pit of his stomach.

'But didn't Chloe say she got it from Alice?'

'No. She says she found it here.'

The fog rolled and descended once more.

'But why?'

'I don't know but I can make a pretty good guess that she was afraid Ros wouldn't let her see Alice again and lied on the spur of the moment. She could not possibly have understood the implications.'

In his imagination Jason watched the story unfold: Chloe returning home, conscious of the evidence of wrongdoing in her bag, longing to hide it, to destroy it, to leave no trace that it had ever existed; her mother chivvying her – 'No. Leave the unpacking now. Come and have supper' – and a reluctant Chloe leaving the bag in the hall; later a furtive Chloe unpacking behind the closed bedroom door, listening for the sound of her mother on the stairs, of an older sibling on the landing; now she has the picture in her hands but where to hide it? In an agony of uncertainty she hears her mother approaching, hesitates in the middle of the room and thrusts the obscenity back in her bag. The door opens. Her mother's cheerful voice: 'I'll just take the dirties.' Chloe freezes and their eyes meet.

Jason's mind now showed him that mother some hours later, sitting alone, her mouth determined, her eyes dark with malicious satisfaction, with malevolent intention, with happy anticipation of the morrow.

'The bitch.'

For a moment Jason could not be sure if it were he or Ed who had uttered the words. Then his colleague was once more speaking but the anger and sarcasm had drained away.

'Apparently it had been downloaded from the net so they took my computer and laptop. I suggested they might raid Alice's house too but they said there were no grounds.'

'You're quite sure the children could not have downloaded it here?'

'Pretty certain. I don't think Chloe would be interested in such stuff. I've always been careful to know what they were doing when they were playing on the computer, not because I feared this but because I didn't want them getting into chatrooms or sending umpteen emails.'

'Chloe is bound to say she got it from Alice when she realises what is happening. She is nine not five.'

'Let's hope so but the longer she leaves it the more difficult it will become.' Ed's voice was heavy with defeat. 'For the time being I am not allowed to see any of them, nor contact them, nor work and the law is not exactly speedy in its process.'

'I don't know what to say.'

'No, but at least you have come here not to say it. It's surprising how quickly the flow of visitors dries up when someone cries child abuse. The neighbours have started to look the other way as if they fear catching the eye of a paedophile might indicate some sort of complicity.'

'I can't believe anyone would think of you in that way. No one at Morton's does.'

Ed did not answer that. He looked moodily into his now empty glass and after a few seconds asked Jason to have another drink. It was at this point that his guest would normally have said no and begun to take his leave but, conscious that Ed had just told him he was lonely, Jason felt obliged to accept and stay longer despite the call of marking and a heap of neglected letters from Alan Parnell.

'How are things with Kat?'

'Hideous. She won't let me sell the house.'

'Can she stop you?'

'Yes.'

'And can you afford not to sell the house?'

'No.'

Ed absorbed that in silence and both men brooded darkly, each on his private misery, until Ed asked about Morton's. Jason told him about Nick Bright's father.

'I didn't see it at the weekend because of Leah's party but apparently Mr Bright got on right at the end so he really is going to be playing next week. So far he is on two hundred pounds.'

'Hope he makes it. Nick's a good kid. Any news

of Harry Jackson and his father?'

'None. They appear to have vanished from the face of the earth. There was a supposed sighting in Spain but it turned out to be a false lead. I admit to some sympathy with Jackson but I know it's misplaced.'

'I'm not so sure. Harry is loved and he always came to school clean and fed. He's been in the school for two years and has never given us a day's trouble. So what have we to teach Jackson?'

'Yes, but until recently he's had a mother who presumably saw to that. Or rather the poor little chap has had a series of mothers. Since the last walked out he's been regularly left alone at night because Dad is out lorry driving and the two elder ones take advantage of his absence to spend the night with their lovers. Jackson knew that and knew that the law required otherwise because Social Services have been trying to find a solution. If anything had happened to Harry nobody would have any sympathy at all.'

Ed shrugged. 'Of course that's true,' he conceded reluctantly.

'Anyway, back to what matters now. What is the next stage?'

'The police will interview Chloe. If she sticks to her story they will prepare a file for the DPP. I still find it hard to believe that they won't go to Alice's house. It sounds to me as if the child is in moral danger at the very least.'

'I would be surprised if, after this, Social Services don't find a reason to make some enquiries but never mind Alice. What about Chloe? Surely she needs to realise the sheer scale of what she is doing before it is too late. Can't someone talk to her? A gran perhaps or some other grown-up she trusts?'

'She has grandparents on Ros's side but not mine – my parents are dead. They are the sort who spend months at a time travelling and minding their own business. They didn't show much interest in the divorce and they've never gone overboard with the children. I can't think they'll want to get involved.'

'There must be somebody.'

'Whoever might talk to Chloe would need to be aware of the nature of what she is saying and I am not too keen to broadcast that at present. I keep hoping Chloe will tell the truth about Alice and this nightmare will end. Or maybe she will confide in one of the boys. Luke would know what to do.'

'Ed, you must be able to contact Luke without Ros knowing? By mobile or something? Tell him everything. Get him to talk to Chloe.'

'I'm not supposed to contact any of them as you know, but I admit I've tried just that. No good. Ros has changed their mobiles. I've thought of trying to get a letter to Luke as he comes out of school but I don't know whom to ask.'

'I'll do it.'

'No, Jason. Thanks all the same but whoever does it must do so without risk, which is to say he or she must be able to plead ignorance both of the content and of the forbidden nature of the communication. You can't. You work at Morton's and you could never claim you didn't know what was happening.'

'I'd still do it.'

'I know but I won't let you. You have trouble enough of your own.'

When he thought about that trouble Jason found himself as trapped as Ed Deacon. He had insisted on a legal separation, despite the costs involved, because he wanted to bring Kat to terms, but she was obdurate over the house and the maintenance payments despite his giving in to her demands in respect of access. Parnell wrote stern letters to Lane and Webb who replied in kind and nothing moved except the bills. He went to bed each night preoccupied by mental arithmetic and rose each morning with the sum unresolved.

On Saturday night he joined Carol, Ben and Debbie at Ben's small house near Trowbridge to watch Nick Bright's father try to win a million pounds. He arrived late and Carol told him that Mr Bright had now won £32,000 and had all three lifelines left. Jason looked round the tiny room in which there were but two chairs, occupied by Carol and Debbie, before sinking down onto a floor cushion next to Ben.

'He wobbled a bit over one and you could see Mrs Bright just willing him not to risk it but he did and it was OK.'

The advertisements finished and the features of Chris Tarrant filled the screen. Carol gave a small whimper of tension and Ben moved fractionally nearer the set.

'Who succeeded Henry the Eighth? Was it—'

'Edward the Sixth,' came the answer before Tarrant could even read out the options. The audience laughed as Bright repeated the same words after listening to the four possibilities which were presented to him and added, 'Final answer.'

'Jasper, you have just won sixty-four thousand pounds.'

The small group of teachers joined in the applause and the cameras panned to the beaming face of Mrs Bright.

'Jasper! What a name!' murmured Debbie, picking up a bottle of Pinot Noir and handing it round.

'The next question is worth one hundred and twenty-five thousand pounds...'

'Don't take any risks,' said Ben to the screen as Tarrant began explaining how much a wrong answer would cost. 'Sixty-four thousand tax-free pounds is pretty good.'

Jason was briefly assailed by a stab of uncharacteristic jealousy. He repelled it only to find it replaced by another as Debbie spoke.

'He's still got three lifelines, darling.'

Darling. The casual endearment sent a small dart of unhappiness and loss into him. *Darling.* It was what Kat used to call him, seemingly long ago in another age, the age in which he had been married, the age when he had been a father every day.

Jasper Bright used two of his three lifelines on the very next question and was rewarded with a hundred and twenty-five thousand pounds. Tarrant asked him if he knew what he was going to do with the money and Jasper said he would move house and have a model railway in the attic for his son.

'I bet you mean for yourself, you cunning

195

devil.' Carol held a cushion over her face as if she could not bear to see anything go wrong.

The next question was about placing British cities on the same lines of longitude. Ben fetched an atlas and they knew the answer before Jasper quietly, confidently, but very slowly worked it out. He did not waver from his answer despite temptation from Tarrant to do so and the audience erupted into long applause as he won a quarter of a million pounds.

'Which of these was not a book by Erich Maria Remarque: *All Quiet on the Western Front*, *A Time to Love and a Time to Die*, *Shadows in Paradise*, *The Grey Seas of Jutland?*'

Jasper looked first puzzled then defeated.

'I haven't a clue,' groaned Ben. 'The only one I recognise is *All Quiet on the Western Front*.'

'And also *A Time to Love and a Time to Die*,' added Jason. 'At a guess I'd say he also wrote the Jutland one but I don't know.'

'I've never even heard of Remarque,' said Carol. 'I would have actually said *All Quiet on the Western Front* because it is so famous I would have expected to have known the author or at least to have recognised his name when I heard it.'

'He doesn't know either,' observed Debbie as Jasper struggled and Tarrant reminded him he had one lifeline left. Jasper used it and asked the audience. The camera showed his wife shaking her head and rolling her eyes in despair. Jason thought that if she could have done so she would have run on to the stage and forcibly stopped her husband playing.

Ben gave a hollow laugh as the audience split

more or less evenly between the last three choices with a small percentage voting for the first. Jasper announced he would take his winnings and in reply to Tarrant's query as to what he thought the answer would be he selected *Shadows in Paradise*.

'Jasper Bright, you have won two hundred and fifty thousand pounds. If you had played the last question and said *Shadows in Paradise* you would have,' here Tarrant gave a long pause, 'just lost two hundred and eighteen thousand pounds.'

Bright gave a great sigh of relief and was enthusiastically clapped from the chair.

Ben switched off the television and Debbie went to the kitchen, followed by Carol with an offer of help with the food.

'We'll need to watch young Bright for a bit. There is bound to be quite a lot of envy and spite around,' observed Ben. 'It's not every day that your dad wins a quarter of a million.'

'He's got lots of friends but of course you're right. Come to think of it, I'm pretty envious myself. Perhaps I should try it.'

'How far would you have got tonight?'

Jason laughed. 'Not as far as Jasper Bright.'

Over a light supper which they ate on their laps they talked about where Ben and Debbie would live when they married and found that Debbie favoured Shepton Mallet, where she worked as a clerk in the prison, and Ben anywhere round Trowbridge or Frome. If Ben moved to Shepton Mallet he would leave Morton's, thought Jason unhappily, and another good teacher would be lost. Angus Gaskill, Ed Deacon and now Ben Fuller with Matt Johnson doing less teaching and

197

more administration. The thought startled him because it suggested he had accepted that Ed was not coming back.

When Ed's name came up in the conversation Jason kept largely silent, afraid of revealing what Ed had confided to him, but thoughts of his colleague kept recurring. He rang him at intervals over the next weeks only to be told on each occasion that there was no progress. He visited Angus once more and found him depressed but rational and Elizabeth looking happier.

By the time the Ofsted inspection started towards the end of May he had persuaded Kat to let him sell the house by conceding that she could keep seventy per cent of the proceeds. Parnell had argued with him but he knew from the estate agent that the Holders were still looking and he was anxious to force the pace, pointing out to the solicitor that if he, not Kat, had left, then he would not have been able to sell the home until Leah was eighteen. At any time Kat might tire of the cramped cottage and try to bring about just that result. The Holders maintained their original offer and a date was set for exchange of contracts.

The estate agent put a large 'Under Offer' notice across the For Sale board and Jason, seeing it as he returned from history club one Tuesday evening, felt a lightening of his step, seeing a small brightness in the dark.

He hummed as he picked up the post from the mat and put it unopened on the kitchen table while he fed Objubjub. He decided on scrambled eggs for supper and a glass of wine in which he would toast the Holders. May their loft be all they could wish for. Light-headed with relief and progress he picked up the small collection of letters.

'One electricity bill,' he informed Objubjub. 'One bank statement. One postcard and one unknown.'

He peered at the one he had called Unknown and felt his heart give a great leap as ice poured into his stomach. His hand shaking, he opened the envelope which bore the stamp of the Child Support Agency. The contents of the letter danced before his eyes, blurring into unintelligibility, mocking his recent mood of optimism. In two strides he was by the hall telephone.

'Dad!' cried Jake in delight at the unexpected call.

Jason did not return the greeting. 'Please ask your mother to come to the phone. *Now.*'

An uncertain Jake returned a few seconds later to say Mum couldn't come now but would phone him later.

'Tell her that either she comes now or I get in the car and come there.'

Jake departed reluctantly and Kat's voice came on the line.

'Jason, this is most unreasonable–'

'Why have you gone to the Child Support Agency?'

'I had no choice. If you are on Income Support and you haven't already got a court order they make you.'

'Income Support? What the devil are you doing on Income Support? You are a teacher.'

'I was but I just couldn't manage the supply work on top of everything else. I've told you before how hard it is. I'm sorry, Jason, but I had to put the children first.'

'I am not sure how giving up a steady income means putting the children first. Do you understand what being on Income Support means? It means you can't even do a day's teaching to get extra money for anything at all.'

'I can work sixteen hours a week as it happens but I won't. I couldn't face even that. I'm stressed out with it all.'

Stressed out, repeated Jason to himself after the call had come to a less than cordial conclusion. He stared at the form in front of him and began to read the accompanying explanation less with anger than with incredulity. He must pay 20 per cent of his disposable income to the Child Support Agency. Disposable income, he read with disbelief, meant money left after his mortgage payments, but fuel, water and sewage charges were not taken into account, nor were the costs of travelling to work unless they could be shown to be unduly and unavoidably high.

Jason turned the envelope over and performed a rudimentary calculation on the back of it. After payment of his mortgage, insurance, car loan, fuel bills, telephone, council tax and credit card repayments he had £450 left each month to buy the groceries, the petrol and to pay the legal bills. After Child Support Agency deductions he would have £90 and even that was not a reliable figure. The money he had already been paying to Kat and which had felt ruinous had not so thoroughly beggared him.

It took him two hours to fill in the form and

assemble the necessary supporting document-ation. He used the school photocopying machine at break next day to make a duplicate set and posted the bundle on his way home. Some vague knowledge of the system told him that delay could result in the calculations of arrears.

Ed shook his head when Jason asked him if he had any experience of the Child Support Agency. 'No. Ros still works. Ironically I tried to persuade her not to when we were together and urged her to give up until all the children were at secondary school but she would have none of it. Indeed when Chloe was born she wouldn't even take the full amount of maternity leave. Nothing would induce Ros to give up work.'

'We've never had a lot left over but with two of us earning and living in the same house it was fine. We both hate debt and pay our cards off pretty well every time. The car loan was just about our only extravagance but one income keeping two separate households is a very different matter. Ed, I just can't believe the formula the CSA applies.'

'You may have got it wrong. Wait until they get back to you and appeal if it's impossible. How's Ofsted?'

'Crazy. I think they know they've come across a pretty horrible failure which should have been spotted last time and they're being even more thorough than usual. They've actually brought in a couple of extra people and I've had one in my classes for two days solid. They are being ultra critical and have had two of the women staff in tears. Even Ben nearly lost his temper with them

201

when they were nit-picking over his positive residuals. Carol Marsh told the staffroom at large that she felt like hurling a meat pie at one of them after he had sat through her cookery class and then realised the inspector in question was there listening! She was in full flood about how she would bet that he was an unreconstructed male chauvinist who had never so much as boiled an egg when her eye fell on him and she stopped with her mouth open. Fortunately he saw the joke and the whole staffroom fell about laughing.'

Jason realised Ed was not listening, that he had no interest in the inspection nor in the fate of Morton's, that his question had been born of duty not curiosity. Even when Jason's anecdote was finished he did not look up, but sat brooding, absorbed in his own anxiety. He had already told Jason that there was no news, that the investigation continued slowly, the police still retained his computer and he was still forbidden to contact the children. His solicitor had now put in a request for supervised access, which would mean he could see the children in the presence of a social worker. When Jason said surely that would alert the children to what was happening, Ed had replied that they must be fully alert anyway given the absence of all contact.

Jason knew that Ed was losing hope. The children must be wondering why they were not allowed to ring their father and Ed had been relying on Luke, at least, to take action when he became aware of what was in train. This did not appear to have happened and he was beginning to fear that Ros had convinced them and that

Chloe was too scared to admit the true provenance of the pornography.

Certainly Ed was thinner now and looked older. The strain was taking its toll and Jason had little idea how to lighten the load. For the first time he wondered if, beneath the seemingly resigned exterior, there boiled a volcano of despair which might erupt unpredictably, trailing devastation and disaster.

Ed's parting words, however, were of worry on Jason's account rather than his own.

'Let me know what happens with the CSA.'

The Ofsted inspectors had departed and the exam season started in earnest and still Jason had heard nothing from the CSA. He rang the local office to find himself in a queue. He held resolutely on and after ten minutes was rewarded with a cheerful voice telling him that Kylie was speaking.

'How may I help you?'

'I sent in forms over a month ago and haven't heard anything.'

'Oh dear. Can I have your name, sir?'

Jason supplied his name and address together with the reference number on the CSA letter.

'Are you the non-resident parent, Mr Kirk?'

Jason gritted his teeth. 'My children no longer live with me, if that is what you mean. I would very happily be resident with them.'

There was the sound of a computer keyboard being tapped. 'We don't appear to have you on record. Just bear with me a moment.'

The moment became three minutes.

'I'm sorry, Mr Kirk, I cannot find any record of

your forms. Could I ask you to ring the regional office? I'll just give you their number.'

Twenty minutes later Lucy was speaking. With mounting irritability Jason supplied the same information.

'Just bear with me a moment.'

Jason listened wearily to the tapping of a keyboard before Lucy asked him to wait while she made some enquiries. He was unsurprised when they bore no fruit.

'I'll have to look into it, Mr Kirk, and ring you back.'

'Thank you but I'm a teacher so I won't be available most of the time. I'll ring you. When will you have the information?'

'It depends,' Lucy prevaricated. Jason bit back the temptation to say, 'On what?'

'Try again in a day or so. I should be able to tell you what is happening by then.'

Jason left it for three days and was surprised to find he was not held in a queue. His pleasure was short-lived.

'Alison speaking. How may I help?'

'May I speak to Lucy please?'

'She's on another call right now.'

'I'll hang on.'

'It may be some time and she already has one call waiting. Can I help?'

Jason reluctantly gave his details and listened to the inevitable tap of the keyboard.

'I can't find anything, Mr Kirk. I'll look into it and call you back.'

Over the next few days he spoke to Zoe, Sue and Christine before Lucy finally answered once more and told him that despite extensive searching there was no trace of his forms.

'But how can that be?' demanded Jason in despair.

'I'm very sorry, Mr Kirk. Did you send them by Recorded Delivery?'

A small knot of cold misery settled in the pit of his stomach. He had filled in the forms, copied them and posted them within twenty-four hours but he had not thought to register the posting, trusting in a service which rarely let him down. Instinctively he believed his forms were lost not in the post but at the Child Support Agency. He would not be able to prove it and it seemed pointless to vent his ire to Lucy. Instead he asked for a fresh set of forms and said he would send copies of the originals in the meantime.

At least the house sale was proceeding smoothly. Kat had jointly signed the contract with him and he expected exchange imminently. He had no intention of making another purchase in the near future and had asked his mother to store his share of the contents. Kat had agreed to take Objubjub.

'Where will you go?' asked Carol.

'I shall rent a single room somewhere until the CSA have done their calculations and the terms of the legal separation are signed and sealed and the lawyers paid in full. Then I shall know exactly where I stand and I can then return to the property ladder, doubtless a few rungs down.'

He had thought of asking Ed Deacon to rent him a room thus enabling him to keep an eye on his colleague but Hillier had asked him to think again.

'I appreciate your care of Ed but I really must counsel against what you are planning, Jason. If you had always lived there that would be one thing but going there now could be seen as giving aid and comfort to a child abuser. I know we all think he is innocent but we must allow for the possibility of his being convicted and that would leave your actions open to question. You are a teacher, Jason, and cannot afford the sort of vindictive innuendo which might appear in the press.'

'He hasn't been so much as charged yet, never mind convicted.'

'And if he is charged it will be banner headlines in the local press and if you are sharing his house at the time you will be embroiled in it all. I beg of you, Jason, to think of all the consequences.'

Hillier was right but Jason felt treacherous merely to concede he was so. Nevertheless he began to seek other options and as the long summer term drew to its end he took lodgings with an elderly spinster two miles from Frome. Mrs Turnbull had recently lost her twenty-year-old cat and Objubjub would go temporarily with him to his new home.

In the week preceding the move Carol Marsh helped him with the packing and Kat visited several times to take her share of the contents. Jason wondered how she would fit so much into the tiny cottage but forbore to say so.

Once he saw Kat drive up just as he and Carol were taking down some curtains. 'Don't mention Frome,' he hissed. 'She doesn't know I'm moving that near. I want completion out of the way before telling her.'

He was disconcerted when he saw a flash of jealousy in Kat's eyes as he introduced Carol, surprised at her reaction, uneasy as to where her spite could lead, wanting to reassure her, uncertain how to do so, obscurely guilty without any cause.

'I thought I might as well take Objubjub today,' announced Kat casually.

Jason thought of Mrs Turnbull. 'I'll bring him over on Friday when I see the kids. You can get him used to his new surroundings without them there. It makes more sense.'

'OK,' said Kat unsuspectingly. 'Where are Jake and Leah going to sleep amidst all this chaos?'

'Where they usually do. The beds aren't going till Monday.'

'Where on earth is your mother going to store it all?'

'In the garage. The car will live on the drive until I'm resettled.'

'She must be a saint.'

'She is. Those boxes over there are yours. Let's get them in the car.'

'Who's the girl?' asked Kat as they pushed the last of the items into the crammed boot.

'Carol? She's not a girl. She teaches at Morton's and, just in case you have the wrong idea, she is not a girlfriend either. It will be a very long time before I trust another woman.'

Kat ignored the sally but when she said, 'Objubjub on Friday then and let me know where you'll be living when you've finally decided,' and he had said 'I'll do that,' he thought that maybe it would also be some time before she could trust another man.

11

One of the earliest actions Jason took on finding himself in lodgings for the first time in his life was to install a telephone in his room. Mrs Turnbull said of course it was important for him to keep in touch with his children but the first six calls he made were to the Child Support Agency from whom he had still not heard. He rehearsed his circumstances with four different people and finally demanded a supervisor who said she would need time to look into what had happened. The assessment finally arrived on a Saturday morning, demanding not only a weekly sum which would put home ownership beyond him, but also a huge total of arrears.

'How,' demanded Jason, after a sleepless weekend in which not even the savage satisfaction of finally letting Kat know that he had settled within a mile and a half of his children had managed to slow the maddened whirr of his hammering indignation, 'can I have accumulated thousands of pounds in arrears when my wife only applied to you in May?'

'It is the difference between what you have been contributing to the upkeep of the children and what we assess you should have been paying Mrs Kirk.'

'The upkeep of the children? I have been paying half the bills on the cottage ever since she left.

I have bought them clothes and, in my son's case, uniform. I have given his godfather money towards a trip to Disney. I have them every other weekend during which I meet all their needs.'

'We have to apply a set formula, Mr Kirk. If you think we have failed to take anything into account as obliged by statute you can appeal.'

Jason applied a profane epithet to the statute and replaced the receiver with irritable force. He could meet the sum demanded and pay off the legal bills from his share of the house proceeds and still have some money left over but it would seriously deplete his small capital, on which a cold inner voice told him he would have to draw to make ends meet in the future if he were not to stay in lodgings until Leah was eighteen. His hitherto orderly lifestyle had collapsed in chaos but, he thought, at least he now knew where he stood and could make plans.

The satisfaction was short-lived as he suddenly remembered the warning that he must tell the Child Support Agency of any change in earnings or relevant liabilities. He had just moved from paying mortgage to paying rent with the specific intention of reducing his outgoings. That meant his disposable income had enlarged and the Child Support Agency would in turn want a larger sum.

Briefly he toyed with conveniently forgetting to tell the authorities but knew that the consequences would be worse in the long run. Kat might tell them out of spite or they might find out another way and the resulting arrears would be crippling. He had no choice but to start the whole miserable process of assessment all over again.

In mid-August Kat took the children away to her parents for a week and upon their return Jason took them on a camping holiday that dissolved into fiasco. It rained steadily throughout the first five days and Leah developed a stomach complaint, which caused Jason to stop the car every half-hour on the journey back. Jake, bored and disappointed, ran into the cottage with no attempt to conceal his pleasure that the holiday was over.

Kat took sufficient pity on Jason to offer him both drink and supper but he refused, instead driving to Carol's flat and finding her out. During the return journey he ran into a delay on the road and realised that this would be his regular journey when Morton's returned in September. His thoughts turned to the children he taught and he wondered what had happened to Harry Jackson.

As if in answer to his musing, Jason opened his newspaper on the Sunday before term commenced to find Harry's picture prominent on the front page. He had been recognised by a fellow pupil of Morton's in, of all places, the Calvinist Cathedral in Geneva, into the bareness of which Harry had slipped to keep cool on a day of blistering heat. He had tried without success to hide behind a pillar and then sprinted away down an aisle. The other pupil, a girl, and her parents gave chase but Harry escaped.

'What on earth is he doing in an expensive place like Geneva?' wondered Carol when Jason rang to find out if she had heard the news. 'I would have expected Spain or somewhere like that.'

'Probably reasoned that Spain and France are

full of Brits at this time of year but that applies to most places. Maybe Jackson has friends in Switzerland. Anyway it looks as if there is a pretty good brouhaha going on over there at the moment. My bet is he was over the border into France before you could say Jack Robinson. Dad must be working illegally unless they've robbed a bank.'

'You don't sound very worried about Harry.'

'He's got his dad.'

'Who first neglects him and then evades the law. You have more faith in that man than I have.'

'Would you have more faith in Social Services? The state has a lousy record as parent. Most kids who come out of care end up unemployed, homeless, on drugs or in prison and quite often they endure all of those fates.'

'Yes, but they come from backgrounds where that sort of thing is the norm.'

His judgement was becoming distorted, thought Jason. A year ago he would have had little patience with the likes of Mr Jackson but now his empathy with anyone deprived of his child seemed to be so great as to overcome any other consideration. He knew he must begin to take a more rational view of the world but of one thing he was still very certain: although Hillier had been right to stop him trying to rent a room from Ed Deacon, he could not believe that Ed was anything but wholly innocent of charges which had proceeded from the spite of a woman who wanted to have his children entirely to herself. It would be good to think that Ed might clear himself comprehensively and return to

Morton's in the coming school year.

Within a week of the start of term Hillier announced that Angus Gaskill had taken early medical retirement. The practical effects on the school were minimal and the news was received with a shrug. Angus was understood to be slowly improving and he and Elizabeth would shortly commence a long holiday. Jason was among those who had visited recently and noted the deputy head's recovery with relief but, recalling that conversation of nearly a year ago when Angus had planned to leave on his own terms, he felt a small stir of regret.

A week later Hillier himself was gone and the school in special measures.

'They didn't waste much time,' commented Ben, approvingly.

The acting head imposed on them also did not waste much time and the staffroom was split between those who hailed his arrival with hope and those who resented the new atmosphere and demands. He sat through a lesson with each teacher and Jason made sure Terry Pepper demonstrated his unnerving skill. He interviewed every member of the school's staff from Matt Johnson to the caretaker.

'It's certainly making a difference,' said Carol happily.

Jason found his new living arrangements were also making a difference and that they had brought unexpected consequences. The distance involved in getting to and from work was a drawback of which he had always been aware but he had not thought through its wider impact. If he stayed on after school he got back a bit too late to see Leah before she went to bed. If he wanted to visit Carol or other friends after school he was always conscious of a sizeable journey yet to come.

Initially he took great delight in arriving at the cottage unexpectedly to see his children, knowing that if he were disappointed it was not far to go home, but Kat retaliated by calling on him when he had the children and, as relations were far from cordial, the tension communicated itself to Jake and Leah. Furthermore they could no longer stay with him overnight and Kat subtly found ways to insist on earlier return times so she could get them ready for bed.

The children did not like the new arrangements. The old house had the virtue of familiarity and they had fitted into it when they visited as though they had never left. They had their own friends to play with, knew where things were and could run in and out of the house as they pleased. The restrictions imposed by Mrs Turnbull's house, where only one room was theirs and from which most of their possessions were absent, cramped their playfulness and left them uncertain and wanting to return to the cottage. Other than Jason himself, only Objubjub provided any continuity between their old home and Jason's new one and he was glad he had, after all, kept the animal with him.

Going in search of Objubjub usually meant finding him with Mrs Turnbull to whom the children took an immediate liking, treating her as a surrogate grandmother. On some visits they spent more time with her than with him, especially as she provided treats and old-fashioned teas of scones and cream cakes on which they fell with loud enthusiasm.

Kat appeared oblivious to the restrictions and the manner in which Jason now lived. He did not think she gloated but she had no conscience about the effect of her actions on them all and certainly showed no embarrassment.

Jason's straitened circumstances received a boost shortly before half-term when the new head announced a reorganisation which increased his responsibilities. His joy was somewhat tarnished by the reflection that he had only recently received the revised CSA demand with its increased weekly payment and increased arrears. He would now have to fill in yet another set of forms and receive yet another assessment demanding yet another increase. As the realisation manifested itself to him, he slumped in his seat in the staffroom and groaned aloud to the surprise of colleagues, who had just been congratulating him on a not insignificant promotion.

Only his work was now stable and reliable. He had no permanent home and at the age of thirty-three lived in a single room which was not his, his finances were unpredictable and severely limited with unspecified legal bills still to come and an ever-changing liability to the Child Support Agency. He could not house his children overnight and was not welcome in their home. He was no longer married, nor was he divorced. The future stretched before him, uncertain, fraught, disorderly.

Jason had thrived, although he had not consciously known it until now, on order, stability and predictability, on exactly the kind of life which had apparently so bored Kat. He had no childish expectation that his life would be problem-free but he held to an underlying conviction that he would be able to deal with what his mother always called the occasional ill wind, because surely it would herald only temporary squalls. Now he found himself at the centre of a storm with his boat upside down and drifting away while he saw neither land nor lifeboat.

Ed's storm was greater, however, and Jason continued to call. Far from moving towards a reassuring resolution, matters had deteriorated with the discovery by the police that Ed's computer had been used to access pornography.

'I can't believe it. I know Alice is more than capable of it but I just can't see Chloe having any interest at all. Indeed the police say it was used for the purpose only once and that was on an access weekend when Alice was here. I remember it well because the next-door neighbours had a minor emergency and I went in there to help. I think Alice must have tried to interest Chloe while I was out of the house and she probably got a disgusted response. Ros was certainly right about Alice.'

'What do the police say?'

'I think they believe me. They have confirmed the story of the neighbours' emergency but, as far as I know, have not been to Alice's house. They have also seen Chloe again who insists that she just found the document here. I am beginning to wonder if she is telling the truth. Suppose Alice brought it, did not show it to her and then left it behind? Chloe would be right to say she found it here.'

'Then she wouldn't have taken it off with her, would she?'

'Yes, if she suspected Alice and thought there was trouble coming. I doubt if she realises what is happening even now. She probably thinks she is the one being punished by not being allowed to see me and that it all has something to do with what Ros found in her holdall. So rather than admit to the influence of Alice, whom her mother cannot stand, she just says she found it and leaves it at that.'

'Chloe is nine. She must understand the involvement of the police is serious stuff.'

'Yes, but she may attribute that to the nature of the document and indeed may be afraid she will get Alice into big trouble. In her mind only grown-ups are allowed to have this sort of thing so the fact that I might have it would not matter.'

'But she must talk about it to the boys? Luke surely would smell a rat?'

'That depends on what Ros had told them.'

'It's just too fantastic. Why won't they go to Alice's house and check the computers there?'

'Because no offence has been committed. The pornography was not itself of a paedophile nature and it didn't involve rape or anything like that and I alone am saying that is where it came from. It is merely the sort of thing that no adult would put in the possession of a child unless he wanted to corrupt her. On its own it wouldn't have sparked an investigation, given that there was a plausible explanation for its presence, but it has been taken in context with all the rest of the things Ros alleges.'

'Looking for bruises on the back of a child who had a nasty fall and making a passing comment on her new underwear? Haven't the police anything better to do? And shouldn't they be worried about Alice seeing this sort of stuff and touting it round her friends?'

Ed shrugged. 'The whole appears to them greater than the sum of its parts and the only evidence against Alice is mine.'

'They must surely have asked Ros about her?'

'I'm sure they have and Ros will have said she is not a nice child but that she has never had any reason to believe she is involved with that sort of thing and it would be a perfectly truthful answer.'

'Truth is more than accuracy of words.'

'Let us hope the CPS thinks so.'

'The Crown Prosecution Service? It's going that far?'

'It will have to when the police investigation is over. I suspect they will recommend no further action but there is such hysteria about child abuse these days that the CPS may be unwilling to take that risk. Look at some of the barmy cases they have taken on when someone has emerged from the woodwork thirty years on and claimed some poor, unsuspecting pillar of society did the unspeakable to him when he was six and it turns out to be all about money or revenge for some completely different grievance.'

'True, but some of those cases have stood up. It's a pretty ghastly crime. Supposing some pervert got hold of Chloe or my Leah, you wouldn't call the reaction hysterical then.'

'Perhaps not, but, in case you have forgotten, Ros is claiming some pervert *did* get hold of Chloe and *I'm* the pervert in question.'

The bitterness in Ed's voice contrasted sharply with the calm manner in which he had predicted a prosecution and Jason looked at him more closely. There was an eczema rash on his hands which Jason had not noticed before and he was yet thinner.

'Are you seeing the doctor?'

'Yes. Sleeping pills and tranquillisers are all he can suggest. I agreed to the first but not the second. This will be a long haul and I don't want to come out of it living on Prozac. It's been months already and it will be many more months with the CPS when the police get round to sending it on. If there is a trial it will probably be a year away. I should like to work but no employer would be likely to want me at present even in those jobs which do not involve children. The sorts of jobs I could once have done at home, such as indexing books, are too often done by computers these days.'

'Why not get away? Just for a couple of weeks or so?'

'Yes, I've been thinking on those lines myself.'

'Let me know when you're going. Otherwise I'll be round again soon. Would you like me to bring someone else? Did you know Carol Marsh?'

'Not particularly well,' said Ed discouragingly.

Jason decided to take Carol anyway, thinking it would be good for Ed to see more people. They arrived one evening in early October to find the house in darkness.

'He must be out. That's unusual.'

'Did you tell him you were coming?'

'No. I've got into the habit of just turning up. This is the first time this has happened. I'm sorry you have had a wasted journey.'

'You said he was thinking of going away. Perhaps he's gone.'

'I think he would have told me.'

They were just turning back down the drive when Jason saw a man enter the neighbouring one.

'Excuse me,' called Jason. 'Has Mr Deacon gone away?'

The man paused and came to join them. 'Not so far as I know. He usually tells us and gives us the key. He was around an hour ago because there was a light on upstairs.'

'He must have nipped out,' put in Carol. 'We'll try tomorrow.'

'It's history club,' said Jason. 'Let's make it Wednesday.'

On Wednesday night Jason and Ben stood staring up at the same dark house. Jason's attempts to telephone in between were met with an answering machine but none of his messages had been returned. Carol had been intending to come with him but at the last moment had been unable and Ben had agreed to take her place.

Jason peered into the porch. There were no newspapers or milk bottles but a pile of letters, unlikely to have been the product of one day's mail, lay scattered under the letterbox.

'He must have gone away. Oh, hello again!'

The neighbour had appeared by Jason's side, saying he was glad to see them because he had been getting worried. Mr Deacon did not appear to have been at home since Jason last tried to visit but he had not handed over a key and there was a bathroom window open upstairs. The three of them walked round the house, looking through the downstairs windows, seeing little in the gloom of the October twilight.

'Perhaps we should call the police,' murmured the neighbour.

Jason looked up at the open window. 'Have you got a ladder?'

'Do you want me to go?' asked Ben when the ladder was in place.

Jason shook his head. Ben was younger and fitter but he, Jason, could still climb a ladder. Getting through the small window was a different matter and the others called up warnings to him as he twisted and turned on the top rung before finally arriving on the bathroom floor in an undignified heap, his hand sending a glass crashing to the floor.

'Ed?'

He did not expect his call to be answered as he switched on the landing light and began to open the doors of the rooms around him. The first was a child's room with an ancient bear on the bed and Winnie the Pooh curtains. The second was a box room full of junk accumulated over decades. There were two more. Jason tried the door of one and found himself in a room with the curtains drawn.

'Ed?'

With reluctance, with premonition, with delayed recognition of why he had not accepted Ben's offer to climb the ladder, Jason switched on the light, his unwilling eyes seeking the scene he dreaded. Ed Deacon lay in the middle of the double bed he had once shared with his wife, with his back to the door. As Jason approached, still futilely saying his name, he saw the glass on the bedside table and the empty cards of pills. He put a hand on Ed's shoulder and the body fell on its back. There appeared to be no note.

A few seconds later Jason looked out through the bathroom window. 'I'll let you in. I'm afraid we will need the police.'

Driven by some atavistic fear of being alone in a strange house with a corpse, Jason ran down the stairs like a scared child and pulled open the front door.

'How?' asked Ben.

'Sleeping pills. He must have planned it carefully – cancelled the milk and the newspapers, made sure nobody would look for him before the pills could well and truly do their work. He said he was going away and but for the open window that is what people would have believed had happened and they would have seen no reason to do other than wait for him to return.'

The neighbour came back from the hall where he had telephoned the police. 'They're on their way. I must go and tell my wife what has happened.'

'Poor old Ed.' Ben's voice was an appalled whisper.

The telephone shrilled a summons and Jason went out into the hall to answer, giving Ed's number which he had come to know by heart over recent months and being met with a surprised pause.

'Who's that?'

'A visiting friend. Is that Ros?' He heard his voice sharpen with hostility.

'Yes. Can I speak to Ed?'

'I'm afraid not.'

'Isn't he there?'

'No.'

'Well, when will he be back?'

'Never.'

There was a short puzzled silence which somehow held some indefinable suggestion of fear. 'I don't understand.'

'Well, try and understand this then: he's dead and you killed him.'

Ben seized the phone and began to babble apologies, saying Jason had been a close friend of Ed and had received a great shock. Ed had died quite peacefully and he was so very sorry for what she must now be going through. He began to make the kind of consolatory sounds with which people respond to crying. Jason snorted.

'That was unforgivable!' Ben's outrage exploded when he put the phone down.

'I know and I don't want to be forgiven.' Less for justification than for information he told Ben all he had learned from Ed.

'But what was Ros supposed to do when she found pornography in Chloe's case?'

'Ask Ed where it came from.'

222

'But Chloe had already told her she found it in Ed's house. Presumably from what you tell me Chloe would not have said too much to her mother about Alice. What choice had Ros but to take it seriously?'

'She could have tackled Ed before going to Social Services. Dammit, Ben, she's been trying to keep those kids from him ever since she left and she suddenly saw the most perfect opportunity to ban him from seeing them. And, before you tell me that she couldn't possibly have foreseen *this*, let me point out that she is a clever, successful, determined career woman and would have known perfectly well what she was unleashing.'

A police siren interrupted Ben's reply and Jason went to the door. He was surprised to see a plain-clothes man who, while his uniformed colleagues went upstairs, introduced himself as Inspector Farrell.

'I happened to be in the station when you called and as I had been involved in the case I thought I would come along. I'm more sorry than I can say that this is how it has all ended. Mr Deacon was of course under the most terrible strain.'

'He couldn't face the delay,' explained Jason. 'When I was last here he was talking about how it might be another year before the trial. The doctor had suggested tranquillisers but he had refused. He was horribly depressed but I wasn't prepared for this.'

'I don't think there would have been a trial, speaking entirely off the record. The child never once suggested that he actively gave her the

223

material, merely that she had found it here. She agreed that she had a nasty fall and complained of back pain and said that was the only time he had been into the bathroom since she was very little, but I am telling you more than I should.'

'Did you tell him?'

'Not in so many words but I think he knew we thought it was all nonsense.'

'Vindictive nonsense. I suppose you will tell me that it is not a crime to drive someone to suicide.'

Ben stirred uneasily and the inspector seemed to recollect himself, becoming suddenly very formal in manner and saying he would have to contact Mrs Deacon.

'I've already told her. She rang while we were waiting for you.'

Farrell looked grave but responded in neutral tones. He was interrupted by the arrival of the neighbour and all three made statements which the constables wrote down in slow longhand. Jason signed his with bitter pressure on the biro and knew that Ben was watching him unhappily.

'Don't let Kat destroy you,' he said when they were once more in Jason's car. 'The Jason Kirk of that phone call is not the Jason Kirk I know. Kat's bitchiness is colouring your view of everything.'

Jason recalled how he had reasoned himself to a similar conclusion when he had queried his defence of Mr Jackson, but he was not yet ready to concede this to Ben. 'Ros has been twice as bad as Kat could ever think of being. I suppose I should count myself lucky.'

Ben ignored the sarcasm. 'Yes, but she now has a suicide on her conscience and that will be a life sentence. Forget Ros.'

'God help the children.'

'Amen. When they realise the full enormity of what has been going on they may never forgive their mother.'

Jason tried to picture Jake and Leah in the same situation and found his imagination unequal to the challenge. At least they still had their father, even if he no longer lived with them, and they had a mother they adored and who in turn loved them. Harry Jackson had no mother, just a father who neglected him possessively while the Deacon children had no father, only a mother who had wanted to be the sole parent.

'Haphazard love.'

'What?' Ben sounded startled.

'I was thinking of Harry Jackson for some reason. That's what he's always had. Mothers came and went, his father has left him to his own devices most of the time but suddenly treats him like recently discovered treasure. At least Jake and Leah are secure in the knowledge that we love them and care for them and always will.'

'Do you remember the Beggs children?' asked Ben suddenly.

'How could I ever forget? The girl was in my form. Went off to Yorkshire or Lancashire or somewhere to some long-suffering relatives. Why do you ask? They're not coming back, are they?'

Ben laughed. 'No, at least not so far as I know. I was just following your train of thought and wondering if they felt loved through the mother's drug haze or when they visited their father in prison? Or did they believe their existence to be

225

an unplanned nuisance?'

'That's pitching it pretty strongly. I doubt if the Beggses would have described it that way. They were just not up to parenting.'

They were talking about anyone they could think of, Jason acknowledged to himself, in order to avoid talking about Ed, to escape the reality of that lonely death and of the intolerable mental agonies which had preceded it, to block out the questions, the self-recriminations. A year ago Ed had been among them in the staffroom every day, often taciturn, sometimes bitter but still there, thinking, teaching, living, oblivious of the cruel blow yet to fall. Jason's own world had just been turned upside down and the path he was then so unwillingly treading had ended in lodgings at Frome, with his children somehow less reachable than when he had lived miles away, and the Child Support Agency darkly menacing his future. He wondered what the coming year would bring and realised that in the thought was an implicit recognition that he had lost control of events, that he was at the mercy of fate and of Kat.

12

The small church seemed full of Morton's staff and pupils but, as the funeral service commenced and the congregation began singing 'The Day Thou Gavest, Lord, is Ended' Jason found his gaze resting neither on his charges nor his hymn book, focusing instead on the four figures in the front right-hand pew. He had glimpsed Ros's face as she entered, noting the haggard lines and red-rimmed eyes beneath her black hat, and felt an unexpected flash of pity, understanding that she was confronting the irretrievable nature of what she had done. Perhaps, throughout Ed's torture, she had persuaded herself that there would be a point when she could withdraw the allegations and release him from the cruel teeth of the trap into which he had fallen. Perhaps she believed, as had the police, that there would be no trial and he would return to teaching, wounded but not mortally so, while she herself had a fresh excuse to limit his contact with his own children, to impose new conditions.

Behind any wrongdoing, thought Jason, was an assumption of control: *I can always pull back at the last minute if I decide I don't want to do it.* It must be what criminals thought as they set out to rob and to burgle, prepared to change plans if the risk suddenly looked greater than anticipated, what murderers thought as they bought the poison: *I can always use it on the weeds instead.* Cheats told themselves they need not use the prompt if the exam looked possible after all. Adulterers believed they could give up their treachery without their wives finding out. Liars were ready to deny their lies.

Now it was the victim who had taken control and left behind a brutal legacy of guilt, together with a wedge between Ros and her children which he would not have sought to drive in life. He had not even left a note, leaving his control over events to speak for itself: complete, too complete to need explanation or justification.

The children stood on either side of her, Chloe weeping inconsolably and leaning against her brother. Not against Ros, observed Jason, as a cold arrow pierced him and he saw the wedge for himself. He uttered a silent, urgent prayer for Chloe who had lost a father and was now uncertain of her mother.

When he had told Carol of the death he and she had spoken simultaneously. 'I don't know how she could do it to Chloe,' Jason had said as he finished his story and 'I don't know how he could do it to Chloe,' had been Carol's response to the news.

Both parents were horribly guilty. He could not deny that but, while Ed had been driven to the deed by the madness of slow and unremitting torture, he could not, even in his most generous moments find any excuse for Ros. He pitied her now and regretted the way he had broken the news to her with a hot shame, which assailed him afresh each time he recollected that telephone call, but he still hated her and mourned Ed with indignation as well as grief. Jason saw other eyes directed towards Ros and thought he detected in them a similar response to his own.

Hillier gave the address, praising Ed's long dedication to teaching. Luke read one of the lessons and the vicar prayed for Ros, the children and all who suffered the loss of a loved one. No one mentioned the manner of the teacher's death.

Jason glanced again at Ros as she left the church behind the vicar. He used the press of colleagues as an excuse not to greet her as he left, uncertain of his reception, not wanting to put it to the test. He recognised the neighbour and conversed with him briefly as the mourners stood about in the chill October air. Fallen leaves, which had not been there when they arrived, now lay strewn throughout the churchyard and the street outside, dry and rustling, blown by a rising wind which caused Jason to pull his overcoat more closely about him.

He was turning towards the coach which had brought the Morton's party when to his amazement he saw Kat. She was wearing boots and a long black coat and Jason felt an unusual stab of regret. His wife looked relaxed and happy, despite the occasion, as she had looked throughout the ten years of their marriage. For perhaps the space of a minute he did not approach her because he did not want to see her long-lost expression change into that of the emotional warrior's with which he was now all too familiar.

He was surprised that it did not do so when she suddenly turned and saw him, but he still approached warily.

'I didn't realise you knew Ed that well,' said Jason when he had asked after the children and been assured they were fine and looking forward to their next visit.

'I scarcely knew him at all, but I taught Chloe for a term when I was doing supply and got to know Ros. It's a ghastly business.'

'Yes. I don't believe what Ros was saying. I suppose you know? The inquest?'

'Yes, I read the reports but Ros hadn't said

anything to me about it.'

'I can tell you that the detail would never have stood up in court.'

'If what you are saying is that she made it all up, then she is a prize fool. The kids are more than old enough to know what is going on and they'll be unlikely to forgive her. Dear God, can you imagine me trying to explain something like that to Jake and Leah? It's too horrible even to think about.'

Kat was reassuring him, he realised. Her words gave him a disguised promise that this was one weapon she would not use in the war she so ruthlessly waged, that it was the nuclear option, not a conventional means of destruction, and she was far too alive to the consequences. She guessed his thoughts and gave him a comradely grin, which he returned as they stood facing each other, drawing their coats more closely about them as another gust of wind hurled leaves and litter into the air, experiencing a closeness which had eluded them for a year. He recalled the vicar saying something about tragedy drawing people closer together. Then Kat caught sight of Carol who was talking to Ben not far from where they stood and said, her tone still friendly but her features stiffening, that she must go.

Jason turned once more towards the coach only to be again distracted, this time by the sight of Angus and Elizabeth who were just turning away from a conversation with Hillier. Jason hailed them eagerly but Angus was already talking to one of the science teachers and it was Elizabeth who came, smiling, towards him.

'You're looking well,' said Jason. 'How is he?'

'Vastly better. The doctor says at this rate he will be back to normal in six months, but I'm just taking each day as it comes. This awful event hasn't helped but he seems more angry than upset.'

'Can't you get away for a proper break?'

'We're going to find some winter sun next month. I couldn't risk going abroad until I knew he really was better.'

'Is there anything I can do?'

Elizabeth shook her head.

'Come on, Sir,' called an impatient voice from the coach. Jason frowned.

'It's nearly lunchtime,' pointed out Elizabeth with a smile.

Snatches of conversation drifted through the coach as it first waited until the hearse and the car following it had commenced their journey to the crematorium and then began a slow reverse among the remaining mourners.

'Remember that field trip when he fell over in that muddy field?'

'Did you see Mr Gaskill? He was with the staff in the front row.'

'Luke used to be in my class.'

'Do you remember how he yelled at Chrissy Beggs that time she pulled my hair?'

'He once showed me how to do a magic trick. It's ace. You tie an empty matchbox to your arm under your sleeve then...'

'He should have been head.'

Jason caught Ben's eye and smiled. Whatever surliness Ed had inflicted on the rest of the staff had clearly bypassed his dealings with his pupils

231

and Jason was glad that he was remembered so fondly. The announcement of his death and the rumours which immediately swirled around its nature had temporarily unsettled both Ed's own form and the wider school, the children at first more distressed than their teachers but, with the resilience of youth, recovering more quickly.

Jason thought often of Ed in the weeks which followed, his memory sometimes showing him the man and sometimes the empty shell lying lonely on the bed. He tried not to think too much of the children but was tormented by the image of Chloe weeping, embraced by a tight-lipped Luke.

His own life was continuing on its unsatisfactory course, brightened by fortnightly visits from Jake and Leah and by a growing but still wary closeness to Carol.

One cold winter Saturday they walked ten miles in the countryside of St Catherine's and Cold Ashton, scrambling over stiles, jumping small brooks, eating pasties for lunch at a small, isolated pub. All day Jason had taken Carol's hand to help her over obstacles but when, as they came in sight of the car, she took his arm saying she felt exhausted, he was immediately alert and uneasy, unsure whether it was her feelings he feared or his own.

Later he was about to climb the stairs towards a hot bath when Mrs Turnbull stopped him and asked him if he ever took on private coaching because her grandson needed a hand with his maths. Jason pointed out that he was unqualified to teach maths and she replied that Henry was only eight and therefore not doing anything very complicated but was being put in for a prep school which demanded a better performance in the subject than he was currently capable of rendering. As he was coming to stay for part of the Christmas holiday she thought it might be an ideal opportunity, there being a teacher on the premises...

Jason, who approved neither of private tuition nor of prep schools, suppressed his political instincts in favour of an unexpected way to pay for Christmas. He was taking the children to his mother's and returning them to Kat for New Year by which time Henry would have arrived. He found some obscure justification in the dovetailing of the arrangements, as if somehow the coincidence indicated a wish on the part of the Deity that he should fall in with Mrs Turnbull's wishes. His only real hesitation was provided by the reflection that his landlady had been so kind to Jake and Leah that he ought to refuse payment, but, to his guilty relief, she would not hear of any proposal to offer his expertise for nothing and he reached a compromise with his conscience by determining that he would give a generous proportion of additional time free.

So predictable had his routine become that he suspected nothing other than error when he missed Leah's nativity play.

'It's on Wednesday,' Kat told him when he returned the children one Sunday evening. 'It's rather sweet. They're doing it in a real stable on a nearby farm.'

Jason wrote down the directions and arrived at two o'clock the following Wednesday to find an empty stable and a puzzled farmhand.

'It was yesterday. It's always on the Tuesday before they break up. Never been on a Wednesday, has it?' His tone, suggesting surprise that anyone could be ignorant of the annual arrangements, would have amused Jason in any other circumstances.

'I told you Tuesday,' insisted Kat.

'You said Wednesday,' accused Jake. 'I heard you.'

'Well, I'm really very sorry. I must have made a mistake but I could have sworn I said Tuesday. How stupid of me. Leah was so disappointed.'

'Oh, thanks a lot.' Jason gritted his teeth.

'I've said I'm sorry. Well, let's make sure we get it right with Jake's carol concert. It's on Friday, isn't it, Jake? It's at six so you won't have to get anyone to cover for you at Morton's.'

Two days later a bemused Jason sat through the hour-long concert without seeing any sign of his son on the stage or of Kat in the audience. The beginnings of suspicion gnawed his peace of mind but when he consulted his mobile he found Kat had left a message: '*Sorry, chicken pox. Hope you get this in time.*'

Fear became certainty. The message was timed at five to six when she would have known he had taken his seat and switched off his mobile. He searched for innocent explanations and found none except the obvious: Kat was breaking the truce which had prevailed since Ed's funeral, was renewing her campaign of obstruction.

'I'm sorry,' said Kat. 'He's been ill all day but I was hoping he might get better. Then just before

I phoned you I saw the first signs of rash.'

'I'll go up and say goodnight.' Jason moved towards the stairs.

'No, he's asleep.'

'Well, I can look in on Leah.'

'Please don't. It took me hours to settle her. I hope she's not getting it too.'

Jason hesitated. 'They may have heard my voice and be expecting me. I'll creep up and peer in quietly, then if they are asleep I won't wake them.'

'I'd really rather you didn't. It only needs one of them to wake and make a noise and I'm the one who is going to have to get them off to sleep again after you have gone.'

What would he have done had they still been together? Reluctantly he admitted to himself that he would have taken Kat's advice.

'OK.'

'Thanks. Let's hope Jake will be better for Christmas.'

Jason felt the cold shock enter his stomach. 'Kat, the children are coming with me to my mother's for Christmas. It's still a week away and there are no other children there for them to infect.'

'Of course, if they are well enough.'

'Kat...'

'Jason, be reasonable. I didn't give Jake the chicken pox.'

'Well, if the worst comes to the worst, I'll have them for New Year again and you can have them at Christmas.'

'I'm sorry but that won't be possible. I promised my parents they would be there for New Year.'

'And I promised my mother they would be there for Christmas. I accept that may now be impossible but that means they come to me for New Year.'

'Let's see what happens. They may be perfectly fit to travel. Jason, you know as well as I do that childhood illnesses don't follow conveniently predictable patterns. Jake and Leah are bound to be ill occasionally and that means that arrangements may have to change at the last minute. Surely you realise that?'

'I'll call in tomorrow night.'

'Jason–'

'I said I'll call tomorrow night.'

The children would not be coming to him for Christmas. He would once again spend the festivities with Eileen, except that this time there would be no New Year visit to which they could look forward. In despair he rang Alan Parnell on the Monday.

'Have you any reason to suppose they are not ill?'

'Kat hasn't said Leah is ill. She doesn't have to be as I would hardly want to split the children up at Christmas. As for Jake, I haven't been allowed to see him. On Saturday night Kat said he had been delirious all day and had only just sunk into sleep. Under no circumstances was I to go up and wake him. On Sunday I went round at lunchtime and she spoke to me through the window saying Jake was very bad and she didn't want me to catch shingles. I told her not to be so damn stupid but she said Leah was calling and she must go. Since then she has resolutely refused even to talk to me on the phone. She seems to be reverting to her old ways just when I thought all that was over. It seems I've been living in a fool's paradise.'

'I know it's easy for me to say this, but please stay calm and, above all, avoid any temptation to force your way to Jake's bedside. You will play into her hands if you give Lane and Webb any grounds for curtailing the access arrangements or worse still applying to the courts for prohibitions or even an injunction. Back off and be sweet reason itself.'

A year had passed since Angus Gaskill had asked him to be reasonable and to take a proper break as the school closed for the Christmas holidays. In that year Angus had himself lost his reason, Ed had killed himself and Jackson had abducted his son. But fate could give as well as take away and Ben had become engaged, Jasper Bright had won a quarter of a million pounds, while Morton's was showing the first significant signs of once more being a school worthy of respect. All he, Jason Kirk, asked of fate for the coming year was to be allowed to be a father to his children. If he were to be granted that and no more then he would remain reasonable.

Accompanying Eileen to church during their childless Christmas he stared at the figure in the life-sized crib and wondered how Joseph would have reacted if Mary had suddenly got up and left the stable with the infant Jesus, saying she was bored and would not be back. The absurd thought sent a surge of amusement coursing through him and Eileen frowned in surprise as he smothered a laugh.

'I can't somehow see Kat as Mary,' commented Eileen when he explained later. 'The Devil, possibly, but not Mary.'

Her words haunted him when he finally saw Jake halfway through January.

'How did you cope with the itching? Did Mum smother you in that horrible pink stuff?'

'Pink stuff?'

'Yes, you know, calamine lotion.'

Jake looked puzzled and Jason thought there must be some new method of treating chicken pox. It must be at least twenty-five years since he had experienced the disease.

He tried to remember his mother as she was then and failed, her features resolutely those of the sixty-year-old he knew now.

'No. Just Lemsip.'

Jason came to an abrupt halt, causing the pedestrian behind to bump into him. Still staring at his son, he was oblivious to both the collision and the apology, which was tinged with a mild resentment. He tried to keep his tone neutral.

'Lemsip? I thought you had chicken pox?'

'So did Mum at first but they weren't the right sort of spots and then the doctor thought it could be German measles. Dad, do measles come from Germany? Then it just sort of went away but Mum said I must still stay in bed until my temperature had gone down.'

'And it did? Before Christmas?'

'Enough for us to go to Granny and Grand-dad's on Christmas Eve. Mum said that you had gone to Nan's by then or me and Leah could have gone with you.'

'Leah and I.'

'OK. Leah and I.'

'Did you feel very ill when you had the rash?'

'I did the first day but after that I didn't. It was really boring having to stay in bed, but Mum said I had to in case the rash came back and I disinfected Leah.'

'Infected Leah. You're not a bottle of Dettol, are you?'

Jake laughed helplessly and Jason forced a smile in response, while his outrage grew and burst in a splutter as he repressed the swearing which had been about to break forth. He hated himself as he saw the innocent mirth die from his son's face.

'What's the matter, Dad?'

'Nothing. I was trying to stop a hiccough. Here we are. McDonald's.'

'Dad, can we go to Longleat again? The monkeys are just great and Leah's too old to be scared of the tiger. Do you remember the seals and that smelly fish we fed them? I'd like to see the elephants a bit closer. I asked Mum but she said not till the weather's better.'

'I'll think about it. Tell me about your friends. Is William still on the scene?'

'Yes. His Mum's just married again. He's got a ... a ... I can't remember. It's like a nearly dad.'

'A stepfather? Surely you know that word? You remember the fairy tales with wicked step-mothers?'

'I just couldn't think of it. A stepfather. It's a funny word. Is it because he steps into the old dad's place? Or is it that he's only a step away from being a real father? It's what they say at school – that someone is a step away from the right answer.'

Jason looked at his son with quickening interest and a feeling of excitement. 'You like words, don't you? I mean you're interested in why things are called what they are? Like German measles and stepfathers?'

Jake shrugged. 'I was just wondering. That's all.'

'But it's very clever to wonder at that sort of thing and to think up explanations as you have just done.'

Jake looked puzzled rather than smug and Jason let the subject drop, but not before he had given his son the extra boost of wondering aloud if all nine-year-olds were as sharp.

Henry, on the other hand, was not at all sharp, although whenever Jason reported on his progress to Mrs Turnbull he used the term potential rather than dullard. He had returned to school earlier in the month, leaving Jason frustrated, conscious of failure and richer. As he banked the cheque he wondered if he should seek out more of such work. Ben, he knew, was giving maths tuition to fund his share of the wedding costs.

Whenever he recalled the conversation with Jake, his memory replaying the crowded Mc-Donald's, the table still stained with the spillage of a previous customer's milkshake, the way his son fell upon his Big Mac as if he had starved for a month, he felt a chill of dread. Sometimes he felt it even before he called to mind the reason. It came to him at unexpected moments in lessons, walking along the corridor at school, eating with Carol, chatting to Mrs Turnbull, marking work alone in his room.

A stepfather. A nearly dad. From the moment that Kat had left him and taken away Jake and Leah he had known that one day another man might take his place in the daily lives of his children, but until now the notion had been but a dim one, fittingly shapelessly in the background of his thoughts, a ghost he need not confront or at least one he could postpone confronting. Kat, for all her restlessness, had always been the more conventional, refusing to move in with him until they were married, and he did not think that she would accept a man in her life or as a surrogate father to her children on any other terms. As they were not yet divorced and there was no sign of any suitor, Jason had felt safe in excluding a stepfather from his imagination.

There was still no suitor and he and Kat had agreed to divorce after two years, on the grounds that their marriage had irretrievably broken down, so he knew it would be some time before he need confront the prospect in reality, but now Jake's innocent definitions tormented him with their picture of the future over which he had no control, which rested entirely in Kat's hands: *he steps into the old dad's shoes ... only a step away from being a real father.*

Jake had described William's stepfather as a nearly dad but Jason felt that the description better fitted the real father, the one who had so nearly been Dad to his children throughout their lives but found his place taken, his role usurped.

241

He would continue to be called Dad, would continue to be recognised as the father for all legal purposes, but it would be the other man, the one the children called by his Christian name, who would bring them up, would see them, hear them, smell them on a daily basis. It would be the stepfather who watched, amused, proud, encouraging, as they took small steps towards adulthood, the stepfather who sorted out their childish squabbles, who later upheld their mother's discipline through teenage years, who would be daily privy to their career decisions, their first love, their laughing, their weeping.

Home was where the children lived most of the time, kept their possessions, found their mother, retreated in times of misery or fatigue, played with friends. Home was love, security and closeness, and home would be warmed by the stepfather not the fortnightly dad, however special the bond between him and the children he had expected to bring to maturity.

If Kat married again then another man would become Dad in all but name. It would be he, Jason Kirk, who became the nearly dad. Jake would be ten by the time the divorce was made absolute but Leah would only be five. It was possible that she would come to regard a substitute father effectively as her own, especially if he was kind and loving. Jason knew it right to wish that any stepfather would be kindness itself while fervently hoping that he would be distant and cool, accepted rather than loved, respected rather than included.

As often as these thoughts came to him Jason

tried to drive them away with logic. His fears might never materialise and he might remain the only father his children knew. Against those fears he deployed every cliché from crossing bridges before arriving at them to letting tomorrow take care of itself; against them he tried consciously to think of other, pleasanter, scenarios, to distract his thoughts by concentrating on work, but still the images danced stubbornly in his mind, refusing to leave.

He thought of another man swinging Leah up on his shoulders to see something better, saw him bending down and mending a temporarily broken toy, saw him leaning over Jake while he showed him a quicker way to achieve some task on his computer, and was full of the ice of impending loss, a loss that must some day be real. Performed by strangers, all these actions would have stimulated gratitude not resentment but performed by a stepfather they became unbearable even to contemplate. Jason raged silently against his fate even as he smiled at Nick Bright, protected Terry Pepper and occasionally worried about Harry Jackson.

He supposed that the intensity of resentment would diminish over time, that he would accept what he now railed against just because it was there, as he might in time accept a disability or a bereavement, hurt or angry occasionally rather than preoccupied with the loss.

But it isn't there. It hasn't happened. Jason tried to reign in the gallop of imagination as it sat astride his thoughts and whipped them into a headlong rush. *But it will happen one day*, cried the

Cassandra of his mind. Then I will make the most of the time in between, thought Jason, before recollecting that his ability to do so rested as much with Kat as with him.

'What on earth are you thinking about?' Jason looked up to see Ben watching him quizzically. 'You've been going through the most amazing facial antics. First you looked furious, then miserable, then you positively brightened up and now you look confused. Meanwhile colleagues have been coming and going and you haven't answered any of the three who spoke to you.'

Ben seemed amused rather than alarmed and Jason smiled back. 'Sorry. Who were the three and what did they say?'

'Sarah and Chris just said hello and Carol asked if you were all right. I suppose you *are* all right?'

'As all right as I'm ever likely to be when I think about Kat. She has gone back to finding excuses for me not to see the children and it turns out that the episode of chicken pox, which was her excuse to prevent my having them for Christmas, was non-existent.'

The laughter faded from Ben's eyes. 'Have you told your solicitor?'

Jason shook his head. 'I've come to recognise the futility of that. Kat kept Jake in bed until I had left on Christmas Eve when she suddenly decided he was well enough to travel to her parents. He had actually been ill and there had been some sort of rash so her story will always sound quite plausible. She thought it was chicken pox and even the doctor thought it could be German measles. The

244

fact that a week later she knew it was neither and didn't tell me is irrelevant because she would say that whatever it was Jake was too ill to leave his bed, even though Jake tells me he felt that bad for only a couple of days.'

'Even so, there must be something you can do to stop it happening again. Shouldn't Kat have to produce a doctor's certificate or something? Damn it, Jason, she's *using* the kids.' Ben's tone was scandalised.

'Reasonable people just manage these issues and that, in my naivety, was what I was expecting us to do. For heaven's sake, who would want to demand doctors' certificates when a child is ill? I suppose I can ask Parnell to seek such a requirement but God knows what the judge would make of it. It's just plain crazy.'

'If you don't fire some sort of warning shot then there is nothing to stop her doing that every year.'

A stepfather might stop her, thought Jason, another adult in the house, someone who understood what she was doing and who disapproved, someone who perhaps wanted her to himself for a while unencumbered with other people's children. Jason laughed aloud and Ben looked startled as the staffroom was filled with the bitterness of his irony.

13

'But it was a one-off.' Jason heard the anger in his own tone and, conscious of Jake and Leah playing on the floor behind him, forced himself to speak quietly.

'I am sorry, Mr Kirk, but all your earnings have to be taken into account.'

'Look, I tutored a child for one hour a day for six days. I have never taken on tutoring before and I am not likely to do so again.'

'That will be taken fully into account, Mr Kirk. We average out overtime.'

'It is *not* overtime. It was a one-off.'

'We still need the details, Mr Kirk.'

Jason's anger turned to despair. 'But if you average it out it can't even make a difference of pennies.'

'I quite appreciate that but we need the forms to enable us to make that assessment.'

'Does that mean that if my wife earns some extra money you will reduce my liability?'

'What your wife earns is her own business, except of course if it affects her Income Support. The CSA's interest is in ensuring that the absent parent takes responsibility for the children even when no longer resident.'

'I was resident. It was my wife who walked out.'

'But the children reside with her. Mr Kirk, I don't make these rules and I do appreciate how

246

you feel but–'

'I doubt if any of you appreciate how I feel. Do you know how many times you have changed my assessment in just a few months? And every time you do it the arrears change as well. You are robbing me so comprehensively that it is all I can do to find money to look after the children when I do see them. How does that promote responsible parenting?'

The room was suddenly quiet as Jake became aware that he was somehow linked to the bad-tempered exchange taking place in the corner and Jason, turning, caught the alarm in his eyes. He brought the call to as civil a conclusion as he could manage, trying to look as if it had been unimportant.

'Shall we go over to the park?' Parks are free.

'OK.' agreed Jake, but Leah grumbled that she did not want to and asked to see Mrs Turnbull instead. When Jason assented she scampered off as if in expectation of a treat.

'Dad, why haven't you got television?'

'Because Mum took the television when I left the old house.'

'Yes, but we've got two now because there was already one in the cottage. You could have the one from my room.'

Jason recalled the comment he had made to the Child Support Agency and realised that Jake had understood only too well.

'It's all right, Jake, but it was a great offer for you to make. I don't need a television because I am too busy in the evenings. Honestly, I just don't, but thanks all the same.'

Jake went on looking at him, not believing him, blinking back tears. 'Dad, it's not fair.'

Jason, hugging his son, was distressed to feel the sobs working their way up through the small body. 'No, it isn't, but life is often not fair. It will be all right, Jake. In the end everything will work out.'

'Dad, I want to live with you.'

Jason smiled sadly. He knew that Jake was not unhappy with Kat, that it was to his mother he turned when he was ill or anxious or upset. His son's words were intended as an expression of solidarity with his beleaguered father. He pretended to misunderstand.

'I would like us to be all together too but that can't happen.'

Jake was not deflected. 'I meant live here with you.'

'Mum would be very sad. She needs you. And what about Leah? Think how you would miss Leah.'

'I wouldn't. She's stupid.'

Jason grinned and began to change the course of the conversation to spare his son the temptation to pursue his demand but he was to re-run it in his mind long after Jake and Leah had departed to spend the rest of the half-term break with Kat and her parents. His son was nearly ten, intelligent and beginning to form his own judgements about the actions of the grown-ups around him. He would soon be able to recognise Kat's manipulative deceits, a thought Jason found disturbing rather than reassuring.

More disturbing still was the question as to

how the Child Support Agency knew about his brief spell of tutoring. The information could have come only from Kat to whom he had mentioned the project when discussing what the children wanted for Christmas. The reassessment would make no difference to Kat: it would be the Child Support Agency which gained from any increase in his payments. Spite alone could account for her action, a wish purposely to make his life as difficult as possible, to give him an unpleasant jolt, but why? Was it that she hated him sufficiently to want to see him suffer or was it because she thought that if she wore him down for long enough then he would agree to anything she demanded in respect of the children?

Jason lay on his bed, worrying, feeling hot despite the chill of the day. He rang Carol Marsh and was disconcerted when a man's voice answered, even though he had half expected Carol to lose patience with him. Unable to return her affection, wanting her as much for comfort as for companionship, unready for a new relationship and unwilling to risk a second major rejection, he had not merely kept the friendship platonic but had shied away from even the most innocent physical contact. He had sensed that Carol understood and did not mind immediately but that she also expected his attitude to change, that he would learn to trust and relax. More than a year later she must now wonder if that were ever likely to happen.

'Idiot! That was the plumber.' Carol's laughter floated along the line when she telephoned half an hour later. 'I had my hands covered in dough and I asked him to take the call and say I would ring back.'

'He didn't sound like a plumber. Anyway, I didn't tell him who it was.'

'What do plumbers sound like? You didn't have to tell him who it was. He said it must be my boyfriend because it was a man who had sounded quite surprised and displeased. He was laughing himself silly.'

'Then I hope he recovered before he mended the leak.'

'It wasn't a leak – just howling pipes. Anyway the dough is now converted into pie crust. Why don't you come and help me eat it?'

My boyfriend, thought Jason, as he found his car keys. He did not know whether to be flattered or unnerved by the description which had not been applied to him since he had courted Kat more than a decade earlier. It was too soon, he told himself, too soon.

As he passed along the hall to the front door he heard laughter from the sitting room. Mrs Turnbull had friends in for Bridge. They would spoil Objubjub, who would then spend the night on Mrs Turnbull's bed rather than Jason's.

The bell rang and Jason opened the door to an elderly lady and a much younger companion who might have been her daughter.

'Oh, thank you, Jason.' He turned to find his landlady emerging into the hall. Through the open door behind her Jason saw a scene of warmth and friendship as people found places to sit and handed round drinks to each other. Objubjub was basking by the log fire.

'Have a good evening,' said Mrs Turnbull. 'Going anywhere special?'

'To Carol's.'

'Then you won't starve. Do give her my love. She's such a nice lady.'

'I will, thank you. Hope the Bridge goes well.'

Jason fought down self-pity as he unlocked the door of the car and sat while he waited for the windscreen to demist. He too had once had a home where friends gathered to eat and drink and be amused. Now his whole life was confined to a single room because what they had was not good enough for Kat. As a student his aspirations had been modest but very clear to him: a home, a family, a stable income. Now at nearly thirty-four he had no proper home, no family living with him and an income so effectively plundered that he could spend not much more than he had as a student. His mind told him that his position was not permanent, that his life would not forever be frozen in the pattern it followed now but, consumed by present misery, he found no comfort in reason.

He thought of Kat, living on income support, managing two lively children in a tiny, rented, only semi-modernised cottage. Was such a life really preferable to the one she had forfeited? Was any privation or challenge a relief from the monotony and predictability of their once-comfortable lifestyle? If his modest aspirations were so boring, what had attracted Kat to him all those years ago? What had persuaded her to consign herself to what she perceived as utter tedium? Had she thought she could change him or had she wanted to experiment with dullness and then found herself trapped?

Jason mentally shrugged. The questions were unanswerable. Perhaps he was boring, easily contented and limited in ambition but if so then Carol did not seem deterred by such attributes. His fault, he recognised, lay less in his own nature than in his failure to understand Kat's, taking it for granted that she was as easily pleased as he, that her vision of a happy future was the same as his. Had his eyes been open earlier he might have pre-empted her departure by arranging one for both of them, moving them to a different part of the country, abroad even, anywhere to change the scenery, the friends, the routine.

He considered this with disbelieving anger. Could so little have saved a marriage? Could Kat throw away a marriage with so little cause?

Carol looked at him with concern when he arrived at her flat with a bottle of wine under one arm and a bunch of flowers in his other hand.

'You look just about all in. Is it Kat again?'

'No more than usual. Just tired and fed up but I feel better already. It smells fantastic.' He followed Carol to the kitchen and began uncorking the wine.

'You look as if you need something stronger. Have a G and T instead.'

Jason hesitated. 'I shouldn't. I'm driving.'

'Not for hours. It will do you good.'

'Well, perhaps a small one. Do you have whisky rather than gin?'

'Yes. Help yourself.'

Jason opened the right cupboard with the

unerring assurance of the regular visitor and located a bottle of Famous Grouse before opening another and extracting a half-used bottle of soda. He shook it gently to see if it had gone flat. It had not and he wondered who had used it so recently, who had been here with Carol. He drank standing up in the kitchen, leaning against the refrigerator, watching Carol as she bent down to take a dish from the oven. She looked round at him.

'Go and sit down. I won't be long.'

'Isn't there anything I can do?'

'No. It's almost ready.'

He woke with a start to see Carol bringing in a pie, her hands in oven gloves. He jumped up and almost fell over in embarrassed haste. 'Sorry, I must have nodded off.'

Carol smiled. 'You really are shattered. It's Boeuf Bourguignon.'

'Wonderful.'

Carol returned to the kitchen and came back without her apron. She placed a dish of carrots and runner beans on the table. Jason looked at her with an appreciation not limited to her cooking, taking in the sandy hair, the lightly made-up face now slightly flushed from her exertions, the trim figure, the healthy, untroubled way she moved, the immaculate creases in the sleeves of her blouse, the crisp light-blue cleanliness of her jeans. By comparison Jason felt untidy and sluggish, as though he had come to school unshaven or was wearing the same shirt as yesterday. He feared he must have all the appeal of an unmade bed with unwashed sheets.

Later Carol said he must stay. He was far too tired to drive and, anyway, had drunk a lot of wine on top of the whisky. He looked at her uncertainly, searching in his befuddled mind for an objection which was not rude.

She read his thoughts. 'That sofa turns into a bed. It's very comfortable and will give you a sound night's sleep.'

He slept till ten and woke to the smell of freshly ground coffee, his head dimly aching. In the shower he looked at the row of shampoos and body washes and tried to select the least scented. Around him gleamed white tiles with a pattern of pale-peach flowers. Looking at them he felt a coldness stir within him, a premonition of an unwelcome thought which he identified as lonely nostalgia when he realised that the colour and shape of the flowers were the same as those which had adorned the church at his marriage to Kat.

Carol had given him a clean towel and a new toothbrush. He should have been feeling restored, vigorous, ready for the day. Instead he was weary and conscious of purposelessness. Life with Carol would be peaceful, comfortable and pleasant but he was as afraid of the prospect as he would have been had she been wild and unpredictable. He did not want his happiness to depend on anyone but himself. He would go home and begin to take some control of his life. He doubted if he should even wait for breakfast.

He remained for lunch and then for tea, saying little and doing less, idling through the newspapers, falling asleep at intervals, aware of Carol's unobtrusive anxiety, of her quiet friendship reaching out to help him. He drove home at six, wondering at his poor conduct, at the burden he had imposed on a friend, at his seeming helplessness. As he drew near to Frome he wondered what Mrs Turnbull had made of his overnight absence, whether she dwelt censoriously on its likely cause or whether she had been worried for his safety. She must have been uncertain whether to draw the bolts on the front door to augment the security provided by the Yale lock, whether she should feed Objubjub. He could so easily have telephoned her, but, overcome with wine and fatigue, the thought had not even occurred to him.

Selfish, irresponsible, immature. The adjectives floated into his mind, briefly accusing him, rebuking him as he might rebuke his pupils. Mrs Turnbull would doubtless ask him to let her know in future if he intended being away all night or suddenly found he could not get home and he would apologise and promise to do so.

So sure was he that this would be his conversation with his landlady that he was taken by surprise when she intercepted him in the hall with horror in her eyes.

'Oh, Jason, they have found that poor little boy.'

He looked at her without comprehension.

'The one you used to teach.'

'Harry Jackson? Where? He's not dead?'

'No. It's not as bad as that but there's a *siege*. His father has a gun and says he won't give him up.'

'My God! Where?'

'In the Irish Republic. Somewhere in County Mayo. He must be so frightened.'

As Jason entered his own room the telephone rang. Ben's voice was pitched high with anxiety. 'Have you heard?'

'Yes. Jackson must be off his head.'

He uttered the same sentiments when Ben's call was followed by one from Carol. Neither said, 'I told you so.' Both thanked heaven that it was half-term and Morton's would be spared the press at the gates. Later, as he watched the television news with Mrs Turnbull, Jason, his incredulity growing as he followed the story, felt their gratitude was premature and that the siege might well outlive half-term.

The Garda appeared to be willing to play a waiting game, negotiating with the gunman, hoping to wear him down as his food supplies ran out. They confirmed that they would not be storming the small terraced house unless they thought Harry was in imminent danger. Their spokesman said several times that there was no immediate fear for the boy's safety.

Harry's brother and sister gave inarticulate interviews, blaming the Social Services and demanding some unspecified change in the law. The new head of Morton's said Harry was a popular boy, a delightful pupil and everyone there would be thinking of him and praying for his safe return.

'He never knew Harry,' Jason told Mrs Turnbull. 'Jackson had done a runner before this chap took over.'

A spokesman for an association which represented parents who were fighting Social Services up and down the country for the return of their children said that although he could not condone

what poor Mr Jackson had done he could understand it. The members of his association were so
desperate that they often threatened to take the
law into their own hands.

A spokesman for Somerset Social Services
denied that officials had acted in a high-handed
fashion, carefully enumerating the occasions
when they had tried to find workable solutions
within the Jackson family.

'I bet you would like to tell the world how that
brother and sister wouldn't help,' Jason told the
screen. He explained his comment to Mrs
Turnbull who made *tch tch* sounds of disapproval
but she sounded resigned rather than scandalised.

The item ended with a trail of a discussion, on
a later programme, about the issues raised by the
case: broken families, the paucity of help given to
men who wanted to look after their children, the
competence of the police hunt and the methods
involved in bringing such sieges to end without
violence.

'They will probably squeeze all that into six or
seven minutes and no one will be any wiser,'
observed Mrs Turnbull. 'I do hope Harry will be
all right.'

'I don't think his father will harm him, but he
has been on the run, presumably with no friends
and no education for months on end, indeed for
nearly a year. Goodness only knows how they
have been living. It can scarcely have failed to
have had some effect on him. He was only
thirteen when it all happened and a pretty young
thirteen at that. He's not streetwise, or at least he
wasn't then.'

Over the remaining few days of the half-term holiday Jason became a frequent visitor to Mrs Turnbull's sitting room as they watched successive news bulletins. The drama at the small terraced house in County Mayo gradually fell out of the headlines and by Sunday evening was not even mentioned. It was however generously covered in that day's newspapers and two of the tabloids devoted several pages to the background of the Jackson family.

Unsurprisingly the leader pages found much upon which to comment. Harry Jackson, pronounced a columnist in one of the broadsheets, was a victim of a society which had lost sight of the basic need of any child for security and stability and which confused instant gratification with long-term happiness. Families these days split themselves up and reformed with all the ease and frequency of amoebas. Harry Jackson had grown up with a procession of mothers and siblings coming and going in a home from which the father was usually absent. He spent hours alone, unsupervised, living on junk food, often spending the entire night on his own in a house on an estate where burglary and violence were rife. Let down at home, he was also let down at school, going to the worst Somerset had to offer.

'Is that true?' asked Mrs Turnbull. 'I thought Morton's was a good school.'

'Once it was the best, but not now. Not for a very long time but the comment isn't fair all the same because the school took good care of Harry.'

Harry's sister, Lisa, had given a long interview

to a tabloid with a large circulation. There was a picture of her pulling a Christmas cracker with Harry, both of them looking at the camera. Another showed her sitting on her father's knee in jeans and T-shirt, a ring through her top lip and several more through her eyebrows. Her comments were the only ones which still sought to blame the Social Services for taking Harry away. The paper's own commentator blamed them instead for not taking him away sooner.

One paper offered the lurid recollections of three of Jackson's former partners. All said he was not a violent man and that he loved his children when he was about but he was always away working (if that was what he was really doing, observed one snidely) and they had all wearied of too many evenings spent alone ('not that I just sat there and waited, like, I used to go the pub and that's where I met Steve, like,' said another).

The papers speculated as to how the siege would end, piously hoping that all the participants would come through safely while preparing for the drama of a death.

One detail held Jason's attention: Mr Jackson was said by one of his ex-cohabitees to owe the Child Support Agency several thousand pounds.

'Enough to drive anyone insane,' he commented to Ben the next morning.

'A lot of people have debts they can't pay but they don't resort to gun sieges. Anyway, I prefer the cost of Jackson's endless fornication to fall on him not the rest of us.'

The primness of Ben's phraseology was uncharacteristic and Jason, glancing around to identify its cause, saw a girl of about seventeen or eighteen sitting in a corner with a book.

'The head's daughter,' mouthed Ben.

A few minutes later the head himself came in and the girl rose to join him.

'I shall be away for the morning taking Natalie to a specialist. Matt Johnson will hold the fort.'

'Is it anything serious?' asked Jason as the door closed behind the head.

Ben shrugged. 'Nothing fatal. She was telling Carol earlier on that she has stomach pain, which one doctor says is a grumbling appendix and another kidney stones. I do wish our esteemed head wouldn't always sound as if he expects the place to fall apart in his absence.'

'Famous last words,' grinned Jason as shouts echoed from the playground. He looked out of the window and discerned a small group of older boys with a younger one in their midst. Matt Johnson was walking towards them and they turned to face him. Something in their manner, which spoke of menace not apology, wiped the smile from Jason's face and sent him racing outside. At first he hesitated, unwilling to escalate the situation, sensing he should let Matt try to defuse it, but then he saw that the younger boy was Terry Pepper and that he was bleeding from the nose. He forced himself to walk slowly, to keep his attitude non-confrontational.

One of the older boys was shouting at Matt, thrusting his face close to the teacher's. Matt stood his ground but put his hands in his pockets. It was as if in slow motion that Jason saw the youth throw the punch and Matt fall senseless to the ground. From somewhere inside the school came a girl's scream.

As Jason reached the group the deputy head stirred. Ben was telling the boys to wait outside the head's office but the one who had assaulted Matt, a Year Eleven student called Ryan Boult, refused to obey, filling the air with profanity and accusation.

'He pushed me, he did. He pushed me. I've got a right to defend myself. I–'

'Rubbish.' Ben made no attempt to conceal his anger. 'He had his hands in his pockets. You were trying to get him to push you.'

Jason helped Matt back to his feet. The deputy head staggered slightly and then said, 'I think this is one for the police.'

The boy turned on his heel and Jason was looking at Matt, an anxious enquiry on his lips, when he felt the blow of Ryan Boult's head butt in his back. He grabbed ineffectually at Matt to steady himself and then fell heavily forward, nearly taking Matt down with him. Shocked, winded, unable immediately to get up, Jason was vaguely aware of sudden activity.

It was Ben who helped him to his feet. Feeling for his handkerchief to mop up the blood of a cut on his forehead Jason found his dazed vision resting on Terry Pepper, who still stood in the centre of a now non-existent group of bullies, staring vacantly before him, seemingly oblivious of the violent scene. Jason's eyes switched to where Ryan Boult struggled and swore in the grip of two policemen, both of whose hats lay on the ground, and then to the immaculate figure of the area director of education standing, briefcase in hand, a few feet away.

'Dear me,' said the area director as if he had just spilled some cake crumbs on a very posh carpet. 'Can somebody please tell me where I can find the head?'

14

'Jason?' Kat's voice was curious rather than concerned. 'Are you all right? It's all over the papers that you were involved in some fight.'

'I'm fine. Fortunately the attack on Matt was witnessed and a girl called the police. Even more fortunately they happened to be virtually passing the school when they got the call. They didn't bother with the niceties, just came in and grabbed the maniac responsible.'

'And Matt?'

'Concussed. They kept him in hospital overnight for observation but he's all right now. Terry Pepper, the kid they were bullying, has got a lot of bruises but is otherwise well enough. At first I thought they had broken his nose because it was bleeding but apparently not.'

'And you? It says you were hit from behind and knocked over.'

'Yes, I've got a nasty cut on the forehead from where I hit the ground. That's all.'

'All! Have you seen the paper? It's awful about Morton's. Says a teacher committed suicide there not long ago, that the deputy head has left the profession with a nervous breakdown and that the previous head was ousted after an abysmal Ofsted report.'

'Yes, I've seen it. No one is talking about anything else at school. It was gross to bring up the Ed business, which was, after all, nothing to do with pressures at Morton's, and even nastier to have a go at the head for not being there when it all happened. He was taking his daughter to a specialist and could hardly have predicted a fracas of that sort.'

'You can't blame the press for making a big thing of it. Even in this crazy day and age you don't expect to find two teachers laid out in the playground – and in nice leafy Somerset too. County must be going ballistic.'

'Oh, they are, believe me. You should have seen Ponsonby's face. He rolled up just as the crucial blow was being struck and the cops were racing into action with half the school peering out of the windows. I think he would have closed us down on the spot had he been able.'

'What on earth did he say?'

'Quite a lot in that mild tone of his. He was doing his usual Victorian stuffed popinjay act and also as usual missing nothing. He sat down in the head's office and his first question, when the immediate kerfuffle had died down, was why was Terry Pepper standing looking vacantly into space when he must have been in pain and why did he not seem remotely interested in the affray breaking out around him? How long had he been behaving in so detached a way and what had we been doing about it? My bet is he'll be in special education by yesterday afternoon. Even autism wouldn't explain oblivion to pain.'

'What are you talking about?'

Abruptly Jason realised that Kat knew nothing about Terry Pepper and had not been privy to any of his worries on account of his pupil. It must have been just after Kat left that he had first noticed anything odd. He wondered that he still had the capacity to be surprised when such small proofs of their diverging lives presented themselves, but he was always taken aback whenever they did so, as if, in some deep recess of his brain, he was refusing even now to accept the reality of what Kat had done.

The active recognition of Terry's multiple problems was, thought Jason, the only good to have come out of the affair. Long after his telephone conversation with Kat had come to an end and he had spoken reassuringly to Jake and Leah, the bitter reflections filled his mind. That very morning Jasper Bright had sent a large list of books he thought should be in the school library and a large cheque to ensure that they would be. Then he had taken his son out of the school.

Nick would be joining a small private school some ten miles away the following Monday. So would the three Patel children whose father ran a minor but profitable supermarket. Five pupils from another form, whose parents must have quickly conferred and arrived at the same conclusion, would be going to other state schools at the commencement of the following term. Jason knew that this was only the beginning, that if in a matter of two days parents had already started reacting, more would do so in the weeks to come. The press had declared open season on the school and its dismal results and he had no doubt that story would follow story, unnerving parents and demoralising staff.

Soon he and Kat would have to look at options for Jake's secondary education. He was glad they lived too far from Morton's for it to be considered. Leaving his current job was now more pressing than before but he felt reluctant to take the necessary steps to abandon his colleagues.

At ten o'clock he heard the chimes of Big Ben announce the television news and then Mrs Turnbull's voice, eager, urgent, calling him. Going downstairs, he looked at the screen to find it filled with the aftermath of an atrocity in Gaza.

'It was in the headlines.' Mrs Turnbull patted her lap and Objubjub leapt into it. 'It's all over and the little boy is quite safe. I expect they'll come to it soon.'

It came as a shock to Jason to realise that, so preoccupied had he been with the fight and its consequences, the fate of Harry Jackson had slipped entirely from his mind.

A few minutes later he stared at the bewildered face of Harry, escorted from the small house by a policewoman, and then at the features of his father, contorted by misery and defeat as he emerged scruffy, bearded and handcuffed. The gun turned out to have been a toy.

'That'll make them angry.' Jason listened to the story of how the Garda had stormed the building in the night and pictured them discovering the harmless device which had kept them at bay for so long. 'It would have been so much more dignified had it been real. Thank God Harry's all right.'

'I wonder what will happen to him?'

Jason thought he knew. Harry would spend the rest of his minority in care with, if he was lucky, foster parents or, if he was unlucky, a whole series of foster parents. He would visit his father in prison and stagger towards adult life not knowing if he was unloved or loved too much. Too old to be adopted, too young to manage alone, he would become a human parcel, passed about and handled with varying degrees of care in an adults' game until the last wrapping of childhood had been torn away and whatever was underneath was left – fragile, ignored, abandoned.

The following day the local papers splashed the story of the siege's end on their front pages. One dwelled heavily on Harry's having been a pupil at Morton's. The same paper ran an account of a court case the following week under the headline MORTON'S PUPIL ON DRUG CHARGES. The youth in question had left the school three years earlier.

'It shouldn't be allowed,' protested an angry Ben, but, when Jason attended his wedding to Debbie, a fellow guest let slip the information that Ben was applying for a job near Shepton Mallett. Jason knew the sense of abandonment he felt to be unreasonable as was his wariness of Carol's remaining at his side throughout the reception. They were the only colleagues Ben had invited from Morton's and, other than Debbie herself, they knew nobody else there, so it was natural for them to gravitate towards each other but Jason could not repress the thought that there was something proprietorial in Carol's attitude, a statement of attachment, of ownership. He was uncertain if he would have been as guarded had the occasion not been a wedding.

His unease descended into irritability and when Carol suggested that, as neither was attending the evening disco, they might search out a local restaurant for a light meal, he declined without any attempt to proffer a convincing excuse. It only served to fuel his ire when Carol misunderstood, thinking that the event had caused him to dwell on how differently he had hoped his own marriage to develop. He repulsed her well-intentioned sympathy with cold courtesy and, as he walked towards his car, he tried not to remember the expression on her face.

At home Jason ignored the attempt of a purring Objubjub to wind himself around his legs and hurried upstairs before Mrs Turnbull could appear and ask him if had enjoyed the wedding and what the bridesmaids had worn. As he pushed open the door of his room there was a rustling sound and he bent to retrieve the envelope which must have come in that morning's post and been pushed under his door by Mrs Turnbull. A familiar lump of dread moved inside him when he recognised the logo of the Child Support Agency.

Tears of frustration stung his eyes as he read the contents. Parliament had recently approved amendments to the Act which necessitated a review of his payments... Jason read the succeeding explanation without absorbing any of its rationale. He threw the letter and its inevitably attached forms on to the bed, turned on his heel and ran downstairs before walking, unseeing, to the local newsagent which had been closed for two hours. Knowing he was acting without logic he returned to the house and retrieved his car.

Arriving at the largest supermarket for miles around some thirty minutes later, Jason searched the newspaper section for *The Times Educational Supplement* and, finding one, sat in the driving seat with the pages spread across the passenger side while he encircled any vacancy, within a radius of fifty miles, which promised a pay point above his own, his eyes straining against the dimness of the car light. A bleep from his mobile announced the receipt of a text message, but, thinking it might be from Carol, he held resolutely to his task.

When he had finished his search, which yielded two posts of likely interest and a third of remoter promise, he reluctantly picked up the telephone and retrieved the message: 'Hi dad mum is out leah is being a pain wot ru doing.'

He glanced at his watch. It was just after ten o'clock. His son was almost certainly in bed and texting him under the bedclothes. Jason smiled, imagining Jake lying on his stomach with the phone propped on the pillow as he earnestly punched out the letters in the weak light of the screen, trying to evade detection by the baby-sitter, while, unbeknown to him, his father also struggled to read in the dark because he was beset by a childish urge to know immediately what might be on offer.

'Time you were asleep. Love to Leah. See you soon. Dad.'

'Gd nite dad.'

'Please spell properly.'

'Tomorrow.'

Jason grinned and replaced the telephone in its hands-free socket. As he was re-folding the newspaper, the strains of *William Tell*, which had been selected by Jake as his ringing tone, filled the car. Jason glanced at the screen, saw the number was Carol's and declined to answer, feeling guilty and assertive, knowing that in reality he was fleeing a decision that he must soon make. As he drew out of the car park, his headlights fell on a woman then getting into her own car, one foot, elegant in a dark high-heeled shoe still resting on the ground. Jason's gaze travelled to the leg which now pulled the foot in, to the slender white hand which reached out to pull the door shut, to her face, half hidden by a cascade of blonde hair made bronze by the street light. He did not look back.

It was not just Carol, but anyone, he thought, not just his reason that told him that it was too soon to become attached again but his very senses, which had been dulled to numbness.

As if that deadening had spread to encompass his every emotion, he watched without reaction as a steady stream of parents removed their children from Morton's or prepared to do so. He taught with vigour but without much hope, he tried to combat the pall of disillusionment which seemed to hang over the staffroom like a city smog but without much conviction, he tried to feel anger each time the school's name was pilloried in the press but the most he could manage was weariness.

By the end of the summer term only the absence of places elsewhere was keeping Morton's alive. The head was moved to solve the problems of another school thought to be worth saving. Matt was made acting head and in its reports of the appointment the press dwelled heavily on its having been he who was knocked unconscious by a former pupil. Morton's was no parent's first choice and the instinctive reaction of those whose children were allocated a place there was to appeal. No replacement had been found for Ben; Carol announced she would be leaving at Christmas.

Jason attended interviews at Bath and Portishead without success but eventually secured his escape by accepting a post at the same point on the pay spine in Radstock. He planned to spend the summer holiday house-hunting in the area between there and Frome and, with Carol's help, he found himself perched on the top of a stepladder decorating a ceiling in his new two-up two-down semi-detached home on the day his divorce arrived in the post.

A week later he and Ben were stacking his possessions in a small van to complete the move from Mrs Turnbull's. The children, after a solemn conference, had voted to leave Objubjub with the landlady. Both Kat and Jason had offered the cat a home but Leah was convinced Mrs Turnbull would cry and Jake decreed it was unfair to Objubjub when he was so obviously attached to his current home. Jason knew that both would in future visit his former landlady on the pretext of wanting to see Objubjub and wondered if, unrealised by them, that was the real reason for their decision.

Mrs Turnbull was sad to lose Jason but had grown used to a long procession of lodgers and waved the van off cheerfully, having first given Jason a freshly baked cake with which to celebrate his new life.

Kat prepared for life as a divorcee by announcing that she would in future be known as Katie and that she would revert to her maiden name, Kat Kirk becoming Katie Johnson.

'I hate it,' whimpered Jake. 'We're all Kirk. I want Mum to be Kirk as well.'

Jason decided to treat the protest lightly. 'People change their names all the time. Ladies change them when they marry, children change them when they are adopted, film stars and authors and–'

'I still hate it.'

'You'll get used to it,' said Jason at the same time as his son, in predictive mockery, uttered the identical words in an imitation of his father's tone.

They grinned at each other.

'Will you miss Morton's?'

Jason looked at him in surprise. 'Yes, a little bit. I've been there for longer than you have been alive. Why?' he asked as he watched Jake absorbing this impressive statistic.

'I wish I hadn't moved schools. I miss the old one.'

'Still?'

'Well, not as much as I did but just sometimes. It's peculiar.'

'That's a good word, but why is it peculiar?'

'Most of the time I don't think of the old school at all and then suddenly it's as if I'm there for a few seconds and then it's gone again. It's the same with our old home. Does that happen to you?'

'It happens to everyone. All sorts of things bring back sudden memories. One of the most evocative is smell. Sometimes when you return to a place after years it is the smell which reminds you what it used to be like.'

So his son did not like change, thought Jason, when he looked back on the conversation. It was not a good omen for a child of ten who might well have many an upheaval in front of him. At the very least he would have to move house again because Kat was unlikely to be content with the rented cottage now that the divorce was settled and the future more predictable. Jason wondered if resistance to change was Jake's way of reacting to his parents' separation or if it was a part of his nature which had made the split all the more painful.

Perhaps his son would grow into one of those people who lived in the same town all their lives, who took holidays always in the same place, who established a routine the breach of which was unthinkable, who worked for the same company or institution from the moment they embarked on gainful employment until they qualified for their pensions. Curry on Friday, roast on Sunday, Christmas cards written by December the first.

In this Jake was closer to him with his preference for stability than to Kat with her unquiet search for sources of new excitement. When his son was old enough to marry he would warn him about such incompatibility. Opposites might attract but like minds were more likely to stay the course.

'Incompatibility is just what most people need,' argued Carol when he voiced the thought at a supper at Ben's new house a few weeks later. 'How dull life would be if both were stick-in-the-muds and how little the children's minds would be stretched, but if both were restless the children would have no anchor at all and that would be equally bad. I think you need a healthy mix, with one supplying the occasional brake and the other the accelerator.'

Jason was unsure whether she saw herself as his brake or his accelerator.

'Of course, there are incompatibilities which must be hell – like smoking or non-smoking,' observed Ben.

'Noise and silence,' Debbie asserted, 'must be the worst. After all, if you smoke you just go out to the garden but if you are one of those people who must always have a background noise then everyone around you is involved.'

'That's true.' Carol's voice had a musing quality. 'There are lots of folk who like to have the radio or music playing all through a car journey while others use the time to think in peace. It would be the same if one partner always came home and immediately switched on the television so it was always on while the other wanted it only when watching something specific.'

The theme continued for a while among the small party but Jason found his thoughts drifting. He and Kat had seemed compatible enough, there had never been any obvious source of irritation and yet there had been a faulty root in their marriage, one waiting to be pulled effortlessly from the soil which he had thought so well nurtured. They had not become incompatible: they had always been so but neither had recognised it.

The evening passed enjoyably but Jason found himself tired and not looking forward to the long drive ahead first to Carol's flat and then to his house. He thought that perhaps there were attractions to city life where buses and tubes ran late and taxis were available twenty-four hours a day, but he knew he preferred the country. City and country had been among the incompatibilities discussed that night.

Kat had always lived in small towns or in the country. He wondered if her search for novelty might one day lead her to London and if so how Jake and Leah would fare in inner city comprehensives.

His own lesser challenge of teaching in a comprehensive school which mirrored the one that Morton's had once been was accomplished smoothly. There was no sixth form and he missed the pleasure of teaching pupils who were both sufficiently interested and sufficiently clever to pursue his subject at a higher level, but the competent, confident, focused atmosphere of the school with its aspiration and receptiveness to new ideas was more than enough to reconcile him to the loss, especially as the sixth form at Morton's had in any event been destined for closure.

Eileen observed that the change was doing him good when he arrived to spend the weekend in Dorset. She had visited his new home twice and had assembled several boxes of items from her own house which she thought would brighten his. As they stacked the goods in the car she commented that she liked Carol.

Jason recognised the tone although it was more than a decade since he had last heard it.

'Not yet,' he said. 'I'm not ready. We're just good friends. In fact sometimes I doubt whether I will ever marry again.'

'Nonsense!' retorted Eileen with the briskness with which she had approached his wilder statements as a child. 'You make a very good husband and somewhere out there is a very good wife waiting for you.'

I never did like Kat. Jason heard the words as surely as if his mother had uttered them and knew they were true. He now wondered if the reason the two women had never bonded was not merely a clash of personality but because Eileen had detected from the start flaws in Kat's character, to which he had been blind until the very hour of her leaving. Surely if that were the case she would have offered at least some tentative warning? Would she not have enlisted her husband to help?

'You never did like Kat, did you?' The words were out before he had realised he intended to

275

utter them.

'Not very much but there wasn't anything I could really get hold of. Your father felt the same way. We didn't like to say anything because it would only have made you angry and then, after Jake and Leah came along, we thought we were wrong, that it was working out well. I am so glad it all happened after Mike died. He would have been devastated.'

There was a short silence before Eileen added vaguely, as if in mitigation of what she had just said, 'But we always liked Alex and Sheila.'

'So do I. They've been pretty good through all this mess. God knows what they must think of their daughter.'

'Their priority will be to stay in contact with Jake and Leah so whatever they think they will not say it to Kat.'

Everyone, thought Jason, seemed to be afraid of Kat, wary of her reactions, eager to placate the wrongdoer in return for any concession, no matter how minor. The children were prizes which could be won only by successfully crossing a minefield, avoiding crippling explosions, gazing worriedly through the smoke of any detonation, puzzling anxiously as to whether the small elusive figures were still there. Her parents knew the safe path across that minefield and would not put a foot on either side of it, not for his sake or Eileen's or anyone's.

Perhaps they would take a risk for Jake or Leah but so long as they saw the children's happiness as best served by continued contact with themselves they were unlikely to disturb the status quo.

He too must learn to work within that status quo. There must be a way in which he could convince Kat that he was not a threat to her future life. They were divorced and he had a new home and a new job. Surely there must be some means of building on that, of finding his own path over the minefield and sticking to it.

'...you never really know someone until you are married.'

He realised that his mother had been speaking and, absorbed with his own thoughts, he had not heard. Focusing on the words she was uttering as his concentration returned, he shook his head.

'No. I didn't know Kat in all the years we were married but I know her now and I am going to work out a way to turn that knowledge to my advantage. It can scarcely be beyond the wit of man. After all, Jake and Leah live only a couple of miles away and I have a court order specifying the access arrangements. It's not as if they live halfway up the Himalayas or are wandering with nomads in Alaska.'

Although he had yet to work out his route over the minefield, the thought that somehow it must be possible returned at intervals to give him a comfort which his mind told him was spurious. Each time Kat successfully frustrated contact with his children he repeated the increasingly meaningless mantra that there was a way if only he could find it. Meanwhile he drew consolation from the reflection that Kat was now behaving so badly that his situation could not worsen.

It was after Christmas when Leah shattered that frail complacency with just one word, when at last she and Jake were visiting for a weekend and the word she uttered was neither Himalayas nor Alaska.

15

Jason froze, his mind rebelling against his daughter's news, telling him that she was confused and that she intended some other meaning even as the shock of truth entered him and he knew that once more Kat had outwitted him, had gulled him into an illusory security, had watched with a small, secret smile as he flew into her carefully woven web. She had waited until he was settled, encumbered with a mortgage and a new job, immobile, rooted in the soil of his own decisions while she had kept her own baggage light, with no commitment to work and able to leave her cottage at will. So long as the rent was paid she need not even remain there through any period of notice.

How long ago had she worked out that by agreeing readily to the terms of the divorce and letting him see the children regularly in the meantime she would lull him into the very course he had so obligingly followed? He could not remember any pretext for denying him access to Jake and Leah since March and by the summer he had been actively seeking both property and new employment, unsuspecting, unlessoned by the past. It was as if he had stroked a purring, contented cat and had woken to find it was a tiger.

No sooner had the thought entered his mind than he remembered Objubjub. How encouraging, how full of praise Kat had been when the children had decided to leave him with Mrs Turnbull! Now he wondered if she had seen the giving away of Objubjub merely as a removal of one complication of leaving. It was fanciful and unlikely but he no longer saw innocence in any of her actions.

Leah was watching him anxiously, unaware of the blow she had dealt, seeing his anger, not comprehending it and preparing to cry. He saw her expression and consciously altered his own.

'Newcastle! Why Newcastle?'

Leah shrugged. 'Don't know. Mummy says it's nice. We are going to have a bigger house and my friends will be able to come and stay. I shall go to the school Mummy teaches at and I may even be in her class. Won't it be funny to call Mummy Miss Johnson?'

Jason struggled to keep his expression neutral and failed, turning away so as not to alarm Leah. When she was once more occupied, absorbed in some computer game, happily ambitious to beat Jake when he should reappear, he went in search of his son. Jake was in his room, frowning in concentration as he tried to decipher the instructions for the model tank he had already half constructed. Jason, remembering the rudimentary aeroplanes which had comprised Jake's early efforts, was aware, with a fleeting mixture of pain and excitement, of the passing years.

Jake would soon be in secondary education – in Newcastle. As once Kat had discussed holiday plans even while she schemed to leave him, so she had now gone through all the procedures for placing Jake in a school she knew he would never be able to attend.

Jason sat on the bed and admired his son's efforts, suggesting a small adjustment, interpreting a faintly obscure instruction. For a while he watched Jake work, listening to his commentary, noticing without rebuke a sliver of glue on the carpet. When he did speak it was in as casual a tone as he could manage but Jake was not deceived and Jason saw him stiffen at the words.

'So what's all this about Newcastle?'

To his distress his son's mouth quivered and tears started in his eyes.

'I don't want to go, Dad. It's ages away. I found it on the map and it's nearly into Scotland. Leah doesn't understand. Mum says they talk funny up there and she puts on a silly voice and Leah laughs and thinks it's all a big joke.'

Jason tried to imagine his children speaking a hybrid of their native Somerset and Geordie. He smiled at Jake sadly.

'It *is* a long way but I hear Mum has a job there.'

'Yes. She says it's cheaper to buy a house there and we'll all be better off. Dad, will you be able to come and see us?'

'Of course. It's not Australia, you know. And you will still be able to come here.'

'If Mum lets us.'

For the second time that afternoon Jason realised that his son was growing up and he now confronted the thought that he had long kept

280

suppressed: Jake would soon be as alive to Kat's stratagems as his father was, might one day recollect the chicken pox that never was and draw the inevitable conclusion. Kat was playing a less drastic game than had Ros Deacon but she diced with her children's affections nonetheless and he determined to warn her of Jake's growing awareness. Possibly she knew already and was unbothered, believing that when she had the children safely to herself in Newcastle she could wean them from Jason with less need of subterfuge.

They could not travel alone and if she brought them she would have nowhere to stay. It would be down to him to travel there and back at ruinous expense each time he wanted to see Jake and Leah. He did not know whether the Child Support Agency would make any allowance for the costs involved. Kat would improve her lot by once again earning but that would not affect Jason's liability. The law, he thought, was an ass indeed, Balaam's ass, which spoke without understanding the effects of its pronouncements.

He repeated the sentiment to Alan Parnell when the solicitor confirmed his misgivings.

'I am afraid there is no way of preventing her taking the children to live in Newcastle. It would, of course, be different if she were proposing to take them abroad but she could relocate to Inverness or John o' Groats and there would be nothing you could do. She has found work and a reasonable property market and no judge would gainsay her efforts to do the best for her children.'

'*My* children. It is not doing the best for them to deprive them of their father.'

'I think, under the circumstances, it would be perfectly sensible to seek to vary the access arrangements. You might agree to have them for the holidays and half-terms and Mrs Kirk, or Miss Johnson I should say now, could have them during term-time.'

'I might agree. Kat wouldn't.'

'The courts would be the final arbiter.'

'The courts can arbitrate till domesday but all they can say is what *should* happen. It is Kat who decides what *does* happen. You know that. If she can frustrate my attempts to see my own children when I live a few miles away what is she going to do when I live a few hundred miles away?'

'But you told me a while ago that things were better?'

'Yes, but yet again I was living in that fool's paradise, Alan. It was all designed to make me believe things had settled down at last so that I would do likewise. I just can't believe I was so hopelessly naïve.'

'When are they going to Newcastle?'

'Next week. Kat starts teaching after half-term.'

'Then we can start with a request for you to have the children over half-term.'

'Nothing doing. Kat says she needs that time to settle them in, buy all the new uniforms etc. I have to admit that I cannot call that unreasonable. I would bet you anything that the next time I shall see them will be Easter.'

He would have lost his bet, he reflected bitterly, when Kat telephoned a fortnight before the Easter holiday to say that Jake would be spending it in the Lakes on a school trip. Meanwhile her parents were going to Spain for ten days and wanted to take Leah. It would be a wonderful opportunity for her given that she had never been abroad and was arriving at an age when she might appreciate it.

'No.'

'Oh, Jason, do be reasonable.'

'It's no. Your parents need my permission as well as yours to take Leah abroad and I refuse to give it. She needs to see her father and she hasn't seen me for two months.'

'The circumstances have been unusual. You know that. You can't reasonably expect to have the children every single holiday and my parents need a turn occasionally. Leah is wildly excited about it.'

'You mean you have hyped up her expectations in the hope that I would feel guilty and give in as usual. Well, this time you have failed. It's no and you can explain to Leah why.'

In disbelief he heard Kat call their daughter to the telephone.

'Leah, Daddy says you can't go to Spain. Come and talk to him.'

Leah, wailing, protesting, howling, refused to talk to him. He gritted his teeth when Kat said, 'Well, now see what you have done and I'm the one who is going to have to calm her down.'

'Kat, how can you use them like this? Don't you care that Leah's in such a state? Where are your feelings?'

'Where are yours? It's you who has upset her, not I. She's not even six yet.'

'Nevertheless it's still no. Leah spends Easter

with me. How long is the Lakes trip? I want Jake to spend time here too.'

'I'm afraid that won't be possible. It is five days but right in the middle of the holiday. There are only a few days each side.'

'A few days will do. Jake comes here either before or after the trip.'

Jason could still hear Leah's tearful rebellion when the call came to an acrimonious end a minute later. He forced himself to be resolute when Alex rang him that evening to plead for flexibility.

'I didn't realise Katie hadn't asked you or of course we wouldn't have got Leah so excited about it.'

Jason wondered at the ease with which Kat's parents adjusted to her changes of name. He had refused to call her anything but Kat and fully intended to continue doing so.

'I'm sorry, Alex, but I haven't seen the kids for two months. It can't go on.'

'Supposing Sheila and I promise to go up to Newcastle and personally bring the children to see you next weekend and the weekend following Easter?'

Jason smiled. 'I'm sorry, Alex, but your daughter has been playing a ruthless game and this time I'm putting my foot down. I hate disappointing you and even more I hate disappointing Leah but if I don't take a stand this time then Kat will do this again and again. I am Leah's *father*, not her far-off uncle.'

His resolve held even when Leah would not come to the telephone when he next rang. It was finally broken, unexpectedly, by Jake: *'Miss you dad pls let L go to spain mum is so cross and L cries all the time.'*

Fury fought with despair as Jason looked at the text message. A passing colleague accidentally jostled him and apologised but he scarcely noticed as he turned into the staffroom, knowing Kat had won, recognising with distaste and loathing that she would always win because she had no hesitation in inflicting petty suffering on her children, blind to the knowledge that it did not seem petty to them. All she would ever have to do would be to maintain the pressure through bad temper at home, dwelling on grievance instead of seeking to distract, promoting rather than diverting resentment, emphasising not compensating loss.

He sent a brief response, 'OK', trying to draw a weak consolation from imagining his daughter's tears dissolve into delight and rapture.

'Many thanks. Know how you feel,' came the answering text not from Jake but from Alex and Sheila.

'You have no idea how I feel,' he snapped and several startled glances told him he had voiced the thought aloud.

As once he had sought out Ed Deacon, to confide and draw strength from a fellow sufferer, so now he went and sat by Guy Anderson, an older teacher just two or three years from retirement who had divorced a persistently unfaithful wife twenty years earlier and had paid the penalty by being deprived of his children.

'They were three, six and ten at the time and no

matter that she probably brings home a different lover every night and gets paralytic on vodka several times a week. She's a woman and so she got the kids. Never mind fault or moral danger or example or anything else so old-fashioned. She's a woman, therefore she has a Divine right to her children.'

Unlike Ed, Guy had spoken the words as one cataloguing a rather regrettable collection of facts instead of one who rails bitterly against a harsh and unrelenting fate.

'Normally I would agree that if there really has to be a choice then children are better off with their mothers but not in Nicola's case. She fed them and kept them clean and she loves them but she ought not to have brought them up. I was lucky. She made every effort to keep them from me and often succeeded but as they grew up they drifted back. Ellen lived with me when she went to Bath University and now the elder two are closer to me than to Nicola. The third is sadly off the rails and into drugs in a big way. I suppose I shouldn't be surprised.'

Now Guy gave Jason the reassurance he needed.

'You have done the right thing. Depriving Leah would not have been the answer to this. Just make sure they know you're there and even though you can't watch them grow up in the same way that Kat can they'll always be your kids.'

It was a counsel of defeat, thought Jason, from a man whose battle was over. He swore that he, Jason Kirk, would not be so helpless. In Guy's place he would have contested custody on the grounds that Nicola was an unfit mother. Indeed, in those days surely, there had been a concept of 'care and control'? He began to wonder if he had been right to cede residence to Kat if she was so ready to use the children so ruthlessly, to torment them with disappointed hopes and promises she knew Jason would disown. He shook his head at the thought, acknowledging that both Jake and Leah needed her.

He looked round the staffroom, his eyes dwelling on the colleagues he was beginning to know after teaching with them for nearly two terms. The other history teacher was a happily married woman of forty-five, the senior maths teacher was divorced with two teenage children who appeared to spend as much time with him as with his former wife to the complete satisfaction of all concerned, but he and Guy were not alone in being separated from their children. The head of the French department fought regular battles to see his children, all four of them under twelve years old.

The head was a woman a few years from retirement who ran a tight ship and subscribed to a strict moral code. Jason suspected that she regarded the marital disarray of half her staff not merely with disapproval but with active resentment that it caused too much diversion from the serious business of teaching. Nevertheless the focused approach she inspired was a relief after the siege mentality of Morton's, in which his fellow teachers showed a lively interest as they had followed the well-publicised dramas of the last few months. Occasionally Jason thought of his former school and wondered how staff and pupils fared but he had quickly adapted to his new surroundings and the images of children he had once taught began to fade, their features no longer finely chiselled in his memory even if they had not had time to become blurred.

The departure of Jake and Leah to Newcastle struck him with fresh pain. Somehow when they had lived but a few miles away he felt they were still accessible even when Kat was denying him access, that if he had to he could turn up on their doorstep and force himself into their presence, that he could respond at once to any text message or telephone call asking for him. Their schools were nearby and he knew the staff who taught them.

He had never met any of their new teachers, had never seen them in their new uniforms, could not picture their bedrooms or their garden for he had not seen those either. He did not know their friends nor much about what they did in their spare time. He still spoke to them regularly on the telephone and received conspiratorial text messages from Jake but beyond that he had no contact and the distance was too great to risk visiting without prior agreement. He could not travel so far to find them all away for the weekend.

He hated himself for doing so but he began to embroil Jake in his schemes.

'I want to come and see you but I need to know you'll be there,' he told his son during one call.

Jake lowered his voice. 'I won't tell Mum. When are you coming, Dad?'

'This weekend.'

'No good, Dad. I've got a sleepover at Jude's.'

'Who is Jude?'

'My best friend.'

'I thought that was Tom?'

'Not any more.'

Jason listened to a catalogue of his son's grievances against Tom while waiting for the opportunity to propose an alternative visiting time. They agreed the weekend after next and Jason warned Jake, unnecessarily he suspected, to say nothing either to Kat or Leah. His son agreed and guilt tinged satisfaction as Jason mentally began the preparations.

He told no one but Carol of his intentions when she rang to announce that Debbie was pregnant and Ben ecstatic. Yes, Ben was thoroughly enjoying his new teaching job, she said in answer to Jason's question and then asked when they could all meet up, suggesting the very weekend Jason had fixed for his trip to Newcastle. He made his excuses and she wished him luck but made no proposal that they should meet in the meantime. He believed she might be seeking a painless end to an attachment which had never made much progress and, saddened but vaguely relieved, he made no attempt to thwart her.

Instead he concentrated on his teaching and on the forthcoming journey. Kat had not settled in the city itself but in Heddon-on-the-Wall, a rural area some distance away, and it needed only a cursory study of the map for Jason to be convinced that he must drive. His only other option would be to hire a car on arrival in Newcastle which would add expense. If he drove he would be free of the constraints of train times and could arrive at Kat's door at a moment of his own choosing. It also meant he had no arrangements to make in advance other than to find accommodation but when he began to calculate the costs of the expedition he was almost tempted to put a tent in the boot of the car, finally settling for a small bed and breakfast in the nearby village of Horsely.

When the Friday of his departure arrived Jason was tired from a week's teaching and dispirited at the thought of the long drive ahead. The M5 had turned into the M6 and he was thinking he ought to stop at the next service station when his mobile rang. Jason touched the answer button with his left hand and his son's voice, conspiratorial, excited, throbbing with hope, filled the car.

'Hi, Dad! Are you nearly here?'

'Not for hours but I'm well on my way. Where's Mum?'

'Next door. She'll be back any minute. I'm ringing on the real phone because she has started checking my mobile to see how much I use it. She still thinks it's bad for the brains and says she'll take it away if I don't save it just for emergencies.'

'Mum's right,' replied Jason, raising his voice slightly against the roar of the motorway traffic. 'Don't use it more than you have to.'

Mum's right. Had he said that because he half shared her fears about children using mobiles or because his instinct was still to present a united front in spite of the circumstances? Or was there some deeper worry now just taking shape, forcing itself into his reluctant mind? Was Kat checking not so much the frequency of her son's use of the telephone as whom he called? Did she study the dialled calls register for his numbers? Did she scroll through the text messages?

As if reading Jason's mind Jake said, 'I know, I know. I won't. Anyway, I delete everything if it's to do with you.'

He must find a different, less secretive means of communicating with his son. Kat had not obstructed calls to their home since the move as if she thought it safe to let Jason talk to his children now that he could see them so rarely. Perhaps she even believed that if he talked to them more he would want to see them less and that a gradual estrangement might grow until she could augment it by restricting telephone calls as well. Whatever her plans, he could not encourage Jake to deceive her. Later, when he was a teenager, Jake could practise what Jason thought of as a natural discretion but for now the line between caution and subterfuge was too thin for a child to discern and he knew he must uphold Kat's authority.

'It might be easier just to use land-lines for a while.'

'OK. Mum's coming. Bye, Dad.'

'Bye. See you tomorrow.'

The morning found him tired and dreading the confrontation with Kat, which he knew must come when he arrived on her doorstep. He had fallen asleep preoccupied with mental arithmetic as he had tried to work out just how often he could afford the journey he had just made but had slept dreamlessly and should have woken with a greater sense of well-being. Instead he washed and dressed sluggishly, avoiding breakfast and embarking upon the day so discouraged that he was oblivious of the sun sparkling on the damp hedges and fields of the Northumbrian countryside.

In Heddon-on-the-Wall he asked a man walking a West Highland terrier for directions to Kat's address. As he turned into her lane he saw, with heart sunk disbelief, Alex's car drawn up outside her house. As he parked and retrieved the children's presents from the back seat he could hear the row. Jake was yelling at the top of his voice that he would not go out with his grandparents, Leah was wailing with distress at the dissension which had broken out and a woman weeding the next-door garden was pausing in her task to listen with ill-disguised curiosity.

Jason rang the front doorbell and waited. It was opened by Sheila looking nervous and unhappy.

'Jason, we didn't know–'

'No, but Kat did.' Jason pushed past Sheila and, following the noise, found himself in a comfortable sitting room which he did not bother to examine.

'You knew, didn't you? You found out and set your parents up as well as me?'

'Jake, Leah, come with me into the garden,' said Alex quietly.

Both hesitated and Alex said in a much firmer tone, 'Now.'

The three went out and after a brief, uncertain hover, Sheila followed. Jason drew in his breath for the luxury of shouting his outrage at Kat, changed his mind and opened a window to speak to his in-laws.

'Take them out for an hour,' he began, but Jake protested volubly. 'Just for an hour. Jake, your mother and I want to talk. Granny and Grand-dad will bring you back and then I'll take you and Leah out anywhere you want to go.'

The four turned towards Alex's car, the adults with alacrity, Jake with reluctance and Leah with bewilderment.

'There is nothing to talk about. You turn up here unannounced and happen to clash with my parents who had the good manners to arrange their visit in advance. What is more, you are teaching Jake to be sly and I won't have it. Why not tell me you were coming?'

'Because on each occasion that I have proposed a visit you have found an excuse for it not to happen. Because I have not seen my children for months. Because even at Easter you would not let me have them for even a few days despite Alex and Sheila offering to bring them to me. This was the only way of ensuring I would see them and you have made quite certain that it would be as fraught as possible. I've given up expecting you to consider my feelings but how can you do this to your parents and above all can't you see what you are doing to Jake and Leah?'

'As my parents will confirm, this visit has been planned for ages. They are staying for ten days and of course want to take the children out after school and at the weekends. None of us knew you were coming until Jake started yelling that he wouldn't go out with his grandparents. Just how irresponsible is that?'

Jason began to wonder if she spoke the truth, if he had indeed been the victim of an unfortunate coincidence rather than a plot, but he would not be deflected.

'If I have been irresponsible it is because I am dealing with a profoundly irresponsible person who has to be outwitted before she will do what the law requires her to do. However, I and not your parents will be taking the children out all weekend and on Sunday evening I shall return with a calendar in my hand and in front of your parents we will arrange the fortnightly access you agreed to in court. We will mark out the weekends on which I will see Jake and Leah and a period of four weeks in the summer holiday when they will come to Somerset and if you break any jot of that agreement I shall instruct Alan Parnell to institute proceedings.'

Kat shrugged. 'Of course we can work out a provisional timetable–'

'To hell with provisional anythings. We will make firm, immutable arrangements. What is more, there will be no more incidents like Jake and Disney and Leah and Spain. I shall give Alex and Sheila a list of the dates when I want the children, Alan will send that list to your blasted Lane and Webb and I don't expect any counter attractions to be set up. You're quite mad to do what you are doing – Jake is already fully aware of the fact that you try to keep him from me and it can only be a matter of time before Leah gets there too.'

Kat looked at him for a few seconds and he waited for the answering explosion but when she spoke it was calmly in a tone somewhere between pained reproach and that appropriate to reasoning a small child out of a tantrum. He had heard her speak to Leah in much the same way.

'If you and I were still married–'

'God forbid,' snapped Jason.

'As you say and indeed He has forbidden it with a little help from me. But *if* we were still married then you would not keep the children all to yourself for an entire weekend every fortnight. They would develop their own interests and be free to pursue them. Saturdays would be for sports coaching, playing with friends, parties and sleepovers. You and I would see them in between and the older they became the less we would expect to see them. We would be bankers and taxi drivers and not much more.

'That is just the reality of children growing up. What you want to do is interfere in that process and absorb them every other weekend. It is just about feasible with Leah but not Jake. What you call excuses are in fact quite justifiable reasons why Jake should be encouraged to forge his own life.'

'I am quite happy for Jake to find his own interests. Quite happy to take him to coaching or matches and to watch his progress. I am equally happy to take him to friends' houses and pick him up but you didn't let me do much of that when I lived pretty well round the corner and it's a bit far-fetched to think that I am coming all the way to Newcastle to find you have quite deliberately filled the weekend up with that sort of activity, which is what you would do given half a chance. So you can arrange as much coaching as you like but the friends can play with him in the intervening weekends. That seems to be perfectly reasonable.'

'It isn't natural.'

'Yes it is if I occasionally include his friends in our outings. Anyway I shall not always take them both out at the same time because there are some things I can do with Jake that Leah could not manage. When it is Leah's turn Jake can be doing other things.'

'Did you know Jake can sing?'

Jason looked startled at the change of subject. 'Sing? I suppose he sings well enough but–'

'Not just well enough – brilliantly. One of the teachers at school who sings in a choir said she thought he had a very trainable voice so I let her try a few lessons with him, not really believing that he had any special talent or that he would be much interested. You know that he has always refused to learn an instrument because it's sissy or as he says naff. You could have knocked me down with a feather when he sang a monumentally good "How Great Thou Art" after only three lessons and seemingly with enthusiasm rather than embarrassment.'

Jason looked at her, wondering how seriously to take what she was saying, his suspicious mind already looking for her motives. He had not far to look. Choirs sang predominantly on Sundays, providing another excuse for Jake to be occupied at a weekend. Nevertheless Kat could not invent a talent or an interest which did not exist in Jake and he suspended judgement till he could listen to his son's efforts for himself.

Later, when Jake stood, precariously balanced on top of Hadrian's Wall, and filled the surrounding countryside with the strains of 'How Great Thou Art', Jason swallowed the lump in his throat and acknowledged that if he was not quite of the standard of Aled Jones his son sang movingly in true notes. His biggest regret then was not the lost Sundays which might follow but that such an ability should have existed for so long unnoticed as war raged between Jake's devoted, angry parents.

He knew, now, that he had lost. His son lived hundreds of miles away and was evincing a significant talent that would need careful nurture, a nurture he would not be there to provide. It would be Kat who would foster Jake's ability, Kat who would choose the teachers, select the choir in which their son would sing, Kat who would balance his life to make sure it was all manageable, that he still played, still learned, still sang. It would be Kat because her status as parent was real while his had been reduced to little more than honorary status. He was what Jake had called in a different context a nearly dad.

A nearly dad. The words rang in his brain through the long journey back to Somerset.

16

'I applied months ago.' Jason tried to keep his voice quiet as he talked to Tracey Speaking of the Child Support Agency. 'And during that time I have gone on paying far more than I should be paying. Any moment now I shall simply not pay at all.'

'I understand your frustration, Mr Kirk–'

'No. You do not.'

'But it still wouldn't be advisable to withhold payment. The law says–'

'The law says that my reasonable housing costs are allowed for the purposes of assessing my disposable income. Those costs changed before Christmas when I bought a house to provide space enough for my children to visit me. Before that I was in one room while my ex-wife took me for all she could get. No one has suggested that my new costs are unreasonable, everyone agrees my payments should be adjusted, no one seems able to get round to performing that adjustment. I want to know how long it's going to be.'

'Bear with me one moment, Mr Kirk.'

Jason listened to the familiar tapping of a keyboard.

'Just let me confirm your details, Mr Kirk. Can you give me your reference number, please.'

Jason reeled it off by heart and waited through more tapping.

'And your address, Mr Kirk?'

'Four, Apple Orchard Close.'

'And your old address, Mr Kirk?'

Jason gave it, forcing himself to be patient, wanting to shout that he had given this to at least half a dozen previous Traceys, Jans and Melanies.

'We only have the old address, Mr Kirk. We don't seem to have any record of any change. When did you send us the forms?'

'November the twenty-sixth in the Year of Our Lord two thousand and five at the main post office in Trowbridge at eleven thirty-four a.m.'

'Thank you, Mr Kirk.' Tracey's tone was that of one who stays studiously polite when spoken to rudely, very lady-like, very calm, superior in the face of ignorance.

'By Recorded Delivery,' added Jason, undeterred.

'Bear with me a moment, Mr Kirk.'

'I have borne with you for more than six months.'

'Thank you, Mr Kirk.'

Jason waited.

'I'm sorry, Mr Kirk. I will need to look into this further and call you back.'

'Please would you put me through to the manager?'

'Bear with me a moment, Mr Kirk.'

Music floated along the telephone line, every so often yielding to a ringing tone before renewing its mockery of progress. Jason glanced at his watch. He was due in class in twenty minutes.

'Good afternoon. This is Christine Weatherby. How may I help?'

'Are you the manager?'

'I am a supervisor.'

'I want the manager.'

'She isn't here. Can I help at all?'

'How about the deputy manager?'

'He is in a meeting. Are you sure I can't help?'

'Quite sure. I have been passed hither and thither for six long months and now I want to cut through it once and for all.'

'If that has happened, then it is quite wrong, Mr Kirk. What exactly is your query?'

Jason gave up and rehearsed his grievance yet again. There was no tapping.

'I see. I will ring you back in twenty minutes if you will give me your number.'

'I shall be teaching by then.'

'What time will you be free?'

'Just before four o'clock.'

'I will ring you at four-fifteen, Mr Kirk.'

Jason did not believe her but had no choice other than to take the promise at face value and to direct his attention and that of his pupils to the Tudors. At four-twenty Christine Weatherby rang to say there was no trace of his forms but she was concerned that they could go astray when sent by Recorded Delivery and she wished to investigate the matter fully. She would therefore be grateful if Jason could take the matter up with the Post Office and of course she would send him new forms in the next post.

'I really do want to see someone to discuss this case. My assessments change every five minutes but when I ask for an amendment nothing happens for six months.'

'Of course you can have a face-to-face interview. I'm very sorry that the system has let you down in this way. Will you be able to come here or would you prefer us to arrange for an officer to see you at your local Social Security office?'

'Either way will be difficult during the working day, but I think I prefer the second. It's half-term next week. I suppose it wouldn't be possible then?'

'We will make it possible, Mr Kirk.'

'Then I'll hand the forms over in person then.'

'A good idea.'

Mollified, Jason drove home in good spirits. The evening was fine and he did not relish spending it alone, finding, to his surprise, that he yearned for Carol. On an impulse he rang her but she was not in.

He opened the back door and decided to mow the lawn. Eileen had planted hollyhocks, roses and honeysuckle but the previous owners had allowed the garden to become overgrown and neglected and it would be a while before it would be a pleasant place to relax, yet it was the garden which had persuaded him to buy the house, for it was big, far bigger than the size of house warranted, and in his imagination Jake and Leah played in it, running its length, hiding in its bushes, arranging barbecues for their friends. One long, lonely Saturday Jason had dug a pit and installed a pond complete with fountain and lilies. Ben had given him a gnome, with a fish on the end of its rod, as a joke. The house itself was likewise run-down and Jason had obtained a large reduction in the asking price. Eileen had contributed some furniture and Carol had proved clever at finding bargains. Already the house felt as if he had lived in it for years, creating in him a feeling of freedom, of being able to start again.

Mrs Turnbull had come to visit and immediately volunteered some bookcases which had not been used since her son flew the nest many years ago. Jason had spent a happy Sunday arranging his books, which had been packed in boxes during his time in lodgings. The modest-sized front room had a fireplace and he walked for miles in the country, collecting wood to burn, sensing the gradual healing of his spirit, not yet quite trusting that his life had entered a phase in which fate would give rather than take away.

At first, when the sensation of well-being warmed him, he deliberately sought out the chill of separation from his children, as if in being happy he was somehow betraying them, betraying his own fatherhood, his own hopes.

His neighbours were friendly, on one side a young couple with a newborn baby who had recently moved in and were busy modernising their house, and on the other a widower many years retired whose grandchildren were of approximately the same age as Jake and Leah. The latter now peered through the neat trellis on his side of the fence and offered Jason a gin and tonic. Jason parted the wild growth of ivy on his own side and accepted with a grin.

They stood and talked until Giles said he must get on with his watering, leaving Jason to resume his mowing. Later he extracted a pizza from the freezer and put it in the microwave which had been Eileen's housewarming present to him. He consumed it in front of the television and watched a film until he was tired enough for bed.

Upstairs he looked at the large double bed which seemed to fill the room and thought not of Kat but of Carol. He drove the image away by pretending to himself that it was Objubjub he missed, unwilling to entertain any complications in his newfound idyll, until he fell asleep still determinedly imagining the weight of the animal on his feet.

He was surprised to feel Objubjub still there when he woke in the morning. The power of imagination was indeed wonderful, he thought, as a purr drifted into his wakening brain. The purr grew louder and Jason looked towards the foot of his bed, taking in the large ginger form curled up there, its eyes regarding him nonchalantly.

'Tigger!' Jason regarded the animal with sleepy amusement. 'Haven't you got a perfectly good home next door?'

Tigger yawned, stretching his limbs, his claws spread wide. By the time Jason had returned from the bathroom the cat had gone through the window by which he had entered in the night.

Normality, thought Jason. Normality was a house and garden to care for, a job he enjoyed, pleasant neighbours and cats which strolled in and out as if they owned the place. If he could only settle his affairs with the Child Support Agency, the Somerset side of his life would be untroubled. He tried not to brood on the Newcastle side just as he tried to ignore the whisper which said that normality was also a loving wife and happy, healthy children.

Such was his faith in the competence of Christine Weatherby that he had no serious doubt his problems with the Child Support Agency would be solved in the course of the interview he had been promised. He was happy to wait for half-term during which Kat had agreed Jake and Leah would visit, subconsciously expecting Kat to find a last-minute excuse, certain that soon he would have a settled CSA assessment. A misty guilt attended the thought because he had successfully applied to mark GCSE papers that summer and he had no intention of declaring it, nor of telling anyone what he was doing. The remuneration would cover several fares to Newcastle.

Kat herself delivered the children, having come south to stay with her parents. She and Jason agreed a time for her to collect them to take them back and even though it meant the children being with him for one day less than they had previously agreed he was happy enough with the arrangement. On the day he was due to see the official from the Child Support Agency he left Jake and Leah playing with Giles's visiting grandchildren in his neighbour's garden.

Jason's feeling of optimism received a further boost when there was no delay at the Social Security office and he was shown into an interview room within minutes of his arrival. He sat down opposite a woman in her early twenties who regarded him without enthusiasm and asked what she could do to help. Jason produced his latest batch of forms and explained his changed arrangements.

'Why was it necessary to move to somewhere so much more expensive?'

'Because I was living in one room and could not accommodate my children on access weekends. In any event I did not myself wish to go on living as a lodger. It was a purely temporary arrangement while we sorted out the divorce.'

'So you have applied for your allowable housing costs to be increased and also for a variation to allow the costs of journeys to Newcastle to be taken into account?'

'Yes.'

'That would involve a very considerable reduction in your liabilities, Mr Kirk.'

'I know and I asked for it more than six months ago. I assume it will be backdated given that I sent the application by Recorded Delivery?'

The woman whose name badge proclaimed her to be Natalie frowned. 'How many journeys have you made in that time, Mr Kirk?'

'One,' admitted Jason.

Natalie raised her eyebrows. 'But you have applied for such costs to be allowed every other week.'

'Because that is how often the law states I may see my children. Unfortunately my ex-wife does not see it that way.'

'Mr Kirk, I am sure you appreciate these forms have to be based on fact. On your own admission you have made only one visit in six months. You cannot expect us to allow for expenses which you do not actually incur. Indeed it is an offence to make a fraudulent claim.'

Jason remained calm. 'If you would kindly

allow me the deductions to which the law says I am entitled then I *would* be up there every other week because I could afford to lay siege to my wife's house until she allowed me to see my own children. As it happens your inordinate delays have merely kept me separated from them.'

'There is no need to be aggressive, Mr Kirk.'

'I was endeavouring to explain why I have been to Newcastle only once since my wife moved there.'

'I will need to take advice on your case. If you could wait a moment please...'

'Why not? I've waited six months.'

Her mouth tightened but she made no reply, instead gathering up the file and going out of the room. Jason prepared to be patient and waited a quarter of an hour before getting up and pacing the small room. Ten minutes later he put his head round the door, more for something to do than in the hope of seeing any action which might be relevant to his own affairs. A youth of eighteen or so was lounging on a scratched, scuffed chair. Another with torn jeans and pierced eyebrows was arguing with a quietly-spoken official. At the far end of the room a girl of no more than sixteen tried to control a bored, misbehaving child.

Jason turned away, depressed as he was so often when dealing with unmotivated children at school. He settled back into the tiny room with the high window and the posters advertising the department's customer service ethos on the walls, aware of mild claustrophobia. There was still no sign of Natalie.

Another ten minutes passed. Jason asked for

directions to the lavatories. He was on his way back when, passing a door marked 'Private – Staff Only', he heard Natalie's unmistakable tones: 'Makes you wonder why the poor cow went to Newcastle, doesn't it? Probably couldn't get far enough away from him... Bet he hits the kids.'

Jason froze, momentarily tempted to throw open the door, then returned to the interview room. He waited, bitterly remembering the optimism with which he had entered the building less than an hour ago.

Presently the door opened and Natalie came in, her mouth disapproving.

'Mr Kirk, I am not going to be able to sort out your case today. I am very sorry but we will get in touch with you soon.'

As she sat down she opened the file, ready to explain yet another delay. Jason looked at the forms in front of her and felt the angry incredulity course through him.

'You have had those forms for six months.'

'Mr Kirk, I fully accept you sent them but as you know we did not receive them–'

'I said you have had *those* forms for six months. They are the originals, not the batch I gave you today.'

There was a short silence during which Natalie stared at the offending papers with embarrassment and Jason with a fury he saw no reason to hide.

'You hadn't even opened the file, had you? I doubt if all those people I spoke to did either. They just tapped in to their computers and when they couldn't find anything new they gave up.'

'I assure you, Mr Kirk, that will not have been the case. I don't understand this any more than you do but–'

'How long before I get an answer?' Jason, knowing that for once he had forced officialdom into defensiveness, tried to turn the situation to advantage, to suggest that he would overlook error in return for speed, to panic his opponent into giving him the decision he wanted.

Natalie wavered and her eyes fell but she would not give in so easily.

'If I could sort this out now, Mr Kirk, I would, but the issue of how much we allow for the visits to Newcastle is not straightforward in the circumstances. It should not take long but it will be a few more days. Given the muddle over your forms I will see that your case has priority. I really am very sorry.'

'I want an exact date by which I can expect an answer and a direct number for you if it does not arrive.'

She would like to tell him to say please, thought Jason, as he watched resentment and uncertainty chase each other across her face, but the discovery of the forms had left her in too weak a position.

'Mr Kirk, I do understand why you are so angry but it is this agency's duty to ensure that absent parents take some responsibility for their children and therefore we have to make the correct assessment–'

Jason found himself towering over her, vaguely aware that he had just banged the desk with his fist before jumping to his feet and leaning forward, feeling an alien satisfaction at the fear which sprang into her eyes. She pushed her chair back, away from him, as he began to shout, his voice filling the small room, bouncing from the walls as the dam of his self-control finally burst and the pent-up anguish and indignation of the past two and a half years issued from him in an unstoppable flow.

'Absent parent did you say? Do you suppose I want to be absent? It wasn't I who walked out on ten years of marriage, who upped and left the family home. Damn you for lecturing me on taking responsibility when all I wanted to do was take full responsibility. Do you hear me? Full responsibility. So your blasted agency is here to ensure that I maintain my children, is it? Well, I *was* maintaining my children. I provided a home for them, I fed them, I clothed them. I kept them in heat and light and entertainment and holidays.

'And all I ever wanted was to go on doing that because I love my children, because there is no one more dear to me than they are. I was daft enough to think that it would always be like that – that I would go on seeing them, hearing them, smelling them, touching them. That I would be there when they were well or ill, frightened or triumphant, happy or upset. Why do you suppose I would have had children if I hadn't wanted to be around while they grew up? If I hadn't wanted to do all of that? I have asked that question many times and no one has yet come up with an answer.

'Well, my ex-wife thought otherwise and the law treats me like a bloody criminal. She can walk out, steal Jake and Leah, take them to the other end of the country and she's the one who gets all the sympathy while I get the bills and the hassle and the disapproving frowns of snooty officials like you who inflict all the anxiety and fear that you can manage and tell yourself you've done your duty.

'And why? Just because I am a man. I suppose you think men have no feelings, that we don't care if we are deserted and our children snatched from us? That our sole reaction to such a barbarity is to avoid paying anything to keep our children? Well, let me tell you–'

'I think you have told us quite enough, sir.'

Jason spun round to see a policeman standing just inside the door which he had not heard open and behind him an alarmed looking woman. He looked back at Natalie who was crying, her hard little face crumpled, her snivels now the only sound in the room. She must, he realised, have pressed some concealed panic button.

He knew he should feel embarrassed, perhaps ashamed, but instead felt only the satisfaction of having shaken her composure. He turned back to the policeman, surprised to find that the angry shaking of which he had been dimly aware during the last few minutes had passed. When he spoke it was in seemingly untroubled tones.

'I'm sorry I lost control, officer, but I was badly provoked.'

Jason thought he detected sympathy in the other's eyes and wondered if he too were unwillingly separated from his children. If so they must be very young as the policeman looked as if he were in his early twenties. It was, however, not he but the woman who answered.

'We take aggression against our staff very seriously. It is not something we are prepared to tolerate, Mr er...'

'Kirk.'

'Mr Kirk. I am afraid I must ask you to leave the premises now or I will make a formal complaint to the police. Natalie is very distressed.'

'So am I but don't let that worry you. It hasn't up till now.'

'I must ask you to leave nevertheless.'

'Certainly – when I have made my own complaint. Suppose we start with conduct likely to cause a breach of the peace.'

The policeman raised his eyebrows. Natalie stopped sniffing and looked up in amazement. The manager merely waited.

'I have been falsely accused by this official of assaulting my children. For the record I have never even smacked them. Indeed I am a teacher and regard allegations of a propensity to hit children as a slur on my professional conduct.'

'I never–' began Natalie.

'Yes, you did and to a third party which makes it slanderous. You said my wife had gone to Newcastle because I hit my children.'

Natalie gasped. A deep blush spread over her face and tears again sprang from her eyes. The manager looked closely at Jason as if trying to assess the meaning behind his words. She succeeded.

'I think, officer, that Mr Kirk has calmed down now. I will talk to him in my office. If you would wait here, please, while I call someone to help Natalie.'

She went out, accompanied by Natalie who threw Jason an angry look as she left. He smiled at her and winked, enjoying her expression of helpless outrage, unseen by either the constable or the manager. He knew that later he would regret his conduct, would wonder that he could have behaved in such a way, that he had so far departed from his normal self that he could have unleashed such a tirade against a woman and rejoiced in it, but for the moment such sentiments eluded him. He knew too that however much regret he might come to experience he would never apologise. He hated Natalie as much as the system she represented.

The policeman discharged his duty by giving Jason advice on his future conduct, which he accepted with a good grace.

'I probably shouldn't say this, sir, and I hope you won't let it go any further, but my brother hasn't seen his kids in two years, so I know how you feel but it's not the fault of anyone here and you did frighten that lassie with your shouting.'

'I know but you didn't hear the conversation before I lost my temper.'

'Well,' murmured the constable doubtfully, 'I hope you've got it all off your chest now, sir.'

'I won't yell at the manager, if that's what you mean. Indeed I've never bawled at anyone in quite that fashion before but it needed saying. The law seems so helpless and the women get away with murder, quite literally so sometimes. I once had a colleague who was driven to suicide.'

He saw the policeman's gaze switch and followed its direction to see the manager who had returned and was standing by the door. He guessed she had heard what he had just said and knew it for a certainty when, as they arrived in her office, she introduced herself as Margaret Spence and offered him a cup of tea.

Jason elected strong black coffee instead and she smiled.

'I think, Mr Kirk, that you had better tell me everything.'

To his surprise he did. He described the moment of homecoming when he found his wife and children gone, the stratagems to which Kat had resorted in trying to prevent contact between him and his children, the long sojourn in lodgings when he did not have a proper home in which to receive Jake and Leah, the way Kat had waited until he had a new house and a new job and had then departed to the other end of the country, the seemingly endless months in which he had not seen his children at all. He told of Ed's bitterness and Guy's defeatism and throughout the long tale he spoke of the Child Support Agency, of its frequent changes of assessments, of delays and lost files, of speaking to a different person each time he rang.

He talked mainly, however, about Jake and Leah and the unlooked-for reduction of his role from father to occasional visitor. They were, he said, effectively growing up without him. On the occasion he had visited Newcastle he had taken them T-shirts and Jake's was a tight fit while Leah was in a phase of preferring pretty, feminine dresses. He was losing touch with their growth, with their likes and dislikes, with them. Kat

313

allowed him a great deal of telephone access and he and Jake sent text messages daily, but he was still conscious of a distance growing that was more than geographical.

Margaret Spence heard him out, occasionally making a note when he referred to the Child Support Agency, but otherwise content to let him talk, to explain both grief and grievance. When he had finished there was silence in the room. He looked down at her hands as they rested on the desk, noticing the immaculate manicure and the sapphire ring on the third finger of her left hand. Below it lay a wide band of white gold.

'Have you got children?'

'I wouldn't normally answer personal questions from a client of the agency, but yes, I have. I've got four and I can't even begin to imagine how James would feel if he couldn't see them.'

Jason recovered some of his spirit. 'Perhaps you should tell Natalie that.'

'We see all sorts of clients here, Mr Kirk. For all I know Natalie may have spent the previous interview being abused by someone who felt it unreasonable to pay more than fifty pence a week towards the upkeep of a child he fathered on a one-night stand. I am, however, very concerned by the inappropriate comments you attributed to her. I have no direct responsibility for Natalie because she works for the Child Support Agency not the Benefits Agency. They merely use that room to interview local clients. I must, however, put in a report if what you said is true.'

'It was mostly true, but, in fairness, I think she said I probably hit my children rather than

314

actually did hit them. It was something like "bet you anything he hits the kids". Frankly I don't want to take matters any further. I just want my payments sorted out. The last straw was when I saw that the forms had been there all the time and then she started to lecture me on my responsibilities. Sadly it looks as if you can't sort it out either as you are not in the right agency.'

'Oh, but I can get it moving for you. I'll personally phone the lady you mention – what was her name? – Christine Weatherby and explain that the CSA have had the forms all along and that the cost of going to Newcastle when your payments have not been adjusted is keeping you from your children. I am afraid I will have to mention Natalie's behaviour but I'm also afraid I should now talk about yours.'

'You don't have to,' said Jason, failing to sound contrite.

Margaret Spence hesitated, then shrugged. 'At least tell me you won't do it again.'

'I can guarantee it. I am never coming back here.'

'Well, I think we'll draw a line under it although if Natalie complains I expect you'll get a stiff letter from the CSA. We do have a duty to protect our staff. Every time there is an incident like this the Union demands screens between staff and the customers. We resist it because it is so dehumanising but it is still very necessary in some offices.'

But not here. Jason's imagination supplied the unspoken words. She was telling him that he had introduced a hooligan element into the leafy surroundings of rural Somerset and he knew the unspoken allegation to be just, as he also knew that Natalie would make no complaint because she herself was also in the wrong. The incident would be ignored and gradually fade from the memories of those involved. In years to come Natalie would perhaps tell her friends that the worst incident she could remember from her time in the Child Support Agency was not caused by any teenage hoodlum but by a nice-looking, respectable, middle-class man, a teacher of all things. The friends would look scandalised and press for details.

Of course, she might recall it quite differently. Perhaps a very different Natalie would look back in ten years' time and warn new recruits to the Agency of the need to understand fathers, telling them how once she had got it so wrong...

Jason tried to picture an older version of the woman against whom he had so spectacularly railed, to see softer lines, a kinder expression, eyes which understood, a mouth that did not curl in disapproval but his imagination failed him.

He became aware that the manager was looking at him. It was time to thank her and make as dignified a departure as the circumstances permitted, to return to his children and retrieve them from Giles's garden.

As he drove home he thought of Jake and Leah running towards him but in reality they ran away because they were racing up and down the garden in competition with his neighbour's grandchildren. Tigger had taken haughty refuge in a tree. To his surprise he found Carol there too.

'All well?' she asked him.

He shook his head and watched the concern and sorrow enter her eyes. He smiled and hugged her and was surprised by the desire which suddenly pierced him, causing him to want her not just as friend and helpmate but as a lover, as a wife. Instead of disengaging in alarm he did so slowly.

Carol also smiled, knowingly, happily.

'Oh, I think some things are better,' she said.

17

Jason watched with resignation as a monkey pulled his windscreen wiper from its socket. Leah was shrieking with laughter and banging wildly on the rear window and monkeys were banging back. One hung from the car roof and peered intently at Jake. Another sat on the bonnet picking fleas from its fur. When it departed Jason saw that it had left a deposit at the same moment that Jake noticed it and cried 'Ugh!' in delight. Rufus, Giles's ten-year-old grandson, had pressed his face to one of the side windows and was pulling faces, imitating monkey chatter.

The monkey studied the wiper curiously then made off with its trophy. Amy, who was squashed between Leah and her brother, was trying to call their attention to the antics of a very small monkey which had attached itself to the car in front. The ancient Morris Minor had, in addition to modern indicators, its original winged kind, which now stood out at right angles to the car. The monkey was swinging from it first with one paw and then with the other. Eventually it wound its tail around the light and hung upside down. Amy stood up and leaned between the front seats to get a better view.

Jason engaged the gears and the car moved slowly forward, the monkeys jumping out of the way, one still clinging to the roof.

'Dad, do you believe in evolution?'

'Yes. Why?'

'You don't believe that God made the world in seven days?'

Jason dared not take his eyes from the road for fear of running down a monkey but there was something in his son's voice which disturbed him, which made him want to turn and look at him.

'There is no contradiction between the order of creation set out in Genesis and the order worked out by scientists. So if you think of it as seven phases rather than as seven days...'

'Steve says it's seven days,' asserted Leah, tuning into the conversation. 'He says we all look like God and God isn't a monkey. He says it's blasterbus to say so.'

'Blasphemous. Who is Steve?'

Jason tried to keep the question casual, believing he already knew the answer.

His children answered simultaneously.

'Just a chap from church,' said Jake.

'He's Mummy's best friend like Carol is your best friend,' said Leah.

Jason knew his son was looking at him but he continued to concentrate on his driving until

318

they were safely out of the monkey reserve. Then he said, 'Seals soon. Lunch first or afterwards?' and used the time occupied by the ensuing argument to gather his thoughts.

'Mr Kirk, why don't the lions chase the car?' Rufus peered intently at a large lioness who looked back at him unperturbed.

'Because they can't catch our scent. That is why we have to keep the windows shut.'

'Steve says Daniel was in the lions' den and they didn't touch him because God looked after him. It's in the Bible.' Leah's tone suggested she envied Daniel the experience.

Jason, who had brought the car almost to a standstill, turned to look at his daughter but she was already distracted by the size of the mane on a nearby lion. He decided to postpone the enquiries he had been about to make of his son until they should be alone, but it was Jake who began the conversation when the others were on the opposite side of the boat they had boarded to feed the seals.

'Dad, I don't like Steve.'

'Why not?'

'He's bossy. We don't have fun on Sundays any more. He won't let Mum cook and we can't watch television. We go to church in the morning anyway because I sing in the choir but he makes us go to his church in the evening as well. He says we can't play outside in case we make a noise and disturb other people's Sabbath.'

'What's his church like?'

'Not bad. It's not boring like the one we go to with Granny. They have guitars and things but it goes on for ever and Leah gets tired and messes about. Then when we get home Steve tells her off and she cries and screams. It's always the same. I hate it.'

'How do you get on with the vicar?'

'They don't have a vicar, at least not a real one. He dresses just like everyone else. They call him a pastor.'

Jason phrased the next question carefully. 'Does Steve stay with you?'

'Oh, there's nothing like *that*,' said Jake dismissively. In other circumstances Jason would have laughed.

'Have you told Mum how you feel about Steve?'

'Yes. She says...'

At that moment a seal burst above the waters beside them, letting out a plaintive cry, and the crowd surged to their side of the boat. Jason only just caught the end of his son's sentence '...I mustn't hate him because that's what the Devil wants.'

Anger and fear fought for supremacy in Jason's troubled mind. Fear won as he recognised his helplessness. Kat could embroil Jake and Leah in any dogma, any sect, any cult even and he would be powerless to prevent it, no matter how oppressive the regime. So long as she and the children lived life in the mainstream, punctual at school, well nourished, appropriately clothed and clean, no one would question the absence of outdoor play on a Sunday, the gradual closing of their minds, the slow, insidious growth of intolerance, of condemnation, of hatred, the bullying of a small child who could not keep still in church.

'I don't care which faith Kat brings them up in – at least not within reasonable limits.' Jason found himself shaking as he described the conversation to Carol on the telephone long after the children were in bed. 'But I won't have them bullied into belief. This Steve sounds ghastly. Jake called him bossy but only because his vocabulary is too limited to include the word bigot. I can't think what Kat is up to. This sort of thing is just not her scene. Any minute now Leah will be telling me the Pope is the Antichrist.'

'Well, if Steve is that committed he will be telling Kat the error of her ways and persuading her to return to her lawfully wedded husband because he won't believe in divorce and therefore won't recognise hers. This can't last, Jason. Either Kat will really come to believe it all and try to come back to you or it will just be a passing fad and she will give Steve his marching orders.'

'I wouldn't have her back.'

'I meant she will try to undo as much of the damage as possible by coming to live nearby and letting the children see you as often as they like.'

'Some chance!'

'Then she must give it up but if you try to force a showdown now she will just become more entrenched. I think you should be a bit more subtle. Get the grandparents to visit and take them out on Sundays, encourage Jake and Leah to spend weekends with friends. Turn up unexpectedly yourself even if it is an expensive gamble.'

'No. I see the wisdom of what you're saying but it can't be done every week and that means Leah being bullied Sunday after Sunday.'

'Well, at least talk to Kat's parents first – and Alan Parnell.'

'I'll think about it.'

Thought gave him little comfort and brought him no closer to any resolution of the problem. Jake was probably old enough to question what was happening but that would merely expose him to Steve's anger and, if he grew sceptical, weaken Kat's authority which Jason did not want at so young an age, knowing it was vital that Jake should respect his mother, that he must not come to resent or deride her decisions, confident that others would share his view. Already his son blamed Kat for the break-up of the home, had seen and understood her deceit, had been aware of her attempts to keep him from his father. He was becoming protective of Leah and Jason recognised that the seeds of dissension were irrevocably sown. To water the ground and encourage the seed to grow and flower was something Jason had promised himself he would never do, yet now it appeared another man was doing it for him without the least idea of the consequences.

Carol's observation that Steve would not admit the validity of a perfectly lawful divorce produced not reassurance but misery. It was not an aspect of the situation which had previously occurred to him but now he saw its truth and he wondered what Kat had told Steve to explain the situation. If she had told him the truth, had said that she had left without warning after ten years of marriage, that she had tried to keep the children from her husband by dint of trickery and falsehood and that she had no reason for any of it beyond boredom, then would such a man have entered into so close a relationship with her?

Perhaps he was, after all, interested only in her soul and the children had misconstrued his frequent presence. Maybe Kat was a part of his mission and he had no intentions beyond converting her to his faith. It was a possible explanation, but not as likely as the obvious alternative which struck Jason with cold and compelling force.

Kat, he now realised, had almost certainly lied, had spun a story for Steve which explained her present circumstances in such a way as to attach no blame to her or at least to minimise any likely censure and she could not do that without attributing the worst possible conduct to himself. She might have presented him in the character of a serial adulterer, a wife-beater, a violent father. Whatever she had said there had to be a risk that it might eventually reach the children's ears, through a careless conversation overheard at home or at church when no one knew Jake or Leah was listening, from a wariness in Steve when he, Jason, was due to have the children, from warnings, however carefully disguised, which he might feel it his duty to give.

Jason would have liked to take Carol's advice and speak to Alex and Sheila but Kat was staying with them and the only opportunity he would have would be when she was already on her way to collect Jake and Leah. He wondered how much they knew of Steve, whether the children had spoken to them about him, whether indeed they knew more than he did. There was, however, one mystery which he could clear up as soon as he saw Kat. It would take only seconds to find out if she was seriously considering active, fundamental Christianity.

Kat looked back at him with lazy amusement when he asked her, having sent the children next door to say goodbye to Giles and Tigger.

'Get real. If I were into that sort of thing there would be plenty of Evangelical churches which are rather more sane.'

'So what is all this about?'

'Steve amuses me. He's a widower with three children at the school where I teach. He came in one day and told the head that none of them were to use computers because they are the Devil's instruments. I want to know what makes people like that tick.'

'And where exactly do Jake and Leah come in to this interesting psychological experiment?'

'They don't. I want them to understand that there are lots of different beliefs in the world and that not everybody thinks as we do but I wouldn't let them near the church if I thought that everyone there was as mad as Steve. The pastor is actually rather a kind man.'

'But it's not the pastor who comes to the house. It's Steve, who, by your own admission, is a lunatic. Jake says he is not allowed to play outside on Sundays.'

'Only when Steve is there. Anyway what Steve does with them is more fun. We play board games and innocent things like Hide and Seek and Hunt the Thimble. It's all perfectly healthy.'

'Leah might enjoy that sort of thing but Jake is getting a bit too old. And I gather you are not allowed to cook on Sundays?'

'Cold food is just as nourishing and probably better for them than a roast.'

'What about the way Steve tells Leah off for not concentrating in church?'

'He doesn't tell her off, just suggests that she tries a bit harder. She can be very difficult sometimes.'

'I haven't noticed.'

'Well, you wouldn't, would you? You only see the children for high days and holidays when you spend all your time asking them what they want to do and falling in with it. I am the one who copes with them on a day-to-day basis and gets all the sulks and tears.'

'And whose fault is that?'

Kat sighed. 'I am not going into all that again. Meanwhile I've had more than enough of this interrogation. I am not answerable to you for my religion and I resent the suggestion that I can't take care of Jake and Leah. I will choose my own friends and if that includes Steve then so be it. At least he's *interesting*.'

Incredulous, exasperated, again outwitted, Jason looked at his ex-wife. 'I am beginning to believe that I never knew you. I spent ten years married to a stranger and didn't even realise it.'

'What a cliché. Just like our marriage, when you come to think of it. That was a cliché too.' Kat yawned, looked at her watch and began to get up from her chair, her eyes on the window, seeking the return of Jake and Leah from next door.

Jason would not be deflected. 'If it were all as harmless as you make it sound then Jake would not be so unhappy.'

Kat's eyes flashed. 'My son is not unhappy.'

Jason recognised fear in her anger. For all her naked triumphalism, all her goading, all her self-assurance, Kat was still beset by dread that Jason might yet take the children from her, might turn the tables and convert her distant nightmare into the daily reality he had faced for so long. He tried to press home his momentary advantage, before she should reason it away.

'Jake has told me he is unhappy and I am prepared to go to law if necessary. What do you suppose a judge would make of it all?'

'He would have no view unless Jake and Leah were being ill treated.'

Jason knew that she was right and that if he argued she would merely become more certain. Instead he sought to plant another fear. 'Jake will soon be old enough to speak for himself and for that matter to decide for himself.'

'Decide *what?* If you think you can lure Jake away...' Kat broke off as the children came through the front gate towards the house and Jason smiled at her, sure that for once he had won and that Steve would shortly disappear from his children's lives.

Something else was tugging at his mind. 'You said Steve has three children. Where are they in all of this? Do they come with him when he visits?'

'No, if it is any of your business. They are being brought up by their grandmother.'

Jason made no attempt to lower his tone as Jake and Leah came noisily into the hall.

'Well, if he can't bring his own children up he can stop pontificating about mine.'

Victory can be more dangerous than defeat, thought Jason later. Steve would no longer torment his son with his Victorian notion of upbringing but Kat would resent his own interference and look for ways to take revenge. She would not see the triumph of his will on this occasion as the result of a minor skirmish in a long drawn-out war, from which she emerged the undisputed winner, but rather as a harbinger of other defeats waiting for her in the future.

Above all it had been foolish of him to taunt her with Jake's growing independence, by hinting that he might prefer to live with his father and was approaching an age when that preference would have force in any legal battle. Kat, he knew, would now scheme to make sure this did not happen, would seek ways of ensuring the preference swung back to her and he knew also that she could best achieve that by driving some fresh wedge between him and Jake.

They were not happy thoughts and nor was his recognition that something within him was changing and that he did not like the shape it was taking. He had never been a cruel man, had never revelled in another's misery, had never relished revenge as a cold dish, only savouring it scalding hot from the fires of immediate fury and indignation. Yet he had smiled at Natalie when she wept, had winked to complete her humiliation, and now he had, scenting a rare victory, smiled at Kat to let her know he was enjoying her fear. He was becoming something, someone, he did not want to be and, if the metamorphosis was completed, he would face the greatest loss of all – the loss of himself, of self-respect, of liking the image his soul reflected to the world, of inner peace.

Once, when he had told Carol how disproportionately pleased he had become with his house, garden and visits from Tigger, she had said that such feelings were akin to recovering from an illness. Some years ago, she told him, she had contracted a serious ear infection and for many months could not balance properly.

'If I turned my head too quickly I nearly fell over,' she said. 'Whenever I ran, the ground seemed to come up to meet me and I felt as if I was perpetually in the early stages of 'flu or had a mild hangover. Somehow the world just didn't look quite normal: distances were distorted and occasionally I would feel as if I were swimming instead of walking. It was horrible and when it finally went I rejoiced in things which I had always taken for granted: being able to run for a bus, to jump on an escalator instead of edging on with one hand gripping the side, to look into the distance and find I was focusing normally.

'Anybody else would have laughed at my being so pleased by such small things but those who had suffered similar problems understood. What you have been through is a bit like that. All the things you took for granted – your own home, a garden to tend, animals coming and going – were snatched from you and it is quite natural that you should appreciate them the more for having lost them. I don't think it's at all odd.'

Jason remembered that analogy now and wondered how Carol would have reacted if, one day, when she was quite well again and had been revelling in the return of health she suddenly found the world once more tilting. Would she not, in an urgent quest to retain her grasp on a normality restored, have fought savagely against the unexpected tilt? Would she not have smiled with grim satisfaction as it faded? Or would she instead have experienced only happiness, relief, gratitude?

He found himself calculating the years before Leah should be a self-confident teenager freeing herself from Kat's manipulative web, before Jake should be old enough to travel alone on the train from Newcastle. His misery was finite, he told himself, but a small, mocking, hard voice inside his head replied that the years before he was released would seem an eternity.

When he thought of Kat he pitied even Steve. He believed he was converting her but she was merely playing with him and his hopes and would cast him adrift as soon as she wearied of exploring his psyche or whenever a more interesting case presented itself.

The more interesting case proved to be a Jehovah's Witness and Jason endured a fortnight's nightmare that his children might be involved in an accident and denied a blood transfusion before he was quickly supplanted by an environmentally conscious social worker who insisted the car stay in the garage while they cycled everywhere.

'It's good for you,' Jason told a mutinous Jake.

'Kat won't stand that for long,' he told Carol. 'She likes her comfort. Anyway Leah cannot pedal for miles and they live in a fairly remote area.'

Jason's worry was not the cycling but that Sam was a social worker and Kat's relationship with him might give her some unfair advantage in some unspecified battle yet to come. It turned out to be a false prophecy. Sam had strong views on what he called parental alienation and, during the three months that he was a part of Kat's life, Jason began to see the children regularly. He tried hard not to believe that was the reason when Kat ended the liaison just before Jake started secondary school.

'I liked Sam,' said Leah sadly.

'I hope you'll still come and see us, Dad,' whispered Jake.

Margaret Spence had ensured that the Child Support Agency had been made fully aware of Jason's circumstances and for the first time since Kat had sought its intervention Jason considered his payments both reasonable and predictable. He had been allowed deductions to take account of fortnightly travel to and from Newcastle and Sam's insistence on contact had meant the journeys were not wasted and that Jason was welcome in the family home. Jake's fear that this orderly pattern should now be in jeopardy was, he knew, only too well founded and, when Kat found a series of excuses to deny him access throughout the entire Christmas holiday, he could only fret impotently. Eileen wept and he suspected that Alex and Sheila had remonstrated but Kat reverted to her old habits with no loss of either ingenuity or ruthlessness.

By Easter, when he had seen Jake once and Leah not at all because she had been ill when Alex and Sheila, who were briefly visiting, were ready to bring the children south to stay first with him and then with them, the name of Dan had begun to crop up in telephone conversations, unaccompanied by any suggestion of undue zeal for religion or environmental fervour.

'I've a premonition this one might last.'

Carol looked at him uncertainly. 'I'm not sure whether you're telling me you like or dislike the premonition but it will probably have to happen some time. What do the children think of him?'

'Jake appears indifferent. I think he has got so used to the frequent changes that he is resigned to just waiting to see what happens next. It's Leah I'm worried about. Kat said something about her being difficult while Steve was still on the scene and, stupidly, I did not take much notice. We were quarrelling at the time and I was a bit too dismissive. Yesterday Alex rang to say they were quite worried last time they were there.'

'I know you don't see that much of her, but have you noticed anything?'

'No, but, as Kat pointed out, I am not there every day and when Leah is with me she is being spoiled with attention and outings and treats. I suspect it would be very different if I saw them all the time. These tantrums appear to coincide with Kat's relationships if Alex is to be believed and this time they are very bad indeed. It's almost as if she has a premonition too.'

'It can't be easy. If Kat is thinking of marrying and they guess it they will see it as changing daddies.'

'Amoebas.'

'What?'

'Amoebas. Families splitting up and reforming all the time. Re-partnering is the euphemism, I think. There was a Tory MP on television last night saying just that and the interviewer accused her of scapegoating single parents. I tell you I was positively cheering her on and I've never voted Tory in my life.'

'I've never voted anything else but it doesn't make much difference to this sort of thing. Government can't do much about individual morals but social stigma can and at the moment there ain't any stigma. Kat and her ilk will never face disapproval from anyone, or at least they will never have to face any disapproval which shows.'

'Meanwhile Jake and Leah pay the price and I'm helpless to do anything about it. Brave new bloody world.'

'Well, at least if Kat marries she will be settled and the children won't have a procession of men coming and going, and Dan sounds quite normal, which has to be a blessing after those weirdos.'

'Sam wasn't so bad, but, yes, you're right. I suppose Leah will adjust.'

Carol got up. 'The casserole must be nearly ready.'

As Jason followed her to the kitchen she said, 'I saw Ros Deacon the other day. She looks as if she has aged ten years.'

'I wonder how the kids are doing. I can't even

begin to imagine what they must have gone through. If Leah is finding it tough, Chloe must think she has gone to hell and back. Oh, hi, Tigger.'

The ginger form squeezed itself through the slightly open window and Carol laughed. 'He smells the casserole. My mother once had a neighbouring cat who only visited when she was cooking a roast.'

Throughout the meal she talked determinedly of the ways of the various animals she had known: of cats and dogs, of tortoises and guinea pigs and of her childhood among them, of the setting up of a farm in a school close to Morton's, of animals teaching children how to take early responsibility through their need of care and nurture, of farming methods and profit, of experiments and vivisection, of cloning and scientists playing God, of endangered species and the ivory trade, of Third World poverty and free markets, of cruel regimes and dictators.

Jason ranged with her, responding, contributing, occasionally disputing, but his words were mechanical, mere repetitions of those he had uttered in similar conversations in the past. His thoughts refused to travel to school farms or scientists' laboratories or sugar plantations, instead remaining resolutely on the ghost of a man dead by his own hand and long since buried. His anger over Ed's death had dulled and in its place lingered the faint wraiths of misery and sadness but there was nothing vague or faded in his indignation about the other ghost which filled his mind, tugging and demanding: the small, living spectre of his tormented daughter.

He made his own attempt to divert his mind from that cold, muddy channel by asking whether Carol had seen anyone else from Morton's since she had left.

'I saw Angus and Elizabeth about two weeks ago. They were back from another holiday and he looked fully restored to health and indeed full of vim and vigour. Elizabeth looked pretty good too.'

'I'm glad. Elizabeth deserves it. I've rather lost touch with them.'

'I heard yet another rumour the other day of Morton's being closed.'

'Yes, so did I. I ran into Matt Johnson, so it was right from the horse's mouth. This time I actually believe it could happen.'

The telephone rang and Jason went to answer while Carol cleared away the plates. When he returned he spoke not to her but to Tigger.

'Seems you'll soon have a rival, old chum. That was Mrs Turnbull. She is emigrating to Spain at the end of the year to live with her daughter and Objubjub will be making a triumphant return to the Kirk household.'

Carol laughed. Jason began to help with the dishes and soon the swish and hum of the dishwasher filled the kitchen. His words rang in his brain. *The Kirk household.* One man and his cat was not much of a household.

He looked at Carol who was scouring the sink and wiping down the draining board, at the busy hands with the short, unvarnished, well-filed nails, at the hair which fell over her face as she leaned forward over her task, at the rising of her neat but short skirt and its fall as she straightened and turned to him.

He found himself saying the words before the thought was fully formed and saw the joy spring into her eyes. Almost at once he was uncertain, remembering how Kat had also looked at him through sparkling eyes with that hint of tears as he had slipped the diamond on her finger. Carol's next words dispelled any hint of similarity.

'You bounder. Couldn't you have found a more romantic setting than the kitchen sink?'

He smiled but when he afterwards re-ran the scene in his mind he wondered whether in that innocent joke Carol had explained Kat's discontent. Surely the kitchen sink must be the most tedious, unromantic setting it was possible to devise for a proposal of marriage and the light-hearted use of that old fashioned term 'bounder' seemed somehow to emphasise his lack of modernity, to root him in the past.

Later, as he lay listening to her steady, untroubled sleep, he thought of his children. He had blamed Kat for being about to inflict a stepfather on Jake and especially on Leah. Now he would have to reconcile them to a stepmother as well. Through the fitful dreams which followed, his daughter sobbed and shook and screamed against her fate.

18

'Hello, sir.'

Jason glanced round and saw a boy in his early teens hailing him from the other side of the street. He waved uncertainly but as the lad crossed the road towards him he recognised Nick Bright.

'Nick! Great to see you. You've certainly grown.'

'I heard you left Morton's, sir.'

'Yes, but there is no need to "sir" me now that I don't teach you. How's school?'

'Brill. I'll be in the fourth in September.'

Jason, mildly disconcerted by the unfamiliar terminology, performed the right translation. 'Year Ten? GCSE coursework? I can't believe it's that long since you were in Year Seven and telling me how to date Roman coins. Don't tell anyone but until you enlightened me I had more or less forgotten how to do it. Ancient History was never my strongest point.'

Nick smiled. 'Do you remember Terry Pepper, sir ... er, Mr Kirk? He can still do Roman dates just like that.'

Nick snapped his fingers to demonstrate the speed at which Terry could convert modern to ancient and Jason looked at him in surprise. Nick had left Morton's for a private school and Terry for a special one.

'You're still in touch?'

'Oh, yes. It was awful. Terry's mum died but his

dad kept them all together and his sister and brother were terrific. Terry boards now at a special school near Bristol but he comes home every weekend. He comes to us quite a lot in the holidays when his dad is working.'

Jason thought of Mrs Pepper cooking, the sister with her head in a magazine, the brother who had nearly collided with him on the landing and had described Terry as a 'good kid'. They had deserved a better fate but it looked as if Mr Pepper, whom Jason had never met, had risen to the occasion with a determination and surefootedness which might have eluded many better educated and more privileged than he. For the first time in a long while an image of Harry Jackson danced into his mind and he saw again a small boy, coatless in the winter chill, weeping by a tree.

A man and a woman came to join them and Jason recognised Nick's parents. For a while they talked, then Mrs Bright reminded Nick of errands still uncompleted and the three moved off. Jason watched them walk slowly down the street. Nick's father drew attention to something in a shop window and they stopped to look more closely, standing in a small, happy group, the man's arm around his son's shoulders. Jason turned away with a renewed sense of loss.

Fate, Jason muttered to himself, trying to quell the sudden bitterness. Fate had given Terry Pepper a lifelong affliction and had snatched away his mother but it had given him also the love of a family which could cope and the friendship of at least one sturdy little ally. By contrast it had taken all from Harry Jackson and given nothing in

337

return while Nick Bright had been blessed with love, stability and modest wealth as well. Three very different fates, three very different fathers.

Jason peered at his reflection in the window of a small café advertising Olde English Teas and thought of his own fatherhood, of what fate had handed Jake and Leah. He had visited Newcastle the previous weekend and had met Dan, a quiet, sensible librarian in thrall to Kat. It won't last, he had told first himself and then Carol. For a while Kat would enjoy the power but such a man would no more be able to keep her interest than he had.

'I hate you, I hate you, I hate you,' Leah had screamed at Carol.

'Congratulations, Dad,' said Jake with listless duty.

Jason realised that his engagement to Carol had abruptly stolen any lingering hope his children might have had of a reconciliation between their parents, that so long as they were single there was a chance that the nightmare would end. Now it was he, Jason, who had pronounced finality and he knew that Jake would experience not misery alone but also disillusionment. Until now Kat had been the villain of the terrible play in which his children were forced to act and he the wronged hero but it was he and not Kat who was ensuring there would be no happy ending.

Four weeks later, when Kat announced that she and Dan were to marry, Leah threw a tantrum in class, hurling pencils across the room, pushing other children and finally biting the teacher who was trying gently to restrain her. Kat, appalled, tried to reason and coax as well as chide, but Leah screamed all the way home in the car. Later Dan found Jake and his sister hugging and crying inconsolably in Leah's room.

'Go away,' said Jake with uncharacteristic rudeness.

Jason begged the Friday from a reluctant head and left for Newcastle as soon as school was finished on the Thursday. There was no sign of Dan when he at last arrived at Heddon-on-the-Wall and, at the invitation of a worn, spiritless Kat, he stayed in Jake's room rather than the Bed and Breakfast at Horsely. For the first time in three years they were all together under one roof. He began to doubt the wisdom of such an arrangement, wondering if it might remind the children of happier times.

'I just don't know what to do with Leah. I would have thought she might have found it easier than Jake. After all she was only three when it all happened and can't have much memory of us being together. There has never been any sign of her disliking Dan. She seems to think that if I marry him she won't see you any more, that you'll just somehow fade away. As if.'

'The problem is that she never really does know when she'll see me, does she? You keep me from them for months at a time and then suddenly it's all sweetness and light again and they see me every other week until you get fed up and decide to go back to your beastly tricks. They haven't seen my mother in nearly two years and you know as well as I do that they adore her. If we had managed to establish a regular and reliable pattern it would be easier to persuade them now that such a pattern would continue.'

'Oh, for goodness' sake. What matters is what we do *now*. If Leah goes on like this she'll be excluded from school. I took her into the head's office and smacked her after the last episode and it was a bit more peaceful for a while but she has started up again and I can't hit her every time. Somehow I've got to find a way of calming her down and reconciling her to what's happening.'

'What does Dan say?'

'That perhaps we should wait a while but I don't agree. Leah cannot be allowed to dictate our lives for us.'

'You mentioned some time ago that she was becoming difficult. That was ages before Dan came on the scene.'

'Yes, and a lot of notice you took at the time. It all started when I was seeing Steve but actually she quite liked Sam and it was better then.'

'Which, if you remember, was the very time when I was seeing them every two or three weeks without fail. You put an end to that so you can hardly be surprised if Leah is afraid of my disappearing altogether. Every time a new man arrived she must have wondered if this was the new daddy and now it has actually happened, God help her.'

'And what about Carol? The new mummy?'

Carol. In his imagination she smiled at him, her eyes no longer uncertain as they waited for that small, regretful twist of his mouth which used to say as surely as words, 'Not yet, I'm not ready, not yet. I'm sorry, my love.' The new confidence conferred by the prospect of nuptials had given a lightness to her movements, a spring to her walk, a playfulness to her caresses.

Once she had said that she wanted to be a full-time mother, that she did not want a childminder, an outsider, to witness those moments in her children's development which she wanted to hug to herself; the first attempts at crawling, standing, walking, speaking. Jason had replied quietly, sadly, hating himself, that he could not keep two families on the pay of a middle-ranking teacher and she had pulled a face of disappointment. Though he spoke of the limitations of money his mind had been very differently engaged, trying to imagine how Jake and Leah would react when Kat brought home a new baby, a half-brother or sister, from hospital and then maybe another. Would they feel themselves usurped, supplanted by children who belonged to both Kat and Dan, to whom Dan was a real father? He pictured them coming to stay with him and finding more half-brothers and half-sisters, the children of the marriage he was about to make to Carol.

'Amoebas,' he said aloud, recalling the Conservative MP.

'What?' Kat looked startled. 'You've been miles away. In case you have forgotten we were talking about your daughter. Leah. Remember her?'

Jason ignored the sarcasm. 'I'll collect her from school tomorrow and take her out, leaving Jake with you.'

'He has a choir practice anyway. What do you think you can achieve with her that the rest of us can't?'

'That depends on you as much as me. I want to assure her that I will be around every two or three weeks and that she will come to stay with me for at least some of every holiday and that we will both go to stay with her grandmother in Dorset. I shall tell her that Objubjub is now at home again and missing her. But I am not prepared to tell her any of that unless it is true and she can really rely on it. Your choice.'

'Tell her what you like,' snapped Kat.

'No. I will tell her only what is true.'

'Very well.'

'You mean it?'

'Oh, do stop nagging. I've said so, haven't I?'

'If I promise Leah all of that and you renege then I really will go to law. I shall invoke Leah's behaviour as proof that she is unhappy and ask for a revised residence order so that the children can live with Carol and me.'

He watched Kat absorbing the words, weighing probability, accepting that whereas it had never been very practical in the past for Jason to look after the children alone, the arrival of Carol, of stable living arrangements, of space put them on a more equal footing. He waited to see if she would wilt or fight.

She fought. 'I'm afraid I won't be blackmailed. Children are better off with their mothers when they are as young as Leah and it is I, not Carol, who is her mother. Anyway, you seem to have overlooked the fact that Leah hates the idea of you and Carol as much as she hates that of Dan and me. I well remember if you do not that she shouted at Carol telling her she hated her. So I don't think you will get very far at law.'

'What do I tell Leah?'

'That you will see her more often but I can't sign up to any particular pattern. They are developing their own lives.'

'You *have* signed up to a pattern. It was all set out in the divorce settlement. I can enforce that much at law and probably should have done long ago.'

'That was before I moved up here. What was reasonable then is impractical now. It is probably I who should have gone to law and applied for a variation long ago.'

Jason sighed. 'None of this will help Leah. She needs security. I am prepared to agree to access once a month instead of every fortnight so long as it is a cast-iron guarantee that nothing will get in the way of it happening.'

'Well, if you must, but frankly your visits here are disruptive. It would be better to allow time after the marriage for them to settle down with Dan and the new arrangements. Say three months.'

'Nothing doing. They would think I had given up on them.'

'Not if you go on telephoning. I've never restricted that.'

The implied threat sent a chill through Jason. If Kat ever tried to cut off his telephone contact he would secretly supply a mobile for Jake and be not in the least troubled by his conscience.

'We're getting nowhere. Indeed we are fiddling while Rome burns. I am going to bed.' Jason got up from his chair and headed towards the hall and the stairs. Kat did not oppose him.

The following morning he drove Jake to school and privately sought out the headmaster. No, he was assured, Jake had shown no signs of any underlying anxiety and his work was well above average. He seemed quite content and indeed these answers had already been given to Miss Johnson. It was, of course, never easy for children when their parents split up and subsequently re-married. Miss Johnson had already brought Jake's future stepfather to the school for a parents' evening.

A dart of jealousy tightened Jason's knuckles but he kept his face neutral. So Dan was already assuming the role of stepfather, that of the nearly dad.

Reassured by Jason's calm exterior the head went on: 'He seemed to relate to Jake quite well. I think you can be confident that he will make a perfectly reasonable father figure.'

Jason knew the words were kindly meant and bit back the retort that Jake already had a per-fectly reasonable father. He thanked the head with what grace he could muster and left the school feeling obscurely disorientated, his world tilting.

It would be three o'clock before he could see Leah. Kat had pondered letting him take her from school for the day but they had decided to keep routine as normal as possible. He intended therefore to return to the house, consult Kat's Ordnance Survey maps and plan a walk. He was in the very act of pulling on his hiking boots when the telephone shrilled. He wondered who

344

would be ringing Kat at home during a weekday and almost ignored it, finally answering as much to silence the instrument as to find out who was calling.

'Hi. It's Dan,' said an uncertain voice. 'I thought you might be at a loose end while the kids are in school. There is a very good pub a couple of miles from you if you would like to join me for a quick lunch.'

Jason was not deceived. Dan worked in the university and there would be nothing quick about a lunch in the country. He wondered if Kat knew.

'I don't know whether Katie would approve,' Dan went on as if reading his thoughts. 'But I thought you and I should talk. The Leah situation isn't good and–'

'All right,' interrupted Jason to prevent himself changing his mind. 'Where is this pub and what time should I be there?'

He wrote down Dan's directions and decided on a different walk which would bring him to the pub after a long detour. He might yet find an ally in Dan as he had once in Sam and if they could agree his right to see his own children then Kat might yet lose the upper hand she had so successfully maintained. Yet he resented discussing Leah with Dan. Leah was *his* daughter, her welfare *his* concern. He knew that he must accept the advent of Dan into her young life, that Dan would administer treats and discipline and advice, would take daily decisions which would bind her, would always be there in the evenings and at weekends, the father figure, the nearly dad, the man who would step into Jason's shoes

345

and wear them until they looked more natural on him than on their owner.

Jason arrived at the pub a quarter of an hour early and ordered a shandy, choosing a table near the door so that he might watch for Dan's arrival, like a soldier not wanting to be surprised by the enemy. Jake sent him a text saying that school lunch was quite good that day and he was having fish and baked beans. He sent a message back, after a quick study of the blackboard above the bar: 'Mine's a ploughman's. See you later.'

He looked up from pressing the send button to see Dan joining him, a glass of lager already in his hand. 'Hi,' they said simultaneously and with mutual awkwardness.

Jason observed the man beside him carefully while he too studied the menu and then went to the bar to order for both of them.

'It's good of you to make the time,' acknowledged Dan. 'I'm genuinely grateful because I want this to work for all of us.'

'I suspect that will rest with Kat rather than either of us.'

Dan did not answer that and there was a short, awkward pause while both searched for words which might take the conversation forward but which would not compromise their positions.

'Jake seems to be coping well but, as you know, Leah is very upset,' observed Dan. 'I can't say I blame her. Divorce must be hell for kids.'

'It was not what I would have chosen for them but I had no say in the matter. Kat just upped and went without any warning. I hope you're luckier.'

Dan refused to be provoked. 'That's for Katie and I to work out. Leah is your concern as well.'

As well? The careless phrase, harmlessly meant, startled Jason. Leah's well-being was surely primarily the concern of himself and Kat. Dan was the *as well*. His mind forced him to face the reality his feelings denied. Dan and Kat would have daily responsibility for Leah's tears and tantrums and he could advise only from afar; it was he not Dan who was the nearly dad.

'I have already told Kat that it would be easier to deal with Leah if my pattern of access was regular and reliable. That is in her hands, not mine. I also told her I had a mind to invoke the law.'

Dan spread some pâté on a piece of brown toast, concentrating closely on the simple task. Jason waited.

'I asked you to meet me because I want us to get on with each other, even if superficially, even if only for the sake of the children, but you can't reasonably expect me to side with you against Katie.'

'No, but more importantly I don't expect you to side with Kat against the children. They need me and every time she refuses contact she deprives them as well as me.'

'I don't think you should see it like that. She loves the children dearly and tries to do what is best for them. It isn't easy for her.'

Jason lowered the glass he had been raising to his lips and stared at Dan in disbelief. 'Not easy for *her*, did you say?'

'I meant not easy for either of you. Look, I'm

347

not after a quarrel. I just want to talk about Leah, about what we can do – all three of us.'

'Kat can let the children see me regularly and also let them visit my mother at least once a year, she can stop lying and cheating. You can stand up for the kids when she is pushing them around the board of her rotten game. As for me, what am I supposed to do that I will actually be allowed to do?'

Dan gave up and a desultory conversation followed before he looked at his watch and said he must hurry back to work. They argued half-heartedly over who should pay with each insisting he had some unspecified obligation to do so. Jason won and, reaching inside his jacket for his wallet, turned towards the bar. When he next looked round Dan had gone.

He had, he acknowledged to himself, acted like a child while Dan had made a genuine effort to calm the situation, to open up lines of communication for the future, to make some progress with Leah's difficulties but he was too full of resentment to feel any shame. *As well*. The words still rankled. He supposed he would have to apologise and learn to talk to Dan for his children's sake but for the moment he preferred to be angry, knowing that Carol would berate him for a fool. Had he not come to Newcastle for the specific purpose of helping Leah? Yet he had repelled the first person to offer a rational discussion as to how to do just that.

'Men!' Carol would say in despair. Jason allowed himself a small smile at the thought but wished she were with him now.

When he collected Leah from school there was no sign of Kat but his daughter, red-eyed and mutinous, was escorted to the gates by an exasperated teacher. Kat's fear that she might be excluded was not without foundation, he thought.

'That's Leah Kirk,' a girl informed her mother. 'She's so naughty that she has to sit outside the class. She threw her lunch-box at Miss Johnson.'

The mother, aware that her daughter had made no attempt to lower her voice, threw an embarrassed look in Jason's direction as she saw Leah join him. 'Shh!' she warned, her finger on her lip.

'Did you throw your lunch-box at Mummy?'

'No,' whined Leah miserably.

'Tell the truth.' He pulled the seat-belt round her and waited for her to fasten it, noticing the trembling fingers, already regretting the severity of his tone.

'She's horrible.'

'You don't mean that, do you?'

Leah began to weep, her small frame shuddering. Jason did not start the car but joined his daughter on the back seat, holding her for comfort, rocking her as he had done five years ago, ignoring the curious glances of parents and children as they passed by.

'Mummy isn't really horrible, is she? It's everything else which is horrible. You don't want her to marry Dan and you don't want me to marry Carol but you can't change any of that by being so badly behaved. Leah, we both love you.'

'I want you to love each other like you used to.'

He could not remember loving Kat. He could

remember numerous incidents, small gestures, whispered endearments that proved he had once loved his ex-wife but he could not re-create the feeling, the flood of warmth, the flutters in his stomach, the onset of desire when he thought of Kat. He could hardly explain that to Leah as she looked up at him, still hopeful that somehow she would wake up one morning in her old home in Somerset and find Mummy and Daddy still there.

Surely Kat must be right when she said that Leah could have little active memory of family togetherness. What she yearned for now must owe more to imagination than to memory but that also was something he could not explain. Helpless, he wished he had been prepared to join forces with Dan, had accepted the olive branch held out to him in the country pub.

Meanwhile he must soothe Leah into a state of sufficient calmness to permit reasoning. He saw that they were now alone, that the other cars, parents and children had disappeared and then that they were not quite alone because Kat was coming through the school gates. She hesitated and he nodded, unfastening Leah's seat-belt and pulling her into the centre of the seat. Kat got in on the other side and, for the first time since she had been plucked from home and father, Leah found herself sandwiched between two consoling parents.

It was an approach they continued throughout the rest of the afternoon and evening and Leah's recovering spirits were first made manifest in a renewal of interest in what was going on about her, then in her participation in family activity and finally in excited volubility. The following day her behaviour was normal but Jason dreaded Sunday and the moment when he must once again leave. Dan joined them for Sunday lunch and he and Jason assumed a cordiality which he hoped might reassure Leah even if it failed to deceive Jake.

Jake appeared content with a certain amount of benign neglect, understanding the need to restore Leah to stability. Consequently he spent a great deal of the time with Dan and Jason found himself grateful rather than resentful.

'Thanks for looking after Jake,' he said as he made his farewells in the evening and was surprised to find he meant it. Both children waved him off but as he glanced back in his rear window he saw Leah in the throes of a tantrum. He was obscurely comforted when Dan began to propel her gently into the house.

He glanced at the car clock and groaned. He had left more than an hour after the time he had appointed and would now be back in Somerset in the early hours of Monday morning. He dialled his home number and told Carol not to wait up.

He broke his journey at a service station, fighting the need for sleep, eating a snack he did not want, walking up and down in the cold night air, pulled back to Newcastle when he thought of Jake and Leah and forward to Somerset when he thought of Carol, until he was ready to commence the second half of his journey. It was in the final stages of the drive, when he had left the motorway and was heading into rural Somerset that he knew he must stop for at least a short nap. He steered the car off the road and parked in front of a gate which led to a field.

In his dreams Leah was banging on her door. Puzzled, he wondered why she did not simply open it. Was she locked in? The noise grew louder and Jason found himself awake and staring into the impatient eyes of a herdsman.

'Why be ee 'ere?' demanded the man. 'Don't ee know cows want milking? You be blocking the gate.'

Jason looked at the clock and a rush of alarm swept through him. His short nap had become a profound sleep and he now had barely enough time to complete his journey, shower and shave and drive to school. As he pulled himself upright in his seat he made a placatory gesture to the angry cowhand and turned the key in the ignition.

A few yards further on he stopped the car and wound down the window for fresh air. Half drugged with sleep, feeling unwashed and stale, he tried to recover himself sufficiently to drive but before he could again move off the car was surrounded by lowing cattle plodding slowly towards the milking parlour, wherever it might be. He cursed freely, recognising yet another delay.

His eyes fell on his telephone and he saw that the screen proclaimed three missed calls. Carol must have woken and realised he was not at home. She was probably even now fretting with anxiety, building pictures in her mind of car crashes, ambulances and hospitals. He rang and was flattered by her tearful relief.

At home she cooked him breakfast while he showered and got ready for school, wondering how he was to face the day in a state of such fatigue, wondering if the head might consider him unreliable with his requests for leave on a Friday and a late appearance on Monday morning.

'I must go,' he told Carol. 'As it is it will be a photo finish with the start of the first class.'

He had said nothing about Newcastle nor had she asked, sensing that the subject might cause him distress. They would talk after school, he thought, but when he put the car away that evening he wanted neither talk nor a meal, only sleep – long, deep, uninterrupted sleep.

He woke at three, brought to consciousness by both thirst and a need to visit the bathroom. In the kitchen Objubjub wound himself between Jason's legs, delighted at the prospect of a feast at so unexpected an hour. Jason obliged, rubbing his hand along the creature's back, listening to the throbbing purr of contentment.

He undid the back door, wanting to stand briefly outside, to gulp some fresh air, to listen to a still world. It was a clear night, the moon hanging low in a D-shaped crescent. A new moon, he realised, remembering the old adage: C for chaperone, D for debutante. Jason identified the Plough amidst the hard, bright stars.

The sounds of the night floated on the still air: the cry of a vixen, the hoot of a distant owl, the barking of a dog. Something crossed the back lawn – silently, slyly – and Jason recognised the outline of a fox.

Leah would be afraid out here, in the dark, with the sounds and the vague shapes. Perhaps even Jake would be uneasy. Jason returned indoors, saddened. His children's lives were full of dark, threatening shapes which only the adults perceived as harmless. Somehow he must persuade them that the night would end.

19

Leah and Jake sat on either side of Eileen, watching with curiosity rather than enthusiasm, as the wedding, which had taken place two hours ago in the local register office, between Jason Andrew Kirk and Carol Fenella Marsh was blessed by the Church. Jason would have been content with the civil ceremony alone but Carol had insisted on a solemnisation and the village church, decked with red and yellow flowers, was full of family and friends.

Leah had sulked a little when Carol had decided not to have bridesmaids. Her tantrums had diminished over recent months but there was some subtle change to her personality which Jason, on the increasingly rare occasions when he saw her, found difficult to pinpoint. Outwardly happy, seemingly easily delighted, talkative, active, she exhibited all the characteristics of the Leah he had once known but he sensed rather than saw that each was somehow blunted, as if a full, throaty roar of laughter in an adult had an edge of nervous giggle. He felt his daughter was somehow looking at a world which retained its vivid shapes and colours but behind the very faintest of mists.

Jake seemed well enough and had shown no particular emotion when Kat had married Dan six weeks earlier. He had stood self-consciously amidst the younger pageboys and bridesmaids at the Service of Blessing, resentful of the kilt he was obliged to wear. Afterwards he waited on the edge of the crowd outside the church, his black, shiny shoes scuffling the autumn leaves, downcast not because his mother was marrying but because he felt a fool. He walked slowly when called for photographs, head down, shoulders hunched.

'It's a bit much for a twelve-year-old,' muttered Alex. 'I don't blame him.'

Meanwhile Leah rejoiced in her pretty blue dress with the old-fashioned smocking and Kat posed in a white gown, long veil and twenty-foot train. Sheila maintained a discreet silence while Jason permitted himself a bitter smile. Kat and purity had long since ceased to be synonymous in his mind.

Kat was not present at his wedding, causing Jason to wonder whether he should be relieved by the absence of a living reminder of past failure or worried over the impression of disapproval or indifference which her decision might imply to the children. She and Dan had timed their wedding so that the honeymoon would coincide with half-term and had made a half-hearted attempt to send Jake and Leah to stay with Alex and Sheila instead of Jason. Kat's parents had resisted with vigour and Jason took them instead to spend the break with Eileen in Dorset.

Jason was now comforted by the presence of Alex and Sheila, who had volunteered to take the children back to Newcastle after the ceremony, but alarmed when he thought he detected in Leah a reluctance to go. The impression of her unwillingness was so hazy that he could not be sure that it existed outside his imagination but it was still enough to disturb his peace of mind on his honeymoon, which took place in Tangier.

When he bought a fez for Jake, it was Leah's face he could see beneath it. When he bargained with the owner of a large tented emporium in the Berber market for a pouffe of the kind Eileen had indicated she would like, it was not his mother's feet but the small form of his daughter he could see resting on it. When he bought her a child's handbag with a motif of fig trees on its side he found himself visualising her reception of it as dutifully grateful rather than gleefully curious.

They had agreed that Carol should sell her flat and move into his house after the wedding and Jason was sure that Leah would resent the change. By contrast Kat and Dan were selling their homes to buy one much bigger. Everything in his children's world seemed to be shifting about and he could hardly believe how wrong had been his vision of a secure, stable upbringing for them as the children of a permanent, healthy marriage between himself and Kat. Was it really only four years since he had believed that vision to be reality, believed that only a harsh blow of fate such as grave illness or bereavement could deny its realisation, its continuation?

Jake greeted life with a shrug, Jason realised sadly. Certainly he was not actively unhappy, as capable of sudden joy and happy expectation as any other child, high-achieving at school, presenting no problems at home, but he no longer appeared to react to the events which the adults in his life inflicted on him. The child of eight who had protested that he did not want to be taken away from his father, from home, from all he had taken for granted in his short life, had grown into a boy of twelve who gave the impression that he was no longer capable of surprise or active resistance.

Jake was waiting, thought Jason, even if he was too young to realise that was what he was doing. But for what did he wait? Until he should be old enough to choose between his parents with their new spouses and living arrangements? Or until he could leave altogether and forge his own, independent, existence? Or did he wait merely for all the upheaval to end, for the world to settle once more into an orderly and predictable pattern, for the war between his parents to dissolve in truce?

He prayed urgently to an unspecified Deity that Leah should not learn to wait, that she should live in the present for the present even if she found it alarming. A child, he knew, should react spontaneously for better or for worse not refrigerate feelings for later retrieval.

'It's a very biblical scene.' Carol's voice

interrupted his unwelcome thoughts.

'What? Sorry, I was miles away.'

'In Newcastle, I suspect, but I'm in Tangier. I was saying the scenes remind me of the pictures in my Bible when I was a child. People in long robes, camels and rows of goods hanging in front of tents.'

'Yes. Timeless in some ways, rapidly changing in others. Do you suppose they ripped off the tourists quite so shamefully in biblical days?'

'Probably,' laughed Carol. 'The New Testament is full of warnings about usury. Now what about locating some genuine native recipes?'

'I doubt if there will be any out here. We will find some in Tangier itself.'

'I meant talk to the people and ask them.'

'Speakee Arabic?'

'Speakee not bad French. Let's try.'

Carol succeeded in fractured English with a young lad of Jake's age who drove a hard bargain and then raced off to find his elder sister who laboriously explained, through the passable translation of her younger sibling, how to cook lamb. Carol thanked her, handed over the money to the boy and pulled a face at Jason.

'Not much different from anything I could have worked out for myself. I think I'll stick to more conventional souvenirs.'

Jason smiled back. He was thinking of the beach but it had rained ever since their arrival and had been too cold for swimming.

'Have you ever ridden a camel?' asked Carol suddenly.

'No, but I've a feeling I'm about to.'

'Yes. Over there.'

Jason followed and left the bargaining for the price of a ride to her. She was, he had discovered on the first day of their arrival, a much less embarrassed and far more ruthless haggler than he would ever be. As the beast rose bumpily to its feet he clutched its hump and mentally calculated the distance between himself and the ground without enthusiasm. He thought of Lawrence of Arabia.

'You don't look very happy,' teased Carol. 'I think you prefer terra firma.'

'I do and the more firmer the less terror.'

Carol smiled at the time-honoured joke, reaching for his hand. For a while the animals plodded side by side while their human cargo held hands across the space between them and looked dreamily about them at the scrubby desert. Jason wished he could relax as thoroughly as the occasion warranted but his children looked back at him from the sand, reproaching him for his own happiness, as they so often seemed to do from the darkness when he made love to Carol.

On his return to the hotel he rang Kat.

'Is Leah all right?'

'Yes, of course. Why?'

'Nothing. Just some sort of premonition. Can I speak to her?' He chatted with both children, certain that Kat would think him a fool and that he should not have betrayed his groundless fears.

Next day they rose at dawn and took a boat for Gibraltar, returning too late for dinner in the hotel, eating instead at a small restaurant, strolling back in a leisurely fashion. The receptionist handed them their key and a message to ring Kat.

'It's midnight there,' said Carol but Jason was already dialling.

'Jason?' Kat's voice was strained. 'You and your premonitions. I had to get Jake to hospital...'

'What? Kat? Hello? Hello? Kat, are you there?'

'Jason?' Kat's voice was a bellow. 'Can you hear me? Jason?'

'Yes, I can. Can you hear me?'

'I said can you hear me? Jason? Hello?'

'Hello, dammit.'

'Oh, that's better. This line doesn't seem wonderful. I was saying there is absolutely nothing to worry about. Are you hearing me?'

'Yes,' shouted Jason. 'What's happened?'

The line went dead. Immediately he rang Kat's number and was amazed to hear the answering machine. Carol was watching him anxiously.

'Jake's in hospital but I don't know why,' he explained. 'There was something wrong with the line and now all I'm getting is the answering machine. I think we should get back home.'

'Tomorrow is Christmas Day. You won't get a flight.'

'My God, I'd forgotten! I wonder what's wrong.'

'Did it sound serious?'

'Kat wouldn't ring me for trivia and she sounded upset. I'll try again later.'

Three more attempts proved fruitless and Jason was persuaded to give up till the morning.

'Get some sleep,' advised Carol. 'The morning will come quicker.'

It was what his mother used to tell him when he

was too excited to sleep on Christmas Eve. He smiled bitterly at the reflection, knowing that Kat had ensured that sleep would elude him for the rest of the night.

'Merry Christmas,' mumbled Carol when he tried ringing Kat at six.

'No luck?' she enquired when he slammed down the receiver after a third failed attempt at seven.

'Perhaps they are not there,' she suggested as room service brought in breakfast.

Christmas Day was a miserable affair with Jason unable to contact Kat and frustrated in his attempts to secure a flight the following day. He tried telephoning Alex and Sheila but they also were not answering.

'Try the hospital,' suggested Carol. 'It will probably be called Newcastle City General or something like that. If Kat is there that will be why you can't reach her.'

'She can hardly be keeping Leah and Dan there all the time,' objected Jason. He did, however, follow her advice and was eventually put through only to be told that there was no record of any Jacob Kirk.

'If he's gone home already, it can't be serious and you said that Kat told you there was nothing to worry about.'

'If he had gone home I wouldn't worry but they say he was never in there. It must be some other hospital.' His mouth twisted regretfully. 'I'm sorry, this isn't much of a honeymoon.'

'No, and I am not a saint.' Carol's resentment broke out suddenly, taking him by surprise. 'This is, as you have just said, our *honeymoon*, not a

361

casual day trip in the middle of half-term. I know what you've been through with Kat and the kids but I am not going to put up with it dominating our married life. We are not cutting short this break unless you receive confirmation that there is something seriously wrong with Jake.'

Jason blinked, then moved towards her but she stepped back at once, gesturing to him to come no closer.

'Do you realise that I waited three years for you to ask me to marry you?'

'I needed a divorce and, anyway, I wasn't ready. I'm sorry.'

'You are still not ready. It's time you grew up.'

Three days later they arrived at Kat's home in Newcastle. It was their first visit to the new house and Carol commented approvingly as they walked up a short drive, 'They seem to have done pretty well for themselves.'

Jason was concerned less with Kat's material prosperity than with the obvious absence of occupation. The day was rainy and overcast but no lights shone from any of the windows and, when he looked through the letterbox, he could see envelopes scattered over the mat.

'They are obviously away which means Jake must have been well enough to travel,' pointed out Carol quietly. 'And as you haven't got through to her parents I think we can assume they have all gone to Dan's parents for a big family get-to-know-each-other Christmas.'

Jason knew she was right, that she was offering a logical explanation, that, despite her protest he had cut his honeymoon short for nothing. As his mind re-ran the events of Christmas Eve he realised he had once more been duped. Kat had been there at midnight and there could have been no question of travelling at such an hour so she would have heard his desperate ringing and had deliberately ignored it, tormenting his mind with fears for his son, wrecking his honeymoon, bringing it to a premature end. Even by Kat's standards it was horribly vengeful, a manifestation not of simple resentment but of active spite, of a desire to wound through mental anguish.

Carol was watching him anxiously and he smiled at her.

'You have married a serious fool. I'm sorry we can't go back to our Arabian nights but Somerset will have to do. As you say, Jake must be well enough to travel so we will have to wait till they return to find out what happened. I haven't got a number for Dan's parents if that's where they are and both Kat's and Jake's mobiles appear to be switched off.'

'It's an ill wind which blows nobody any good, as they say. Let's ring up your mother and invite her for New Year.'

'I suppose Objubjub will be pleased to see us as well. Come on, let's go.'

The journey home was slow and troubled with long tailbacks from two separate accidents, fog and driving rain. Jason was relieved that Carol seemed in good spirits, seemingly not resenting the curtailing of their honeymoon and the fruitless drive to Newcastle. He wondered how Kat might have reacted to such events and thought that she too might once have been sanguine, concerned only for him, willing to endure disappointments and reverses for the sake of his peace of mind. Now she mounted assault after assault on his mental well-being, apparently deriving satisfaction from it.

He tried to imagine Carol turning into a character of fiendish cruelty but reassuringly failed and he could only hope that there was no icy disillusionment awaiting him in the shades of the future. It seemed impossible but so it had once seemed also with Kat.

When the M1 became the M6 Carol took over the driving and he drifted into sleep, occasionally waking briefly to see rain pouring down the windows of the car and the tail lights of other cars in the darkness. At Bristol he again took the wheel while Carol dozed and he thought, with active hatred, of Kat. It was not in his nature to wish ill on anyone but now he found himself fantasising that Kat was dead and the children had come home to live with him and Carol.

He repelled the thought, asking himself angrily if he really wanted Jake and Leah motherless, but the reply his mocking mind sent back was not the absolute denial he had expected, the fantasy returning with its dark comfort. It was not one he could share with Carol and his tortured spirit accused Kat of driving a wedge between them almost before their marriage had begun. He groaned, causing a small stir from his wife but she did not wake.

They arrived home in the early hours of the following morning. The house was cold and seemed empty despite the swift appearance of a purring Objubjub. Carol switched on lights and went upstairs to turn on the electric blanket while Jason activated the central heating and began unpacking the boot of the car. Carol had purchased milk, bread and cheese from a service station when he had stopped to fill the petrol tank and Jason realised he was hungry, that neither of them had eaten since lunch-time. He imagined the neighbours being woken by the sounds of their return to wonder what might have gone wrong.

He glanced at the post which Carol had dropped in a disorderly heap on the kitchen table, recognising a communication from the Child Support Agency and another from the Inland Revenue. He postponed opening either until he had slept for what remained of the night but he did look briefly at the writing on numerous envelopes which contained different sizes of Christmas card, seeing nothing to inspire him to an early inspection of the contents. He took a similar view of their luggage and they fell into bed with most of it not merely unpacked but unopened. In Jason's dreams a dismissive, shrugging Kat told him that she simply could not understand what all the fuss was about. As he woke and the image of Kat dissolved, he knew the reality would not be much different.

'But I told you there was absolutely nothing to worry about and you said you had heard me.' Kat's voice was weary and incredulous when she answered the telephone three days before the beginning of term.

'But you said Jake was in hospital.'

'I most certainly did not. I said I had been

obliged to take him to the hospital. He fell over and cut himself sufficiently badly to need stitches and an X-ray. He has sprained his wrist, not fractured it, and the cut is healing well. I just can't see why you had to come tearing back from Tangier. It was completely over the top.'

'Because you didn't tell me any of that and you weren't answering the phone.'

'I wasn't here to answer it. We left immediately after your call was cut off.'

'At midnight?'

'Yes, at midnight. At a quarter past midnight to be exact. We were going to leave that morning but all the hospital stuff took hours and then when he came home Jake went into a deep sleep and Dan wouldn't have him woken. Of course we thought about going on Christmas Day itself but decided to drive overnight instead. Not that any of this is your business.'

'You must have known I would phone back. You need have waited only a few seconds.'

'Why? I already had one foot out of the door when you rang and Dan and the children were waiting in the car while I talked to you. I repeat that I had already told you there was nothing to worry about and I had made sure you had heard. I don't see that I could have done much more.'

'I tried your mobiles. They were switched off.'

'You make it sound like a crime against the state. I left mine behind by accident and Dan had confiscated Jake's.'

'What? He has no right to do that.'

'Of course he does. Jake was running up inordinate bills and Dan decided to teach him a lesson.'

'So I couldn't speak to my own son over Christmas. You didn't even tell me you were going away or give me a number to call.'

'Jason, I can do without all this nonsense. You had better ring back when you are in a more reasonable frame of mind.'

'I want to speak to Jake and Leah.'

'Of course, but it isn't possible now. Dan has taken them out to get some things for school. It's term in a few days.'

'*Dan* wouldn't have him woken, *Dan* has confiscated his phone, *Dan* has taken them out to buy gear for school,' Jason told Carol morosely when the call had come to a not particularly cordial end.

'I'm sorry that bit's so hard.' Carol pulled him down onto the sofa to sit beside her. 'What was the matter with Jake?'

'He fell and sprained his wrist and cut himself. You know, I just don't believe we ever were cut off. There was nothing other than Kat's bellowing to indicate anything wrong with the line and I didn't have any difficulty with any of the other calls we made.'

Carol did not respond and Jason, seeing himself through her eyes, knew she thought his reasoning paranoid. Only time and experience of Kat's manipulative antics were likely to give her a different perspective and he did not seek to insist on the likelihood of what he had just said. Instead he suggested they make the most of the last days of their break by planning some walking and soon their heads were lightly touching over Ordnance Survey maps.

He was in the middle of a field trying to take a photograph of Carol with the new camera he had purchased for their honeymoon when he heard the single bleep which told him he had a text message. He reached into the pocket of his anorak for his phone, holding the camera and his right-hand glove in his other hand.

'Hi dad please ring.'

His son answered the call immediately.

'I'm only allowed two calls a day unless it's an emergency,' he explained.

Jason grinned at the disgust in his son's voice. 'Don't text messages count as calls?'

'Not so long as they are short and to members of the family.'

'Dan's rules?'

'Yes, but Mum agrees. I wasn't even allowed to call you at Christmas.'

'Couldn't you have used a real phone? Mum had the number of my hotel.'

'Dad, you mean a land-line. Mobile phones *are* real phones, as Dan keeps reminding me. He says it's time I realised that the bills are real too. Anyway I did try to phone but you were always engaged and Mum said we had tried long enough.'

'I'm sorry. I was trying to phone Mum but I thought she was at home. What were Dan's parents like?'

'All right.'

Jason's mouth tightened as he absorbed the lack of enthusiasm in his son's voice but he did not enquire further. He had learned by now that if his son had anything he wished to confide he would impart the information in his own time.

'How's Leah?'

'All right.' This time there was an edge to Jake's voice which alarmed him.

'You sound upset.'

'No. She's just spoiled but who cares?'

You do, thought Jason, but he kept his tone casual. 'So who spoils her? Dan?'

'A bit but Stepgran thinks the sun shines out of her–'

'Jake!'

'OK, OK.'

Jason grinned. 'Does Stepgran have any other grandchildren?'

'Thousands. Well, six. They were all there. Dan has a sister who married an Irish Catholic.'

This time Jason laughed aloud but his son did not respond. He put the next question as neutrally as he could.

'Any other little girls?'

'You must be joking. They're all boys.'

Jason longed to be with Jake, to put an arm round his shoulder, to take him to a football match, to walk with him by the sea, to make him feel special, loved, the centre of someone's universe, not one of seven who competed unequally with a small girl. Eileen had always maintained that he had married not only Kat but her family too and now it seemed that Jake had acquired not only a stepfather but an entire stepfamily as well, with all its emotional baggage.

He tried to lighten the conversation, to enquire about presents and meals and fun, about the impending return to school, the lessons and the teachers. He discussed the latest Harry Potter, asked which films Jake had seen, told him he had learned a new piece of magic and would show him the trick next time, gossiped about pop groups, television and some of Jake's old friends of whom he had news. His son's monosyllabic replies were, he knew, verbal yawns. Jason would have known how to handle the mood better if he had detected any likelihood of his son suddenly breaking out in bitter protest but the listlessness was a prelude to nothing. There was no sudden outpouring of complaint, no hint of tears, of resentment, of fear.

By the time the call was finished he had completed his slow traverse of the field to find Carol sitting on a stile.

'Is everything all right?' Carol's tone suggested concern, perhaps curiosity, but beneath it Jason thought he detected an uncharacteristic note of impatience. *For goodness' sake, you've already wrecked our honeymoon. Can't you manage even a country walk without agonising about your children?*

He could not have blamed her if she had said those words; he was certain she thought them. *You have another marriage to work at now. I'm Carol. Remember me?*

'Yes, it all seems fine.'

'You don't sound very convinced and why are you looking at me like that?'

'Like what?'

'As if I have just frightened you in some way.'

Jason attempted a smile which he knew probably looked more like a grimace. He opted for truth. 'I was wondering for how long you will put up with me, or at any rate with my problems.'

'Let's just relax and enjoy this walk.' She sprang down from the stile and began to walk ahead of him, fast, purposefully, without any sign of the relaxation she had just urged.

Jason followed, climbing the stile and running to catch her up, thoughts of his children pushed resolutely aside.

'We can go to Newcastle next weekend,' said Carol as he drew alongside and he knew it was an apology, that she was trying to make up the quarrel before it even began. He looked at her gratefully, realising that was not what she wanted; that she would prefer him to look at her with hungry not humble eyes.

When a second loud ping announced another text message she took the phone from his pocket and switched it off.

'After the walk.' Her tone allowed no argument and his reason told him she was right. Jake could not expect instant availability on every occasion but, recalling the joyless conversation which he had just had with his son, Jason was unable to banish the desolate little ghost which flitted at the back of his mind.

It must have haunted Carol too for half a mile further on she said grudgingly, 'You had better see what it says.'

'No. It can wait. Are we going through that wood or round it?'

'Through it. It's about to rain and we'll get less wet. Anyway, I need to go the loo and there will be more cover.' *And you can read your wretched text message and phone your son while I am thus occupied.*

371

Jason's imagination supplied the words. He was tempted to leave the instrument off to repudiate the obsession she attributed to him and then wished he had actually done so.

'I hate dan, love leah.'

He rang at once and Jake answered. 'Don't worry, Dad. Dan just told her off, that's all.'

'Jason?' Kat's voice abruptly superseded his son's. 'You know I don't like the children using mobiles. It's dangerous to their brains. You have our number so please use it and for heaven's sake, stop giving in to every tantrum. I have quite enough trouble with Leah as it is.'

'I know. Sorry. She just sent me a miserable message and–'

'If this goes on, I shall put an end to Jake's having a mobile at all. You are becoming a slave to their every whim.'

'Kat. Please. If I saw them regularly I would be a much better judge of what is going on and would react less anxiously.'

Kat terminated the call just as Jason saw Carol emerging from the bushes. She looked at him, then at the phone.

'I don't want to know. Tell me later.'

'There's nothing to tell.'

'Good. Let's get walking.'

Jason fell in beside her but the mood they had shared when they had set out was gone and he was unsurprised when Carol eventually suggested cutting the outing short. He proposed they dine out but she said she was not in the least tired and would not mind cooking. When the meal was over they worked on preparation for the first lessons of the imminent term, retiring to bed at different times, politely volunteering for the remaining chores of emptying the dishwasher, feeding Objubjub, locking the doors, while the air was heavy with anger, hurt and disappointment.

He would go to Newcastle alone next weekend, thought Jason. Carol could stay in Somerset and see her friends. Ten days ago they had been on their honeymoon and already he was trying to ensure their separate lives. Leah, he reflected, was only seven and the years of strain yawned ahead of him, dark and cavernous, swallowing his children and his marriage to Carol.

20

Jason watched the little group moving towards him, the small girl holding the man's hand, looking up at him as she talked eagerly. They drew nearer and Jason first heard the sound of her animated chatter and then began to discern individual words. The boy did not seem part of the conversation; he moved with hunched shoulders, affecting a lack of interest, looking at the ground rather than at either of his companions. He was the first of the three to notice Jason.

'Hi, Dad!' At once he began to run towards his father. Leah broke away from Dan's hand and followed suit, her conversation forgotten. Jason swung her up into his arms briefly before replacing her on the ground with relief, noting her increased heaviness. Jake gave him a mock punch.

Their stepfather joined them. 'Katie says can you keep them till seven instead of six? We may not be back till then.'

Jason nodded agreement, made a perfunctory enquiry as to Kat's well-being and a rather more genuine one about Alex and Sheila. Dan said they were all well and asked after Carol and Eileen. Jason said they too were well. The two men stood regarding each other with nothing to say and no wish to prolong the courtesies, but neither wished to be the first to terminate the exchange. In the end it was Jake who did so by sounding the horn loudly enough to make Jason start and Dan frown with irritation.

'He's not allowed to play with the horn,' announced Leah smugly. 'Dan says it's rude and it's called noise pollution.'

Jason glanced towards Dan who was getting into his Mondeo at the other end of the car park. 'He's quite right.'

He raised his hand in a wave when Dan drove past. Leah shouted goodbye through the open window. As the vehicle passed him Jason could see Leah's scooter in the back and a red sweater he recognised as belonging to his son.

'Yelling is pretty good noise pollution too,' Jake observed to his sister and Jason recognised amusement rather than resentment in his tone. His recently acquired teenage status gave him an aloof superiority: he would no longer condescend to argue with a seven-year-old.

'The baby will yell,' retorted Leah, 'and there will be nothing you can do about it. When babies cry you have to pick them up and cuddle them. Mummy says. You are not allowed to be cross or the RSPCA will come and take you to court.'

'The NSPCC, dumbo.'

'Do you want a brother or a sister?' intervened Jason hastily.

'It won't be either,' pointed out Jake. 'It will be a *half*-sister.'

'So Mum knows it's a girl?'

'Mummy saw a photo of it. It's called a scan.' Leah put in before Jake could answer. 'I don't like its name. I think it's stupid.'

Jason raised his eyebrows at Jake. 'Tabitha,' he muttered. 'I hate it too. It's what Gavin called his cat.'

'Tabitha Carter,' Leah explained. 'Not Tabitha Kirk because she belongs to Mummy and Dan.'

A sudden recollection of Harry Jackson explaining to a confused Ed Deacon the various relationships of his parents and siblings came into Jason's mind. By the time he recalled himself to the present the children were no longer talking about Tabitha.

Relieved, he concentrated on edging the car out on to the main road. He knew he was simply postponing what he had come to Newcastle to do but there was something in Jake's attitude, some formless misery, which made him turn from his task and seek refuge in delay.

Leah supplied an unexpected impetus about ten minutes later when he and Jake were talking about Objubjub and an impending visit to Eileen to spend a fortnight in Dorset over the Easter holiday.

'Will you and Carol have a baby?'

Jason half expected an explosive rebuke from Jake but none came and he realised that his son was waiting to hear the answer too but that, where Leah was merely curious and possibly hopeful, her brother was tense, unwilling to hear the answer he suspected would come.

Jason hesitated and Jake seemed to shrink with disappointment. 'Yes, babies come with marriage.'

'Not always,' protested Leah happily.

'No, but usually.'

'When?' Jake breathed the question and Leah suddenly became still, her voluble exclamation checked, uncertainty replacing excitement as she sensed a tension she could not identify.

'About the same time as Tabitha, perhaps a bit later.'

'Will it be a boy or a girl?' demanded Leah.

'We don't know. We are doing it the old-fashioned way and finding out when it arrives.'

'Why?'

'Because that's how Carol wants it. I don't really mind when we know or what it is so long as it is fit and healthy.'

Leah embarked on a long series of questions. What would they call the baby? If Tabitha was her half-sister and Daddy's baby was also a half-something then what was the relation between Tabitha and the new baby? Would it be christened in a long white gown as she and Jake had been? Tabitha had a granny who wasn't their granny, would the new baby have a special granny too?

Jason answered patiently, admiring the ingenuity of some of the enquiries, smiling at others, watching Jake out of the corner of his eye as he drove. He had not expected his son to be enthusiastic about another upheaval, another readjustment of a world already made chaotic but the quiet rigidity was beginning to disturb him as Leah prattled heedlessly and Jake went on looking out of the side window, withdrawn but not oblivious.

He still had not spoken when, deep in the Northumbrian countryside, Jason at last parked the car and pointed to the place where he proposed to position the tent. It was Leah's latest craze; a bright yellow tent, assembled and erected by an obliging adult, a small stove, melamine crockery, plastic glasses and a large picnic. Jake climbed out and began extracting items from the boot while his sister ran wildly amid the moorland growth, attempting cartwheels unsuccessfully, calling attention to her efforts, speculating on the contents of the picnic.

Jason moved round to the boot to help Jake but, as if sensing that some question was about to be asked, some confidence sought, some reassurance attempted, the boy made purposefully for the campsite, lugging equipment and the carrier of cool drinks. Jason extracted some of the heavier items from the car and followed his example.

It was not till they had eaten and gathered up the used plates and Leah had wandered over to explore a felled tree which she thought made an interesting low-level climbing opportunity that Jason tackled his son.

'You don't seem too happy about the baby.'

Jake shrugged but his father was not deflected. 'What's the problem? Surely you don't think

Leah and you will somehow be squeezed out because there's another child on the way? Mum and I might have had another if we had stayed together. Indeed, I am sure we would have produced a brother or sister for you before now.'

'That would have been different. We'd have all been the same.'

Jason, understanding his son's meaning, tried to find the right words, words which might soothe or reassure even if they could not magic away the misery, but Jake spoke first.

'If it was you and Mum having a baby, we would all be the same family. It would be a proper brother or sister and you and Mum would be all our parents not like it is now. Tabitha belongs to Mum and Dan and whatever you call it will belong to you and Carol but Leah and I only have half a mum and dad in each place.'

Jake paused for breath and moved sharply away from the comfort of Jason's arm round his shoulder. He struggled on, trying to find a way of conveying the unhappy confusion of his mind. 'I want it like it was when we were all Kirks. I don't like *now*. I was happy *then*.'

Jason hesitated and Jake, drawing up his knees, rested his head on them so that Jason could not see his tears. 'I don't want to be a half-anything. I want Mum and Dad like Sheena and Paul and Gavin and ... and...'

Jake's voice dissolved. From somewhere in the distance came a shout from Leah and a loud splash. Jason jumped up in alarm and guilt and sped towards the tree trunk on which she had been playing when he had last seen her. He slowed down as giggles reached him followed by squeals of delight. When at last he could see what was on the other side of the tree he found his daughter trying to entice a Yorkshire terrier into a small stream. From somewhere in the distance an unseen person whistled hopefully and commandingly. The little dog hesitated, looked regretfully at Leah and then ran in the direction of the sound. Leah pulled a face of disappointment.

'You must be where I can see you,' Jason told her. 'Stay on the camp side of the tree.'

Leah didn't argue and Jason spent a few moments watching her run along the trunk and then, more ambitiously, try to balance on a sturdy but not especially wide branch. By the time he was walking back towards his son, Leah was flat on her stomach endeavouring to wriggle under a different branch which was no more than eight inches from the ground.

There was no sign of Jake. At first Jason felt no very great anxiety on his son's account. Saddened but not fearful he looked about him, calling, coaxing, unease stirring only faintly when he could not see him. At thirteen Jake was old enough to retire from the scene to recover his composure without being harassed and after a while Jason decided merely to wait until his son should return of his own accord.

He glanced back at Leah but she was still happily occupied with the challenges presented by the fallen tree. She waved but did not appear to require his attention and he did not join her in case the sounds of his engaging in cheerful play might augment Jake's sense of isolation. A

379

memory of his own far-off schooldays drifted into his mind and he recalled reading *The Wind in the Willows* and how Toad had listened to the contented purring of a cat as he underwent a joyless encounter with the forces of law and order.

He had once been summoned to see the headmaster to account for some misdemeanour he could not now recall and had felt the warmth of the electric fire playing on his legs, which were still cold from the winter playground, and he had reflected miserably how he would have found the fire comforting, cosy even, but for the circumstances of his being in the head's study. Jake, he thought, would feel as lonely as Toad or the young Jason Kirk if father and daughter were to play loudly together.

After twenty minutes or so the first wisps of fear floated into Jason's stomach. Where had Jake gone? Was he waiting for Jason to go in search of him? Would he, perhaps, believe himself betrayed if nobody came to look for him? He was, thought Jason, far too sensible, too down to earth, to have indulged in some dramatic gesture such as running away or commencing the fifty-mile journey home on foot, expecting to be overtaken and persuaded into the security of the car.

Yet was he so sensible? Was not this the child who had said with conviction, as if he believed the course of events reversible, that he wanted *then* rather than *now*, as if he hoped Jason could wave a wand and all the intervening years away. How much did he really know about the extent of his son's maturity? Had he not dismissed Leah's moods when Kat had complained of difficulties and claimed that he had seen no trace of such behaviour?

You are not here, Kat had said, demanding to know how he dared to oppose his opinion to her own when she had daily charge of their daughter. Of course Leah was not going to play up when she was being treated, her every whim indulged. Why then should he be any more satisfactory a judge of Jake's reactions? Jason called out to Leah.

'Did you see where Jake went?'

'No. He was with you.' Leah looked momentarily surprised and then resumed her acrobatics on the trunk.

'I think we had better go and look for him.'

'You go.'

'I can't leave you alone in the middle of nowhere. Come on, it won't take long.'

Preoccupied with his anxiety for Jake, he took Leah's compliance for granted and was taken aback when his request was met with voluble protest. He tried to explain more fully: Jake was upset, had wandered off and might be lost, and it really was necessary that he, Jason, should try to find him but he could not leave her alone and she must come too.

Leah sulked but gave in and unwillingly set off with him. First they went to the car but Jason had not seriously expected to find his son there, the vehicle being locked. Then they walked about, calling fruitlessly, before he decided to drive along the route Jake would have taken if he had started for home on foot. After two miles he turned and drove in the other direction but with as little result.

When they returned to the site of the tent, Jason left Leah locked in the car with instructions to sound the horn if anyone tried to open it. Freed from the limitations of Leah's pace, he ran, scrambling over bush and scrub, calling his son. The terrier suddenly reappeared and ran beside him barking. Jason looked at the harmless creature in fear. Who was the owner who lurked so near them on the moor? Why had he not continued his walk? Had he waited, watching, looking for a moment when one of the children should be alone, unprotected, easy prey?

A whistle, made faint by distance, caused the small dog to pause in its antics, ears alert, gazing in the direction of the sound which it decided to ignore. Jason continued his fruitless quest but when a second whistle reached them the terrier bounded off and he headed in the same direction. Less than two hundred yards on the other side of the stream was a gypsy encampment, illegal, untidy, threatening in its ugliness, in its manifestation of a contempt for the social norms.

It was in the opposite direction from where he had left Jake and, unless he had walked in a huge circle, his son was unlikely to have stumbled upon this camp, but it did not follow that all its occupants were at home. Any of them might be wandering on the moor and could have met Jake.

Jason was unsure exactly what he feared from such an encounter and was unwilling to let it take form in his mind. He stood looking uncertainly at the dilapidated caravans, at the battered cars of which two bore no number plate and at a thin, unkempt dog tethered to a towing bar. It eyed him balefully, too dispirited even to bark. There was no sign of the terrier and Jason could not associate it with the scene now before his eyes.

No sooner had the thought entered his mind than the animal reappeared, leashed now and panting as it fought with its owner for the return of its freedom, running and straining. The girl came to a halt when she saw Jason and he ambled towards her, afraid to hail her aloud in case the inhabitants of the camp should hear.

'You haven't seen a boy, have you? About thirteen with a red jacket?'

She shook her head. As they both turned away from the camp she looked at him with concern.

'Is he alone? Lost?'

'He is certainly alone. I don't know whether he is lost or hiding. I've been looking for ages and I have a small daughter alone in my car. If I was worried before I'm fairly panicking now I've seen those gypsies.'

'I don't blame you. I was frightened for my dog but ... a child! Where is your car? I will stay with your daughter while you look for Jake. That is his name, isn't it? I heard someone calling it earlier so it must have been you.'

'Yes. My daughter is called Leah. I really would be very grateful but it's a terrible imposition...'

'Nonsense. By the way, my name is Alison.'

'Jason.'

'This is Yogi.'

Jason bent down to give Yogi a pat of introduction. Then he began to call his son, the name echoing around the moors and dying in the answering silence. As the brightly-coloured tent came into view so did a man, heavily built, his dirty T-shirt pulled down over a bulging stomach. Jason felt Alison draw slightly closer to him but Yogi bared his teeth and lunged at the end of his lead. The man regarded the dog's antics with amusement rather than contempt and Jason relaxed.

'That your boy?' he asked them.

'You've seen Jake? Where?'

'Over there, talking to our Hughie.'

Jason followed the man's nod and saw nothing but empty moor.

'Go on a bit and up that hill and there's like a dip and they're there rabbiting with Dorcas.'

'Thanks. I thought he was lost.'

'Nah. Just rabbiting like.'

To Jason it seemed unlikely that his son, who was sentimental about animals and had owned pet rabbits, would be engaged in such an activity but at least he was in no danger and he grinned at Alison in relief. Five minutes later he was wondering at his naivety as they discovered the car unlocked and Leah gone.

As he leaned weakly against the vehicle it was Alison who called his daughter. When there was no reply he roused himself and in a voice of both fear and anger repeated the summons. A moment later Leah appeared from some bushes.

'You shouldn't call people when they're doing something private,' she reproved him. 'It's very rude.'

Alison began to shake with laughter. 'You go and retrieve Jake. Leah will be OK with me.'

Fifteen minutes later he found his son alone and sobbing where the man had indicated. He tried and failed to keep the fury of relief from his tone. 'Where on earth have you been? I've been half mad with worry and I had to leave Leah on her own.'

Jake sank down on the grass and continued crying, swallowed up by some grief which made him oblivious to rebuke, until Jason took sufficient pity to enquire the cause.

'Dorcas caught a rabbit. It was horrible. It screamed and she ran off with it in her mouth. Hughie said they'll eat it for supper. He called me stupid.'

Jason, sinking on to the bracken, put an arm round his son's shoulders. 'But you have eaten rabbit, Jake. It too had to be killed. So do the lambs and the cows and the pigs. You know that without my telling you.'

'It screamed.'

'I'm sorry but people do have to eat. Dorcas was only doing what terriers do naturally.'

'But you hate hunting. You told me so.'

'For sport, yes, but this was for food.'

'I'll never eat meat again. From now on I'll be a vegetarian.'

'That's up to you, but Mum won't cook two different meals every night. It would be too much for her after a busy day.'

'I don't care. I'll get my own.'

'Fair enough. Come on, we have to get back to Leah. A very kind lady volunteered to stay with her.'

They found Alison and Leah playing I Spy in

the car with Yogi tied to a nearby tree. She at once offered to stay there while Jason and Jake went to dismantle the tent, sensing that they would want to move on, to put a distance between themselves and the gypsies. As they walked side by side Jason found himself thinking warmly of the man who had directed him to his son: harmless, despite his unprepossessing appearance, a father himself.

'Dad!' cried Jake in disbelief. 'It's gone.'

Jason stood still, staring with incredulity and indignation at the place where the tent had been. There was no tent, no stove, no plates, no picnic.

'Who's taken it?' demanded Jake in angry bewilderment.

'Hughie's father.' As the grimness in his tone changed to helpless laughter his son looked at him with incomprehension.

'Can we get it back?'

'No. There was nothing there that is valuable or sentimental. We'll just have to replace it all. People like that can be dangerous, Jake. It is better to let sleeping dogs lie.'

'Bobby is sentimental. Leah loves him.'

'Loves him so much that she took him to the car with her. He is all right.' Jason thought of the cuddly bull from which Leah would rarely be separated and wondered what he would have done if that too had been stolen. Confronted the thieves? Involved the police?

It came to him now that Leah, at nearly eight, was too old to need such a toy all the time and he wondered if it was her protest against the fate her parents had inflicted on her.

Jake turned back with him unwillingly, still half

386

inclined to challenge Hughie and his family. It was he who explained, furiously and indignantly, what had happened, somewhat consoled by Leah's gaping surprise and Alison's scandalised exclamations.

Alison said her car was further along the road and Jason drove her to it, thanking her again. Leah hugged Yogi goodbye, forgiving him even an attempted mauling of Bobby. For a while the two cars moved in convoy but eventually he ceased to see Alison in his mirror and turned his mind to the problem of how to spend the rest of the day. In the end they went to Newcastle and bought a new tent and stove together with other camping items which Jason did not consider strictly necessary but which Jake and Leah felt no respectable tent could possibly lack.

They stowed the purchases in the car and found an early supper at a café where Jake carefully selected vegetarian dishes. Jason formed the impression that he secretly yearned for sausages and bacon but thought it unfair to tempt him. His son would, he was sure, not eschew meat for long.

He returned the children an hour late and half expected an explosion of protest from Kat, who was engulfed in a storm of explanation from Jake and Leah who vied with each other to provide the most shocking details of the day's events. Dan glanced at Jason, looked at him more closely and offered a drink.

Kat eventually joined them in the sitting room and listened to Jason's story of a lost son and momentarily missing daughter. He expected her to remonstrate, to say he had been irresponsible and silly and had better not take the children camping again.

'Poor you,' said Kat. 'And thank God for Alison.'

Jason was too surprised to respond.

'I will have stern words with Jake. He should not get away with wandering off like that,' continued Kat. 'No wonder you are so white.'

Jason realised that both Kat and Dan were looking at him with concern, that the afternoon's shopping and supper had not restored him as fully as he assumed.

'He didn't have such a wonderful time of it. He saw a terrier catch a rabbit and it upset him.'

'He should be a bit more realistic at his age. Why did he go off in the first place?'

'Because I told him Carol and I are starting a family. Leah had been going on a bit about your own impending arrival and I think it all got too much.'

Kat sighed. 'Whatever have we done to them?'

'You mean whatever have *you* done to them. You walked out and you tried to keep them from me and still try whenever the mood takes you.'

Dan stirred uneasily but Kat shrugged. 'I wanted a clean break. It would have been better than this.'

For a moment Jason was too angry to speak. He rose to leave but as he did so he saw the fleeting expression which crossed Dan's face, a look of amazement and distaste. He knew then that Kat's second marriage was also doomed, that a child was about to be born into a home which would one day be a battleground or a desert.

Jason did not know what Kat had told him about the reasons for her departure but, whatever she had said, she had now revealed a motivation, a meanness, a callousness of which her husband had been previously unaware.

Dan would fear for his own fatherhood too, thought Jason, would wonder if Tabitha would be snatched from him as carelessly as Jake and Leah had been taken from their father. *A clean break.* The words would haunt him.

'Leah is only eight,' whispered Carol when Jason repeated the conversation to her. 'In fact not quite eight and if you are right then she could see a second break-up before she is old enough to cope with it.'

'Kat and I lasted ten years so Leah might well be grown up if anything does go wrong. Still, the scales didn't fall from my eyes until she walked out. If I read his expression accurately Dan is already seeing her through something less than rose-tinted spectacles and Tabitha isn't even born.'

'One can read too much into a single glance. Now, I've got a whole series of messages for you. Eileen rang and wants us to go and stay before the baby is born. Ben also rang to tell us that Debbie had twin sons on Friday, David and Noah. Mrs Turnbull rang all the way from Spain to ask after Objubjub, and Giles looked in to say that his grandchildren will be here for half-term and wondered if Jake and Leah would be around.

'Yesterday, I took Objubjub to the vet because he came in with blood pouring from his shoulder and front paws. He is fine but needs antibiotics for five days. The washer in the tap has been fixed. Alex and Sheila rang just before you got back because they had already heard from Kat that you had lost both Jake and Leah and that all the camping gear had been stolen—'

'Spare me,' protested Jason. 'It can all wait.'

Later he returned to the conversation with Kat, telling Carol that, until she had made her remark about the clean break, he had actually thought there might be a thaw in her attitude. After all, he observed, she could so easily have berated him for losing sight of not one child but two when he was supposed to be taking care of them. She might have asked, quite reasonably, why he had not checked the area before setting up the tent there.

Instead she had sympathised with his anxiety and had appeared to blame not him but Jake. It had puzzled him but, in his weakened state, he had been ready to be reassured and had not questioned her reactions.

'You may well have been right not to question them.' Carol was looking at him thoughtfully. 'Perhaps it was all quite genuine and was only ruined by the subsequent quarrel.'

Jason shook his head but Carol persisted.

'Consider how settled her future must look now. She is married to a responsible man, has a baby on the way to cement the relationship, is secure in an agreeable house big enough to accommodate all three children, has a job if she wants to keep on working. She can afford to relax a bit. I think you should give the thaw a chance.'

Jason was not persuaded but he woke in the middle of the night, Carol's words ringing in his brain. *Settled. Settled. Settled.* Behind the sound was an echo, faint but insistent, and he raised himself on his elbow in an attempt to identify it.

Then he remembered and he laughed aloud, triumphantly, maliciously, rejoicingly, full of sudden hope as the solution to his loss was suddenly presented to him. Beside him Carol stirred and mumbled a question but he didn't answer and she fell back into sleep.

'Dad!' called the dream images of his children.

'Coming,' he called back and knew it was at last true.

21

'It's very odd. I still can't get hold of Jason and now they're telling me that number does not exist.'

Dan frowned in puzzlement. 'What about the mobile?'

'It's on answer but I've left dozens of messages and he hasn't returned one of them.'

'Perhaps you should try a neighbour.'

'I could have done at the old house but I've never had any numbers for neighbours at this one.'

'You said there was one called Giles. His grandchildren played with Jake and Leah and he had a cat called Tigger.'

Kat shrugged aside the suggestion with impatience.

'Sorry, only trying to help.'

'I know but it really would help if you could

remember Giles's surname. I can't ask Directory Enquiries for Tigger's number.'

Dan risked a laugh but there was no answering amusement from Kat.

'It's very odd,' she repeated.

'Get Jake to text him. He always answers Jake.'

'I've already thought of that. Jake has sent *"Please ring Mum"* half a dozen times. Jason simply replies *"As soon as I can"*. What on earth is that supposed to mean?'

'I don't know but I'm sure all will be revealed in due course. Meanwhile there is no emergency which makes it imperative to contact him, is there?'

'No, but...'

'But what?'

'I just wish I knew what was happening.'

'What is happening at this moment is that Tabitha is crying.'

Kat turned and went towards the stairs, still thinking of Jason and his sudden elusiveness, convinced he had some reason which would not be to her advantage, that it was all part of a plan she would not welcome.

Frowning, Kat lifted Tabitha from her cot but her mind was engaged less with the immediate needs of her child than with Jason's evasiveness. It was unsettling and she was beginning to feel humiliated. Accustomed to having the power, to being in control of events, to being able to dictate terms, she sensed that Jason was somehow play-ing with her, that she was the mouse to his cat.

Her reason told her she was over-reacting but her antennae, which had always been reliable and had never yet failed her, were providing quite a different interpretation. She tried now to pick up the right signals with them but they played only to her instincts not to her intelligence.

Tabitha quietened and Kat looked down at the child with love. If anyone tried to take Tabitha she would fight like a lioness, not caring whom she hurt so long as the baby did not slip from her grasp. Could Jason feel like that? Was there some desperate counsel to which he was preparing to resort?

'Don't be silly,' she muttered to herself.

It was six years since she walked out. If Jason had not managed to defeat her in all that time he was unlikely to start now. Anyway, his outrage and misery must have dulled over such a period, especially as he now had a new life with Carol and the baby. There must be a dozen reasons why he was temporarily unavailable on the telephone and perhaps he thought it funny not to answer her, a form of revenge, maybe, for the times when she had deliberately avoided him.

If that were the case she would try no longer. Let him get in touch when it suited him. He couldn't be aloof for ever if he still wanted to see the children. She wished the silence from him could be permanent. It would be a welcome break from his wearying and importunate demands to see her children. If only Dan would take a tougher line with him it might be easier and so much more settled for Jake and Leah.

'I'll live with Dad when I'm sixteen,' Jake had said bitterly only last week when she had refused some petty but inconvenient request. It was too bad of Jason to come between them like that.

'He's not my real daddy,' Leah had said with feeling when an adult had innocently assumed Dan to be her parent.

'Don't say it like that. You'll hurt Dan's feelings,' Kat had remonstrated to the person's embarrassment but not to Leah's.

'It's true,' she had insisted with indignant force.

Dan was such a good stepfather they really should be more grateful instead of which Jake was polite but distant. Kat sighed. Jason had been so difficult over it all. Why wouldn't he help them settle properly?

Jake came in now, looking down at Tabitha with curiosity rather than affection. 'Mum, when can I next see Dad?'

'Oh, not again. Jake, of course I want you to see your father but you know very well he is not answering the telephone.'

'You never want me to see him.' Kat was chilled, not by her son's words with which she was all too familiar but by the tone in which they were spoken. Once Jake would have fairly spat the accusation at her in childish rage. Now he spoke unemotionally as one stating a simple fact.

'Don't be rude, Jake. That is very unkind.'

Jake shrugged and she knew she would have preferred an argument, hot resentment, insolent defiance, a childish walking out accompanied by slamming door.

'You will turn them against you,' Dan had warned after he had witnessed one such confrontation.

That, she thought, must be nonsense. Who had

been there throughout their lives, cooking, comforting, caring, counselling? Who put plaster on their knees when they fell over or marched to the school to put right injustice? Who filled the hot water bottles when they ailed? Who had an ever-ready ear into which they could pour their troubles? They would always love her as she had loved them. In time they would bring their own children to her to be loved in the same way as she had brought Jake and Leah and now Tabitha to her parents.

On the rare occasions that Kat felt guilt it was on Eileen's account not Jason's. She had never really liked Eileen, being well aware that Eileen in turn did not like her. Sometimes she thought the older woman was trying to peer into her very soul. Yet she valued the relationship between Eileen and her grandchildren and knew that she must have suffered greatly when they were withdrawn. Often a memory of Eileen's expression danced unbidden into her mind, an expression she had seen and loved when grandmother and grand-children were playing together. When this happened she would drive both it and the cold guilt, which it never failed to bring, into the past.

'Hello, Kat,' Jason would taunt her in her dreams.

'Goodbye, Jason,' she would utter with grim relief when she woke.

Jake had wandered out of the room again. In his own he found a text message: 'See you tomor-row. Tell Mum.'

Jake whooped with delight and rushed to tell not his mother but Leah. He broke the news to

Kat over supper, feeling safer for Dan's presence. His mother stared at him but it was to Dan she spoke.

'Now what? He hasn't made any arrangements and Jake has a choir practice tomorrow afternoon.'

'I can miss it,' said Jake promptly, sensing danger.

'Let's see when he turns up,' temporised Dan.

Jake saw no reason for any such uncertainty. 'When? I have choir at three,' ran the message he sent to his father as soon as he could be alone.

'Fiveish,' came the reply.

'Let's both go and collect Jake from church,' suggested Kat the following day at four o'clock. 'We can take Leah.'

'Shouldn't I stay here in case Jason comes?'

'No. Let him wait. If he can't consult us before making these peremptory arrangements there is no need to put ourselves out for him.'

Dan shrugged. 'You're probably right, but I'd like to stay anyway and finish this letter.'

Kat did not oppose him and shortly afterwards he heard her car start up. He finished his letter, sealed it in an envelope and decided to walk with it to the post box, which was situated at the end of the road. His task completed, he stopped to talk to a neighbour and was just turning once more for home when a car drew alongside him and Carol hailed him from the passenger seat.

She and Jason climbed out and the three stood looking at each other, while Dan wondered why they had not simply invited him to get in the back for a lift even if it was only a couple of hundred yards.

'We've been expecting you,' he told Jason. 'Was it a hell of a drive?'

For some reason this seemed to amuse Jason but Carol looked slightly uneasy.

'Not really. After all it's only two streets.'

Dan stared, an inkling of the truth beginning to enter his brain.

'Two streets?'

'Yes, we couldn't find anything nearer although we did actually see a house in this street but we thought that might be a bit much. It could so easily give rise to gossip – you know, the wife next door syndrome.'

'You mean you've come to live here?'

'Yes. To be near my children.' The banter had dropped from Jason's tone.

'But what about your job?'

'I'm teaching near Hexham. Carol also has one a bit nearer but only part-time because of the baby. It's all settled.'

Settled. It was Carol's use of that word, when she had pointed out how settled Kat now was, which had shown him the way out. He had recalled how he had once bitterly reflected that Kat had waited until he had settled into a new house and new job before leaving behind her own much lighter baggage and taking the children to Newcastle. He had known that he too could take advantage of the permanence of her present arrangements, that she would not be able to persuade Dan, even if she could persuade herself, that they should move house and his job and Jake's secondary schooling away from Newcastle just to escape him, Jason Kirk.

It had not been easy but, with Carol's support and a steely resolution, he had accomplished the move. Eileen too planned to exchange the Dorset countryside for that of Northumbria and would move later in the year.

Jason watched Dan's reaction carefully, knowing that on it depended all. The other's expression changed from amazement, to admiration and then to something akin to amusement.

'Well done, Dad,' he conceded. He looked down the road in the direction of his own house. 'They've just arrived. I suggest you take the kids off to see your new house while I tell Kat what's happening. It might be just a tiny bit difficult and I would rather Jake and Leah were not there.'

'Dad!' yelled Jake, seeing him as he got out of the car.

'Daddy!' shrieked Leah in ecstasy.

Jason turned and watched his children run towards him.

This Large Print Book for the partially sighted, who cannot read normal print, is published under the auspices of

THE ULVERSCROFT FOUNDATION

BRITTANY
AND NORMANDY

Mary Elsy

BRITTANY
AND
NORMANDY

B. T. Batsford Ltd London

First published 1974
Copyright © Mary Elsy, 1974
ISBN 0 7134 2811 2

Printed and bound by Cox & Wyman Ltd
Fakenham, Norfolk
for the publishers, B. T. Batsford Ltd
4 Fitzhardinge Street, London W1H 0AH

.74.

Contents

Illustrations

Acknowledgements

The Author and Publisher would like to thank the following for the illustrations appearing in this book : Bavaria Verlag for no. 2; Anne Bolt for nos. 1 and 13; Pat Brindley for no. 19; Douglas Dickins for nos. 4, 15 and 16; the French General Tourist Office for no. 18; J. Allan Cash for no. 5; A. F. Kersting for nos. 3, 6, 7, 8, 9, 10, 11, 12, 14, 17, 20, 21, 22, 23, 24 and 25.

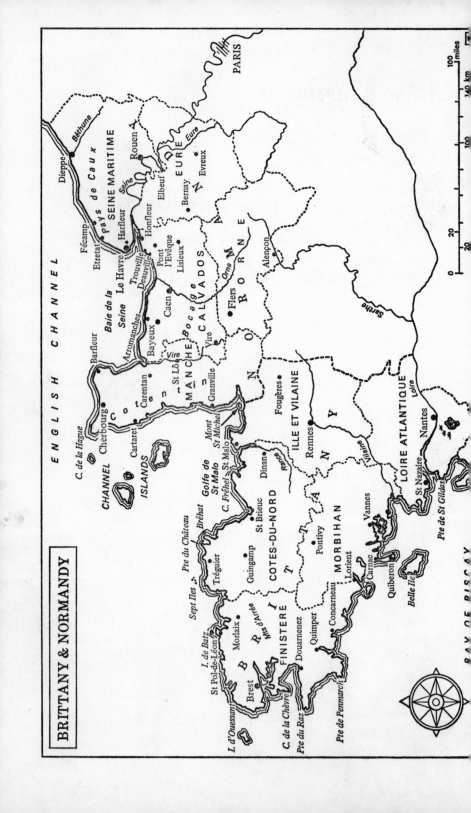

1. History and Introduction

Although it may seem strange to put two provinces so different as Normandy and Brittany into one book, they do have some things in common. The greater part of the two regions were once joined as Armorica and then, in Roman times, as Lugdensis Secunda. Both provinces had ties of blood and trade with Britain. Both (although Brittany to a lesser extent) were later used as a springboard for English invasions of France. Also the sea has played an important part in the lives of both provinces, helping to produce sailors, explorers, emigrants – and pirates. Finally, as part of France, their adjoining coastline forms one of the most popular areas in Europe with British holidaymakers.

While we owe so much of our early institutions to Normandy, Brittany, whose name means 'Little Britain', is part of our ancient history. Its quiet countryside is reminiscent of Devonshire, its craggy coast of Cornwall, while the barren moors in western Finistère (*finis terrae* – 'land's end') are similar to Scotland.

Brittany's history has been determined by its isolated position. This maritime land with the long head, the Brittany peninsula, pointing 180 miles out to sea, on one side the English Channel, on the other the Atlantic Ocean, was once cut off from the rest of France by forests and desolate moorlands.

Little is yet known about its earliest inhabitants, a Mediterranean people. Those in southern Brittany had a fairly prosperous trade in tin and copper, controlling the sea routes from northern Spain and the British Isles, and land routes along the Loire Valley towards the Seine and central Europe. They left behind their culture in the shape of megaliths – menhirs (long stones), dolmens (stone tables) and cromlechs (circles of standing stones), the most numerous and famous being those at Carnac in the Morbihan. Like those of Stonehenge, they were most probably connected in some way with the sun, but the definition of their exact purpose is still controversial.

The Celts, who arrived on the peninsula in the sixth century B.C. and who probably intermarried with the previous inhabitants, divided the land between five tribes. Interestingly enough, this division is very similar to the division of the province into five departments in 1794. The Redones occupied, roughly, Ille et Vilaine, having their centre at Rennes; the Namnetes inhabited Loire Atlantique (but since 1964 this is part of the Pays de la Loire and is no longer in Brittany officially); the Coriosolitae of the Côtes-du-Nord had their centre at Corseul (this is now an unimportant village): the Osismi occupied an area somewhat larger than the present Finistère and had their centre at Carhaix (now quite an important town), while the Veneti occupied Morbihan, with their centre near Vannes. These Celts, who introduced iron, built boats 30 metres long and based their livelihood on the sea.

The Veneti, especially, were particularly fine sailors, as Julius Caesar found to his cost when he tried to make Brittany part of his Roman Gaul. That he succeeded was due chiefly to guile and good luck rather than to superior seamanship. In 56 B.C., one year before his invasion of Britain, a famous sea battle took place near Port Navalo, off the southern coast. The wind dropped, becalming the Veneti in their sailing ships, but favouring the Romans in their oar-propelled galleys. The Romans tied sickles to ropes. Whenever one of their boats drew alongside an enemy sailing ship, a sailor heaved it into the rigging. Then the galley swept on. As the rope was dragged tight, so down came the rigging and sail. The sailing ship was then attacked and boarded. This sea victory over the powerful Veneti, who were most barbarously treated, enabled Caesar to subjugate the rest of Brittany.

Even so, this impenetrable peninsula was only superficially Romanized, as was its later Christianization. The Celts used the menhirs they found in their own religion, as did the earliest Romans, who carved pictures of their gods on some of them. Brittany was still predominantly a pagan province when the Romans left in the fifth century A.D.

The next wave of invasion, which took place during the fifth and sixth centuries, was a peaceful one. It was of fellow Celts from Britain across the water. Whether they were driven out by Anglo-Saxons settling there, or whether they were merely emigrating has not yet been properly researched. But these new colonists, chiefly farmers, gave Armor (land of the sea) its present name Brittany. With them came Celtic missionaries, especially from Ireland and Wales, who completed the provinces' conversion to Christianity. They sanctified many of the pagan menhirs by crowning them with a cross, and divided the country into large parishes – forerunners of today's communes. Many of them were made saints by the Bretons who named towns and villages after them: St Malo, St Brieuc, St Pol-de-Léon are a few.

Under Charlemagne Brittany became an outpost of the Frankish empire and was divided into petty lordships. Its colonization, as under the Romans, was only a superficial one. One Carolingian emperor, Louis the Pious, gave Nominoé, Count of Vannes, the job of keeping the Bretons under control in A.D. 826 in the hope that they would be more likely to obey one of their own kind. Nominoé did quell a riot in 836, but would not allow Frankish troops into Brittany. Later, when Louis died and fighting broke out among his sons, Nominoé promised loyalty to the one called Charles the Bold and even supplied him with soldiers up to 842. This squabbling amongst the brothers enabled him to strengthen his own position and declare his independence. In 845 he managed to throw off the Frankish domination in a battle near Redon. An old stone cross and a modern statue of Nominoé, father of Brittany, stand near the site, now a hamlet called La Bataille. Nominoé died on 7 March 851, near Vendôme, but his independent dynasty was to last for more than a century.

Norman invasions of Brittany took place in the tenth century. In 937, the young Alain Barbe Torte ('crooked beard'), heir to the

Breton crown, returned to Brittany from his sanctuary at the English court of King Athelstan, and rallied the people. Many of these pirates were slaughtered on the Loire below Nantes. The rest were driven out of the country. Alain rebuilt Nantes and made it the capital of the duchy. However, in spite of the victory the battle with the Norsemen had weakened his dynasty, enabling the Breton nobles to defy his successors. Internal strife and poverty were to last until the end of the fourteenth century.

Brittany continued to have many contacts with England across the sea. One duke, Alan the Red, who accompanied William the Conqueror to England in 1066, was later granted Yorkshire lands, formerly belonging to Edwin Earl of Mercia, where he built Richmond Castle. Another duke, Alan III, the first duke to be formally styled Earl of Richmond, fought beside King Stephen at the battle of Lincoln in 1141. Yet another, John I, fought for Edward I in the Welsh wars in 1277.

Brittany remained fiercely jealous of her independence; France's kings had to wait a long time before they could make themselves felt there. By the Treaty of Gisors in 1113, Louis VI had to abandon direct overlordship of Brittany to Henry I of England, also Duke of Normandy. Later, the marriage of Henry II's son Geoffrey to Constance, daughter of Count Conan of Brittany, brought the province even further into England's orbit.

However, Philippe Auguste showed himself to be an astute statesman as well as king. He put himself in the rôle of Brittany's protector by taking the part of Constance and her son Arthur when Arthur claimed the throne of England in succession to his uncle, Richard I. He later abandoned Arthur at the peace of Le Goulet on 2 May 1200, by which Arthur was left only in possession of Brittany, which he held as a fief to his uncle John. But Philippe was only biding his time. Two years later John was disinherited by the French royal court. The seizure of most of his French possessions enabled the king to confer Brittany on Arthur as a royal fief. The Treaty of Gisors was set aside and Brittany returned to France's royal overlordship.

The unfortunate Arthur, a mere sixteen-year-old pawn in the

2 *The calvary at Guimiliau, near Morlaix*

3   *St Thégonnec, Finistère*

royal game, was later captured by John at Mirebeau, and eventually murdered, probably at Rouen castle, by his uncle John. The heiress was his sister, Eleanor, then living at Bristol and the ward of King John, who, as her guardian, claimed the right to administer her inheritance. This, of course, would have delivered the province into the hands of the king of England, just as undesirable to the Bretons as being in the hands of the French king. So her claim was set on one side by an assembly of Breton lords and prelates at Vannes in 1203. Her half-sister, Alix (daughter of Constance and her third husband, Guy of Thouars) was set in her place. Her father, Guy, was made ward of the fief. Later, because Guy was proved to have been involved in pro-English intrigues, Philippe had the excuse to take the governorship of Brittany into his own hands.

Alix was married to a member of the French royal family, Peter of Dreux (grandson of Louis VI), usually known as Peter Mauclerc. However, although Peter did liege honour to Louis VIII for Brittany in 1213, during the regency that followed this king's death he also became involved in rebellious feudal coalitions, and even did homage to Henry III of England in 1229, supporting him against the French king. But his ambitions came to nothing and when his son, John I (the Red), came of age, he relinquished the governorship of Brittany to him.

John I (1237–86), John II (1286–1305), Arthur II (1305–12) and John III (1312–41) were all obedient vassals to the French crown, yet were sufficiently adroit to retain the honour (territory) of Richmond. In 1297, the French king, Philip the Fair, conferred the rank of duke on John II and admitted him to the peerage of France. Their loyalty, however, enabled the French king to intervene freely in Brittany, which he could treat like a royal domain, and obtain services in men and money when needed.

This line of French dukes, ruling from Rennes, ended on the death of the childless John III in 1341. The resulting war over who was to succeed him brought England and France into open conflict again.

The contestants were Charles of Blois (1319–64), married to

John III's niece, Jeanne de Penthièvre, who was supported by the French, and John of Montfort, John III's brother, who was supported by the English Edward III.

The matter was finally resolved in 1364 at the battle of Auray when Charles of Blois, although backed by the great Breton military leader, Du Guesclin, was defeated and killed, and John of Montfort's son (John of Montfort himself now being dead) became John IV. A peace was signed in Guérande in 1365. Charles of Blois, incidentally, was regarded as a saint by the Bretons and a cult grew up round his grave and relics at Grâces, near Guincamp.

This war of succession had brought Brittany to near ruin and the de Montfort dukes (John IV, V and Peter II) tried to secure her neutrality during the rest of the Hundred Years' War (1337–1453). These dukes governed the province from Nantes almost as an independent country, paying homage, but only in theory, to the king of France. They proved good rulers, restoring the ravaged duchy, which then entered into one of the most brilliant periods of her history.

François II, duke of Brittany from 1458 to 1488, continued this policy of maintaining Breton independence against any encroachments by the French king, even if it meant relying on foreign support. He allied himself with England and made a treaty with Edward IV, whereby his eldest daughter, Anne, should marry the Prince of Wales.

The future of the Duchy was dependent on her marriage; many rival claimants sought her hand. Anne herself favoured Maximilian of Austria, whom she married by proxy. But, unfortunately for her, his own country's affairs prevented him from defending his bride.

In 1488 the Bretons, who had supported a federal coalition against the regent of France, Anne of Beaujeu, were defeated at St Aubin du Cormier. François was obliged to sign the Treaty of Verger in which he undertook only to contract marriage for his daughters, Anne and Isabelle, with the French king's permission. François died a few weeks later, it is said of a broken heart.

4   Pont-Aven, near Quimperlé

A few years later, in 1491, the youthful Anne was besieged at Rennes by Charles VIII, whose terms included the rupture of her marriage with Maximilian and her marriage with himself. Anne had little option but to agree. Also, by the terms of her marriage, if he died without issue, she would have to marry his successor. And this is what happened! The ugly, rather stupid Charles died in 1498, and Anne was then obliged to marry the prematurely aged Duke of Orléans, the next king, Louis XII. He in turn had to divorce his first wife.

Anne, who died in 1514, has always held a very high place in Breton history. She was a devout Catholic and a patroness of the arts. She also devoted herself to the administration of the duchy, jealously guarding its autonomy. She tried to arrange a marriage between her daughter Claude (by Louis) with Maximilian's grandson, Charles, but eventually had to agree to her betrothal with François d'Angoulême, the future François I.

Shortly after Claude's marriage in 1515, the young duchess found herself Queen of France. She was persuaded to yield her duchy to their son, the Dauphin. Claude died in 1524 and in 1532, the States (Council) meeting at Vannes proclaimed the perpetual union of the county and duchy of Brittany with the kingdom and crown of France. So, at long last, Brittany was united with France. Even so, the duchy retained many of its rights and privileges and its provincial autonomy was to survive until the French Revolution.

The mass of the Bretons, staunchly Catholic, were not much affected by the ideas of the Reformation. Even so, the country was the scene of much fighting. Bandits, such as the notorious La Fontenelle, were able to flourish unchecked. In 1588, the duc de Mercoeur, a governor of Brittany, took advantage of the anarchic situation to lead a resistance against the Protestant French king, Henri IV. Spain sent 7,000 Spanish troops to help his cause. He set up a parliament at Nantes and even put forward his son Philip to be duke of Brittany.

Mercoeur won a victory at Craun in Anjou in 1592, but lost ground when Henri IV was 'converted' to Catholicism (you will probably remember his 'Paris is worth a Mass'). The Bretons, worn

5 *Mont Saint Michel*

out with Mercoeur's ambitions and their country's disorder, sent a pressing appeal to the King to come and restore peace. Mercoeur finally resigned Brittany in 1598. Henri IV put an end to religious strife – for the time anyway – by the Edict of Nantes, signed 13 August 1598, at the great castle of the Dukes overlooking the Loire.

The seventeenth century was a time of prosperity. Brittany, emerging at last from isolation and conflict, benefited from her union with France. Sixty towns were created, trade developed, especially fishing, textiles and printing. Castles and châteaux were built and enlarged. The ports of St Malo, Lorient and Nantes were expanded. Brittany, organized politically as a French province, did sometimes come in conflict with the crown. The Stamped Paper Act of 1675 (the minister, Colbert, decreed that all legal acts should be recorded on stamped paper) led to an indignant uprising, but this was put down.

At first, many Bretons welcomed the Revolution, but soon became disgusted by its excesses, especially the execution of the King and the notorious drownings of royalists at Nantes in October 1793. The new republic also tampered with their autonomy and privileges, persecuted their priests, and tried to enforce conscription. Many rose against it, joining the *chouans*, a name given to bands of peasants, also smugglers and dealers in contraband salt, who added their support to the rebellious Vendéean royalists. *Chouan* means 'screech owl' in Breton for the chouans were also night birds who used the hoot of an owl as a signal.

Chouanism was finally put down after the defeat of the royalist exiles landing at Quiberon Bay in 1795. The wild countryside in which they hid was cleared. Even so, chouanism still smoulders on, but now in the form of Breton nationalism.

The construction of roads, railways and canals over the last hundred years have helped to bring this individualistic province more in line with the rest of France. Brittany lost many soldiers and sailors in the First World War. In the Second, she contributed the largest number of men in France to the Free French Forces and the Resistance movement. Some of the fiercest battles that followed the allied landings in 1944 took place in Brittany – Lorient, Brest, St Nazaire and St Malo were all badly damaged in the fighting.

Since 1945, thanks to the Common Market, Brittany has become more outward-looking. Even so it is still a relatively undeveloped province with poor communications when compared with the rest of France. Although the birth-rate is high, the country is under-occupied because so many Bretons emigrate to work in Paris.

Industrialization has considerably advanced since the Fifth Plan (1961–70) as the zone qualifies for the highest amount of assistance. Some of today's important industries are shipbuilding, building and civil engineering, electronics and electrical engineering (fairly recently introduced), mining and quarrying, fish, fruit and vegetable canning and motor manufacturing (Citroën has two large factories at Rennes). Then there is the thermal power station run on fuel oil at Brest, a nuclear power station at Mont d'Arrée and the 540,000,000 LWH tidal power station on the river Rance, near Dinard. There are also smaller industries, such as textiles, shoe manufacturing, tanning and papermaking, as well as numerous local crafts.

About 30 per cent of the population still live by farming (more than 60 per cent of the land surface is under cultivation), but many of the holdings are too small, although thanks to organizations such as SAFER and FASASA they are gradually being merged into larger units. Brittany's soil is very varied, ranging from scrubby moorland to rich soil. Much market gardening (especially of leaf artichokes and cauliflowers) takes place along the sheltered parts of the coast, where the climate is influenced by the Gulf Stream, and around the Loire. There are many apple orchards, especially for cider apples, and stock-raising farms (particularly cows and pigs). Brittany is France's leading milk producer. Much of the agricultural and dairy produce is sold abroad or in other parts of France.

The Bretons still have many similarities with the Cornish and Irish and especially the Welsh people. About one million of her approximately three million inhabitants, who live chiefly in the western half, speak or understand Breton, which is very like Welsh. Although Breton is not taught in the schools, Rennes University does have a chair of Celtic studies and there are regular broadcasts in Breton on the regional ORTF network.

However, Breton has never been an official language, even during the days of the province's independence. From about the eleventh century onwards, upper-class Bretons wrote first in Latin, then in French. Since the Middle Ages works in Breton have been mainly translations from Latin or French, or fifteenth-century mystery plays. There was a revival of interest in the nineteenth century when many poems and ballads were written in Breton. But although Brittany has produced many writers, some as renowned as Chateaubriand, Ernest Renan and Jules Verne, they usually chose to write in French.

The Bretons are an imaginative people with a love of the fantastic, the eerie and the supernatural. The province is well-named the land of legends, the home of magicians, fairies, demons and saints. Especially saints. Each town, village and hamlet can claim its own saint, usually made without any reference to the Pope or Roman Catholic church. It is said that there are more saints in Brittany than there are stones in the ground.

The sea has played, and still does, a large part in many of the people's lives. Most of France's sailors and fishermen come from Brittany. There are innumerable fishing villages, strung out all along the rugged rocky coast. The seafood gathered – oysters, tunny, mackerel, lobsters, prawns, shrimps, sardines, to mention a few – make it a fish-lover's paradise. In the past, especially, the price paid was a high one : the sea claimed many victims.

So the Bretons have a great respect for the sea. Every year the boats are blessed. Priests lead processions which wade through the waters to the fishing boats and their nets; they pray for a good catch and a safe return for their crew from all their expeditions.

The Bretons, especially those from western Brittany, are a deeply religious people. Mystical and joyous festivals, called Pardons, are held all over Brittany in honour of the saints of a particular chapel or church. The name comes from the churches' custom of granting indulgences to pardon people's sins on a Saint's Day. There is often a legend woven round the Pardon of many of these places.

The Pardon starts with a mass. Then comes an open-air service when people pray before an altar of the saint in whose honour the festival is being held. A procession of priests and villagers chanting and singing, carrying candles and banners and a shrine of the saint, winds through the streets. The traditional costume of the region is worn on these occasions, especially by the women. Very often the Pardon ends with a fair. You would probably see dancing to bagpipes and wrestling, a traditional Breton sport.

Because of poverty and long periods of internal strife, Brittany has far fewer fine cathedrals and churches than Normandy. Only a few small churches were built during the Romanesque period of the eleventh and twelfth centuries. Also the style of building was much influenced by the use of local granite, which is a hard and difficult stone to work with. The construction of large churches and cathedrals was usually held up by financial difficulties, with the result that they tend to incorporate the architectural features of many centuries. Examples of this are to be seen at St Pol de Léon, Tréguier, Quimper, Nantes and Dol.

Except on the eastern border and along the coast, there are few great castles in Brittany. Kerjean, Josselin and the ducal castle at Nantes are three half palace-fortresses. With the exceptions of the ruling dukes and a few great families, most of the Breton nobility were poor and lived in simple manor farms.

Art in Brittany reached its highest expression in religion, especially in the size and decoration of the parish churches. From the fifteenth to the eighteenth centuries Breton sculptors, usually local men, worked in wood and stone to decorate church interiors. Rood screens, baptismal fonts and pulpits are particularly finely done in many Breton churches, as are many of the stained glass windows and pieces of gold plate.

The parish closes, mostly built during the seventeenth century, are a typical Breton feature. There was a tremendous rivalry between neighbouring villages about the grandeur of their closes.

The cemetery, which is often reached by a triumphal arch, is surrounded by the church, the calvary and ossuary. The calvary, a tall decorated structure, most probably a descendant of the menhir, which later gave way to the cross, was used for religious teaching by the priests. As its name implies, these monuments are carved to depict the Passion of our Lord, the events leading up to the crucifixion and the events that succeeded it. Jesus on the cross is usually the focal point and around him are gathered the persons who took part in this great drama, such as the apostles, the Virgin Mary, angels and archangels.

But Brittany's greatest attraction for tourists is its 3,500 km. of jagged coastline, tall cliffs and wide sandy beaches. The shore and the fertile land behind is still known as the Armor (land of the sea), while the interior, also attractive, with its wooded hills, moorlands, cultivated fields and pastures is still the Argoat (land of the forest: because so much of it was once covered in trees).

Brittany's climate – mild, humid, windy and variable – could be called oceanic. There are differences, although not very great, within the regions. The north is colder than the south, which is warmed by the arrival of waters from the tropical areas of the Atlantic into the Gulf of Gascony. Mediterranean plants, such as palm trees, mimosas and magnolias flourish along the southern shores, as they do along the part of the north coast influenced by the Gulf Stream. The climate also grows colder as one moves eastwards. Brest is a few degrees warmer than Rennes. It is also wetter. But although Brittany has the reputation of being a rather wet province, its annual rainfall is lower than in many other parts of France. This is because its rain, although fairly frequent, is also fine.

Brittany, which represents about five per cent of France, divides roughly into two areas, higher Brittany in the east, and lower Brittany in the west. These names are odd in that higher Brittany is low, while lower Brittany is hilly. Millions of years ago higher Brittany was covered by a shallow sea, while lower Brittany was an island. Today even the highest hills in the west do not reach 400 metres. The highest in the Monts d'Arrée is 385 metres, in the

Montagnes Noires 326 metres, while the Menez Hom is 330 metres.

When France was divided into 21 regions in 1964 Brittany, as a peninsula lying between two seas, with all its customs and historical traditions, was the one with the greatest geographical unity and homogeneity. Except that the department, the Loire Inférieure, later called the Loire Atlantique, has now been controversially incorporated into the Pays de la Loire, its divisions are much the same as they were before the Romans arrived. Because of this, I have divided the book into the departments, Ille et Vilaine (capital Rennes), Côtes-du-Nord (capital St Brieuc), Finistère (capitals Morlaix, Brest and Quimper), Morbihan (capital Vannes), still throwing the traditional Loire Atlantique (capital, Nantes) in for good measure, and moving in an anti-clockwise direction round the province.

2. Ille et Vilaine

Rennes and its surroundings

Rennes, capital of the department, Ille et Vilaine, and Brittany's major city, is also the province's front door to France, the main entrance to the western peninsula. Strategically situated at the junction of the Ille and Vilaine rivers in stockfarming and agricultural country, it is also a commercial and industrial centre, possesses an important university, and is the seat of an archbishopric. It has expanded considerably over the last half century: in 1936 it had a population of 98,000; in 1976 this will be 200,000.

Rennes, centre of the Celtic Redones, was the commercial centre of Armorica under the Romans, who surrounded it with a wall. It became the seat of the dukes of Brittany in the tenth century. After the union of upper and lower Brittany it was proclaimed capital in 1213 and the dukes came here to claim their crowns. The *Parlement* of Brittany was held here from 1561 to 1675 when, because of the uprising against the unpopular stamp act, it was transferred to Vannes until 1689. The Rennes *Parlement* opposed the *ancien régime* on several occasions, as also it did the decrees of the Constituent Assembly of the French Revolution. It later became reconciled with the Revolution and Rennes was the headquarters of the Republican army during their fight against the army of the Vendée.

In spite of its age and although its history is closely bound up with Brittany, Rennes, stately, cultured, coldly classical, appears more French than Breton.

The reason for this is that on 22 December 1720 a great fire, which lasted a week, swept through its old medieval buildings, destroying much of the town. The story goes that a drunken carpenter set fire to a heap of shavings with his lamp. As there was no running water or proper way of putting out a fire in those days, and with the wind acting like a bellows, the blaze grew worse. About a thousand buildings were destroyed.

Because of this catastrophe much of the town had to be rebuilt, mostly at the crown's expense. The two architects, Jacques Gabriel and his son, Jacques-Anges (he was also responsible for the Place de la Concorde in Paris) had it built *à la* Louis XV, quite an innovation at that time – very uniform, with tall houses set in wide rectangular streets.

Even so, there is still a little bit of old Rennes with its maze of cobbled street, fifteenth- and sixteenth-century gabled houses and superior eighteenth-century *maisons* with sculptured façades for you to see. One tourist speciality is the pancake shop (pancakes are particularly popular in Brittany), 22 Rue du Chapitre. Near by is the eighteenth-century Hôtel de Blossac, which has a particularly fine staircase. The house called Ti Koz, which is supposed to have belonged to Du Guesclin, is now an attractive and expensive pancake restaurant.

The 'kings' and 'queens' of Brittany rode through the old gate, the Porte Mordelaise, which is fortified by two towers, to the cathedral. They entered the town by this route when travelling in special processions to be crowned in the cathedral.

Rennes cathedral is dedicated to St Pierre and is the third to be built on this site since the sixth century. The present one was finished in 1844, after 57 years' work. But its façade, granite and imposing, dates from 1540 to 1703. The interior, a mixture of Roman Byzantine and Renaissance styles, seems rather dark, but has a mellow atmosphere and beautiful ceiling. Pink granite pillars blend well with the mauve of the stained-glass windows. The organ is worth looking at, as is the high altar, decorated by Flemish craftsmen showing scenes from the life of the Virgin Mary, in a chapel at the rear. For interest, look at the statue of the bishop of Rennes who died in A.D. 505 : it is dressed in robes and lies inside an ornate *châsse* in the chapel of St Amand. Whenever there was a calamity threatening the town this holy man's statue was carried through the town in the hope that he would use his influence with the powers above.

But the imposing Palais de Justice, overlooking the Place du Palais, is Rennes' most famous building. You enter first the Salle des Gros Piliers, a large vestibule with rather austere columns, where it is not too difficult to imagine markets being held. The fine double staircase leads to the first floor and city hall (1734), empty, unused and still a little shabby. But all around it lie a number of magnificent rooms, decorated by painters such as Jouvenel and Coypel.

The most impressive of them is the Grande Chambre, Rennes' parliamentary debating chamber. Sixty feet long, 30 feet wide and 22 feet high, it has particularly beautiful panelling, paintings, gilded woodwork and ceiling. Tapestries on the wall show important events in Brittany's history, such as the marriage of the Duchess Anne and Charles VIII of France. Although the originals were destroyed during the French Revolution, these modern Gobelins, which took 24 years to make (one person doing one metre a year), are priceless. A box overlooking the chamber was used sometimes by Madame de Sévigné, who took a great interest in the proceedings.

The Palais was also the supreme court of 2,300 Breton tribunals and so played an important legislative as well as political rôle. Most of the counsellors and presidents were chosen from the noble families of the province. Members of the Rennes *Parlement* were much respected and traditionally had large families. A seat could be bought for something like £21,000 in today's terms. Salaries for court officials were low, but judges received 'spice' (this was chiefly sweets and preserves) from their clients. Today all the Palais is used for law courts.

When in Rennes you should visit the Thabor Gardens, reckoned to be the second-best flower garden of France. It shows a variety of garden arrangements, such as a formal French garden growing flowers from all regions, a skilfully designed landscape one, an attractive rose garden, also a botanical one. For children there is a miniature zoo with monkeys, guinea pigs, parrots and other birds, set around a pagoda. The whole park covers an area of about 25 acres, and its nucleus once belonged to the Benedictine Abbey of St Melaine (Melaine, a famous bishop, was also a great healer and adviser to Clovis). The church is worth a visit.

Rennes' Musée de Bretagne is worth seeing, too, as it shows the history of the province and has some good examples of Breton furniture, kitchen utensils (those most enormous pans must have fed giants), and most interesting of all, a collection of the colourful costumes of the region.

Rennes is an excellent centre for tours by rail, bus or car. On its east side lie the border castle towns, such as Vitré, Fougères and Combourg.

Walled Vitré, situated on a spur overlooking the Vilaine valley, with its impressive castle perched watchfully high above, has preserved its medieval character. Its heyday was from the sixteenth to the eighteenth centuries when it was renowned for its textiles, woollen cloth and cotton stockings. Today, although it still has factories, it acts chiefly as a market for farm produce.

The best view of the town is from the castle watch path. English visitors will be interested to know that the suburb of Rachapt was occupied by their compatriots for several years during the Hundred Years' War, while they were besieging the castle and town. Eventually the frustrated inhabitants paid them to go away. So when you cross this area, whose name translates into 'repurchase', you will know how it got it. The museum, installed in three of the castle's towers, is worth seeing.

The Château des Rochers, home of Madame de Sévigné, whose lively letters tell much about country life and Vitré during the time of Louis XIV, is not far from here. Les Rochers is still owned by members of her family, but you can see the chapel and her own room, known as the Green Room, which is filled with her possessions. The garden beyond was laid out by Le Nôtre.

Also near by is the village of Champeaux with its charming square and attractive fourteenth- and fifteenth-century church.

Fougères, set beside a forest (3,900 acres of trees) about 46 km.
to the north-east of Rennes, stands at the intersection of the main
roads linking Brittany with Paris and the Channel ports. So you
are likely to pass through it if you come into Brittany via
Normandy.

Like Vitré, it is set picturesquely on a promontory overlooking
a valley, the Nançon, but its castle, one of the most famous in
France, is situated below, almost surrounded by water. It has a
history as romantic as its appearance. Victor Hugo introduced
Fougères into *Quatre-Vingt-Treize* and Balzac put it into *Les
Chouans*. Both authors obtained their copy by visiting the castle.
Balzac even talked to survivors of the rebellion.

However, in spite of its hugeness – 13 towers connected by
ramparts – the castle has often been captured. Henry II of England,
Pierre Mauclerc (not for long though), Du Guesclin, Charles VIII,
Mercoeur, the Vendéeans, are just a few who have held it.

Fougères the town has been more successful than its castle and
Vitré. It switched from manufacturing sailcloth to ladies' shoes,
for which it is particularly famous, readymade clothes, lingerie
and other light industries. But because of its greater industrialization there is less of interest to see. The best way to spend an afternoon there is to walk round the castle's outer fortifications and
have a guided tour of its interior.

The castle at Combourg, rising above a little old town set beside
a lake, looks like a theatrical set-piece, which is as it should be
since it was the home for a period of Du Guesclin, Brittany's most
famous military leader, and also of Chateaubriand, her greatest
writer. Built in the eleventh century, it was enlarged in the fourteenth and fifteenth centuries.

Chateaubriand, born at St Malo, had a chequered and up-and-
down career. He fought for the royalists at Valmy, then escaped
to England, where he lived in great poverty. During the Restoration his fortunes rose again, when he became France's ambassador
to England. He spent two years at Combourg as an impressionable
and dreamy child, so perhaps its gloomy atmosphere and the then
rather desolate surroundings of woodland and heath helped to

mould his later mystical style. He slept high up in a turret called the Tour de Chat (Cat's Tower), because it was supposed to be haunted by a former Lord of Combourg, who returned each night in the form of a cat. You can visit his room, which has been turned into a museum and from which there is a good view of the surrounding countryside.

About 37 km. west of Rennes lies the Paimpont forest, covering an area of about 40 sq. km., and part of the eastern remains of Brittany's Argoat. Here still grow the old ashes and beeches, also firs and pines, although many of these have been fairly recently replanted to counteract the spread of broom and gorse scrubland.

This is King Arthur country, where this legendary king is supposed to have lived with his knights, ladies, hermits, magicians, not forgetting the Korrigan (the Breton leprechaun), and to have sought the Holy Grail.

It is a region of lakes and legends. A stone from the fountain of Baronton could unleash a wild storm, while the fairy, Vivianne, who captured the wizard Merlin in a magic circle, was born in the now empty château of Comper. Morgane, Arthur's sister, and a pupil of Merlin, ruled over the picturesque Val sans Retour, where she is supposed to have captured, imprisoned and punished people, especially naughty boys. Only the bold Sir Launcelot could deliver them from her witchery.

The village of Paimpont, set beside a pool and surrounded by trees, only dates from the Revolution. A seventh-century monastery, then a twelfth-century abbey once stood here. But of all this only the thirteenth-century church remains.

Sleepy Dol, lying to the north of Rennes, can quickly be reached by train. It is also situated on the tourist route between Mont St Michel and St Malo.

Old timbered houses and the most interesting part of the town lie along the Grand' Rue des Stuarts. Steep side turnings on the right lead up to its old cathedral, St Samson, a curious structure, a large sprawling mixture of centuries, with towers and turrets somehow putting one in mind of a Norman fortress.

Dol has no right to a cathedral as it is no longer a bishopric.

That it ever was one is due to the fact that until some time between the fifth and eighth centuries the marshland and Bay of St Michel were covered by a great forest. St Michel and Dol stood on hills but became islands when the sea flooded over this area. When the waters fell, leaving marshes, they were not drained until about the twelfth century onwards. But by then there were bishoprics at both St Malo and Dol although they were only about 24 km. apart.

Dol, lying on the frontier between Normandy and Brittany, was often besieged by the Normans. In 1076 William the Conqueror was defeated by this proud little town. In 1203, John, murderer of Prince Arthur, took Dol, burned its Romanesque cathedral, and occupied the town for a year. Later, perhaps overcome by remorse, he sent funds for the construction of the present cathedral, which dates from the thirteenth century. Altogether about 80 bishops have occupied the see of Dol. The first was St Samson in the sixth or seventh century; the last was M. Hercé, who distinguished himself by being shot along with other royalist supporters at Vannes in 1795 after the failure of the Quiberon invasion.

Inside the cathedral there is still much to remind one of its bishops. Unfortunately, when I visited it, it was undergoing repairs : some things were missing and it was not at its best. The interior is long, cool and grey with a particularly fine stained-glass medallion window in the chancel. The 80 fourteenth-century stalls are fascinating. Each arm-rest has a face carved on it, of nuns, monks and some which look suspiciously like devils.

Behind the cathedral lies the Promenade des Douves, a pleasant place to picnic and enjoy a good view of the Marais, the drained salty marshland, now a fertile area and renowned for its mutton, which stretches rather monotonously towards the coast. You can also see Mont Dol, a 200-foot granite mound, from which many prehistoric animals and flint implements have been excavated.

According to legend, the devil and the archangel Michael were once engaged in mortal combat here. You can even see the marks made by the devil's bottom and his claws. It seems that the devil was worsted because he was thrown injured into the Trou du Diable. Even so, he did somehow manage to appear mockingly on

Mont St Michel, about 19 km. away. But the archangel leapt after him, giving a mighty spring and leaving his footprint for ever on the mount. The mystery, of course, is where did the devil go next?

The Chapel of Notre Dame de l'Espérance on Mont Dol, which replaced a signal tower put there in 1802, is today the centre of a popular pilgrimage.

On the other side of Dol is the Champ Dolent, which boasts a 63-metre menhir, one of the finest in Brittany. Its name means 'field of pain' and refers to a legendary struggle which took place there.

St Malo, its surroundings and the Emerald Coast

One's first view of St Malo, Brittany's sea gateway, should be from the deck of a ship in early morning, when the old walled city of the corsairs, so strategically placed on its small peninsula, slowly slides itself out like a hazy mirage from its place between sea and sky.

Perhaps the most remarkable thing about this ghostly image that gradually takes flesh is that it really no longer exists. St Malo died during a two-week siege in 1944 when it was pounded to death by the American forces in Cherbourg. What you see now is merely a restoration. The pinkish granite towers, turrets, houses and twisting cobbled streets, even the twelfth- to seventeenth-century cathedral of St Vincent, have all been painstakingly put back.

St Malo was named after a sixth-century priest from Wales, who settled in the Gallo-Roman town of Aleth (now St Servan), situated beside the Rance, behind the island peninsula. He converted the inhabitants to Christianity and became their first bishop. However, later Norman invasions forced the people to settle on the more easily defended rock to their north. The bishopric was transferred there in 1144, and strong ramparts were built round the town. Because of its impregnable position, it was able to develop along its own independent line, under the loose control of the church. Its motto is '*Ni Français, Ni Bretons, Malouins suis*', adopted between 1590 and 1594, during the wars of religion, when its inhabitants even managed to establish a republic.

St Malo became renowned for its traders, its seamen and its pirates. For its size it has produced quite a number of eminent men, such as Jacques Cartier, who discovered the mouth of the St Lawrence river and Canada; Duguay Trouin (1673–1736) and Surcouf (1773–1827) privateers who inflicted very heavy losses on the English, Dutch and Spanish fleets; not forgetting Chateaubriand, who was born here, the tenth and last child of a St Malo shipowner.

St Malo's best feature is still its oldest – the ramparts. Tides here are very high, and waves sometimes rise to as much as 40 feet. The battering-ram effect of the sea is tremendous and vibrations can be felt miles away. No wonder that the old walls, which have stood up to centuries of bashing, managed to survive the destruction of the town.

A walk round the ramparts, starting from the St Vincent gateway, takes about an hour, and gives you magnificent views of the bay. You will see the islands – Fort National (built by Vauban in 1689), the Ile du Grand Bé (this isolated spot, which contains the tomb of Chateaubriand, can be walked to at low tide) and the Petit Bé Isles. There is also a grand view of the Emerald Coast to the west of Dinard across the Rance river.

After passing the Grande Porte you will have a good view of the narrow isthmus, which joins the walled city to its suburbs, the harbours and St Servan. The ramparts, which skirt the houses of the rich St Malo shipowners, pass numerous little stairways and ramps from which you can descend to the town again if you wish. There are also many little parks with seats where you can rest and look out to sea.

Near St Thomas's gateway is the aquarium, which is built into the walls of the ramparts in the Place Vauban and which contains fish found around this part of the coast.

By now, you are near the Place Chateaubriand, the main part of St Malo, and close to its famous waxworks museum (Quic en

6 *Château de Combourg, childhood home of Chateaubriand*

Groigne), where you can see carefully reconstructed scenes from the history of St Malo. The words '*Quic en Groigne*' come from an inscription the sparky Duchess Anne had carved on the tower during a dispute with the Bishop of St Malo : '*Qui-qu'en groigne, ainsi sera, car tel est mon bon plaisir*', meaning 'Whoever may complain of it, it shall be so, for such is my pleasure'.

St Malo's museum is situated in part of the castle. There are guided tours in English during the season, but it is useful if you can read French.

The first gallery shows the three aspects of the Malouins, as traders, as pirates, and as explorers. Their exploits were particularly terrific during the seventeenth century. They did not cease their war against England until 1815 and were not finished finally as privateers until 8 July 1856. The corsairs' weapons – pistols, daggers and swords – are shown along with some of their loot, such as captured coffers. One great prize was a bell taken from the English frigate *Hercules* in 1777.

An interesting model shows St Malo at the time of Jacques Cartier. Its ramparts were pierced by two gates, Grande Porte and St Thomas, and enclose the manor, cathedral, houses, cemeteries and fields.

The cathedral, St Vincent, has only recently been reconstructed. Dignified, spacious and Gothic, it blends old with new, being somehow modern yet old at the same time. The stained-glass windows, designed by Max Ingrand, are particularly fine. The cool grey interior is constantly warmed by shafts of yellow-mauve sunlight filtering through. There are a few old statues to be seen, but many empty niches are still waiting to be filled. Unfortunately the descending steps are not easy to see, and notices have been set up to warn the unwary to look where they're going.

Jacques Cartier's black slab tomb is very simple. He is also remembered by stones marking the spot where he stood in the cathedral on 17 May 1535 to receive the benediction of the Bishop of St Malo prior to his departure for the New World.

Apart from its quaintness and history, St Malo, which joins up with busy St Servan (which faces the Rance river and has shingle

7   *The beach at St Briac, Côtes-du-Nord*

beaches) and the spa resort Paramé (good beach), is a yachting
centre, has a casino, and is particularly renowned for its seafood.
It also makes a good centre for expeditions, both by land and
sea.

Rothéneuf, a few miles farther to the east, within easy reach by
bus, has picturesque pines, dunes, cliffs and good beaches and is
a pleasant place for a family holiday. Cancale, farther on, is a
picturesque fishing port and seaside resort (shingle beach). If you
go there by car you should drive via the Pointe du Grouin, a wild
rocky headland, from which there is a good view of the coast from
Cap Fréhel to Mont St Michel.

The local bus to Cancale deposits you beside St Méen, its main
church. Not far from the inside door is a book whose pages turn
automatically after you have inserted a franc, and give information
in three languages about the area. There is also a sailors' chapel
dedicated to the 508 local men who were drowned at sea between
1846 and 1967.

If you descend the hill via the Rue de Port you will soon find
yourself at the harbour below. Grey stone houses, hotels, bars,
restaurants, cafés and shops lie along the roadway overlooking the
sea. Cancale is especially a place for seafood gourmets. For centuries it has been renowned for its shellfish, particularly oysters,
the beds of which are cultivated in the shallow bay stretching
towards Mont St Michel.

Cancale is also renowned as the birthplace of Jeanne Jugan,
founder of the worldwide order of the Little Sisters of the Poor.
Jeanne was one of seven and the daughter of a Cancale fisherman.
She was left fatherless when still young and worked as a domestic
for an elderly lady, who left her 400 francs when she died. Jeanne
used this money to buy a home where she could give shelter to poor
elderly people. With friends she founded an order which obtained
subsistence for their charges entirely by daily begging. This organ-
ization, helped by some members of the church, slowly grew. Today there are many thousands of these sisters, working in various
establishments, helping to look after the poor.

From St Malo you can make sea excursions to the Channel

Islands, the Ile de Cézembre, the Iles des Chausey (a wild rocky archipelago), and also to Cap Fréhel (a magnificent sea trip) and St Cast.

You can also go by boat down the Rance river to Dinan, a very pleasant trip, as is the bus journey there. The disadvantage of the boat trip (which only takes place during the season) is that it doesn't really give you enough time to see Dinan properly if you intend returning the same day by boat.

Dinan, with its *vieille ville* of half-timbered houses, attractive squares, twisting narrow streets, gardens and trees, is one of the most delightful and best-preserved medieval towns in Brittany. Strategically placed at the head of the Rance estuary, a road-centre of north-east Brittany, it is often referred to as Du Guesclin's town.

This famous Breton military commander, who became constable of France, occupies a rather ambiguous position in Breton history. Although he is esteemed for his success, he cannot really be said to have served the cause of Breton independence, which was preserved by playing off the English and French kings against each other. Du Guesclin's allegiance to the French king disturbed this delicate balance. He had a hectic career and was taken prisoner several times. On one occasion the French king paid 40,000 crowns for his release, a tidy ransom, proving how useful he found Du Guesclin.

Du Guesclin, who married a Dinan girl, literally left his heart behind him in that town. He had asked to be buried there, so that when he died in 1380 near Châteauneuf de Randon the funeral cortège obediently set off for Dinan. Alas for his wishes, there were many stoppages on the way. His body was embalmed at Le Puy and his entrails left behind in a church there. But as the embalming was badly done the flesh had to be boiled off the bones at Montferrand and buried in a church there. Then a message was received at Le Mans from the king that his skeleton was to be taken and buried in the royal church at St Denis, near Paris. So, in the end, Dinan only received his heart.

It resides in the north arm of St Sauveur's church. If you draw the white curtain before a cenotaph, you will see a carved stone heart, behind which it lies.

Beyond St Sauveur's is its churchyard, now converted into a garden and named rather ironically after Du Guesclin's arch enemies, the English. The Jardin Anglais slopes down among the town's old ramparts towards the river and picturesque old port, not much now used. Above this strides the viaduct bridge, which carries the main road from Paris.

Dinan castle, which has many connections with the Duchess Anne, contains a very good local history museum and is well worth a visit. A lively market is held every Thursday morning in the town.

Elegant Dinard, facing St Malo across the Rance, can also be reached either by boat or road. The road there passes over the top of the famous Rance dam, completed in 1967, the turbines of which use the exceptionally high rise and fall of the tides here to produce electricity. Economically the dam has not proved particularly successful. Nevertheless, as the first sea-powered generating station in the world it is an interesting experiment. There is a car park near by and you can, if you wish, go on a guided tour of the power station.

Dinard, queen of the Emerald Coast, is Brittany's smartest sea resort. It is expensive and staid, yet at the same time gay, with plenty to do (in season, that is; out of season, and this includes June and September, it is rather quiet). It now boasts a new casino with a magnificent dance hall, a large, warmed seawater Olympic swimming pool as well as three splendid beaches, all perfectly safe for bathing. Then its climate is equable, never too hot and never chilly, so that palm trees and exotic flowers grow along its rocky coast.

Unlike St Malo, Dinard is not very old. In fact, if you had come here about a hundred years ago, you would only have seen a small fishing village. Dinard owes its growth to a rich American, a Mr Coppinger, who while out hunting one day with a party from St Malo, unexpectedly came across it. He was so delighted by its good position and wonderfully sandy beaches, that he decided to stay there. Others joined him, and Dinard eventually became a centre for English-speaking people.

It still is, although now many Belgians, Dutch and Germans come, too. There are tea rooms and shops where English is spoken, also an English church and an English library.

One of its chief attractions is that you can walk along its rocky coast without being disturbed by cars. The most famous walk is the Promenade à clair de la lune, which leads down twisting paths to the Pointe du Moulinet (here the Rance meets the sea), from which there is a very good view of Cap Fréhel (on the left) and St Malo (on the right), the Rance Estuary and even Le Grouin in the far distance.

If you continue past here you will come to the Grande Plage, an enormous stretch of sand, overlooked by the new piscine and casino. The main part of the town and the Boulevard Féart lie behind the Grande Plage (also known as the Plage de l'Écluse).

Dinard, like St Malo, is a good centre for excursions. It is also within easy reach of St Lunaire, a smart resort with two beaches, and St Briac, which, along with its picturesque port and pretty pine-fringed beaches, has one of the finest golf courses in Europe. Sailing is popular all along this stretch of coast.

3. Côtes-du-Nord

The Côtes-du-Nord, part of Brittany's northern coastline, with its rocks, cliffs and splendid beaches, is the most popular area of Brittany with British holidaymakers. The people here live chiefly by farming, especially in fertile Tréguier, where you will see fields and fields of yellow ripening corn; and coastal fishing, particularly shellfish, from the countless little ports. The former deepsea and cod fishing were ruined by the fierce competition with Iceland and Norway. Tourism, too, is becoming increasingly important in summer so that numerous villas and hotels now stand beside the small grey stone houses. These are likely to increase now that Britain has joined the Common Market. Perhaps in the future Brittany's ports will connect directly with British ports across the water, as I am sure they must once have done.

However, although the sea, beaches and bathing are such an important feature of this part of Brittany, prospective holiday-makers should bear two things in mind when choosing their place and time.

Firstly, in some places the sea goes out so far that it virtually disappears, leaving behind it a magnificent stretch of golden sand. The swimmer will have to trudge a long way to find it. In fact, there may only be a few hours a day in which to take a swim. So, if you are keen on swimming, find out about tides before choosing your resort.

Secondly, the season is rather short. Out of season includes June and often September. Although the resort will be less crowded, a visit then, even to a large place, will mean that there will be little to do in the evenings. Even the casino may be closed.

The Emerald Coast

As the Emerald Coast lies between the Pointe du Grouin and Val André, it is partly in the Ille et Vilaine department, and partly in Côtes-du-Nord. Although the tourist road does not run beside the sea the whole way, the journey beside this rocky coastline, with its cliffs, wide sandy beaches and high points such as Cap Fréhel, makes a wonderful drive.

Lancieux, first stop of the Côtes-du-Nord when coming from Dinard, is pretty, peaceful, has excellent bathing beaches, and is very suitable for family holidays, as is Jacut-de-la-Mer, situated on a long peninsula projecting into a sheltered bay, safe for boating and with a number of small beaches. It has a picturesque little port. The Guilde, a village surrounded by rocks and cliffs and situated at the mouth of the Arguenon, has a port, too. It also boasts the ruins of a castle, Le Guildo, near by, once the seat of a gallant fifteenth-century poet–noble named Gilles, who was tragically murdered by his brother.

The popular resort of St Cast sprawls out over the peninsula of the same name, which lies between the Arguenon estuary and the bay of Frénaye. It is made up of four parts: Les Mielles, where most of the hotels are to be found; L'Isle, a rocky area, bordering the northern end of its long beach, also with many hotels and villas; Le Bourg, which contains the main public buildings and the old Gothic church; and La Garde, at the beach's southern end, resembling a pretty wooded park. From its point and that of St Cast, there are superb views of the Emerald Coast.

The name St Cast could be Cado or Gattwg (Welsh) and belonged to an Irish priest, born in A.D. 522, who became a bishop. He travelled a great deal, even visiting Palestine and Rome, but finally settled in Brittany, where many places have been named after him. In the Rue de la Colonne you will see a monument surmounted by a greyhound (France) trampling on a leopard

(England). This commemorates the time when British troops who had previously landed in the Bay of St Malo were defeated on St Cast's long beach by French troops under the command of the Duc d'Aiguillon, Governor of Brittany in 1758.

Fort la Latte, which juts out from the next peninsula across the bay of la Frénaye, is best approached from the village of La Motte. Its massive circular keep looks very picturesque and feudal perched on its rocky mound, entered by drawbridges. The castle was built by the Goyon Matignon family in the thirteenth and fourteenth centuries, then restored in the seventeenth. There is a good view of Cap Fréhel from its watch gallery.

Cap Fréhel, over 180 feet high, with its tall red, grey and black cliffs, fringed by wave-battered reefs, is the grand spectacle of the Emerald Coast, and indeed, the finest natural feature of Brittany. It is especially beautiful on a clear evening, when from its top you can glimpse the Channel Islands. You can visit its lighthouse, walk round its cape, and watch the noisy gulls swooping round the curious-shaped Fauconière rocks below.

South-west from Cap Fréhel lies Sables d'Or les Pins, a fairly sophisticated place with a good golf course. It is not a village, more a collection of hotels set amongst pine woods and dunes and with a gorgeous (almost) 3 km. of golden sand beach, all this contributing, of course, to its evocative name. The climate is excellent. But families would probably find Erquy, a near-by pleasant picturesque little fishing port with three beaches, cheaper.

Val André, also a family resort, is very popular with the French, an added recommendation. Its sheltered sandy beach is superb, and one of the best on Brittany's north coast. There is much to do here – tennis, riding, fishing, shooting and especially sailing. There is also horse-racing, a casino and two cinemas and it makes a good centres for walks and excursions.

For history lovers there is the near-by ancient Celtic village of Pléneuf, and a tumulus, dolmen and cromlechs where victims were once sacrificed to the sun. The old fishing port of Dahouët, which lies in a creek beyond the Pointe de la Guette to the west of Val André, was used by the Vikings. Later Breton fishermen practised sailing round here in preparation for their long fishing trips to Newfoundland and Iceland.

The Bay of St Brieuc and the Pink Granite Coast

St Brieuc Bay sweeps down in a rough curve from the Pointe de l'Arcouest, the beginning of the Pink Granite Coast, to Val André.

St Brieuc, situated on the bay of the same name and about 4 km. from the sea, is the business and commercial centre of the Côtes-du-Nord. Busy, prosperous and expanding, with many factories (chiefly for treating and preserving meat and dairy produce), its population has doubled since the end of the war. This once rather charming country town is now surrounded by factories, industrial buildings and estates, so you are not likely to want to spend a holiday there. Nevertheless, because of its airport, railway station, and since it is the point of departure for buses going to seaside resorts or on excursions, you might well find yourself there, perhaps with enough time for a look round.

St Brieuc, founded in the fifth century, is one of the oldest cities in Brittany and is therefore an interesting mixture of old and new. The best place to start your tour of it, is from the Place de la Grille, beside its cathedral, St Étienne (St Stephen). This heavy building is certainly not beautiful, but has a sort of sturdy attraction. The turrets, towers and pepperpot roofs put one in mind of a château-cum-fortress rather than a place of worship. It looks as if it has lived, as indeed it has !

The cathedral occupies the site of an abbey, which was founded at the end of the sixth century by St Brieuc, who came from Cardigan in Wales. Its history has been one of destruction, fire and degradation. It was sacked by the English in 1353, set on fire, used as a fortress, destroyed, rebuilt, damaged again when the Constable de Clisson besieged and captured the town. After being restored and reconstructed during the fifteenth century it was used by the Catholic Leaguers as a refuge for three days in 1592. Its nave nearly collapsed in the eighteenth century. The city's Mayor, Poulain-Carbion, was shot in front of it by the Chouans in 1799.

It was turned into a saltpetre factory during the Revolution, when many of its treasures were burned. It later became a stable for cattle, then a place for storing weapons. As you would expect, such treatment has resulted in a veritable pot-pourri of styles, interesting, but not beautiful. However, it does have a rather fine sixteenth-century organ loft.

If you follow the recommended route through the town, you will next climb the near-by Rue Fardel, passing the old houses, Le Ribault's (fifteenth century) and No. 15, the Hôtel des Ducs de Bretagne (1573), where our James II stayed in 1689. You follow this up to Rue Notre Dame and after continuing along here for a while, turn right into the Rue de la Fontaine St Brieuc. Here a lane leads off to where the old fountain stands, presided over by the Virgin Mary and protected by railings and wire netting. It was once a place of pilgrimage where many sick people came to be cured of their diseases. Behind it is the quaint little chapel of Notre Dame.

If you continue on down the Rue de la Fontaine St Brieuc, and eventually cross over into the Rue Gouet, you will soon find yourself back in the Place de la Grille, opposite the cathedral.

If you still have time to spare, you can visit the Boulevard Lamartine; from the roundabout at its end you will have a good view of the valley. A better view still can be had from the Tertre Aubé at the opposite end of the Boulevard Lamartine, continuing along the Boulevards Gambetta and Pasteur. From here you can see the valleys, the Bay of St Brieuc and the Tour de Cesson in the far distance. This is the remains of a fourteenth-century fort which was built on the site of a Roman camp. It was captured by de Mercoeur's Catholic forces after much difficulty during the Wars of Religion, but after 1598 was returned to Henri IV. On the request of the people of St Brieuc the French king had it blown up.

St Brieuc is situated on a plateau divided by two waterways, the Gouëdic and the Gouet. A good view of the Gouëdic valley with its viaducts can be seen from the Rond Point Huguin, not far from Tertre Aubé. From here you can also see the coast as far as Cap

Fréhel. A granite monument to Anatole Le Braz, Brittany's great folklorist, stands in the little park. He is shown in a familiar pose, listening to his companion, Margaret Philippe, who is telling him an old Breton legend. From here, you can return to the town by Rue Victor Hugo, Boulevard Thiers and the Grandes Promenades, an attractive public garden which encircles the Courts of Justice. There is an open air theatre and children's playground here.

St Brieuc is useful for shopping. Campers should note that there is a fish market every day in the Place du Martray, also a market for fruit and vegetables.

Northwards from St Brieuc the road is somewhat uninteresting. The coast is not much indented and there are only a few ports and family resorts.

Binic is a small, quite attractive fishing port. Étaples is a family resort with two good sandy beaches. St Quay-Portrieux, a fishing port and resort which have joined together, is larger, popular with people of fairly modest means (especially those with small children), has good sandy beaches, a casino, miniature golf course, cinemas and facilities for tennis, fishing and sailing. Plouha, situated about 3 km. from the sea, where there are good safe beaches, is quieter and also suitable for family holidays. Brittany is France's chief reservoir for sailors and many naval pensioners live around this area, who supplement their income by cultivating plots of land and letting off parts of their houses in summer.

Paimpol, which gained fame through Pierre Loti's novel *Pêcheur d'Islande*, is a picturesque port with quaint old streets and houses. In its heyday it was the base for a great cod fleet, whose ships ventured as far as Newfoundland and Iceland. Today, although coastal fishing still continues, as does oyster cultivation, its harbour is mostly filled with yachts. The town is also a centre for early vegetables. Still, there is a bit to remind you of its former grandeur, such as a museum of the sea and oyster cultivation, and a merchant seamen's college. Paimpol attracts many artists and writers and will appeal to those who like rugged holidays with plenty of fishing, sailing and boat trips.

From here you can visit the rocky seascape, the Pointe de

l'Arcouest, then take the ferry boat across to the island of Bréhat. You can also take a boat direct to Bréhat from Paimpol.

Bréhat, which is about $3\frac{1}{2}$ km. long and $1\frac{1}{2}$ km. wide, is really made up of two islands joined by a narrow strip of land. Surrounded by islets and reefs its rugged pink granite coast makes a strong contrast with the blue-green sea.

It is a little Eden, where mimosa, fig and palm trees flourish, its peacefulness undisturbed by mundane cars, for they are not allowed on the island. It seldom rains as the rain clouds usually miss it out on their way to the mainland.

You will arrive at Port Clos, about a kilometre from Le Bourg, the 'town'. You can tour the island through the rocks by boat, or you can just wander over it, perhaps visiting the lighthouse, the Phare de Paon. But everywhere is interesting.

Bréhat was once a busy port for sea traffic. Tradition has it that a sea captain from here, while staying in Lisbon, met Christopher Columbus and told him how the island fishermen made their way to the New World, via Newfoundland.

The drive from Paimpol, crossing two bridges, to Tréguier, an old town and port overlooking the junction of the Jaudy and Guindy rivers, is a pleasant one. This area is part of the Trégorois, which is renowned for the production of early vegetables.

Tréguier, once the capital of Trégor and an episcopal city, is an interesting old town with plenty of quiet character. Its cathedral (although now termed a church) of St Tugdual, is one of the best known in the province. This fine Gothic building with its three towers (one Romanesque) and beautiful cloisters (a frequent subject of paintings), dominates the town from the centre of its square.

Its patron saint is St Yves, one of Brittany's most popular saints, for he was traditionally the righter of wrongs and advocate of the poor.

Yves Hélori, born in 1253 at Minihy Tréguier not far from the town, was the son of a country gentleman. He was always interested in religion and after studying law in Paris, where he stayed for 13 years, returned to Brittany to become a priest. He also became a magistrate and advocate in the Bishop of Tréguier's ecclesiastical court, which tried civil cases as well. He soon became famous as the poor man's lawyer, choosing only to help the most wretched cases. He was canonized only 45 years after his death. Since then he has always been known as the patron saint of lawyers. You will see many statues of him in Breton churches. The favourite one shows him standing between a poor man and a rich man, whose purse he is refusing.

A church has been built over the manor in which he was born and died, and which is now the scene of a famous annual Pardon. Pilgrims are expected to scramble through a low thirteenth-century archway, known as St Yves's 'tomb' in the centre of the cemetery on their knees.

Tréguier was also the birthplace of another Breton celebrity, but one of a rather different type. Ernest Renan, philosopher and historian, made science his religion. His book *The Life of Christ* and others were roundly condemned by the Roman Catholic church. Even so, his statue has the place of honour in the square in front of the 'cathedral'. His humble home and birthplace have been turned into a museum.

Perros Guirec, on the coast, not easy to reach by bus from Tréguier, is one of Brittany's largest resorts. From here begins the Corniche Bretonne (Breton coast road), one of the most interesting parts of the Pink Granite Coast. Around here granite rocks have been chipped and chiselled by that great artist the sea, helped by the wind and the rain. Locals have given these strange shapes names, some eerie, such as The Witch and Death's Head; some are creatures, such as The Rabbit and The Tortoise; others are more mundane, such as The Thimble, The Umbrella, The Corkscrew, The Armchair, and there is even a Napoleon's Hat.

Perros Guirec, like Quay-Portrieux, was formed by two joined-up villages. The name Perros comes from the old word Pen Roz, while Guirec was called after an early priest, St Guirec. Today, it is an expensive and fashionable resort, boasting a casino and two good beaches, but rather dull out of season.

I liked its odd-looking, squat, sturdy little church partly

Romanesque (twelfth century) and partly Gothic (fourteenth century), built out of granite and topped by a tower and spire. Also, the pinkish chapel, Notre-Dame-de-la-Clarté (sixteenth century) on a hill is worth seeing. Apparently a Breton noble, whose ship was lost in a fog off this coast, vowed that he would build a chapel on whatever part of the coast showed first to give him his bearings. To commemorate this, the chapel was named Our Lady of Light.

The Plage Trestraou, an enormous sweep of sand, with a casino behind, reminded me of Dinard, except that the very solid granite seats on the promenade were proof positive that one was now well and truly into Brittany. Perhaps, too, the sand is a little paler.

However, the best part of Perros Guirec, the real *pièce de résistance*, in my view, anyway, is the fascinating walk along the Sentier des Douaniers (the Coastguards' Patrol).

Its start lies behind the Rue de la Clarté, or you can take the steps up beside the left of the Ecole de la Voile, on the Plage Trestraou. This walk, which takes about one and a quarter hours, follows the cliff, first along winding grassy paths, then slopes down to the rocky shore and varied-shaped, pink and grey rocks. They are all fantastical, out-surrealizing any creations by Barbara Hepworth and Henry Moore. Some must surely be crouching, petrified monsters, left stranded by the sea, others, piles of pink stones, are perhaps the start of some piscine palace, left carelessly to be used later. You pass many little caves and pools, secret and private, while in the distance looms the lighthouse. A park, a sort of rock reserve, lies behind granite posts. On the far side, near the beach of St Guirec, stands the small oratory dedicated to this saint, who is supposed to have landed here in the sixth century.

When I visited this place one evening, it was at its eerie best, an enchanted and ageless spot, surrounded by an atmosphere of primitive, prehistoric magic. One expected the wizard Merlin in his tall cap suddenly to emerge from the shadows and dance round with the ghoulies and korrigans. Perhaps the few crosses that have been planted on the rocks have been put there to offset their mischief and protect the unwary visitor from their attentions.

My path eventually led me to a secluded silent beach, which led into a small port and the little town of Ploumanach. From here, I was able to catch a bus back to Perros Guirec.

Trégastel Plage, the next resort to Ploumanach, also has its share of strange-shaped rocks. To the right of its Coz Pors beach are a pile known as the Tortues ('tortoises'). Above them stands a statue of the eternal father, and below, caves with a prehistoric museum in one. From the Grève Blanche (white shore), which you can reach by taking the rocky path round the promontory, you can see Rabbits Island and the Triagoz islands, also the rock called The Corkscrew, and the great shape supposed to resemble a crown, which is known as the Roi Gradlon crown.

At Trégastel Bourg, a few kilometres from the Plage, is an interesting twelfth–thirteenth-century church and its seventeenth-century ossuary. Just outside the village is a calvary, standing on a little hill. From here there is a very good view of the coast.

There are many islands off this part of the coast, the largest being Ile Grand, which is connected to the mainland by a road. The most distant, the Sept Iles about five miles out at sea, have a lighthouse and a bird sanctuary.

Trébeurden, lying farther south along the coast, is another larger seaside resort, also rocky and with good beaches. The Tresmeur beach is the most popular.

Lannion, which lies inland on the Léguer river, is the commercial centre of this area, linking as it does both with Tréguier and Guincamp, and is a good place from which to start on excursions farther afield. There is not much to see in the town itself – medieval houses in the Place du Général-Leclerc and the Brélévenez church, which was built on a hill by the Templars in the twelfth century. Near by, are the châteaux of Kergrist (you can only visit outside) and Tonquédec (an impressive ruin) and the Chapelle de Kerfons (fifteenth-century, prettily situated). Or for those who are more interested in the present and future, there is the space and telecommunications centre at Pleumeur-Bodou, whose white plastic sphere can be seen from afar.

For trips into Brittany's interior, the town of Guincamp makes a good centre. From here you can get to Mur-de-Bretagne, just in

Côtes-du-Nord, which makes a good starting place for a tour of Lake Guerlédan (see chapter 5).

The Corniche de l'Amorique (Amorican coast road) starts from St Michel-en-Grève, a small seaside resort, renowned for its sailors' church and cemetery, prettily situated beside the sea. Next to it stretches a magnificent three-mile beach, the Lieue de Grève ('league of shore'). The road here is very picturesque as it follows the wooded coast, passing the Grand Rocher, then St Efflam, which joins up with Plestin-les-Grèves, farther inland. The road between St Efflam and Locquirec, following the ragged coast, is particularly attractive. When you arrive at the little fishing port and resort of Locquirec Côtes-du-Nord has ended. You are now in Finistère, the mysterious land of the west.

8   Quimper cathedral from the southwest

4. Finistère

Finistère, the old west Brittany of legends, of winds and wide skies, or rough seas and rocks, of rivers, forests, and 'mountains' is for those who like rugged yet relaxing holidays.

It does not have one central town you can pinpoint as capital, but three, Morlaix, capital of the north, Brest, capital of the north-west, and Quimper (pronounced Kempair), capital of the south.

Morlaix and its surroundings

Morlaix, an attractive old town, climbing steep valley walls, lies at the foot of a high viaduct bridge crossed by a railway. The town grew up round the Rivière de Morlaix, beyond the viaduct, and was once quite a prosperous and important port. Today, its harbour is used chiefly for pleasure yachts, or boats carrying market produce, such as fruit and vegetables, especially strawberries.

Sleepy Morlaix existed during Roman times. During the twelfth century it was one of the residences of the counts of Brittany. An incident which took place in the early sixteenth century enabled its inhabitants to add a lion facing a leopard (English) and the probably practical if rather unchristian motto *'S'ils te mordent, mord les'* ('If they bite you, bite them') to their coat of arms.

The English fleet, which sailed up the estuary in 1522 to anchor below the town, had been told that the nobles and merchants, its chief defenders, were away attending the great fair of Noyal, near Pontivy. No doubt they thought they had a good chance of getting some easy booty.

9 *Dinan*

According to local legend, they enjoyed themselves too much and stayed too long and were therefore caught red-handed by the returning people. They were too befuddled to defend themselves, so victory was easy. A further attack, this time in 1532 by corsairs, decided the Morlaisiens to construct the Château du Taureau ('Bull's Castle') strategically at the entrance to the estuary in 1544.

Because of its many old twisting, steep, narrow streets, Morlaix can really only be explored properly on foot. It is a pleasant place just to wander round in. I suggest you first visit the Syndicat d'Initiative, placed very conveniently at the foot of the viaduct in the Place des Otages, where you will get a map and much helpful information. Nearby is quite a cheap restaurant and bar, the Café Moderne.

If you climb to the right of the viaduct, passing an old seventeenth-century house with dormer windows, you will find yourself outside St Melaine, a fifteenth-century, Gothic Flamboyant church. Its square steeple, shouldered by buttresses, is topped by a modern spire. Inside, the chief treasures are its modern stained glass windows and a colourful tableau representing the descent from the cross.

St Melaine was originally an old priory, founded in the twelfth century, as was St Mathieu, on the opposite side of the old part of the town, which was demolished in 1821 and rebuilt (except for a sixteenth-century tower) in 1824. St Mathieu possesses rather an unusual treasure, a fifteenth-century statue of the Virgin, which opens to reveal a figure holding Christ on the cross inside (over the altar to the left of the high altar). The thirteenth-century church of the Jacobins in the Place des Jacobins was badly damaged during the Revolution, when it was used as a stable and storage loft; it now contains a museum.

In spite of numerous depredations over the centuries, Morlaix still has some attractive sixteenth-century gabled houses. The gracious house of Duchess Anne, 33 Rue du Mur, with three overhanging timbered stories, is the best. Its closed court inside has a lantern roof. There is also a very fine carved staircase and a remarkable chimney along one wall. Other picturesque old houses and low-fronted shops with broad windows are situated in the narrow street, rather ironically named the Grande Rue.

Morlaix is especially the happy hunting ground for history-loving holidaymakers. All around and within easy reach are some of Brittany's finest churches, chapels and most elaborate calvaries. One of the most popular excursions you can take from this centre is the one to the *enclos paroissiaux*, the parish closes.

During the season there are special excursions; otherwise you can drive round them by car, or take a local bus. The chief parishes to visit are St Thégonnec, Guimiliau, and Lampaul.

When staying at Morlaix, I took a local bus to St Thégonnec, the best of the three parish enclosures, standing magnificently in the centre of its village. As it was out of season the priest who usually showed people round was absent, but he had thoughtfully left all the relevant information on the chapel steps.

It told me, of course, what I already knew, that these buildings were an open air museum and formed the most complete and splendid enclosure in all Brittany. They had taken two centuries to build (1550–1750) and were a masterpiece in praise of God, built by local people who had not hesitated to devote a large part of their wealth, acquired by flax growing and weaving, to its construction.

'Now stand in the middle of the road, but mind the traffic,' the notice said, which I obeyed, although fortunately there wasn't much around just then.

The rounded triumphal arch before me symbolized the victorious entry of a Christian, redeemed by Christ into the immortality of a heavenly Jerusalem. A statue of the Heavenly Father stood in its centre to welcome me inside.

Once through its arch, I examined the calvary, built in 1610, which tells the story in carved figures of Christ's trial, crucifixion and redemption, and it was quite fascinating. It was easy to see how a priest could use it as a teaching aid – also as political propaganda. Henri IV, because he was a Protestant and anti-Leaguer (Catholics), is shown as an executioner. The face of Christ and the faces of his friends always looked divine and at peace, while those of his enemies wore foolish and malicious grins. Above the carved tableaux of figures rose three crosses and two horsemen who kept watch over the crucified figure at its summit. Below the crosses four angels collected blood in chalices.

The church was fascinating, too, and its tower (begun 1599 and still incomplete in 1626) is one of the best examples of a Breton Renaissance tower. The most beautiful thing inside it is the exquisitely carved pulpit 'fit for a pope and not an inch of oak wasted', which was done by two brothers, François and Guillaume Lerrel in 1683. Above it is a canopy, covered in carved cherubs and roses, on top of which fame blows a trumpet.

The statue of St Thégonnec stands in a niche over the pulpit, while on the left-hand side of the church is the colourful St Pol-de-Léon (patron saint of Léon), with the defeated dragon of paganism lying at his feet.

St Pol-de-Léon also stands above the entrance door to the ossuary outside the church. Ossuaries were originally bone houses: bodies were removed from their coffins after a number of years of burial, and their skulls arranged along the shelves, the name of each owner being written across it in black paint. Later the ossuaries were turned into chapels of rest where bodies were kept before burial.

St Thégonnec's ossuary, built in 1676, is now an ornate and magnificent chapel. Below Joseph and the boy Jesus, surmounted by the eternal father, steps descend to an extremely vivid tableau of life-size figures. It shows the Descent from the Cross, the most popular of Breton religious scenes. The crucified Christ is surrounded by mourning figures, among them Mary Magdalene, particularly overwhelmed by sorrow.

Guimiliau is the next place to visit after St Thégonnec, that is if you are doing the tour properly, or have a car. But if you are relying on local transport, you will be unlucky. It seems that the rivalry between St Thégonnec and Guimiliau is so great that you must make your choice, and visit either one or the other. There is no public transport link between them although a train runs through St Guimiliau (no ticket office, though, you must pay on the train or at the other end). St Thégonnec's station is about five kilometres from the village. The walk from St Thégonnec to Guimiliau is about 10 km.

Guimiliau's calvary, with its 200 figures (built 1581 to 1588) is the largest and certainly the most famous in Brittany. On its uppermost part is a large cross; the four statues on its shafts are the Virgin and St John, and St Peter and St Yves. There are scenes from the passion on its platform and a tableau showing the story of Catell Gollett (Kathleen the Lost). As this story was quite often told as a warning to naughty flirtatious girls by priests, I will relate it.

Kathleen was a young servant girl, who didn't TELL ALL at confession. From this small beginning and lapse, she started on the slippery slope and became really wicked, one day actually stealing some consecrated bread to give to her lover. Unfortunately for her, he was really the devil in disguise. For this dreadful deed she was condemned to eternal hellfire.

The sixteenth-century church, rebuilt in flamboyant Renaissance style at the beginning of the seventeenth century, is worth seeing, especially its south porch and the fine carved oak baptistry, pulpit and organ loft. The ossuary chapel is quite interesting, but not up to the standard of St Thégonnec.

Lampaul, not far from Guimiliau, also has a parish close worth seeing. The interior of this church is particularly harmonious and contains some treasures, such as a very fine baptismal font, a decorated sixteenth-century rood beam crossing the nave, and a representation of the entombment.

For those who prefer rocks and wooded walks, Huelgoat, in the Monts d'Arrée, about 29 km. from Morlaix, can also be visited by local bus. Picturesquely situated beside a lake and forest, the remains of the old Argoat, it is renowned for its odd-shaped rocks, grottoes, underground river and waterfalls.

Huelgoat, with its large square with an old fountain in the centre, does not itself have very much to offer the tourist. There is the Renaissance chapel of Notre Dame des Cieux, rather dilapidated outside and bare within, which has some bas reliefs of

life of the Virgin and Passion which are of interest, as are the
curious faces sticking out of the wooden beam running round the
top of the walls. The church in the square is very plain, although
it does contain a rather good example of St Yves, patron saint of
Huelgoat, receiving a poor man's petition while refusing a rich
man's purse. This church also has a very loud ticking clock, which
must make services difficult to hear.

So when you arrive by car or bus the first thing to make for is
the rocks. Follow the Rue des Cendres down as far as the white
Café du Chaos, opposite a garage, and not far from the large
lake. I am putting in these instructions because the path, in spite
of a plaque beside the café, is narrow and easily missed.

You follow it and suddenly find yourself in another world, a
world of enormous mossy green boulders humped around the
noisy underground river, a place well-named the Chaos du
Moulin.

It is slippery and slimy and you have to squeeze past boulders
and scramble up and down rough stairs. But the places to see are
well-marked – La Grotte du Diable, to which you descend some
steps, then a ladder, to gaze into the grotto and underground
stream below. There is also a Théâtre du Verdu, set among trees
and surrounded by rocks. Beyond this are steps and paths leading
from a wide path over the hill, all finding the way eventually to
the Roche Tremblante ('trembling rock'), a large 100-ton boulder,
which is supposed to sway when touched but I'm afraid I did not
have the knack. If you return to the wide path and continue along
it you come to the next natural sight – the Ménage de la Vierge
('Virgin's kitchen'). There are certainly some strange indentures in
the rocks round about, but you will have to use your imagination
about this.

The wide path also leads to the Sentier des Amoureux 'lovers'
path') on the left. It is easy to see how this got its name, as the
path seems to wander vaguely in many different directions, which
mostly end nowhere in particular, such as tiny glens, and one soon
loses one's way. However, if you bear right at the first fork and
keep on what looks like the main path, you will eventually find

first. La Grotte d'Artus, a large grotto, made from a tumble of boulders, then the Mare aux Sangliers ('Boars' pool'), a pretty pool fed by two small waterfalls, crossed by a bridge. The Allée Violette, which is approached from the main path, is a very pleasant forest walk, beside the underground river, which, after roaring below the boulders, gradually widens out into a visible stream. The path ends on the road, which you can take back to Huelgoat.

Or you can continue on down it, through the forest. If you intend to do any further walks, it would be as well to get a map and booklet from the Syndicat d'Initiative in the main square. The walk alongside the canal is a very popular one.

Apart from its strange-shaped rocks, and forest walks, Huelgoat makes a good starting place for a tour of the Monts d'Arrée, Brittany's highest 'mountains'. This range, once much higher, has gradually been eroded down the centuries, some parts turning into rounded hills (*ménez*), others becoming sharp, fretted crests (roc'hs). They are often hidden behind mists and appear rather bare and bleak, although those to the east are more wooded. From the heights there are some good views of the surrounding countryside.

The heights of the Monts d'Arrée can be toured by car (about 120 km.), starting from Huelgoat, passing Roc Trévezel, very picturesque against its mountain background, then to Montagne St Michel and the oak and beech forests of Granou. From Le Faou, a picturesquely situated town at the head of the Faou estuary, which looks best at high tide, you can return to Huelgoat via Pleyben, renowned for its splendid parish close and calvary. Brasparts also has an interesting parish close, as does St Herbot. St Herbot's church is of interest because he was the patron saint of horned cattle, and before St Herbot's Pardon, in May, farmers place tufts of hair taken from their cattle's tails on two stone tables beside its carved oak screen.

Huelgoat is about 21 km. from Carhaix, which was an important town in Roman times (the old capital of Finistère). It is still a junction of roads and now of railways, too, and as it lies in the centre of a cattle-breeding area it is renowned for its cattle fairs. Carhaix also makes a good centre to start on a tour of the Montagnes Noires.

Lying to the south-east, this range has somewhat lower and less steep slopes than the Monts d'Arrée. Dark firs cover many of its sides, which is why it is called black. Here you are in the real heart of Brittany and are likely to hear Breton spoken. If you wish to tour this area, Châteauneuf du Faou, a pretty village, is a good place to stay at and use as an excursion centre. Both the Montagnes Noires and the Monts d'Arrée are excellent areas for fishing.

Morlaix to Roscoff; St Pol-de-Léon

Roscoff, which can be reached quite easily by bus or train from Morlaix, also makes a pleasant car drive. At first, that is when the road follows the river, passing Carentec, a delightful seaside resort, situated on a cape between the estuary of the Penzé and Morlaix.

Later though it becomes rather dull. You will pass through St Pol-de-Léon, now an important market town for artichokes, cauli-flowers, onions and potatoes, but whose cathedral and Kreisker tower bring a touch of grandeur to the surrounding flat country-side.

The name St Pol comes from Paulus Aurelianus, a Cambrian monk who landed here in the sixth century from Wales. He founded a monastery, became an abbot, then bishop. St Pol-de-Léon had the honour of being the first bishopric in Lower Brittany.

The present cathedral, built in the thirteenth century, replacing an earlier Romanesque one, has great elegance, especially in the façade with its huge porch and three high windows above. The whole building has a great purity of style. The interior also shows harmonious design – a nave of seven bays with a network of 12 slender columns and sixteenth-century Gothic stalls.

St Paul's bones are preserved in a chalice opposite the great rose window. There are tombs of many bishops, including that of Jean

François de la Marche, an émigré along with Chateaubriand in London who helped to administer a fund for the assistance of dependants of those killed in the Quiberon expedition. He died in 1806, when his remains were taken to his see in St Pol-de-Léon. English people might be interested to know that he wrote 'The generosity of the English nation surpasses all the instances of benevolences recorded in the history of nations'. Alas, the bishopric of St Pol-de-Léon did not survive Napoleon. The old palace of the bishops is now the Town Hall.

The chapel of the Kreisker, near by, dates from the fourteenth century, but was altered and enlarged in the following century and was used as a chapel by the Town Council. Now it is the college chapel, but it is its beautiful belfry, so delicate and slender, a marvel of balance which has served as a model for many other Breton towers, which has made the Kreisker chapel famous. It may be climbed – 169 steps if you feel energetic – and you will be rewarded by a very fine panoramic view of the surrounding countryside.

Roscoff

Roscoff, with its mild climate and streets of sturdy grey stone houses, is one of my favourite little seaside towns in Brittany. It is likely to become many other people's favourite, too, now that the shipping line between it and Plymouth for travellers and cars together is in action. Holidaymakers coming to Brittany will find it a convenient place to land in if they intend staying in Finistère or the western end of the Côtes-du-Nord.

The port looks out across seaweed-covered rocks to the island of Batz. To get there is very simple. You just walk down a long narrow way, which eventually drops down, covered in green slime, into the sea. Near its end is a little white boat with a blue cabin, the *Santa Anna*, which makes a 15-minute journey to the island about once every hour.

From a distance, Batz looks quite an important place. Its tall lighthouse put me in mind of Nelson's column. But on closer acquaintance it is a mere fishing village, with tiny grey stone houses divided by narrow cobbled streets, bleak yet attractive. Most of the men are sailors, while the women work in the fields or collect seaweed. This, when processed with shells and sea mud, is used as a fertilizer, and its collection is quite an important industry all along this part of the coast.

Batz, sheltered by reefs on its north side, is treeless, but to prove that it is on the Gulf Stream it has a garden of tropical plants on its south-west point. It has some sandy beaches, unlike Roscoff's, which are shingle. If you like rugged picturesqueness and extreme quiet, you might enjoy a holiday on Batz.

Most people connect Roscoff with onion sellers, and certainly it is a great centre for vegetables, especially cauliflowers and arti-chokes, grown all around in the area known as the Ceinture Dorée ('golden belt'); fish, too – apart from being an important lobster port, Roscoff's Charles Pérez Aquarium, which shows sea creatures in their natural environment, is the most important marine laboratory in France.

Roscoff has another claim to fame in that it possesses an enor-mous, nearly 360-year-old fig tree, which can produce as much as 1,000 lbs of figs a year; it grows in a Capuchin convent garden.

Like St Malo, Roscoff was once a centre for corsairs. Sculpted ships and cannons decorate the outside walls and towers of its sixteenth-century church, Notre Dame de Kroaz-Baz, around which the old town clusters. It also has a remarkable Renaissance belfry with three towers representing the Trinity, reckoned to be one of the finest in Finistère.

Roscoff should be of interest to the Scots for it was here that the five-year-old child, Mary Stuart, landed in 1548 on her way to her betrothed, the young French dauphin. A turret marks the place where she landed – the old harbour has been considerably changed since then. But you can still see the plain grey stone house where she is supposed to have spent her first night in France. Nearly 200 years later, another Scot, Charles Edward Stuart, the Young Pre-tender, also landed here after his disastrous defeat at Culloden, pursued to the last by English ships.

My last impression was of Scotland again, because there were bagpipes playing what sounded like a Highland Fling as I sat on a bus waiting to go to Brest. The driver reminded me that bagpipes were Breton, too, and that the International Bagpipe Festival, held for three days in Brest every August, is one of the biggest folklore festivals in Brittany.

So we started our journey, most appropriately to the skirl of pipes and with seagulls whirling overhead in a grey sky. The driver was an amusing fellow, very cheerful and friendly, shaking hands with all who got on the bus, and waving to those who didn't. Even the dogs weren't left out – he barked at them. Nor for that matter were the cows; every time we passed a field of them he made a noise on his mouthpiece which sounded just like a moo. They all stared at the bus with uncomprehending astonishment. Our drive to Brest first through flat fields of vegetables, later through a more varied undulating countryside, was certainly a spirited one. He almost danced the bus down the road. Fortunately, there was little traffic about at that time.

Brest and its surroundings

I am afraid I have a rather jaundiced opinion of Brest. This is partly due to the fact that it was pouring with rain when I arrived and partly because I had difficulty in finding a hotel; the Syndicat d'Initiative, when I found it, was closed, and the people who should have been there were all away attending a fair somewhere else. I also met a dripping wet young American couple at the station who told me they hated the place. 'It's really dull. We're just getting the hell out of it.'

But I think their judgment was a bit harsh. Brest suffered very badly during the last war and has been completely rebuilt. It is now a modern, well-laid-out city with good shops, parks and wide boulevards. But although all this probably makes it more comfortable to live in it is rather featureless, and not for the tourist in search of local colour.

It owes much to Colbert (1619–83), one of France's great

ministers, who made it the maritime capital of France. The marine and administration office, now known as the Inscription Maritime Office, set up by him, still exists today. He also founded a school of gunnery, a college of marine guards, a school of hydrography and a school for marine engineers. Out of all this emerged France's powerful fleet. Other things were added later, such as better dockyards, buoy moorings, and Vauban's strong fortifications.

Brest, although now an important commercial centre with a well-known university, is still predominantly a city of the sea. Its position is uniquely good : the harbour, the total anchorage of which covers about 50 square miles and is 40 feet deep in parts, connects with many inlets and also with the Atlantic through the Goulet channel.

Unfortunately, Brest's first-class strategic position was also her undoing. During the Second World War she was invaluable to the Germans as a submarine base, and a great worry to the Allied convoys sailing between Britain and America. The result was a long and intensive bombardment. All this, added to the Germans' destroying much of the centre before the Americans moved in, resulted in a devastated, almost gutted city.

The Bretons are proud of the new one that has arisen from the ashes. In fact, it was often quoted to me as being the most beautiful city in their province. Whether it is or not, I do not feel competent to judge – most of the time I stayed there it was shrouded in mist.

On my second day there, when it had lifted just enough to allow one to see where one was going, I walked to the Cours Dajot, a small park on the hill, from which there is a grand view over the roadstead and harbour. That you can see see the mouth of the Élorn river, the Ménez Hom and the Pointe du Portzic I take on trust : the viewing table said you could.

There are some quite good excursions by bus, car or boat from Brest. You can drive, or take a bus, to the Pointe St Mathieu, whose tall lighthouse stands amid the ruins of a sixth-century Benedictine abbey, and then visit Le Conquet, a rugged picturesque little fishing port and resort, the southern extremity of the grim northern promontory of Finistère. Or, going in the opposite direction, you can drive over Pont Albert Louppe to the Plougastel peninsula, a little old-world area of Brittany, famous for its strawberries. Plougastel-Daolas, the chief town, possesses quite a famous calvary, built at the beginning of the seventeenth century as a thanksgiving for the ending of the plague. The modern church beside it has a brilliantly coloured interior.

Then there are the Abers. *Aber* is the Breton word (Welsh, too) for estuary. This north-west promontory of Finistère, bleak and wild, is broken by rivers and innumerable shallow streams, which wind across its low-lying hills. Its rocky coastline is dotted with tiny islands, rich in seaweed. This coast of legends, often hidden behind mists, has a sort of melancholy charm, and makes quite an attractive tour.

L'Aber Wrach on the west side is a smartish yachting centre. Le Folgoët, lying inland on its eastern side, is particularly renowned for its large, square-shaped church and beautiful belfry (a copy of the Kreisker one at St Pol-de-Léon). Its Pardon, which takes place in September, attracts some of the largest numbers in Brittany. Find time to visit the church. Note the delicate rood screen, also the fountain in the chapel porch, presided over by the Virgin Mary. Its waters come from a spring under the altar.

And herein lies a story. According to tradition, a simple fellow, named Salaün (Solomon), usually known as Folgoët ('fool of the wood'), lived near a spring in the wood. He only knew a few words, which were 'O, Lady Virgin Mary' (in Breton, of course), which he was always repeating. He died eventually but the people were surprised to find a white lily growing in the woods with these words showing in the design of its pistils. Curious, they dug up the lily and were utterly amazed to discover that the flower was growing out of the fool's mouth. The War of Succession was taking place then, and the Duke of Montfort had made a vow that if he won, he would build a great church to the Virgin. After his victory at Auray, it was decided that this would be the place to put it. The altar was set over the spring from which the idiot drank.

South of the church lies the sixteenth-century manor house, called the Doyenné, now containing a museum. This was where the Duchess Anne stayed when she came on a pilgrimage here in the early sixteenth century. There is also an inn near by where pilgrims stayed.

Not far from Le Folgoët stands the château of Kerjean, partly a fortress, guarded by a moat and thick walls, and partly a Renaissance palace with decorated rooms, colonnades, park and fountain. Kerjean, which was bought by the state in 1911, now contains a small museum of Breton furniture. The *lits clos* (box beds) are like tiny rooms in themselves. There are also some amusing stories connected with the old residents of this house.

If you wish to make a sea trip from Brest (weather permitting), the Port du Commerce lies on the left-hand side of the station and about 1 km. down the hill. You will pass the red granite obelisk in the Cours Dajot, erected by the United States to commemorate the achievements of the French and United States naval forces during the war. The original monument was to World War One, but was destroyed by the Germans in 1941. This one was erected in 1958.

There is not much to see in the port for the most interesting part of the harbour – the naval dockyards, arsenal and castle – are not for prying foreign eyes. However, if you walk as far as the wall on the right you will see gaunt grey battleships lying in dock, below the old château on the other side of the town and bay, while loudspeakers shout instructions to sailors engaged on various mysterious naval activities.

Tickets for the Vedettes Amoricaines are obtained from a new blue-and-white office beside a small port. You can go to Le Conquet by boat as well as bus, and the Ile d'Ouessant (Ushant) if you have the time (it takes about four hours to get there) and a strong stomach, for the sea can be very rough.

Ouessant, the rocky island on the extreme north-west corner of Brittany is notorious for the perilous currents and reefs surrounding it. It is particularly dangerous to approach in winter because of fog and high winds, and has been the scene of many shipwrecks.

Even so, its climate is very mild. If you managed to get there in January and February you would find yourself in one of the warmest parts of France. It is familiar to British sailors because its powerful Créac'h lighthouse, along with the one on Bishop Rock, marks the beginning of the English Channel.

On the way there the boat stops at Le Conquet and the tiny island of Molène, lying amid an archipelago of rocks and islets. Ouessant is about 16 square km. and Lampaul is its largest settlement. Here, you should have a meal of shellfish and salt mutton, the island's two culinary specialities. Most of the land is given over to grazing sheep. As with Batz, the women cultivate what crops there are, while the men are sailors or fishermen (mostly of lobsters).

The Crozon peninsula can be reached either by road (quite a long journey) or by boat (three-quarters of an hour), but you can only buy your ticket half an hour before the voyage in case of bad weather. I left Brest this second way and caught the small white steamer to Le Fret opposite. From here I was told there would be a coach connection with Crozon and Morgat beyond.

It was a pleasant crossing giving one a good general view of the roadstead, also Brest, with its old castle, busy docks, and tall modern buildings. Eventually, one could see the coast in outline as far as Pte. St Mathieu and Pont Albert Louppe, which links the mainland with the Plougastel peninsula.

The Crozon Peninsula

The coach at Le Fret turned out to be a small van into which everyone was squeezed, along with a pig (fortunately, dead). The countryside through which we drove was rather wild and wooded with frequent stretches of ferns and gorse and appeared deserted.

The Crozon peninsula, which stretches out like a tongue between Brittany's western extremities, the Abers and Cornouaille, has one of the best and warmest climates in Brittany. Moreover, it is still largely undiscovered by British holidaymakers.

Morgat, once a sardine port, is its most popular resort, because of its large, safe, sandy beach, set in a sheltered bay. I found it attractive and homely, a good centre for walks along the cliffs, sailing (there is a yacht club and school), fishing and seafood restaurants. Then there are its grottoes. The small caves which lie at the foot of a spur between Morgat and Le Portzic beaches can be reached at low tide, while the large ones have to be visited by motor boat (you can get one from the port and it takes about three-quarters of an hour). There are two groups of these. The best grotto is the beautifully coloured one called the Altar (250 feet deep and 45 feet high).

The chief drawback about Morgat, though, is its bus service (only one a day when I was there), so if you want to make excursions farther afield and you have no car, you will have to walk three kilometres to Crozon, the administrative and geographical centre of the small peninsula.

There was once a Crozon–Morgat railway station. This is now, alas, a mere façade standing in front of a derelict track, a reminder that it was one of Brittany's uneconomic lines. The plain grey ex-railway station now houses an SNCF bus office: the yard in front is the starting place of Crozon's few buses.

Crozon, old, grey and typically Breton, was known in the fifth century as Crauthon, which later became Crauzon. It is built round its long plain church, the rounded tower of which peers like a prim governess above the houses, a landmark for miles.

Unlike so many churches in other places, Breton ones are often in use, even on a weekday morning. There are no plaques or statues inside to important people, apart from Bishops, who have usually got promoted to sainthood anyway. Church interiors are generally crowded with the tall, colourful (or gaudy) statues of saints, set around like silent, passive friends, amongst whom ordinary people can sit, perhaps to draw comfort and inspiration for their own lives.

Crozon church's most famous feature is the reredos to the 10,000 martyrs, on the right-hand side of the main altar. This large and brightly coloured carving is supposed to depict the martyrdom of 10,000 Christian soldiers, who died for their faith

10   *The beach at Beg-Meil, Finistère*
11   *The church at Tronoën, Finistère, from the south (see overleaf)*

12   *The calvary at Tronoën – the oldest calvary in Brittany*

during the reign of the Emperor Hadrian. It has 12 panels of pictures in the centre and six panels of pictures on shutters either side. That they were done about the end of the fifteenth century, probably by two local artists, is all that is really known about them. Why they are here and their connection with Crozon is a mystery.

Opposite the reredos is a more recent memorial, a modern painting showing a girl with her head in Christ's lap, while listed below are the names of all those of Crozon Morgat who died during the war (1939–45), listing how they died and their ages. On a wall beside the chapel on the other side of the church is a list of names of those who died in the 1914–18 War, a tremendously large number for such a small place. But this is fairly typical of most Breton towns and villages.

If you have a car, and this is really a necessity on the Crozon peninsula unless you like long walks, you should do a grand tour, visiting the small isolated hamlet of Landévennec with its ruined abbey and museum, and the various points, such as the Pointe de la Chèvre (view over the Atlantic), Pointe des Espagnols (this was defended by a Spanish force against English and French combined); the Pointe de Dinan (shaped like a dog's head and with fantastic and colourful caves); and particularly the Pointe de Penhir.

Not far from the Pointe de Penhir is Camaret sur Mer (the name comes from the Breton word, *kamélet*), one of the most attractive of Brittany's fishing port/resorts. Whitewashed, grey slate-roofed houses climb the hills behind its peaceful harbour. Lobsters are the chief catch, but the fishermen now have to search for them farther afield than the coastal waters. Underwater fishing and sailing are the two most popular sea sports at Camaret; there are also regular boat services to Molène, Ouessant and Brest (via Le Fret).

The yachting harbour lies on the other side of a long esplanade on which stands a quaint little chapel and Vauban-fortified tower, entered by a wooden bridge across a moat. This holds the honour of having repulsed an Anglo-Dutch attack in 1694, when troops tried to make a landing here. Louis XIV, in recognition of Camaret's valour, had a medal struck to commemorate the occasion, and gave the town the title, *Custos Orae Amorocae* ('custodian of the Breton shore'). Also, and probably more popular, he excused the inhabitants from paying the detested hearth tax. The tower now houses a museum.

The chapel, picturesquely spelled Roc'h-am-a-dour, was burned down in 1527. Its bell tower was broken off in 1694 by an English cannon ball. It was also accidentally burned down in 1910, but was rebuilt again, keeping to its old style. Inside it is a truly nautical little chapel. Apart from the usual painted statues, there is also a sailing boat suspended from the central beam, a fleet of steamers in a glass case before the side altar, along with anchors, lifebelts and oars. A Pardon is held here on the first Sunday in September, following the blessing of the sea.

The walk to Pointe Penhir from Camaret is uphill and passes some menhirs arranged in three sides of a square. The Crozon peninsula was a prehistoric dwelling place, but unfortunately most of the old stones have disappeared, having been used for other buildings. The last few kilometres out to the end of the peninsula lie along a path through heather, the sea either side. From the farthest point you can see the left-hand shape of the coast, the Pointe de Dinan, and in the very distance, Europe's farthest point, the Pointe du Raz.

However, the best view of the sea and the Tas des Pois ('heap of peas') – a famous string of rocks – is from the platform to the right of the granite monument. From here, you can see the shape of the coast, Pointe du Toulinguet, Pointe St Mathieu, and in the dim distance, the island of Ouessant. The monument, incidentally, is dedicated to the Bretons of the Free French army, and was inaugurated by De Gaulle in 1951. A pilgrimage is held here each year by Bretons of the Resistance.

A walk to the Pointe du Toulinguet leads through pretty country but ends disappointingly in a military fort, which you are forbidden to enter.

The drive from Crozon eastwards and inland towards Châteaulin is a particularly pleasant one, through undulating countryside, past woodlands and fields and villages, complete as usual with church with tall towers and surrounded by an enormous churchyard. Although I was travelling in November, the gardens and churchyards were still crowded with flowers – even roses – on this beautifully warm and sunny day.

Then, first in the distance, but later on the left, loomed Ménez Hom, Brittany's highest mountain. From its top, which can be reached by car, there is the most splendid view of the entire Crozon peninsula, also of Cornouaille (the Pte du Van) on the left, and of the Brest Roadstead on the right.

Châteaulin, lying on the bend of the Aulne river, is one of the chief salmon-fishing centres in the Aulne valley. There is even a salmon on the town's coat of arms. Situated beside a railway line and with regular bus services, it makes a good excursion centre, being within easy reach of Pleyben and the Monts d'Arrée, as well as connecting with the Crozon peninsula and Quimper, capital of the Cornouaille.

Cornouaille

This old kingdom, later the medieval duchy of Cornouaille, the French Cornwall, once stretched far farther north and east of its capital, Quimper, than it does today.

But it is still a real old corner of Brittany, a country of Pardons and calvaries, and where you are more likely to see women wearing the traditional black dress and white coiffes – flat lace caps or miniature menhirs – than in any other part. Its seacoast is rocky and exciting. Its interior is flat and well-cultivated with field after field of vegetables or green pasture for grazing cows. You will see many little hamlets of grey or white stone houses with usually a white mist billowing gently in the distance.

Like the Abers, it has its quota of legends, the most famous one being about its king, the Roi Gradlon, who lived during the sixth century, when a town named Ys was the capital of Cornouaille.

This town, which was very beautiful, was protected from the

sea by a dyke. The king always carried the golden key which opened its lock about with him. Alas, this good man had a lovely but dissolute daughter, who had fallen in love with a young man who was really the devil in disguise. He begged her to steal the key from her father and open the gate. This she did, while he was sleeping, and the sea rushed into the town. Although the king woke in time, and mounted his horse, pulling his daughter up behind him, the angry waves followed. They would have swallowed him, too, had not a celestial voice ordered him to throw his daughter back behind him into the water.

The king obeyed with aching heart, and the sea withdrew. But the town still lay buried beneath its waves.

Gradlon chose Quimper for his new capital. The good St Corentin, its first bishop, became his guide and chief adviser. But his daughter, who was turned into a mermaid, and known as Maria Morgane, is still supposed to lure sailors to their death. According to tradition, the curse will only be broken and the city of Ys come back on the day that Mass is celebrated in one of the churches of the drowned city. However, to make things even more difficult, Ys is claimed to be in three different places – beyond the Baie des Trépassés, the Baie de Douarnenez and Pen Marc'h.

Quimper, lying in a pretty little valley, a town of towers and spires, is an attractive, almost elegant place, compared with most of Brittany's plain homespun towns. Its name means 'confluence' and comes from its two rivers, the Odet and Steir, which converge here.

The river Odet, which has been tamed to run neatly behind railings with pavements lined with trees either side, makes its sluggish, smelly, yet dignified way straight through the town. While the Steir, which cuts across the opposite way, is narrower, less formal, livelier, and has more character, especially when it splashes below the old jutting-out houses and turrets.

There are so many quaint narrow cobbled streets running up and down hills and over bridges that Quimper is a town just to wander through, especially the *vieux quartier*. But if possible choose a time when there is no traffic about. The lay part of the city, as opposed to the episcopal part, lies chiefly beyond the Place Terre au Duc.

St Corentin's cathedral (thirteenth to sixteenth centuries) lies in the episcopal area, its twin spires being the city's landmark. Although they only date from 1856, they blend in so well with the rest of the cathedral, that no one would have guessed that they had not been built earlier. To pay for their building the bishop asked the faithful of the diocese to pay one *sou* a year each for five years.

Before the cathedral stands the statue of a man on horseback, who, as you might guess, is King Gradlon. The street leading to the cathedral is named after him, while the square is called after his bishop.

The cathedral's façade with its large flamboyant portal, the high windows of its towers and openwork balconies, is very elegant, as is its interior, in spite of the fact that the thirteenth-century choir is out of line with the fifteenth-century nave. The fifteenth-century stained glass in the upper window is particularly fine. There is a little garden attached to the cathedral with lawns, flowerbeds and seats, and even a paddling pool and sandpit thoughtfully provided for children.

Quimper has some good museums, especially the Beaux Arts, which possesses Rubenses, Bouchers, Fragonards and Corots, amongst others. Quimper is also renowned for its pottery and you can visit a museum and working pottery if you wish. Quimper is probably most famous as being a centre of folklore: if you should happen to be there on the fourth Sunday in July you will find the whole town celebrating the Great Festival of Cornouaille, the biggest folklore festival in France.

Moreover, it is a grand centre for excursions and expeditions by bus, car or train, most of which do not entail much travelling time (though a popular drive in Cornouaille is that around the rocky, indented coast – approximately 320 km.).

Visit Locronan first, a little jewel of a town, set between forests on a steep hill. Its fine Renaissance square tells of wealthier days, when its inhabitants made their money from the manufacture of sailcloth. Taking into account all the places that manufactured it in Brittany, there must have been a great demand!

Locronan means 'holy place of Ronan' and refers to St Ronan, an Irish hermit, who lived in the wooded hills above the town. And it is to this place that the Petit Tromény (another word for Pardon) comes on a Sunday in July, rewalking St Ronan's everyday barefoot route. Every sixth year there is a Grand Tromény, which lasts a week, and in which many other villages take part.

Douarnenez is a large and busy fishing port (also seaside resort if you include Tréboul with it), lying either side of an estuary, and giving its name to the whole bay between the Crozon Peninsula and Cap Sizun. Cap Sizun, known as the Cap, incorporates the famous Pointe du Raz and the Pointe du Van, and is Europe's westernmost peninsula. Cap Sizun also contains a bird sanctuary, which can be visited between the 15th of March and the 31st of August (10 a.m. to noon and 2 p.m. to 6 p.m.; the conducted tour takes half an hour).

St Tugen (you will have to make a detour to visit it) has an interesting sixteenth-century chapel and a saint (his statue stands near to the high altar on the right), who was renowned for his bizarre habit of carrying a key that when touched by another key would drive away mad dogs!

Audierne is another attractive fishing port set picturesquely at the foot of a wooded hill round the mouth of the Goyen estuary. One of its fishing specialities is crayfish, delicately flavoured, which you might care to try.

After Plouzévet, which has an attractive thirteenth–fifteenth-century church, you are approaching the low-lying Penmarc'h peninsula, which, in contrast to the steep indented coastline of Cap Sizun opposite, sweeps round in a coveless 12-mile bay. The famous and very powerful Eckmühl lighthouse stands at the extreme end of the peninsula.

Strange to relate, the Penmarc'h peninsula was once one of the most prosperous parts of Brittany, when its inhabitants chiefly made their living by cod fishing. Then disaster followed disaster.

The cod deserted their coastal waters and a tidal wave wrought great destruction. Finally, during the anarchy produced by the religious wars a notorious brigand, named La Fontenelle, took advantage of the situation to attack this area. Many houses were destroyed and people killed. La Fontenelle loaded his booty on to ships and returned to his island, La Tristan, which he had captured, in the bay of Douarnenez.

Still, he got his deserts in the end. He was seized in 1602 (during reign of Henri IV), and was sentenced to be broken on the wheel, then to be publicly exposed until he died. But Penmarc'h never really recovered from all this.

Not far from the town of Penmarc'h is the calvary of Notre Dame du Tronoën, much weather-beaten because of its exposed position, but having the honour of being the oldest calvary in Brittany.

Pont l'Abbé, with its shady quays, situated at the head of an estuary, is the chief town of the Pays Bigouden, and is famous for its traditional costumes, particularly the tall white lace caps worn by the women. Apart from market gardening, one of the main industries is making little dolls dressed in the traditional costumes of the different French provinces. Its name Pont l'Abbé comes from the bridge built by the monks of Loctudy between the *étang* ('pool') and the harbour. From the little port of Loctudy you can take the boat up the river to Quimper.

In fact, the river trip starting from Quimper down the Odet is one of the most delightful excursions you can take from Quimper. The boat stops first at Bénodet, a very pretty and fashionable sea-side resort and yachting harbour. Then if you want to, you can continue on to Loctudy, then the Glénan Isles, an archipelago of nine islets and home of a famous sailing school.

Local buses from Quimper (bus station in the Boulevard de Kerguelen) go to the Monts d'Arrée and the Montagnes Noires, also to places along the Cornouaille coast. I took one via Audierne to the Pointe du Raz.

The journey there ended rather disappointingly in a car park. Ahead and all around lay billowing mist. I could only just distinguish the long line of buildings and the word 'café' through the fog.

'Voilà l'Atlantique. Next stop America,' said the driver. I was his only passenger – the only person probably mad enough to come in November. Dismounting, shivering and turning up his coat collar, he made quickly for the café and a warm drink.

In spite of my frustration, I was determined to see more of this famous headland, and made my way stumbling towards the edge of the grass, not sure what lay beyond, and hoping that I wouldn't fall over the cliffs.

However, my luck was in. As I walked, so the large pile of rocks before me gradually extended itself into the beginning of a spur and the mist rolled slowly backwards rather like a curtain lifting to reveal the most wonderful views of headlands, high cliffs and foaming water below.

A fisherman made his way along the spur of rock to a pool, just out of sight. Concluding that it was now safe enough I followed him forward over the rocks and might, had there been time, have reached the end of the spur. But perhaps I should add that there are guides, whose office is near the café, who will take parties along the Pointe du Raz unless there is a mist or it is very windy. It is not unknown for people to be blown off the Pointe in a high wind.

Far out at sea and beyond the lighthouse lies the island of Sein, which can be reached by boat from the mainland. It is low and bare with no trees or bushes, but vegetables, especially potatoes, and barley are grown. The houses are tiny and lie along narrow streets. Not surprisingly, the inhabitants lived here in complete isolation until the eighteenth century, when they were converted to Christianity by the Jesuit fathers.

Up to then they were greatly feared by the people living on the mainland because of their habit of looting wrecks, of which there were usually plenty. Today, they are more renowned for their skill at life-saving, although they do still obtain benefits from ship-wrecks off their coast. Much of the furniture in their houses is made from shipwrecks. The lighthouse on the island was built in 1881 to warn ships off this dangerous area.

The men, mostly sailors and lobster fishermen, are very independent. In June 1940 they all put to sea and joined the Free French Army in England. In 1946 they were awarded the Liberation Cross by General de Gaulle for their valour.

The Baie des Trépassés, an innocent-looking stretch of sand to the right of the Pointe du Raz, was supposed to have got its name, Bay of the Dead, from the number of people washed up in it after being drowned off this coast. Although according to another theory it is because, according to ancient tradition, this was the bay from which the corpses of druids were taken to the island of Sein for burial.

Another place which can be visited not far from Quimper is Concarneau, a large fishing port and lively sea resort, with the added attraction of a wonderful old walled town, the Ville Clos.

This is approached from the quay by crossing two bridges which pass under a gateway into a fortified courtyard laid out with flowers. From here, if you like, you can enter a white gate beside the entrance (a charge is made) and walk round part of the ramparts, which give a good view of the harbour and fishing port.

Another gateway leads from the courtyard below into the Rue Vauban, passing the Musée de la Pêche, which is installed in what was once part of the town's fortications. Here you can learn how fishing techniques developed and the history of the town.

Like other such places, Concarneau is just pleasant to wander through, up and down its narrow cobbled streets, and peering through the occasional archways, which lead on to tiny quays and out at the sea beyond.

In the centre square is a green crocodile swallowing a fish holding aloft a lantern, doing duty both as a fountain and a light. Not far from here an arrow indicates another viewpoint and another part of the ramparts, from which to watch the yachts and fishing boats in the bay and Atlantic beyond.

According to a plaque on the wall nothing has changed here since Louis XIV's time, when Vauban improved and added to its fortifications. Before that, however, Concarneau lived through some stirring times.

Some sort of fortress, although primitive, has existed on this island rock since about the ninth century, when it was used by the fishermen and people living round about as an easily-defended place of refuge. By the thirteenth century it was surrounded by a stone wall and reckoned to be one of the strongest fortified places in Brittany. During the War of Succession, it was held for Montfort and was occupied by an English garrison for 30 years. In 1373 it stood up to two assaults by Du Guesclin, but was conquered by the third in 1378. It was reconstructed and improved by two dukes of Brittany, Peter II and François II. During the Wars of Religion it was mostly held by the Catholic Leaguers, except for a short time when, after it had been taken by surprise, it was held by a group of Huguenots from Morbihan. Later, royalist troops assaulted and seized it for Louis XIII and France. Louis XIV had his military architect, Vauban, turn it into part of France's seaboard defences. Today, its mild climate and tranquil atmosphere have turned it into a peaceful haven suitable for harbouring the sick and recuperating. I noticed two hospitals within its sturdy walls.

After visiting the Ville Clos, you can stroll round the fishing harbour, along the Pierre Guéguin and the Quai Carnot. Concarneau is one of the most important fishing harbours in France – tunny fish, sardines, herrings, shrimps, etc. – and on the last Sunday but one in August, the Fête of the Filets Bleus ('blue nets'), one of the oldest of Brittany's folklore festivals, is held here.

If you walk the other way you will pass the Quai de Croix, the lighthouse and the fifteenth-century chapel of Notre Dame de Bon Secours and eventually reach the Plage des Petits Sables Blancs, and the Plage des Grands Sables Blancs.

La Forêt Fousenant, a small peaceful village, surrounded by orchards – the best Breton cider is produced here – lies farther along and inland at the head of a creek. Cap Coz has lovely sandy beaches, good bathing and a sailing school. Beg Meil, a high-class resort, now very popular with the English, can also be reached by boat from Concarneau, as can the Glénan Islands.

The Pointe du Cabellou (a good viewing-point of the coastline) lies the opposite way, as do Port Raguenès Plage, Port Manech (an unspoilt little fishing port), Pont-Aven (picturesquely set where the Aven meets the estuary, beloved by the Impressionists, especially Gaugin, and still much favoured by artists), Riec-sur-Belon (famous for its succulent oysters) and Le Pouldu (also a favourite haunt of Gauguin).

Quimperlé, a small town situated at the junction of the Isole and Ellé rivers, connected by rail and road with Quimper and Vannes (Morbihan), and within easy reach of the Argoat and most of the south coast seaside resorts, makes a good centre for excursions.

5. Morbihan

The Morbihan, which is situated in the centre and south of Brittany, takes its name from the Gulf of Morbihan (which means 'little sea'). Winters are mild along its coast, which is less indented than the north and west. Fishing is an important industry, especially for sardines and tunny, and oysters are bred in the Gulf. As the land is not very fertile farming is chiefly confined to cattle-rearing and dairy production, and orchards for cider apples. The Morbihan is something of a rural backwater and is considered a backward area of France. Breton is still spoken in its western part.

Inland Area

The village of Le Faouët, not far from Quimperlé, lies on the edge of the Montagnes Noires. But its vast sixteenth-century market-place built out of wood and roofed with tiles makes it seem more like a town. The surrounding country is attractive and the two nearby chapels of Ste Barbe and St Fiacre are worth seeing.

Ste Barbe (St Barbara) is a very popular Breton saint, and quite a busy bee. Not only is she the patron saint of all to do with fire, buildings and stone masons, but also of artillerymen and grave-diggers.

Ste Barbe is really a cluster of buildings, which stand on a wooded hillside looking over the Ellé river, for it incorporates an inn, a small bell tower in which pilgrims can toll to attract heaven's blessed attention, as well as the small fifteenth-century

Gothic chapel (this possesses some delicately-carved panels and fine Renaissance stained-glass windows) and a monumental classical stone staircase which leads to an upper terrace. From here a balustraded bridge takes you to a tiny oratory, St Michel, perched on a rock above. According to local tradition, Ste Barbe's chapel was built by a local landowner in gratitude for being saved from being crushed by a rock which had been dislodged by lightning.

Pearly-grey St Fiacre, also fifteenth-century, and more of a church than a chapel, is dedicated to the patron saint of gardeners. Its best features are its triple tower and its superb lace-like carved wooden rood screen, decorated on the nave side with the statues of the archangel Gabriel, the Virgin, St John and Adam and Eve. The figures on the chancel side show various sins, such as theft, lust, drunkenness and laziness and are quite extraordinary and fascinating to look at.

St Fiacre has a curious connection with Kernascléden, about 21 km. to the east. Although its church was consecrated in 1453, about 30 years before St Fiacre, there is a legend that they were built by the same workmen, who were somehow conveyed through time and space from one site to the other by angels.

This Breton church is famous for the perfection of the detail of its workmanship. Its façade, with its gable and rose window surmounted by a slender steeple, has elegance and a purity of line. Inside are some remarkable fifteenth-century frescoes (restored), portraying scenes from the life of Christ and the Virgin. For those who like the lurid, there is a *danse macabre* in the south transept giving a most fantastic representation of Hell and showing a variety of tortures.

Busy Pontivy, situated where the river Blavet is joined by the Nantes–Brest canal, is the principal market town of central Brittany. Its name comes from the bridge built by the monks of Ivy, whose name in turn came from an early Celtic bishop. The town is also linked with the ancient and noble family of de Rohan, one of whose dukes, Jean II, built its castle (only recently restored) in 1485.

Pontivy is an intriguing mixture of centuries. Its Flamboyant Gothic church and Place des Martyrs, old houses and surrounding narrow streets with names such as Rue du Fil (Yarn Street) and Rue de Perroquet (Topgallant Street), recall the Middle Ages, when sailcloth was one of Brittany's chief productions. While the Place d'Armes, Avenue Napoléon, and straight streets lined with austere buildings recall the newer, military spirit of the First Empire.

During the Napoleonic wars, when Britain still ruled the seas, Napoleon decided to build a canal across Brittany, linking Brest with Nantes. As Pontivy lies about halfway between, it seemed a good idea to make it the strategic and military centre of a province of uncertain loyalty. Roads, barracks, a Town Hall, a court and school as well as the canal (now no longer used above Pontivy), were all constructed. The town even changed its name to Napoléonville. However, after the fall of his empire building stopped and, except for a period during the time of Napoleon III, the name Napoléonville was dropped; Pontivy returned to its role of provincial town. Even so, the layout of its wide streets, often named after Napoleonic battles, recalls more heroic times. If its buildings are not particularly noble, then the gorgeous flowers and shrubs planted round about are compensation.

Pontivy, linking as it does with the Montagne Noires and places of interest such as Vannes, Josselin and the Lac de Guerlédan, makes a good excursion centre.

The long lake of Guerlédan, one of the sights of inland Brittany, is really in Côtes-du-Nord, but I have put it in this Morbihan chapter because it is more easily approached from there. This magnificent stretch of water is a reservoir made from the abandoned canal which once flowed through the deep gorge of the Blavet river.

The large village of Mer-de-Bretagne, set amidst trees, is a good place to start on the 40-km. tour of the lake. There is a good panorama of the big dam and the canal linking Nantes to Mer-de-Bretagne via Pontivy, if you leave the village on the D18 and walk or drive about 2 km.

You will then have to return to Mur-en-Bretagne to start the grand tour of the lake from the south. You take the D35 on the right and after the canal turn right on to the D31.

At St Aignan there is a pretty little church and if you make another detour about one kilometre down to the lake, you will find another good viewing point looking out over the dam.

Back on the road again, you will eventually come to the Quénécan forest, undulating and green. The surrounding hills, waters and trees form a landscape which is known as the Suisse Bretonne. However, the forest, once much larger, has been gradually eroded, so that a lot of it now is just scrubland and heath. Most of the oak and beech groves lie around the Forges des Salles.

This is an attractive leafy hamlet which got its name from the iron ore which was smelted here until the beginning of the last century. The ruined castle, now converted into a farmhouse, also lies in this valley. Not far from here lies another 'has been', a roofless overgrown ruin, which was once the twelfth-century Abbey of Bon Repos and, in its heyday, was under the charge of Cardinal Mazarin.

You should not miss going up the gorges of the Daoulas by the D44. Here the river cuts deep and swift through rocks to join the Blavet. The narrow, winding, steep-sided valleys are covered in gorse, broom, heather and foxgloves, with birch trees growing gracefully near the water's edge.

You join the N164 about 1½ km. along the valley on the left and continue about five km. to Keriven, where there is a very good view of the lake, then rejoin the N164 at Caurel. You can now return to Mur-en-Bretagne by the N167, or continue along the N164*bis*, then turn up the D63 to the narrow, rocky and wooded Poulancre gorges and St Gilles du Vieux Marché.

Josselin, about 34 km. to the east of Pontivy is one of Brittany's loveliest medieval towns. Its château is a must for every visitor to the province.

You should see it first from the bridge over the Oust, coming from the direction of Malestroit. It is a truly fairytale castle, with strong walls and tall pointed towers, all seeming to grow straight out of the rocks, proudly mirrored in the dark waters below.

You will have to climb steps and follow passages round to its entrance on the other side. Josselin, still owned by the de Rohans, is a real stately home. Its gardens lead into an inner court and the long, low Gothic façade, a masterpiece of Flamboyant carving, makes strong contrast with the grim but picturesque defences outside. Inside are stone walls and heavy beamed ceilings, which underwent considerable restoration at the end of the last century.

The first château was built here in the year 1000 by the Viscount de Porhoët and was finished by his son, Josselin, who gave his name both to the castle and to the town which grew up round it.

The castle played an important part during the War of Succession and the Hundred Years' War. By the middle of the fourteenth century it had already been razed and rebuilt. It then belonged to the King of France and had as its captain Jean de Beaumanoir, who was also Marshal of Brittany for Charles de Blois. Nearby Ploërmel (a town now famous for its pig markets) was held by John Bramborough for Montfort, who was supported by the King of England.

The two garrisons ravaged the countryside. Although they had frequent encounters, neither side could ever call itself victorious. Eventually, to end this stalemate, Beaumanoir sent the English captain a challenge, which was accepted. A battle between 30 picked men would take place. The result would mean the defeat and withdrawal of one of them.

So, on 27 March 1351, a fight between Ploërmel and Josselin took place at Mi Voie (a stone pyramid now marks the spot). On Beaumanoir's side were 30 Bretons; on Bramborough's side, 20 Englishmen, six German mercenaries, and four Bretons. The battle was fought with lances, swords, daggers and maces.

The fight was hard and bitter. At one stage, when the wounded Beaumanoir called for water, Geoffrey de Blois shouted to his wounded leader, 'Drink your blood, Beaumanoir; that will quench your thirst.' Victory was decided when Gillaume de Montauban

13 Pardon *in the rain at Bénodet*

mounted his horse and overthrew seven of the English champions. Those remaining were forced to surrender. Most of the combatants were killed or seriously wounded, Bramborough himself being among the slain.

Amongst the owners of Josselin the most famous was Olivier de Clisson, who succeeded Du Guesclin as Constable of France, and who married Marguerite of Rohan, the widow of Beaumanoir. He strengthened the castle's fortifications, building eight towers and a great keep. He died here in 1407.

François II of Brittany seized Josselin in 1488 and to punish its owner, Jean II de Rohan, for having sided with the French king, he had it dismantled. However, when his daughter became Queen of France she was obliged to compensate him for this by helping him rebuild it. Because of this you will often see the letter 'A' among the castle's decorations : a token of the family's gratitude, and also a proof of their Breton loyalty. The dukes of Rohan transformed the castle into a worthy noble seat during the sixteenth century, when it became a masterpiece of Renaissance art, well justifying the family's motto, 'I cannot be a king; I scorn to be a prince; I am a Rohan'. Quite a wise one as it turned out, for they are still there, while France's royal family has long since relinquished its throne.

One of the Rohans, Henri, was a leader of the Huguenots, arch-enemies of Richelieu. So, in 1629, during the reign of Louis XIII, the Cardinal saw to it that its great keep and four of its towers were demolished. Its exterior today is much as it was then.

To take a stroll round Josselin, wandering through its cobbled streets and up and down stairways, is like turning the pages of a history book. Many street names recall important happenings, such as the Rue des Trente (Street of the 30), or people, like Rue Olivier de Clisson.

Its basilica of Notre-Dame-du-Roncier (Our Lady of the bramble field) got its name from an old legend. About 808 a work-man discovered a statue of the Virgin Mary hidden under some brambles. He took it home, but the statue disappeared to be found later in the field. He took it home again. Again it disappeared, but was found in the same place. This continued until he got the

14   The standing stones at Carnac, Morbihan

message. The Virgin wanted a sanctuary built on the site where he'd found her. So this was done.

The present basilica was founded about the fourteenth century, but has been restored and rebuilt many times. Its name only dates from the fifteenth century. The old statue of the Virgin was burned in 1793 during the Revolution, but although only a fragment remains, this is enough for the pilgrims who come here on Pardon day. Olivier de Clisson, who did much to improve the church, is buried there, as is his wife, Marguerite de Rohan, in the mausoleum in the chapel to the right of the chancel.

Not far from Josselin is the famous Guéhenno calvary. Built in 1550 (since restored) it shows many of the characteristics of the parish enclosures of Finistère. The ossuary behind has been transformed into Christ's tomb, guarded by soldiers: above it stands the triumphant risen Christ.

Vannes and the Morbihan Gulf

Vannes, relaxed, friendly yet dignified, lying on the Morbihan Gulf, is a city of old walls, gardens and flowers. It is the smallest and also has the honour of being the first and last of Brittany's capitals.

For Vannes had its own independent counts as early as the sixth century, and it was here that Nominoé, as Count of Vannes, declared himself ruler of Brittany. Centuries later, in 1532, the Council, meeting at Vannes, proclaimed the perpetual union of the county and duchy of Brittany with the kingdom and crown of France.

The best place to start a tour of the city is from the helpful Syndicat d'Initiative, beside the Hôtel de Limur (this has a magnificent staircase and garden) in the Rue Thiers, just outside where the ramparts of the old town once stood.

This leads up to the Town Hall Square, where stands the mounted statue of Arthur Richemont, born in nearby Suscino in 1393, Duke of Brittany, a Constable of France, and who also had the distinction of fighting with Jeanne d'Arc. The Town Hall behind, formal and Renaissance in style, was built at the end of the last century.

If you leave the square by the Rue Emile Burgault, you will find yourself in the old part of the city. The Place Henri IV is surrounded by timbered fifteenth- and sixteenth-century houses, between the rooftops of which looms the Romanesque tower of the cathedral, St Pierre.

St Pierre, which was built between the thirteenth and nineteenth centuries, is difficult to see properly outside and is disappointing within. Better to visit the round Renaissance chapel, built by Canon Danielo when under the influence of the classical monuments he had seen in Italy, at the beginning of the sixteenth century. This is in the Rue des Chanoines, which skirts the north side of the cathedral.

To the right of the cathedral is the Rue St Guenhaël, named after a Celtic saint and bordered with medieval shops. If you take this back to the Place Henri IV, then the Halles, you should come out into the Place des Lices.

Here, at the top on the left, is the fifteenth-century house of Vannes and his wife, the city's mascot. Two merry faces stick out from a wooden beam. Exactly who they are is still a mystery. Most probably, they once lived here, as it was sometimes the custom for medieval people to have themselves carved on their houses. According to old records, there was a family in the town who took the name of Vannes as a surname. One was a coiner, another was a bishop, another was president of the duke's exchequer, yet another was a captain in Duke Jean V's bowmen. The man's head may refer to any or none of these.

Almost opposite stands the fifteenth-century Château Gaillard, once the residence of Bishop Jean de Malestroit, then a meeting place for Brittany's refugee parliament, which was exiled from Rennes by Louis XIV after revolting against the Stamp Act in 1675. Times change. Now the tower staircase leads to a room devoted to the prehistoric treasures found in the Carnac region, one of the best museums of its kind in Brittany. There is also a Natural Science museum here.

In nearby Valencia square is an interesting old house, which contains the death chamber of St Vincent Ferrier, now transformed into a chapel (his tomb and relics are in the round chapel of the cathedral).

Vincent Ferrier was born in Valencia, Spain, and came to Vannes in 1419, where he preached and later died. Historically he is quite an important figure, as it was largely due to his efforts that the schism which divided the papacy in the fourteenth century was healed. He was canonized in 1455.

Although St Vincent only spent two years in Brittany he had an important evangelizing effect, using a combination of homely stories and rhetoric to put across his message. From him dates the religious fervour which led to the establishment of so many calvaries, crosses, churches, chapels and Pardons, and was maintained by those two great seventeenth-century missionaries, Le Nobletz and Maunoir.

Although the old part of Vannes is interesting to wander round, particularly if you know a little of its history, in my view the best part of the city lies on the east and south sides. Here medieval ramparts, interspersed with towers, blend well with the eighteenth-century formal gardens, especially when floodlit.

If you take the Rue St Guenhaël, beyond the cathedral, you will come out to the fourteenth/fifteenth-century Porte Prison. Next turn right down Rue Alexandre le Pontois, which eventually leads into the Place Gambetta and the harbour.

You will first pass the gardens of the Préfecture, then Les Ramparts, with its attractive flower beds (on the right) and the garden of the Garenne (on the left). Here you will see a very fine cenotaph to the two world wars. There is also a commemorative plate in memory of those who were shot here for the part they played in the Quiberon landing. These 22 were the most important ones and included the Bishop of Dol. They were imprisoned in the nearby sturdy granite Constable Tower, built during the War of Succession, after Vannes had been besieged four times.

The garden once belonged to Jean IV, Duke of Brittany, who built the Château d'Ermine on what was then reclaimed marshland. The castle got its name from the emblem of Breton chivalry, the Order of the Ermine, which Jean IV founded. However, the present Château Hermine with its grand formal façade was rebuilt in 1800 for a Vanetoise trader, replacing the old residence of the Duke of Vannes.

More mundane, but very picturesque, are the old washing places that border the stream beyond the walls and garden. Here the washerwomen of long ago chattered and clattered at their humdrum but necessary task.

Beyond the southern Porte St Vincent is the port of Vannes, a wide quay with a broad canal, but some distance from the open waters of the Morbihan. It is not now used as it is silted up. Even the little motor boats which make trips to the Morbihan islands start from Conleau, about 5 km. away.

You will notice many CTM (Compagnie de Transports du Morbihan) bus stops around Vannes from which you can catch a bus to the Conleau peninsula. Once there, you walk through a wood to a village and down to a small jetty. The boats are supposed to link up with the buses, and are fairly frequent in the season.

You can, of course, drive round the shores of the gulf by car: westwards to visit Auray and Locmariaquer, or eastwards visiting the Rhuys peninsula (the better trip). But the boat journey across the gulf makes the more interesting expedition.

The Morbihan, which came about by a comparatively recent re-settling of this part of the coast, is about 19 km. wide and 16 long. There are innumerable little islands – about 365 – of which only 40 are occupied. They are low, flat wooded and often hidden by mist. At high tide many of them look as if they are just floating above the water, while some of them do actually disappear. At low tide, which seems more frequent, they resemble long low sandbanks. The area is famous for its sunsets and beautiful light effects. Although peaceful, much boating activity takes place – fishing, sailing, pleasure craft and regattas in summer – on this wide stretch of inland sea.

If you take the vedette from Vannes round the gulf, you can visit the two main islands, Arz and Moines, and Port Navalo and

Locmariaquer, perhaps stopping at one of these places and catching another boat later.

In a way, I preferred the little island of Arz (about three kilometres long) to the larger Ile aux Moines, which is more popular, and therefore gets very crowded in season. Arz's tiny village, Gréavet, is about two kilometres from the landing stage, but you can arrange transport to take you there if you don't feel like walking.

The Ile aux Moines (monks), about six kilometres long, was originally known as 'Izenah' in Breton. The monks, who were from Redon, were given it by Erispoe, a Breton 'king' about A.D. 854. The monks have now departed, but their memory still lingers on in their name.

There are now about 750 people living there, who mostly make their living from the sea – fishing, oyster-culture, boats for transport and pleasure, and, of course, tourism. About a century ago, the population was much larger, but many families left, although some people have returned to retire here. Also, quite a number of people live here for part of the year, particularly in July and August, when the number of inhabitants rises to about 5,000. So should you decide to spend a holiday here, come in spring at daffodil time, or in autumn, when the broom is out.

Moines boasts some prehistoric megaliths, as does Arz, but they are not easy to find. One kilometre to the south of Bourg is the Kergonan Cromlech, one of the largest in France, and further along the same road is the Boglieux dolmen, near a magnificent view of the gulf. To the north of the town is a calvary, looking towards the Rhuys peninsula. There are other dolmens and menhirs to be seen, but the megaliths mentioned are the most famous.

Moines has some good hotels, restaurants and cafés, and has regular boat services and car ferries to the mainland. There are also a number of local festivals. Sailing, water-skiing, walking and sunbathing are the main activities. Its pretty little woods have the most evocative names. Bois des Soupirs ('wood of sighs'),

Bois d'Amour ('wood of love') and Bois des Regrets ('wood of regrets').

Arzon-Port Navalo, a fairly busy seaside resort with harbours and lovely sandy beaches, is situated on the Rhuys peninsula. This attractive region, on the eastern arm of the Gulf of Morbihan, has some small but endearing resorts, and is just now coming into its own. The climate is mild – mimosa, palm and fig trees flourish – and there are numerous beaches and many small harbours. It is warm and particularly attractive in May. Also, it is the only region in which Breton wine is produced (you can't now count that produced in the Loire Atlantique). This is cheap, rough and highly intoxicating, and may be the reason why the Morbihan has the highest rate of alcoholism in France.

Sarzeau is its capital and commercial centre. St Gildas du Rhuys has a particularly wide and beautiful beach, Les Govelins, also an old Romanesque church with a remarkable chancel. Among its treasures are the arms, legs and head of St Gildas, who founded the monastery, which gave its name to the town. Peter Abelard spent an unhappy period here during the twelfth century and was eventually obliged to escape through a secret passage after vain attempts to control the hostile and disorderly monks.

There is also Le Tour-du-Parc, which gets its name from the fact that noblemen who lived at Suscino near by used to make a tour round this area on horseback. Perhaps I should mention that Suscino (a corruption of *Souci n'y ot*) was a château built in 1218 and used by the dukes of Brittany as a summer abode intended for pleasure. In fact, it had quite a hectic time. It changed hands several times during the Wars of Succession, was captured by Du Guesclin, fortified by Mercoeur during the Wars of Religion and was occupied by the chouans and émigrés for a short time in 1795. It was later sold and partly demolished, its stones used for building. Today, its remaining towers and thick stone walls hide an interior as bare and melancholy as the surrounding countryside.

Locmariaquer, which is situated on the smaller western peninsula opposite the Rhuys peninsula, is a fishing village and pleasant family seaside resort. It is chiefly renowned for the Dolmen Mané

Lud and the great menhir (broken into five pieces weighing about 350 tons each, it is the biggest in France) and the Merchant Table Dolmen (three flat tables with 17 supports) near by.

The tumulus of Gavrinis, situated on the island of Gavrinis, at the mouth of the Gulf of Morbihan, can be reached by boat from Larmor Baden to its north (which can be reached by bus from Vannes), but only on certain days. Here in a lovely setting of gorse lies a Celtic king in his tomb, 25 feet high and 100 yards round. You can go inside and from on top there is a good view of the Gulf.

Vannes, situated so near the Gulf, with its boat, train and bus services, and within easy driving distance of many interesting places, makes an excellent centre for excursions.

However, if you are contemplating buses, BEWARE, for there are at least three companies running bus services here and they use different stopping places. C.T.M. does the trips to the Morbihan; Tomine to Josselin, and Drouin Fr. to Quiberon, Carnac and Auray. The best thing to do is to inquire at the Renseignements at Vannes railway station, or at the Syndicat d'Initiative in the Rue de Thiers, and find out *exactly* where the bus you want to use stops.

Auray, Carnac and the Quiberon Peninsula

You can visit Auray by boat across the gulf and up the Loch river, as well as by bus from Vannes. This old town, about 17 km. west of Vannes, also has its store of medieval houses, along with a flourishing and busy port. The oyster beds you will see along its estuary are among the largest in France. A good view of the port and river is to be had from the Loch promenade.

It is easy to pass through Auray, missing the best bits, for its most attractive part is hidden away. So leave the car or bus and explore it further on foot.

Take the steep narrow street from the busy Place de la République down the hillside to the long low bridge crossing the river. Downstream is a port for fishing boats and beyond the broad stone quay is the ancient quarter of St Goustan. Here alleyways and steps climb and twist in and out between a jumble of fifteenth- and sixteenth-century houses. Americans may be interested to know that Benjamin Franklin landed at this quayside while evading the British warships in 1776, when he was seeking aid from the French for the colonists in revolt. The house where he stayed bears a tablet.

Auray has played an important part in Breton history. While here, you can make an interesting 16-kilometre expedition to the Carthusian convent of Auray, the Champ des Martyrs and Ste Anne Auray.

The Carthusian convent, La Chartreuse, lies on the N168 along the Avenue du Général de Gaulle, and is about two kilometres to the north of Auray.

It was near here that the battle which ended the War of Succession was fought in 1364, and where Charles de Blois was killed. Although his death was necessary to John Montfort, the latter was greatly distressed when his body was picked up from the battlefield. He had him buried with great magnificence near Guincamp, and founded a chapel and collegiate church on the battlefield which later became a Carthusian monastery. Today it is a place where the Sisters of Sagesse devote themselves to the care of the young deaf and dumb.

The convent also contains a chapel, built during the restoration in 1823, which contains a mausoleum holding the bones and skulls of the 350 exiles and chouans who were shot in the nearby Champ des Martyrs after the ill-fated Quiberon landing. You can visit the actual enclosure in which they were shot. There is also a small expiatory chapel, built in 1828, near by.

Ste Anne Auray lies beyond the Champ des Martyrs and the Kerso bog on which the battle of Auray was fought (Charles's bad position was the chief reason why he lost) on the D120. Then you turn right on to the D19.

It is only a little place, yet it attracts more people to it in a year than probably anywhere else in Brittany. The reason for this is that it is the most popular place of pilgrimage. The first Pardon takes place on March 7th. Then from Easter until October parishes from all over the province have a jaunt here, partly religious and partly to celebrate (they have a very fine banquet in her honour).

This is the story behind it. In 1623 Ste Anne, mother of the Virgin Mary, appeared to a peasant named Yves Nicolazic, and commanded him to rebuild a chapel dedicated to her, which she claimed had stood in a field 924 years earlier. This was never proved and was unlikely anyway; nevertheless, Yves did find a statue of the saint while digging in the field on 7 March 1625. Since then a Pardon has taken place here every year on that date, along with the local ones and the greatest Pardon of all Brittany on the 26th of July, which is the feast day of Ste Anne, the province's patron saint.

Ste Anne's statue stands in the nineteenth-century Renaissance-style basilica in Ste Anne Auray (the original one was burned during the Revolution). Part of the original face was saved and this has been set in the base. The chapel walls are covered in votive offerings, some dating from the seventeenth century. The fountain in the square, surmounted by a statue of Ste Anne and supposedly miraculous, is rather lovely.

Carnac, which lies about 13 km. to the south-west of Auray, is the district *par excellence* of megaliths and pre-history. Several thousand stones cover this area, the most famous and easily reached being those of Ménec. This alignment lies along the D196, off the main road, just outside Carnac Ville. You can view them and the Tumulus St Michel (about three kilometres) by car, or better still, walk.

You come across the Ménec alignment suddenly and unexpectedly, behind a farmhouse and haystack, an amazing sight of upended boulders, all shapes and sizes – the tallest is 12 feet high – arranged in rows beside the roadside. Altogether there are 1,009 of these menhirs here. Their exact purpose and how and when they were constructed is still a matter of controversy.

If you have a car, the time and the inclination, you can continue along the D196 to pass the alignments of Kermario, also those of Kerlescan (D186) and the Tumulus of Moustoir and finish off at the Tumulus of St Michel (D119) on the outskirts of Carnac Ville.

If you are walking you will find that the road which runs along-side them eventually forks and you take the D119 back towards Carnac Ville. There can be no mistaking the Tumulus of St Michel, whose hill is on the left, for you will see it from afar. Various little lanes lead up to it, but if you continue you will reach a crossroads, and you should turn left up the Rue du Tumulus.

From the top of this mound there is a wonderful view of the fields, woods and houses of the surrounding countryside, especially the Quiberon peninsula beyond and its coastline. The table of orientation, set up by the Touring Club de France, tells where everything is. There is also a little chapel (locked) to St Michel, and a small calvary on the mount.

The tumulus, about 120 yards long and 40 feet wide, is a pre-historic tomb and its mound of earth and stones covers several burial chambers which can be explored – the entrance is through the iron door, under a porch of leaves, opposite the Hôtel du Tumulus. You have to apply at the hotel for a guide.

There are, of course, other alignments and groups of menhirs to view. Locmariaquer, which I have mentioned earlier, is only about 25 km. away, but the ones I have spoken of are the main ones to see.

A visit to the little museum in Carnac Ville is a must for anyone interested in archaeology, and it will certainly enrich your visit to the megaliths. If you should find it closed, you can call on its *gardien*, M. Jacq, who lives near by at 10 Rue du Goh Lore, who will open it for you.

The Museum is called the Musée Archéologique James Miln–Zacharie Le Rouzic. James Miln was a Scot who, after spending much of his life in China and India, returned to Europe when he was about 50. When he visited Carnac in Brittany about 1873, he was completely fascinated by the strange grandiose stone dolmens, menhirs, cromlechs and tumuli. Also, the rocky countryside re-minded him of his native Scotland.

However, it was the Roman remains he stumbled on while out

walking which were to take up most of his attention. As he was a free agent, and sufficiently well off to indulge his interests, it wasn't long before he obtained the peasant-owner's permission to dig up his land. He then started on what was to be his life's work, the uncovering of a Gallo-Roman site with local assistance. His methods were unscientific and he must have dislodged a large number of objects without first measuring their position, doing considerable archaeological damage. Still he was first in that particular field, and one learns by the mistakes of others. And James Miln was certainly well-meaning. He kept a journal of his observations and published a work. Carnac became his home and he toured the whole area. The bedroom which he had rented in the Hotel Lautram soon became an overcrowded depository of finds; he was starting to think about acquiring somewhere more permanent to put them in when he unexpectedly died while in Edinburgh in 1881.

Fortunately, his brother Robert came to the rescue, and as James Miln had often stated he wanted to leave his collection to Carnac, he built at his own expense a place to house it. From then onwards there was a museum open to the public.

The other half of the museum's name belongs to Zacharie Le Rouzic, who was born at Carnac in 1864, the ninth child of a weaver. After leaving school at ten, he was taken on by James Miln to help him in his research and carry his equipment. Although he was not more than 17 at the time of his master's death, Robert Miln appointed him the museum's guardian under the direction of the mayor.

Like James Miln before him, he devoted his life to the cause of archaeology. Unlike his former master though, he was more interested in the ancient stones – which he believed belonged to a much earlier period than previously supposed – and their meaning, than the Gallo-Roman remains. He also had a more scientific approach and tried to classify the periods of the finds. Archaeologists of all nationalities were attracted to Carnac. So, as guardian, conservator and archaeologist, it was only just that his name be added to the museum's title.

Carnac is not only renowned for its megaliths. There is also its church of St Cornély, patron saint of horned cattle, whose Pardon is held in September. On the day of the fair, the priest blesses the cattle at the Saint's fountain. Then there is Carnac Plage, a gently sloping shore which is one of the finest and most popular beaches along the south coast of Brittany.

Carnac Ville and Carnac Plage were two villages which have expanded and joined together. You can drive to Carnac Plage from Carnac Ville down the Avenue du Salins, passing the Marais Salants, square pools of water, then down and round into the Avenue des Druides.

All roads to the right of this lead on to the long Grande Plage, bordered by villas, cafés, hotels, and pine trees. This rather formal seaside resort, much favoured by the English, has everything necessary for conventional holidays – amusement arcades, discothèques, riding, tennis, sailing, miniature golf, even a zoo. All this, with the menhir land behind, qualifies it to be called 'Stonehenge-on-Sea'.

The Quiberon peninsula, lying to the south-west, is often referred to as an island, because that is what it once was. Now it is connected to the mainland by a long, low, narrow sand bar, with pine trees pinning it down into the dunes. Its most attractive part is the Côte Sauvage, which faces towards the Atlantic. But it is on the east side, protected by that great gulf, the Bay of Quiberon, and in the south that you will find the resorts.

Quiberon, situated at its southern end, is the best place to stay, as not only does it have the largest beach, but it is from here that excursions can be made. Then it is blessed with a very good climate, which it owes to its position, its refreshing sea breezes and the fields of seaweed surrounding it. A luxurious sanatorium has been established there, where seawater cures are used to treat a variety of physical and nervous diseases, especially victims of road accidents.

The name Kerberoen goes back to the Breton emigrations of the sixth century, but excavations show that this strip of land has been occupied for many thousands of years. Earlier even than the megalith men, about 4,000 B.C., there was a race of small, long-legged people living here. Up to the eleventh century Quiberon was covered in forests, for records show that Duke Alain Canhiart hunted the deer here. It suffered the usual Viking invasions, then later attacks by English, Dutch, Germans and Portuguese. The year 1746 was a particularly black one for Quiberon, when France and Britain were at war. On the 12th of October an English fleet disembarked on the peninsula. Most of the inhabitants fled. The English remained eight days, and did so much damage that when the Duc de Penthièvre came to inspect it, he released the inhabitants from their taxes for two years.

But apart from the sea battle of 1759, when Admiral Hawke defeated the French fleet under Conflans, Quiberon is probably most renowned in history for the ill-fated battle which took place on one of its beaches, when the Breton Blues, commanded by Hoche, defeated the émigrés and Chouans in 1795.

A statue to Hoche now stands at the entrance to the pleasant little park near the front; to one side of it is the Syndicat d'Initiative. This square makes a good starting place for walks and expeditions.

The best expedition is the one westwards towards the Côte Sauvage (about 12 km. return), which can be done by car. However, the cliff is so soft and easy to negotiate that walking over it is a pleasure.

After Port Maria, noted for its sardines, you will eventually find yourself on a lowish stretch of cliff, where the sea pounds the grey-brown rocks. But this gradually becomes higher as you proceed.

I found it really beautiful, with its coves, grottoes, tiny inviting beaches and roaring water, as the sun sank slowly down over the horizon. Time seemed unimportant as I was lured farther and farther on. First to the Pointe Beger Goalennec, then the delightful little ports of Kerné, Guibelleo and Pigeon, until finally I just had to reach Pointe du Percho. By then the sun had practically sunk into the sea and it was almost dark.

When I did this walk, I did not know that this coast with its strange-shaped rocks, and where some of Brittany's oldest pre-historic remains have been excavated, has a very old reputation of luring people along it: a siren who tries to tempt people to try its waters. I suppose I might have guessed it was dangerous by the many notices I saw along the coast, warning people against bathing and fishing. Some days later, a Breton friend introduced me to the widow of a man who had fallen in while fishing from this very coast, and whose body had not been found until a week later.

Fortunately, I had enough sense to return to Quiberon via the more prosaic road, rather than risk stumbling back the way I had come in the dark.

The next best walk from Quiberon is the one going in the opposite direction (about eight km. return), turning leftward along the Boulevard Chanard, skirting Quiberon's great beach in the direction of Pointe de Conguel. At its tip is a viewing table from which you can see the islands – Belle Isle, Hoëdic, Houat. If you continue past Fort Neuf and just before Port Haliguen, you will find yourself on the beach where the émigré army met its end. An obelisk marks the spot where they surrendered to General Hoche. The road running behind the beach bears the name Boulevard des Émigrés.

The émigrés had planned to join up with the chouans, and the landings began at Carnac Plage, lasting several days. But the enterprise was badly planned, unlucky and took too long. The Republican army was ready for them and they were driven back to the Quiberon peninsula. When the exiles tried to disembark at Port Haliguen, a heavy swell prevented the British ships from getting near enough to land. About 1,500 men were killed. The wounded were taken to Fort Penthièvre and to the Locmaria church, which was turned into a hospital. Hoche did try to save the lives of those taken prisoner, but the Convention in Paris refused to pardon them.

Boat trips from Quiberon leave from Port Maria or Port Haliguen (weather permitting). You can visit Belle Isle, Hoëdic and Houat, Belle Isle's two small neighbours.

Belle Isle, 84 square kilometres in area and Brittany's biggest and most beautiful island, is a must for anyone staying at Quiberon.

The steamer, quite large and comfortable, does the 15-km. journey in about three-quarters of an hour. You can take your car, but as this is quite expensive anyone making a short day-trip would find it easier and cheaper to hire a car or even a bike on Belle Isle for the day. There are also coach trips round the island during the season.

As you approach Belle Isle's coastline it appears at first as long rocks, emerging out of the sea, dotted with houses and trees; then the Vauban citadel, looming above Le Palais, its main harbour and town, comes into view.

Like Quiberon, Belle Isle has a good climate. Its countryside is varied: sometimes undulating, sometimes wooded, sometimes with desolate stretches of gorse and heather, or cut up into cultivated fields and pastures. There are about 140 'villages' (often hamlets) of whitewashed or grey stone houses, and quite a few hotels and camp sites. Its chief and most attractive feature is its beautiful beaches, stretches of sand fringed with trees and rocks, and many little coves along its rugged and picturesque coast ideal for picknicking and bathing.

Rather surprisingly this apparently peaceful place has had quite a stormy history, chiefly because it was difficult to defend. It was invaded by both Saxons and Normans and then in 1006 it was given by Geoffrey I, Duke of Brittany, to the monks of Redon, who owned it for the next five centuries, when it was under continual attack by enemy fleets. Although Henri II had a fort built there in 1549, it did not prevent the English from landing and occupying the place for three weeks in 1572. Then Charles IX, reckoning that it was too strategic a place to be left in the care of monks, gave it to the Duke of Retz, who improved its fortifications. Later, in 1658, Nicolas Fouquet, Superintendant of Finance for Louis XIV, became its seigneur and built himself a château there, also a fleet, hoping perhaps to make it his own private kingdom. However, his later arrest prevented him from finishing the island's fortifications.

After 1674, when the Dutch had descended on the island, Vauban was charged with improving the fortifications (the citadel and its principal redoubts, Ramonette and Grand Rocher). Even

15   Lace seller at Le Croisic

so, it was blockaded by the English and Dutch from 1696 to 1704. It was blockaded by the English in 1761, when it was finally forced to surrender. However, by the Treaty of Paris of 1763 the English agreed to exchange Belle Isle for the return of Minorca, captured by the French.

In 1765, 78 French Canadian families arrived from Canada (many Bretons had emigrated there in 1632). The eastern province, known as Arcadie, had been surrendered by France and was re-settled by Scots, who re-named it Nova Scotia. These emigrants in reverse were quickly re-integrated into the community, and today Arcadian ancestry is regarded with pride.

Belle Isle suffered during the last war when 10,000 Germans occupied the island, and many of her people were forced to leave. Also, as part of the Lorient pocket zone, Belle Isle was one of the last places in France to be liberated.

In my view, Belle Isle is an ideal place for a family holiday or for those in search of peace, quiet and pleasures such as swimming, sailing, fishing, lazing, walking. But it is definitely not for those who want night life and sophisticated amusements.

Unfortunately, when I visited it, I had chosen the windiest and stormiest day of the year. Each time when my guide and I left the little grey Citroën on the clifftop, I expected to see it picked up by the wind and hurled into the sea.

We started our tour from Le Palais, but I never managed to find out how this town got its name. Surely it could not refer to the grim stark citadel, or even to Fouquet's ruined château beyond. Fouquet's proud family motto – 'How high shall I not climb' – was probably the cause of his very long fall from favour.

We stopped to look at Sauzon (its name means Saxon, after the Saxons who settled there), a very picturesque fishing port, famous for its lobsters and sardines, and situated on the Sauzon river. The Pointe des Poulains ('Colts' Point') was our next stopping place. Near here once stood the actress Sarah Bernhardt's château, over-looking a creek, surrounded by rocks; it was destroyed by the Germans during the war. The fort-like building standing in its place commands a wonderful view of the bay and its

16 Vannes – part of the walls

strange-shaped rocks, such as Les Cochons and the Rocher du Chien, which resembles a crouching dog.

Unfortunately, apart from the wind, it was high tide, so that we were only able to peer down into the famous Grotte d'Apothicairerie on the west side of the island. This got its name because cormorants built their nests along the rocky walls and were supposed to resemble jars on the shelves of a chemist's shop. Alas, these birds have long since flown off, and no longer nest there.

On the next part of our drive towards Port Donnant, we saw the island's two menhirs, affectionately known as Jean and Jeanne. Port Donnant is the prettiest of the island's bays, but rather dangerous for bathing, as are all the coves on the west side, the Côte Sauvage of Belle Isle. The Aiguilles de Port Coton, with its strong waves and line of needle-shaped rocks, stretching out to sea, got its name because the sea there is supposed to build up foam like a mass of cotton wool.

The village of Bangor is the oldest on the island, and its church, dating from 1071, is much plainer than most Breton churches inside. The church at Locmaria is also old, but more attractive, and is the proud possessor of two paintings by Murillo – The Virgin and the Virgin and Child.

Port Andro marks the beginning of the *douce*, the calm sweet side of the island. From here onwards are the bathing beaches, such as the Plage des Grands Sables, Belle Isle's finest and largest stretch of golden sand, backed by low hills.

Quite soon after, we were back at Le Palais. Its main church is worth a visit, as is Vauban's great fort, which has an interesting museum inside. This includes mementoes of Sarah Bernhardt and of the island's occupation during two world wars. In the prison behind, now empty, bleak, ruined and desolate, some important Germans were held after the war, as were some Algerian leaders, such as Ben Bella in 1959.

6. The Loire Atlantique

The Guérande Peninsula

The west side of the Guérande Peninsula is known as the white country because of the heaps of salt collected there from the sea.

As recently as Roman times, the sea stretched between the rocky island of Batz and the Guérande ridge. A change of level turned this gulf into marshes. Batz was linked by sand brought down by currents with the mainland, on the strip of which Le Pouliguen and La Baule now stand.

There is still a gap between Le Penbron, west of Batz, and le Croisic opposite, through which at high tide the sea flows into the old gulf, the Grand and Petit Traits. Mussels, winkles, clams and oysters are gathered from their beds in the mud at low tide. Another part has been laid out in squares whose sides are bounded by low banks of clay soil. These are the Marais Salants (salt pans), where salt crystallizes and is collected and put to dry on little platforms, before being stowed away in sheds.

La Baule, lying eastwards beyond the rocky Pointe Penchâteau, sprawls all around a wide shallow arc of coast. More international than Breton, it comes into the Biarritz/Cannes class, a seaside city of casinos, boulevards, parks and pavilions, and rows of grand hotels. It is expensive, although it claims a wide range of accommodation pricewise.

Its chief attractions are its climate and its five-kilometre sweep of sandy beach. Then there are its sporting facilities – sailing, swimming, tennis, golf, riding (especially horse-racing) and night life – cabarets, night clubs and smart restaurants.

Like Dinard, its north coast counterpart, it is a comparatively recent resort. Up to about a hundred years ago there were only a few villas scattered among its sand dunes and pine groves. It has grown and grown. Today its west side extends and joins up with Le Poulinguen, fishing village and smart yachting harbour, while eastwards lie the scattered groves of La Baule-les-Pins, whose pines help pin down the sand dunes and give shelter from the strong winds.

La Baule, with its excellent communications – road, rail, and air – make it a favourite place for conferences, and a good excursion centre for trips all over Brittany.

Near at hand, you can tour the Guérande peninsula (Drouin Tours do this trip during the season). Drive first to Le Poulinguen, then skirt the Grand Coast, where high cliffs and grottoes make a strong contrast to the low coast round La Baule. Batz, another resort, has an interesting church, St Guénolé (rebuilt in the fifteenth and sixteenth centuries), the tall 180-foot belfry of which can be seen from afar.

Le Croisic, larger, whose picturesque fishing port (sardines and shellfish) is divided by islets, has some attractive seventeenth- and eighteenth-century houses, and a Town Hall built during the reign of Henri IV. Also intricate old alleys lead to its sixteenth-century church, Notre-Dame-de-la-Pitié. Le Croisic is becoming an increasingly popular resort. It faces south, has a good climate and has managed to retain its Breton quaintness in contrast to the more slickly sophisticated La Baule. From its artificial mound, Mont Esprit, which is quite amusing to climb, there is a good view of the salt pens and marshes, and even Belle Isle and the Rhuys peninsula on a fine day.

To get to the salt village of Saillé, you will have to return to Batz (N771 and 774). From Saillé you can drive through the salt marshes to Sissable, or take the D92 to the sardine port of La Turballe, then the D99 to the Pointe Castelli, from which there is a good view of the Rhuys peninsula (right) and the peninsula of Le Croisic (left). The D99 and V9 take you to Piraic, another resort and fishing village. From here, you take the D333 and D99 to Guérande.

The old medieval fortified town of Guérande is another Concarneau, only it stands on a ridge overlooking flat country, lagoons and marshes. It is remarkably well-preserved; its ramparts are complete as are its four fortified gates and eight towers. Guérande is chiefly famous in Breton history as the place where Montfort's victory at Auray, ending the War of Succession, was confirmed. It was here, in the old church of St Aubin, surrounded by a maze of old streets, that the Treaty of Guérande was signed in 1365.

Guérande, immortalized by Balzac in *Beatrice*, is another place best just to wander through. But first walk round its ramparts, then enter the fifteenth-century Porte Michel, the most impressive of the gates. Its towers hold a local museum of Breton furniture and costumes, and also information about the workings of the salt marshes, which in the old days were the city's main source of revenue. The great hall leads back to the ramparts. Should you not have time to visit the town you can drive round the wide, tree-lined promenade which has replaced most of the moat (a bit remains in the north-west), filled in by the Duc d'Aigullon, a Governor of Brittany in the eighteenth century, and which formerly surrounded the town.

After Guérande, before returning to La Baule, you can visit Careil manor house, built in the fourteenth century and restored in the fifteenth and sixteenth centuries; it is renowned for its fireplaces, ceilings, and the collections of Renaissance furniture and seventeenth-century porcelain.

To the east of La Baule lies the Grande Brière, the Black Country, whose swampy land, fed by freshwater streams, produces not salt, but peat. It is a melancholy but picturesque region, of swamps, islets and shining expanses of water, framed by reeds, tamarisks and willows.

The Grande Brière, approximately 20,000 acres, was once a large gulf, rather similar to the Morbihan, but fed by the Vilaine and Loire rivers. Deposits of alluvial soil washing down into it gradually raised its shallow floor, turning it into marshy woodland.

Also the Vilaine and Loire changed their courses. The trees were later to become peat.

During winter, the Grand Brière is flooded, but during spring, when drying, it is covered in flowers. The granite islands, now small hills, have become settlements surrounded by dykes. Of these, the Ile de Fédrun is the most typical and complete of these Briéron 'island' villages. A road within it encircles the low, white-washed cottages. Houses have their own docks and boats (*blains*) for travelling along the canals which now drain the marshes.

Peat is getting rarer. Some people make a living by fishing, hunting water-creatures, raising poultry, or grazing sheep on the patches of pasture land. Others grow reeds for making baskets and chairs, or thatching roofs. Villages all around this area are urged to have a few of their houses thatched in order to preserve their picturesqueness and encourage this industry.

The region is particularly popular with anglers and wild fowlers, who punt through it in the white flat-bottomed boats. There is also a bird sanctuary and nature reserve.

You can circle it by car, starting from St Nazaire. On certain days between June and September, Drouin buses do a tour of it. If you are driving from La Baule you should take the coast road via Pornichet Ste Marguerite and St Marc. You can also go this way by local bus, but check first, as not all of them go via the coast.

Nantes

Nantes, with its cathedral, university, factories, port and aero-drome, sprawling either side of the wide Loire, is a true metropolis, and a great city of France. It has played an important part both in French and Breton history.

Nantes, both Gallic and Roman, was involved in many struggles between Frankish kings and Breton dukes. In 843 it took the brunt of the first Norman attack, before they started on their onslaught of Brittany. But it was below Nantes, nearly a hundred years later, that the young Alain Barbe Torte rallied the people to turn the Normans out of Brittany. Later, as duke, he made Nantes his capital, and rebuilt the city. Nantes, in rivalry with Rennes, was Brittany's capital more than once in the Middle Ages. François II and the Duchess Anne governed as sovereigns from its massive castle on the Loire. Then during the Wars of Religion it was to Nantes that Henri IV came to re-establish and guarantee peace – for a period, that is – by signing the 92 articles of the Edict of Nantes.

Nantes chiefly owed her good fortune to her position on the Loire, which for centuries was a natural highway into the heart of France. Her greatest prosperity was during the sixteenth, seventeenth and eighteenth centuries, and came mainly from the sugar and slave trade (known as the ebony trade). Slaves were sold in the Antilles and cane sugar, bought with the profits, was refined at Nantes, then sent up the Loire. By the end of the eighteenth century Nantes was the first port of France. Fine mansions, built by the shipowners, still line the Quai de la Fosse and the former island of Feydeau.

The abolition of the slave trade, the substitution of French beet for Antilles cane sugar, the silting up of the river, making it difficult for large ships to reach Nantes, brought a decline to Nantes' prosperity and importance. Nantes became an industrial city, turning to metallurgy, iron and steel works, brewing, flour mills and food canning, etc. She is still the heart of a wine-growing region. The vineyards of the flat open country south of the Loire produce Muscadet. You will find plenty of this dry white fruity wine in Nantais cafés and restaurants, as you will all over Brittany.

Today, Nantes with her wide boulevards and parks is a big and busy city with the air of capital. Yet the maze of old streets, little squares, especially around the cathedral, and the stairways and alleys leading down to the port, have retained the Breton quaintness of a provincial centre.

Nantes' medieval and classical architecture are conveniently divided into two districts, which were originally separated by the river Erdre, which flowed into the town from the north (Quai de Versailles), but whose last stretch of water now runs below the wide and curving Cours des 50 Otages. On its east side is the old medieval part, on the west is the newer, classical part.

At the southern end of the Cours des 50 Otages lies the wide Cours Franklin Roosevelt. On a map this area's large shape looks like a boat. The old Rue Kervégan and Avenues Duguay-Trouin and Turenne lie along the old Ile de Feydeau, once an island, but now part of the town. Instead of shining water, they are surrounded by rows of shiny cars in a massive car park, and noisy bus stops.

Brittany has royalist traditions and in the Place Maréchal Foch, once the Place Louis XVI, still stands a column surmounted by this guillotined king's statue.

On the left is the Porte St Pierre, a massive gateway, built at the end of the fifteenth century, and which now holds a museum of pictures illustrating the history of Nantes. Just beside it are some Gallo-Roman remains.

The nearby cathedral of St Peter and St Paul was badly damaged by fire in January 1972. Unfortunately, when I visited it, most of it was barricaded off to the public because the roof was considered unsafe.

Built between 1434 and 1893, it has followed the Breton tradition of slow building. Fortunately this has not damaged the final effect. It has an imposing Gothic façade and an interior of white stone instead of the usual Breton granite. The use of this stone has enabled the builders to build higher and the vaulting, 120 feet high, outstrips even that of Notre Dame in Paris, which is only 110 feet. Fortunately the fire didn't damage the statuary and near the inside door are two of Nantes' heroes, St Rogatian and St Donatian, two young Gallo-Roman soldiers, martyred about A.D. 290. These brothers are represented in the towns' processions by two young men dressed as Roman warriors, walking with their arms round each other's waist.

The most important object in the cathedral, the tomb of François II, a Renaissance objet d'art carved in the early sixteenth century, unfortunately I could not see. Anne of Brittany commissioned it to receive the remains of her father and mother,

Marguerite of Foix, too, and it was originally placed in the church of the Carmelites. During the Revolution the Tribunal ordered its demolition, but the town architect hid various pieces of the tomb in his friends' homes. After the Revolution it was put together again, and in 1817 placed in the cathedral. Alas, the gold cask supposed to contain the heart of Anne of Brittany was found to be empty. This casket is now kept in the Dobrée museum.

The château of the dukes is not far from the cathedral. If you turn left down the Rue Mathelin-Rodier, you will soon arrive at this imposing medieval structure, surrounded by a narrow strip of water, then grass and a wall, and entered by crossing a draw-bridge. At one time the south, east and north-east overlooked a branch of the Loire.

The present building was begun by François II in 1466, and his daughter Anne continued the construction. During the Wars of Religion, the Duke of Mercoeur improved on its defences. It was taken over by the military in the eighteenth century, who destroyed some parts of it and added others. Eventually, in 1915, the city of Nantes restored what they could and added two museums.

The castle, like some of the museums in Nantes, is closed on Tuesday, so if you are making a day trip to the town, and you want to see it properly, choose another day. The large courtyard is open every day. You can visit the two museums inside the court-yard, but if you want to see over the castle, you will have to find the *gardien*, as these parts are kept locked. They are worth seeing.

As with so many Breton châteaux, once inside the courtyard the atmosphere changes to that of a palace. Jousting, tournaments and all sorts of performances once took place in its large square. One of the first things you will notice is the rather beautiful well, the delicate iron framework of which is shaped like a ducal crown. If you look down under the netting, put there to prevent children falling in, you will see a crown reflected in the water below.

Behind the well is the Grand Government (the governor's palace), which was rebuilt after a fire in 1684. Next to it, is the Renaissance Gothic *grand logis*, which has five beautifully carved dormer windows, and which was used as a dwelling place for the men-at-arms.

I visited two of the castle's towers, one quite large, with barred windows, where Fouquet (remember Belle Isle) stayed in 1661 before being seized by Louis XIV's men. The other, much larger, its ruins now occupied by pigeons, was a grim and sinister place. It housed many prisoners during the Revolution (priests, Vendéeans, royalists, and other suspects). The interior is now much higher than it was then, because it had once held two floors. Of most interest was the magnificent church carved by prisoners out of the thick castle wall beside the barred window.

At one stage of the Revolution, when Nantes' prisons were over-flowing with suspects, the deputy Carrier was sent by the Convention in Paris to purge the town of 'rotten matter'. Carrier solved the problem by arranging to have them all drowned. The prisons were emptied by putting the condemned men in barges, which were conveniently scuttled in the nearby Loire river.

The two museums in the château are worth a visit. One, the museum of local and popular art shows an interesting collection of costumes and especially of the lace caps worn in different parts of Brittany; also there are displays of Breton furniture and interiors of Breton houses. The Salorges museum, which is situated in the lower part of the building opposite, is more technical. Here you can learn about Nantes' slave ships, privateers and navigation on the Loire during her seafaring days of the eighteenth century.

If you are spending the day in Nantes and want to have a picnic lunch, there is a pleasant park (the Jardin des Plantes) not very far from the castle. If you go down the Rue Richebourg and cross the Rue Stanislas Baudry, you will come to it, nearly opposite the station.

It is large, formally laid-out with many rare and exotic plants and trees, numerous pools with pretty little waterfalls, and sheltered arbour walls. There is a statue of Jules Verne, who was born in Nantes, at one end of the garden.

Apart from the château and castle, there is not a lot to see in Nantes, and heavy traffic makes walking through the old town hazardous. Still it is a pleasant city, if you can manage to forget the cars. The following route makes a fairly representative walk.

Start outside the cathedral in the Place St Pierre, continue down the Rue de Verdun into the Rue de la Marne and the Place de Change (you will find the Syndicat d'Initiative here). Near by is the old church of St Croix. Then continue and cross over the wide Cours des 50 Otages and up the Rue d'Orléans to the Place Royale, a very pleasant square with a large fountain in the centre (1865), representing the Loire and its tributaries. To one side of the square is the church of St Nicholas, which you might care to visit. The Place Royale leads into the Rue Crébillon, narrow, steep, and generally crowded for it has some good shops. The Place Graslin, which it leads into is quite a fine square. The Grand Théâtre is situated there.

From here you can either continue along the Rue Voltaire to the Dobrée and Archaeological museum, named after a Nantais collector of that name (manuscripts, ceramics, enamels, ecclesiastical jewellery, paintings, furniture, weapons and a historical section, etc.) in the Place Jean V, and the museum of Natural History in the Place de la Monnaie, or you can walk from the Place Graslin into the Cours Cambronne, a wide tree-shaded walk, very French, and lined with trim eighteenth-century houses, all alike. In its centre stands the aggressive figure of the Nantais general, after whom it is named, and who is chiefly remembered for his answer, which included '*merde*' (very rude word in French) when called upon to surrender to the English at Waterloo. What happened next, I did not discover, but he survived until 1842.

Turn right from here into the Rue de Bréa and along the Place Sanitaire, down the Rue Mazagraw into the Place St Jean l'Herminer and the Quai de la Fosse. You should now find yourself beside the port. If you find harbours and shipyards interesting, you might enjoy turning right in the direction of the Belvédère Ste Anne. But it is rather a smelly, dirty and noisy walk.

You will see the road leading up to the Belvédère Ste Anne after about 15 minutes of walking. At the top is a garden and table of orientation with a good view of the river and the busy harbour below. The table will tell you which of the various steeples and towers you can see is which, but the tangle of cranes and funnels provides a fairly formidable curtain. You can see the cathedral, but not the château. To the right of centre is the Cité Radieuse, built by Le Corbusier, and an experiment in modern living. The 300 flats have their own infant school, cinema and swimming pool.

Further along to the right, but impossible to see from this position, is Chantenay, where in June 1793, the notorious drownings in the Loire took place.

Part 2
Normandy

7. History and Introduction

Normandy divides into two geographical sections; higher in the east and lower in the west. Higher Normandy, with its rich open chalklands and orchards, lies chiefly to the north of the Seine and is made up of the two departments, Seine Maritime and Eure. Lower Normandy, less fertile and merging with Brittany, is made up of Orne, Calvados and the Manche.

There are probably few other places in the world where an English person would feel more at home than Normandy. The fields and hedgerows, sleepy farms and villages, ruined castles, cathedrals, churches and old manor houses, even the damp mild climate, would remind him of southern England, especially Devonshire. Normandy has played an important part in our island's history and much in our culture originated in this lush green maritime province of northern France.

Normandy owes its name to the Norsemen who settled there in the ninth century. They held the mouth of the Seine and steered their dragon-prowed boats up its wide loops as far as Paris, which they raided four times. Finally in 911 the French king wisely made a treaty at Clair-sur-Epte with their leader, Rollo. This gave them the right to settle over a large area of the province we know now as Normandy. In return, the Vikings were supposed to accept Christianity and perform military service for the Carolingian kings.

Although Rollo was baptized in 912 he is said to have died a pagan, as were most of his Norsemen. However, his son, William

Longsword (William I), was converted and extended Norman rule, wresting territory from the Bretons in the west.

It took the Norman dukes about 150 years to consolidate their power and position. They had to withstand the attempts of the French kings to bring their duchy more under their own control, establish their rule over the Frankish population already living in the duchy and over their own Norse nobles, as well as keep out other dukes from the province.

The Normans retained many of the Viking characteristics. Ruthless and reckless, courageous and crafty, a mere handful of them could vanquish an enemy of far larger numbers.

They were also quick to imitate and adapt. They didn't invent castle building, but soon became masters of it, while they took to horse-riding as if to the manner born. They proved efficient and progressive rulers, adapting and improving on the institutions they found in newly-conquered territories. Under their rule Sicily became one of the most prosperous states in the Mediterranean.

These former pagan pirates became the advocates of the civilization they had previously attacked, becoming strong exponents of feudalism and champions of the Church. The patronage of their dukes enabled the religious centres of Benedictine learning to flourish. Pilgrimages to Rome and the Holy Land, although inspired more by love of conquest and adventure than religious devotion, were very popular with the Normans.

Also, the growth of the Norman population soon outstripped its territory. As many Norman nobles and younger sons had few prospects of inheritance at home, they were obliged to seek their fortunes farther afield.

Fortunately, the Normans had integrated well with the Frankish population. Their dukes, who had unusual political ability made their province one of the best organized feudal states in Europe. Although still technically a fief of the French king, it was independent and strong enough in 1066 to launch a successful attack against England.

William II of Normandy (William I of England) did have some

17   Rouen cathedral from the east

18 *Coutances Cathedral, Manche* 19 *Old still and pots of herbs at the Bénédictine distillery of the monastery at Fécamp*

justification for his claim to the English throne. When he learned that Harold had been made king, he sent emissaries to remind Harold of his former promise – that he should renounce the throne in favour of William. Harold ignored this and William called in the Pope to support his claim. The Pope did so, and excommunicated Harold. William then convened a meeting of his barons at Lillebonne and won their support; he next persuaded Harald Hardrade of Norway to attack Harold in the north.

Harold, after destroying the Viking army at Stamford Bridge, hurried south to do battle with William on 14 October near Hastings. By nightfall he and his earls lay dead, and his army was defeated. William's coronation took place in Westminster Abbey on Christmas Day. He celebrated Easter in Normandy. In 15 months he had conceived an expedition, launched it, and captured a kingdom and a crown.

However, England was a pretty sizeable lump to digest quickly, and he still had to keep his own province in order. While he was abroad William's cousin and consort, Mathilda of Flanders, had ruled Normandy with the help of their eldest son, Robert, who, aided by the French king, rebelled against his father. William died in 1087 during an expedition against the French king.

The union of Normandy and England was broken. Robert became duke as Robert II, while England passed to his brother, who became its king as William II. The two brothers were not long at peace. Robert was supported by the French king and William II was helped by his brother, Henry. On William II's death, Robert's designs on England were frustrated by Henry, who became its next king as Henry I.

Despite negotiations, the quarrels continued. In 1106 Henry, after defeating Robert at the battle of Tinchebray, became Duke of Normandy himself.

The then French king, Louis VI, took up the cause of Robert's son, but Henry I had his own son recognized as the heir of Normandy. In 1119 Louis VI and Robert's son were decisively defeated at Bremule in the Vexin. However, Henry's son was drowned at sea and Robert's son died in 1128; when Henry himself died in 1135 it was the end of the male line of the house of Rollo.

The Norman succession was in dispute until 1144, when Geoffrey Plantagnet, Count of Anjou and second husband of Henry I's daughter, Mathilda, won Normandy from the rival house of Blois. He and Mathilda gave the duchy to their son, Henry, in 1150. Henry inherited Anjou and Maine from his father in 1151, then acquired Aquitaine by his marriage with Eleanor in 1152. He became king of England as Henry II in 1154.

This union of England and Normandy had considerable effect on both their histories. Norman rulers had remained true to the Conqueror's promise in Westminster Abbey – the structure of English government remained Anglo-Saxon, but was under efficient Norman direction and innovation. England had a centralized government and well organized church and, most important, had been made safe from invasion. Norman French, at first the language of the ruling class and the legal language until 1400, was gradually incorporated into English, greatly enriching it.

Normandy was a model feudal state. Because the king could not be in both places at once, he had to delegate and institutionalize many of his functions, thus enabling political institutions to develop in both countries.

Then the Normans were great builders. Towns, abbeys, cathedrals, churches and castles were erected. The material was near at hand. Around Rouen was the soft stone found in the chalky cliffs bordering the river. Around Caen in the Calvados was the oolithic limestone known as Caen stone. Farther west were sandstone and granite similar to those found in Brittany. The Benedictines, protected by the dukes, had a long tradition of architecture, inherited from the Romans, but which they improved on. The Norman style, an imitation of Romanesque, was of bolder proportions, with pure lines and sober, geometric-type ornamentation.

However, Henry II's marriage with Eleanor was to cause deep trouble between France, Normandy and England. The French king had no option but to try and weaken such a powerful vassal. Although it was agreed that the French king's infant daughter should marry Henry's eldest son, taking with her as dowry the Vexin Normand and Gisors, warfare between the kings continued. The next French king, Philippe II (Philippe Auguste) demanded the surrender of Vexin in 1187 on the grounds that Henry's son had died in 1183 and that the newly projected marriage of the latter's brother, Richard, to Alice, another French princess, had not taken place.

Philippe also supported Richard, then a close friend, against his father in the rebellion which hastened Henry's death. However, Philippe and Richard did not remain friends long. In spite of a Treaty made in Sicily in 1191 on the way to a crusade, Philippe tried to annexe the Vexin and the town of Gisors with the aid of Richard's brother, John, while the Lionheart languished in a prison in Germany.

On release Richard won a great victory over Philippe at Fréteval, near Vendôme, in 1194. To protect the Vexin and bar the French king's way into France along the Seine, he built Château Gaillard, a massive fortress overlooking the river, in 1196. After another victory at Courcelles in 1199, Philippe only had the border town of Gisors left in Normandy.

Philippe didn't have to wait long. After Richard's death his brother John inherited the Norman and English crowns. But Philippe, like the Bretons and many Normans, supported the claims of Arthur, John's nephew. John's later alleged murder of Arthur gave him the excuse to invade Normandy in 1202. Château Gaillard fell after a long siege and Rouen capitulated in 1204. By then all Normandy belonged to the King of France, a fact finally acknowledged by the English crown when Henry III (England) and Louis IX (France) signed the Treaty of Paris in 1259.

The French king's administration found much to learn and admire about good government in Normandy. Communes with their own charters were already established. Arbitrary levying of taxes and services was much resented. The French kings were obliged to abide by the *Charte aux Normands* (1314–15), guaranteeing the duchy's rights and privileges.

By the Treaty of Paris Henry had retained the Duchy of Guienne, for which he had to do homage to the French king, and was allowed certain territory which protected its borders. Later kings tried to evade this agreement. French officials often interfered in Guienne. There were skirmishes at sea, kings who refused to do proper homage, destruction of forts, retaliations.

The spark that was to set off the fire was the question of the succession to the French throne. When Charles IV died in 1328 leaving no male heir, the principal claimants were Edward III (through his mother) and Philippe VI (then Count of Valois), son of Philippe IV's brother, Charles.

An Assembly of Magnates decided in favour of Philippe. Edward at first protested, but later withdrew his claim. He did simple homage for Guienne in 1329, but Philippe demanded liege honour and refused to restore lands Edward was claiming. The cold war began in earnest. Edward intrigued in the Low Countries against Philippe, Philippe intrigued in Scotland against Edward.

The Hundred Years' War could be said to have started when Philippe confiscated Guienne in 1337, and Edward declared that France should be his.

Hostilities began at sea between privateers. Edward III went to Antwerp, where he got the support of the Low Countries and defeated the French fleet at Sluis in 1340. Operations next shifted to Brittany where Edward supported John of Montfort against Charles de Blois. He also fomented rebellion in the west of France.

Edward landed in the Cotentin in 1346 and took Caen, crossed the Seine at Poissy, and set out for Picardy. Philippe caught up with him at Crécy where the French army was defeated. It seemed as if everything was going for Edward. The Scots were defeated at Neville Cross while Charles de Blois had defeats in Brittany. However, the Black Death, which favoured neither side, brought the war to a temporary standstill.

Hostilities broke out again in 1355 when the Black Prince

landed at Bordeaux, ravaged the countryside, defeated the French king, Jean II, at Poitiers, and took him prisoner. The period that followed was one of ravaging and pillaging and of great misery for France.

By the Treaty of Brétigny in 1360 France ceded the whole of Aquitaine, also Calais and Guienne, to the English but not Normandy. Charles V (who had been made Duke of Normandy in 1355 by Jean II) began his reign as king of France by sending Du Guesclin to drive the English out of Normandy. This time the English armies and fleet were defeated.

The following years were relatively peaceful. Edward III and the Black Prince died. Richard II and the next French king, Charles VI, were only boys when they came to their thrones and were later too busy with their own countries to take up the squabble.

However, this was changed when Henry IV succeeded Richard, and Louis, brother of a now partly insane Charles VI, tried to make trouble for Henry by helping the Welsh Owen Glendower. Henry IV started on the reconquest of Aquitaine, lost by Richard II. This was continued by Henry V, who landed at the Chef du Caux in 1413. He took Harfleur in 1415, then routed the French army at Agincourt.

In 1417 Henry began the methodical subjugation of Normandy, town by town, district by district. Caen, Alençon, Evreux, opened their gates to him. Henry seized Rouen, the Pays de Caux and Vexin. His next step was to try and disinherit the French Dauphin and make his own house rulers of France.

By the Treaty of Troyes in 1420 Henry was to marry Cathérine, one of Charles VI's daughters. The resulting child would rule both countries. It would be a dual monarchy with each kingdom retaining its own institutions. Again nature took a hand. Henry V died in 1422, as did Charles VI. The son of Henry V and Cathérine was still a mere child.

Then the Dauphin, son of Charles VI, proclaimed himself king of France as Charles VII. The Duke of Bedford, chosen to govern the French territories in the name of the infant Henry, invaded the Loire Valley and in 1428 laid siege to Orleans, which he intended to use as a base against further attacks on Charles's stronghold in the south.

This was where the legendary Joan of Arc came upon the scene. She persuaded Charles VII's captain to send her to Charles's court at Chinon. After she had gained the king's confidence she went with a small force to relieve Orléans. Whether the English would have gone anyway is a matter of conjecture, as their force was only a small one, but their departure probably had a psychological effect on French morale. In 1429 the English were defeated at Patay and Charles VII was crowned at Rheims.

Joan took part in several expeditions. In 1430 she went to Compiégne to help strengthen the defence against the Burgundian ruler, Philip the Good, who was in alliance with the Duke of Bedford. During a sortie she was captured by the Burgundians, who sold her to the English. She was later tried at Rouen, adjudged a heretic, and supposedly burned in the market place on 30 May 1431.

From now onwards English fortunes in Normandy faltered. Philip the Good signed a treaty with the French king, Charles VII, ending the war between France and Burgundy. The very capable Duke of Bedford died in 1435.

Although the English had established a Council of Normandy emphasizing the duchy's separateness from France, and although they had founded a university at Caen, there had always been a certain amount of resistance to their régime. After all, Normandy was attached to France, the people now spoke the same language. There were risings in the Pays de Caux and the Val de Vire.

Also by now France and England were exhausted and wanted to negotiate. By a truce England retained Maine, Bordelaise, the Pas de Calais and most of Normandy. But because they were slow in honouring their agreement the French took several towns from them and started on the reconquest of Normandy. Sir Thomas Kyriel landed in Cherbourg supposedly to reinforce the Duke of Somerset at Caen. Instead he besieged Valognes, giving the French time to close in on him, and forcing him to give battle at Formigny. His defeat there marked the end of British rule in Normandy.

Louis XI, now king, gave the duchy to his brother, Charles, in 1465, but soon took it back. In 1486 he persuaded the French Estates General at Tours to declare Normandy inalienable from the French crown. After this Normandy was governed as a province, although the *Charte aux Normands* was theoretically maintained.

Little was created architecturally during the Hundred Years' War. After it, the style known as Flamboyant Gothic was particularly popular in Rouen and Upper Normandy. Rich merchants built tall houses, partly timbered, partly of stone, with wide eaves and decorated corbels and beams. Good examples of these can still be seen at Rouen, Bayeaux and Honfleur.

Georges d'Amboise, Archbishop of Rouen, who introduced the Italian Renaissance into French building, had much influence on Norman architecture. Examples of this luxurious, exuberant, sophisticated style are to be seen at his castle, Gallion, another is the west door of Rouen cathedral.

The Renaissance style reached its greatest heights in domestic architecture. Older buildings, such as the Château d'O and Fontaine-Henri, were ornamented and added to; parks and gardens replaced fortifications. Gothic survived chiefly in the small manor houses – Renaissance mansions, where a plain outer façade often hid a richly designed inner courtyard, were usually built in towns.

As many Normans were Huguenots, the province suffered badly during the Wars of Religion. There was particular bitter fighting between 1561 and 1563, and from 1574 to 1576. Caen, with its new university, was a particular hotbed of Protestantism, as were the seaports, which had many contacts with England and Holland.

Protestant Henri IV vanquished 30,000 men of the Catholic League in 1589 at Arques and the Leaguers of Mayenne in 1590 at Ivry-la-Bataille. The Edict of Nantes, which he signed in 1598, brought religious peace – for a time anyway – to the province and to France.

Later, in 1685, the Revocation of the Edict of Nantes by

Louis XIV led to a massive emigration of Huguenots from Normandy. As many of them were well-to-do, hard-working and highly skilled, it severely damaged the Norman economy. However, the province was too fertile and its inhabitants too industrious for it to suffer long. By the eighteenth century it had recovered its prosperity.

The seventeenth century had been a time of exploration and expansion overseas: both Quebec and New Orleans were founded by Normans.

Another architectural rebirth had taken place after the Wars of Religion, when many beautiful châteaux were built. A strong Catholic reaction during the first half of the seventeenth century had led to the Jesuits building many colleges and chapels, but in the formal classical style. However, the grand century of building in Normandy was the eighteenth, especially in the towns, where magnificent episcopal palaces and town halls were erected.

As in other parts of France, revolutionary ideas fomented in Normandy. Many Normans served in the new republic. But although they favoured reforms they were naturally hard-headed and conservative with a dislike of excess. By 1793 Caen was the centre for the Girondists, the party of moderation, who opposed the extremists, the Montagnards, based in Paris. During the trial of Louis XVI, 30,000 citizens of Rouen demonstrated in favour of appeal. However, the King's execution and the French army's reverses in the Netherlands led to the ruin of the Girondist party. On 2 June 1793 the Convention in Paris, surrounded by 80,000 armed insurgents, capitulated and ordered the arrest of 29 Girondin deputies. Most of them managed to escape, and tried to raise Normandy, Brittany, Franche Comté, and the south and south-west of France against the government.

Charlotte Corday (1768–93) was living with her aunt in Caen when these refugees arrived, calling for separation from the government and urging military action against the capital. The young Charlotte, deeply moved by events, set off for Paris. She managed to get an interview with the notorious Jean-Paul Marat in his bath, drew the knife from under her dress, and stabbed him through the heart. On the same day insurgent Normans marching on Paris were defeated at Pacy-sur-Eure. Charlotte was sentenced to death by the revolutionary tribunal and executed on 17 July, while in October of that year 31 Girondins were executed.

In November, the army of the Vendée (a coastal department in west France), composed mostly of Catholics and Royalists marched north to raise the Cotentin, but were unsuccessful in capturing the town of Granville. Although they retreated and were finally defeated at Savenoy, opposition to Paris and its interference still remained strong. Warfare continued in the Cotentin and the wooded Bocage, where it was easy to hide. It took the form of ambushes, surprise attacks and raids on government forces and officials, under the direction of Count Louis de Frotté from Alençon. He was eventually caught and shot with five of his companions at Verneuil in 1800.

The nineteenth century was an era of prosperity and peaceful expansion for Normandy. A railway was built between Paris and Rouen in 1843. The Duchess of Berry started a vogue for sea-bathing at Dieppe. The Côte Fleurie became a popular playground for the wealthy of many countries. Good light, wide skies, broad rivers, estuaries and attractive seascapes attracted many artists, especially impressionists, to work on the Normandy coast. Two of France's best-known nineteenth-century writers, Guy de Maupassant and Gustave Flaubert, were both Normans and worked in Normandy.

Normandy's greatest disaster came in the mid-twentieth century, in World War Two, when beaches along the Côte Nacre and the nearby Cotentin peninsula served as a bridgehead for the allied invasion of Europe. More than 200,000 buildings were demolished. Towns, villages, farms and railways had all to be painstakingly rebuilt, a massive task.

Nevertheless it is still a prosperous province, renowned chiefly for its agriculture, especially wheat and dairy produce. It is the home of many famous cheeses; its butter is reckoned to be the best in the world, as is its sparkling apple cider. Livestock rearing, especially horse-breeding, predominates in Lower Normandy.

There are also some important industries – cars, ships, steel, to mention a few; and some small local ones, such as pottery, woodwork, ironwork, copperware and basketry.

Because of its geographical position Normandy acts as a natural corridor from its ports, Cherbourg, Le Havre and Dieppe, to Paris and other parts of France. Many Britishers pass through it on their way south. Although many of the fine old Norman cities and towns suffered so badly in the war, a number of the cathedrals and churches were spared, and the rest have been restored with great care. There is still much old and interesting to see.

Most of this pleasant province is worth exploring, either by car, bus, or – even more leisurely – by bicycle. Less cut off from France, its people are more mixed racially than the Bretons. Even so, you will still see many tall, blue-eyed, fair-skinned people, the unmistakable descendants of those long-ago Vikings.

8. Seine Maritime

Dieppe and its Surroundings

Dieppe, one of France's busiest and most attractive ports, is the best place to start in Normandy.

One's first glimpse of its spires, tall houses and hotels, set between high cliffs, should be more exciting than it is. Unfortunately, the only frontal position from which you can see the town emerging over the horizon is from Sealink's Smoking Lounge, through a glass window, past a barrier of rope coils and all the varied paraphernalia of a large ferry boat.

However, to compensate for this the port is a long one. The ship seems to sail right into the town, cutting deep into Normandy, past gardens, beaches and picturesque old streets and houses.

Dieppe, France's oldest resort, is always regarded as an eighteenth-century town. It suffered two disasters during the seventeenth century : the first was a plague, which broke out in 1668 and in which 10,000 people died, the second was when the English and Dutch fleets bombarded the town in 1694, reducing all the wooden houses in the centre to rubble. Only those buildings made of stone survived; most had to be rebuilt. The eighteenth century was a fortunate period for architecture and the brick houses, built by the architect M. de Vertbroun, were of a sombre elegance, enhanced by the Louis XIV and Louis XV wrought-iron balconies, made by the renowned ironworkers of Arques and Dieppe.

Dieppe became famous as a sea-bathing place after the Restoration, when it was made fashionable by the Duchess of Berry. Later, unattractive hotels and boarding-houses mushroomed up alongside its dunes, shingle beach and sea. Even so, there was enough of the picturesque around the town to attract many artists, especially English ones such as Sickert, Bonington, Beardsley and Turner, to paint there.

Fortunately for Dieppe its war damage was chiefly confined to the unattractive hotels and boarding-houses along the front, while the picturesque part lost only a few buildings. A new front has been laid out, a new casino built, as have many new flats and hotels, also a new Town Hall. All this, plus its port, which although not a great one manages to combine many activities – passengers, fish and fruit – makes it a lively place to visit, and particularly popular with English day-trippers. Incidentally, the best day on which to visit Dieppe is a Saturday, preferably in the morning, when the big market is held.

Dieppe's cafés and restaurants are probably its greatest draw, especially to eat the seafood: sole, mackerel, herring, fish soup and particularly coquilles St Jacques. It is reckoned that two out of every five shellfish eaten in France will have been caught by Dieppe fishermen. The most reasonably-priced restaurants, though perhaps a little shabby to look at, are those along the Quai Henri iv to the right of the Gare Maritime. At Chez Lola you can get a good meal for just under a pound.

Apart from day-trippers, most English travellers to France will have passed through Dieppe at one time or another. It is usually regarded as a milestone, marking the way into or out of France. Nevertheless, it is worth looking round.

The best old thing to see is the sixteenth to nineteenth century collection of ivory in the castle, which was occupied by the Germans during the war and stands atop a hill overlooking both town and front. (The castle was built between 1435 and 1635, and replaces an earlier wooden one burned down during a battle in 1195; it survived the bombardment of 1694.) Many craftsmen came to Dieppe to carve the ivory tusks imported from Africa and the Orient. By the seventeenth century there were 350 of them living in the town. Today, there is only one!

The best old church to see is St Jacq, which has been considerably restored and combines a mixture of centuries. Its nave is thirteenth century, its central doorway fourteenth, its façade tower fifteenth, its east end and their chapels sixteenth, the dome above the transept, eighteenth. The whole could be called a mixture of Flamboyant Gothic and Renaissance, the interior being much plainer than the exterior.

For interest note the little window through which the priest could look down on the people below; it is above the choir, the woodwork of which is so fine that it resembles lace. Also note the frieze above the sacristy door, which shows a line of Brazilian Indians and commemorates the explorers of Dieppe. It was originally in Jean Ango's palace, which was destroyed in the bombardment of 1694.

Jean Ango was a master shipbuilder who during the sixteenth century constructed a fleet of privateers in answer to the Portuguese, who treated as pirates any ships found off West Africa other than their own. Jean Ango's fleet captured 300 Portuguese ships and forced the Portuguese king to change his policy. When Jean retired from the sea in 1530 he built himself a splendid palace in Dieppe, but alas, of wood. However, his country residence, the Manoir d'Ango, can still be visited.

Dieppe's chief tourist attraction is its front, one and a half kilometres of beach, which lies between sea and town. It is difficult to believe that this stretch of shingle and grassy promenade was one of the landing points between Berneval and Ste Marguerite when Operation Jubilee was launched on 19 August 1942. The objective, the capture of Dieppe, was not achieved, but it was the dress rehearsal for the allied invasion of Europe two years later. Over 5,000 men were killed or taken prisoner. Of that number about 1,000 Canadians died in this stretch of water.

Beside the bathing beach are now situated the children's playground, a miniature golf course, a roller-skating track, tennis courts and swimming pool, not forgetting the casino.

Altogether Dieppe has had five casinos, their dates of construction being 1832, 1857, 1887 (very Eastern this one with a dome and minarets), 1928 (this was dynamited by the Germans in order to improve their defences in 1942) and 1961. This last was designed by the architect Tougard, to fit in with the general layout of the front. Open all the year round, it contains a cinema, theatre, dance hall, restaurant and club as well as the rooms where boule, roulette, baccarat and blackjack are played.

Dieppe is within easy reach by car of the forests of Eu and Eawy. Eawy forest, 16,000 acres, is one of the most beautiful stretches of beech woodland in Normandy. Nearer still to Dieppe is the forest of Arques. It was here, incidentally, that the V2s were launched at England in World War Two. The small industrial town of Arques-la-Bataille played an important part in Normandy's history as being the place where Henri IV with only 7,000 men defeated the 30,000-strong army of the Catholic League.

Tréport, about 30 km. north of Dieppe, is Normandy's last town on this coast. It is set on the south side of the river Bresle, which for most of its course marks the boundary between Normandy and Picardy.

Tréport, a small fishing port and popular family resort, is still picturesque with its long shingle beach backed by tall cliffs, as is its twin, Mers-le-Bain, on the opposite bank of the Bresle and in Picardy.

Chair lifts at Tréport transport people to the top of the cliff behind the town. From the terraces there are fine views of the coast and harbour below. Both Tréport and Mers are good places to stay at, as they have all amenities, plus very nice air. The chief snag is they tend to get very crowded during the season as they are within too easy reach of Paris.

Tréport has a long history and was a maritime port even in Roman times. Up to the twelfth century it even disputed supremacy with Dieppe. Then it became silted up owing to a diversion made to the course of the river Bresle. It was burned down several times by the English during the Hundred Years' War and again in 1545. The town and port came into its own again during the time of Louis Philippe and even Queen Victoria twice honoured it with her presence. Tréport had a bad time during the

Second World War, when it suffered severe bombardment and many people were killed. It was awarded the Croix de Guerre with a star of bronze for the courage shown by its inhabitants.

The Alabaster Coast

Southwards from Dieppe lies the Pays de Caux, a rolling chalk country of prosperous farmland, majestic and green, and stretches of beech woods. Particularly attractive are the large, half-timbered Tudor-looking farmhouses with their old stone barns. You will probably notice many tethered cattle in the fields, a custom peculiar to this part of the province.

The tall white cliffs of the Alabaster Coast, continually eroded by sea and weather and cut by deep narrow leafy valleys, make up the most impressive part of Normandy's coastline. That there are few sandy beaches along here may have been to its advantage, preventing over-development and excessive commercialization. The resorts along here are much smaller than those farther south.

Pourville, very pleasantly situated near jagged cliffs and severely damaged during the Dieppe raid, has now been rebuilt. Both Varengeville and Ste Marguerite are a little distance from the sea, but as if in compensation, they are set in very pretty wooded surroundings in a typical Norman countryside of old timbered farmhouses, thatched cottages and small manor houses. Not far away is the splendid, carefully restored Ango manor, mentioned earlier. Ste Marguerite has a particularly attractive twelfth to thirteenth-century church with a beautiful interior. At Quiberville, about 5 km. away, is a sandy beach.

Veules-les-Roses, situated in a sheltered valley with cliffs either side, manages to combine casualness with smartness. Its beach, shingle at high tide, becomes a broad stretch of sand at low. This village resort caters particularly for children. St Valéry, once a fishing and coastal trading port, has only fairly recently become a seaside resort. Its centre was razed in 1940 by units of the British 10th Army, driven back to the sea by the Germans after the collapse of the Somme front. Two memorials to this event stand on the Aval and Amont cliffs. Veulettes, spread over a wide green valley between cliffs, is an attractive if quiet resort.

The most picturesque part of this coast lies between Senneville and Fécamp. Fécamp, due to its famous fishing port – France's fourth largest and the most important for cod – and Holy Trinity church, is a well-known town.

Its quays, old houses and narrow streets lying between long and narrow cliff-like hills have a sort of charm, but it is too commercial and industrialized a place to spend a holiday there. Its church, larger than many a cathedral, is worth a visit, as is the Benedictine distillery and museum. Bénédictine is supposed to have originated at Fécamp : in 1510 a monk called Vincelli had the idea of distilling liquor from the aromatic plants which he found growing on the nearby cliffs.

The church of the Trinity owes its size to the fact that it was the abbey church of a Benedictine foundation. There had been a monastery here since the seventh century. Its main task was to provide shelter for the holy relic of some of Christ's holy blood, lost on the cross. According to tradition, this had been miraculously found in a hollowed-out fig tree beside a spring, which has now been made into a fountain.

Richard I built the church, but it was rebuilt in the twelfth and thirteenth centuries after being struck by lightning, then reconstructed several times between the fifteenth and eighteenth centuries. The monastery, some of which is now restored and forms part of the Town Hall and museum, became very important when Richard II persuaded monks of the reformed Cluniac Order to take up residence there. For a time it was the leading place of pilgrimage in Normandy. Pilgrims still come even now on the Tuesday and Thursday following Trinity Sunday to worship the Holy Blood relic.

Etretat, about 20 km. farther along the coast, is my favourite of the Alabaster Coast resorts. It was particularly popular with artists and writers, such as Maupassant, in the last century, and is an intriguing mixture of character and smartness.

20   *The college chapel at Eu, Seine Maritime*

Its beach, unfortunately shingle, lies between two rocky cliffs. From the right-hand side one, the Amont, surmounted by a small chapel, the first and unsuccessful attempt to fly the Atlantic was made. On the left is the Aval, whose rocky arch, the Port Aval, has been compared most aptly to an elephant plunging his trunk into the water. The sea here is very rough.

An attractive and elegant town lies behind the beach. Note the old wooden market place, housing fruit, vegetable and antique shops and an art gallery, topped by a tower with a splendid old granny clock, wrong of course! It also did good service as a hospital for British and American soldiers in the First World War.

Le Havre

The first time I visited Le Havre, I travelled by bus, and arrived, so to speak by its back door. It was a come down. First, in the distance, loomed the tall skyscrapers, then suddenly, the bus came to a halt in what seemed to be the middle of nowhere in particular, surrounded by half-constructed buildings, untidy land and ugly hoardings. I was quite amazed when I was told that we were actually there. '*Centre ville?*' I asked, non-believing. '*Centre ville. Ici.*' A man beckoned me to follow him through the dilapidated bus station and out the other side. And there it was! Which goes to show that one should never judge by first impressions.

The best way to approach Le Havre is to come down into it from the coast. Then it does really look like what it is, a splendid, brand-new, well-laid-out city. The area that I had first seen was still in the process of becoming part of this.

Le Havre owes its existence to the French king, François i, who ordered its construction in 1517 to replace the older ports of Harfleur and Honfleur. It was first named after him, being known as Francispolis, and was given his coat of arms, a salamander on a red field. This last the town still retains, but the name was soon changed to Le Havre ('the harbour') de Grâce (the name of this piece of the coast).

21 *The Abbey of Jumièges, near Rouen*

The town prospered. By the end of the eighteenth century it had a population of 20,000 people. Trade with the West Indies, and especially with America during the War of Independence against England, brought considerable wealth to the town. It grew richer still in the nineteenth and twentieth centuries. During the First World War its harbour was one of the main supply bases for the Allied armies. During the Second World War it was less fortunate. Le Havre had the dubious honour of being the most badly damaged port on the continent, losing something like 10,000 buildings. The battle for Normandy by-passed it – even Paris was liberated before Le Havre. Even so, although the Germans had blown up all the harbour installations before it was finally taken, the Americans managed to use it as a base. But it took two years to clear away all the town's rubble.

The building of the new town was entrusted to Le Perret, that father of modern architecture. The result, considered a model of all a town should be, includes the residential area of Ste Addresse, the old port of Harfleur, and combines France's most important transatlantic harbour with a busy industrial centre.

Le Havre, like so many of Normandy's newly-constructed cities, which seem to be built more for traffic than the careless saunterer, is best explored by car. I have two criticisms to make about its streets. One, from the point of view of the pedestrian, is that the yellow-striped zebras across wide roads without traffic lights make crossing very hazardous, especially as French drivers aren't noted for their patience. The other, from the point of view of the motorist, is that street names, often in the same beige colour as the buildings, are difficult to read. A driver might well need a telescope.

The best place to start on a tour of the town is from the Town Hall square. The Town Hall, a plain, no-nonsense building with a tall clock tower, overlooks a formal symmetrical garden, surrounded by a wall of plane trees, quite pleasant but rather noisy to sit in.

From here you drive down the Rue de Paris, smartish shops either side, into the Place Général de Gaulle with its large war memorial in the centre, and a dock for boats on one side, spanned by a modern bridge, itself resembling some sort of super-yacht.

The square seems to be surrounded by boxes, all beige and similar, but then the whole of Le Havre is like a city of big horizontal or vertical boxes.

It is also a city by the sea. If you drive back to the Town Hall, then leftwards and westwards down Boulevard Foch, most grand with grass verges and park to one side, you will arrive at the sea front. The beach is pebbly, but sandy further out and popular for bathing, as all the rows of white bathing huts testify.

Then turn left into the Boulevard François 1 towards the ultramodern St Joseph's Church, the steeple of which resembles a well-sharpened pencil pointing to the sky. This is regarded as one of Auguste Perret's greatest achievements. When you enter, the interior seems to be lit by a milliard coloured lights, streaming through the glass panes. In all there are 12,768 pieces of glass, in 50 different shades of colour, but with gold predominating, and in many different shapes, sizes and patterns. Each colour has a meaning, as does its position; the light within the church varies according to the time of day. The church furniture has been specially arranged to induce a community spirit. The altar is in the centre, while the pulpit is part of the circle of surrounding seats, thereby giving a greater feeling of intimacy.

If you continue along the Boulevard François 1 you will come to the Fine Arts Museum. This is built entirely of glass and steel and has a roof specially designed to let in as much light as possible to the picture galleries. Two artists who painted in Normandy – nineteenth-century Eugène Boudin, forerunner of the Impressionists, and twentieth-century Raoul Dufy – are well-represented here.

If you next turn down the Boulevard Clemenceau, you will arrive back at the seafront. Incidentally, it is possible to do a boat trip round the harbour and even go over one of the great Atlantic liners. To do this, you will have to apply for information at the Syndicat d'Initiative, near the Town Hall.

The Seine from Le Havre to Rouen

The Seine, 776 km. long, rises in Burgundy and passes through Champagne, Île de France and Normandy to the sea. It flows through flat countryside, wooded or pastureland, and below tall cliffs, not unlike those along the coast. These heights, dropping sheer to the river, were sometimes crowned by castles such as Château Gaillard, while in the curving bends, where the river was deep, ports were sited, such as at Rouen.

Since early times, when a wooded countryside made travel difficult, this highway has linked Paris with the sea. In the Bronze Age, when tin was brought along the Seine from Cornwall to mix with copper, it was known as the Tin Road. From the sixth century, monasteries, centres of learning, were built beside the Seine, as well as small towns and settlements which during the ninth and tenth centuries produced rich booty for the plundering, pillaging Northmen. Later, after Rollo had made his treaty with Charles the Simple, it became one of the most civilized areas of France. The Normans, ashamed of their ravaging ancestors, outstripped all others in their generosity and support of the Church.

Today, although the Seine is highly industrialized with petrol refineries and factories along its banks, some of it is still picturesque, especially part of the drive along its banks between Le Havre and Rouen, a journey which takes about three hours. This can also be done by local bus, but should you decide to do this, see that the bus trip is *à bord de la Seine,* as there are two routes to Rouen. There is also a boat trip between June and September. This visits Honfleur (some also visit Trouville) on the other side of the estuary as well, the whole journey taking about ten and a half hours. The boat, the *Duc de Normandie,* leaves from the Quai de l'Yser, Le Havre.

The outskirts of Le Havre are ugly and sprawling. You will pass but not cross the new Tancarville bridge, the largest suspension bridge in Europe, linking Le Havre and the Caux promontory with the south side of the estuary. There is not much interesting to see until Lillebonne, and then only the shape of a Roman amphitheatre, a semi-circle of stone covered by grass, in its main square. Lillebonne was known as Juliabonne after a Roman proconsul, and was then an important port, but it is now silted up. It was here that William the Conqueror met his barons and planned the invasion of England.

After this comes a particularly ugly and smelly bit, the petrol refinery and factories of Port Jérôme. Things improve after Norville. First comes Villequier, situated at the foot of wooded hills, crowned by a castle. Then comes forest, and the river appears, very pleasant now, lined with nice old-timbered houses and gardens, backed by white cliffs, and Caudebec, with its attractive old church, built between 1475 and 1539, just visible through the trees. This delightful town and river resort was once the capital of the Caux region.

It was at Caudebec that, when a great tide was running, the sea entering the estuary met the river flow. The sea current reversed the stream one, causing a 'bore', an enormous tidal wave, which was most exciting to watch. However, special engineering work on the river banks has reduced the size of the bores and danger.

The abbey of St Wandrille is not far from here. This old ruin, founded in 649, has little of its abbey church left except a few tall Gothic pillars and the bases of columns which supported the main arches of the nave. However, the galleries of its cloisters, dating from the fourteenth and fifteenth centuries, are still in good condition. But only men are allowed inside.

St Wandrille is named after Wandrille, a wise and handsome count at Frankish King Dagobert's court. He was about to be married when both he and his bride decided that they would devote the rest of their lives to the service of God. The bride entered a convent and Wandrille, to the great despair and displeasure of his king, joined a group of hermits. He eventually went to St Ouen in Rouen, where he was ordained. Because of his magnificent physique, he was known as 'God's true athlete'.

When Wandrille founded the abbey, a stream, the Fontenelle, passed over the site, and it was first called after this. The Fontenelle library and school became a renowned centre of saintliness and learning. After being destroyed by the Northmen, it was restored in the tenth century, when it took the name of its founder, and became one of the most famous centres of the Benedictine Order. St Wandrille survived the wars of religion, but fell into ruins after the Revolution, when its monks had been dispersed. It passed through various hands, the Benedictines themselves returned in 1894 for a few years; the author, Maurice Maeterlinck, lived in the abbey for a while.

The monastery church to be seen there now is an old fifteenth-century tithe barn, which was transported from La Neville du Bosc in 1969, and is in use.

Le Trait, which has a lot of villas, is quite a pretty place, with an attractive grey-steepled church. Jumièges abbey nearby, beautifully situated on a bend of the Seine, one of France's greatest and loveliest ruins, is now under the supervision of the Fine Arts Department.

Jumièges abbey, founded by St Philibert from the Benedictine Order in the seventh century, and later destroyed by Northmen, was rebuilt by Duke William Longsword in the tenth century. Like St Wandrille it was also a centre of learning, but became so famous for its hospitality and charity that it became known as the Jumièges almshouse.

Its great glories are the roofless nave of the Church of Our Lady, where massive pillars and rounded arches rise to a height of 27 metres, and the delicate stonework of the transept and chancel. Charles VII, Jeanne d'Arc's king, often stayed at Jumièges with his favourite mistress, Agnes Sorel, who died there in 1450.

The Jumièges monks were dispersed at the Revolution and the abbey was sold at a public auction to a timber merchant. This vandal used it as a stone quarry, blowing up part of it, which accounts for the present ruin.

Du Clair is another riverside resort, but it is somehow more formal and solid than Caudebec. As one drives out of it, the chalk cliffs and wooded hills beyond are rather pretty. The river bends away again and the road runs through a picturesque wooded valley, then snakes through forests to Canteleu.

From this height there is a good view of the Seine river, Rouen and its busy port below. But the best view of Rouen is to be had from the Corniche de Rouen on the Mont Ste Cathérine, on the opposite side of the city.

Rouen

Rouen, the Ville Musée, which lies along the northern bank of the Seine, occupies a natural amphitheatre in the hills bordering this part of the Seine valley and is within easy reach by train of most of the Norman coastal resorts. I would recommend a day trip there rather than an overnight stay (unless booked beforehand); there is a chronic shortage of hotels in this popular tourist city, due chiefly to the number of old buildings in the centre.

Rouen, known as Ratuma by the Gauls, Rotomorgus by the Romans, and captured twice by the Northmen in the ninth century, became capital of the Norman duchy in 912. The Norse leader, Rollo, proved an able planner. His improvements to the river, narrowing and deepening the bed, linking islands with the mainland, and reinforcing the banks with quays, lasted until the nineteenth century.

It was at Rouen that John was supposed to have murdered Arthur, thus giving the French king, Philippe Auguste, the excuse to invade Normandy; the city was taken after an 80-day siege. The town prospered greatly during the following years, chiefly because of its good position and the trading pacts made first with Paris, then London, the Hanseatic cities, Flanders and Champagne. Rouen offered a stubborn resistance to the English Henry v, though he entered it in 1419; the city became French again when taken by Charles vii in 1449.

Much building took place during the period that followed, especially during the time of Cardinal d'Amboise (1460–1510), who introduced Renaissance architecture to Normandy. Although Rouen suffered badly during the Wars of Religion – it was sacked by the Protestants in 1562 – the Revocation of the Edict of Nantes was a worse disaster. After 1685 more than half its Protestant population, who were mostly employed in the textile industry, emigrated.

Like Le Havre, Rouen was badly bombed during the last war. Her famous cathedral and churches were badly damaged. The industrial district of St Sever and the area between the cathedral and the Seine were the worst hit.

The damage has now been repaired. St Sever has been rebuilt as a residential area and a university was built there in the 1960s. Rouen combines being an important industrial centre (especially for the spinning and weaving of cotton) and port with being Normandy's historic capital.

Rouen's most attractive feature is still its towers, spires, old streets and houses. Although bomb blast caused such havoc in the town centre, the houses' robust timber framing managed to withstand it, so that it was only the lath and plaster fillings which were blown to dust. As this has been put back and façades remounted, the intrinsic character of the streets still remains.

Many of these are so narrow that they are best explored on foot. Incidentally, for three francs you can get from the Syndicat d'Initiative (opposite the cathedral) an earpiece, which gives a commentary on the town in English.

For a tour of the town, the official guide starts from the Place du Vieux Marché, which is as good a place as any as you can leave your car there.

The Vieux Marché is a bit of a muddle, incorporating as it does a car park, a flower and food market (very useful for campers), as well as what looks like the beginning of an archaeological dig, and all surrounded by a mixture of old gabled houses and fairly new shops. A statue of Joan of Arc stands towards one end with fresh flowers either side. Nearby a plaque states that she was burned here on 30 May 1431, while another one shows the layout of the town at that time. Not far away a square of gilt mosaics claims to show the exact place where the pyre stood.

Jeanne d'Arc, about whom approximately 3,000 books have been written, occupies a curious position in French history. French armies and generals as esteemed as De Gaulle have been inspired by her; Napoleon, who was chiefly responsible for her re-interment about 1803, was another. After the First World War she was appropriated by the Right Wing as a symbol of national renewal. During the Occupation, she was used by the Germans as propaganda against the English, and became the symbol of the Collaborationists. Then, although she undoubtedly existed, that she was burned at the stake is now questioned. There is a museum to her in the Tour Jeanne d'Arc, a remnant of the old castle, which contains waxwork scenes from her life.

At the end of the square is the Rue de la Pie in which stands the rather grim house and birthplace of the author, Pierre Corneille (1606–84), now a museum of books and manuscripts. Rouen also has a museum to the writer, Gustave Flaubert (1821–80), who was born in its old hospital, where his father worked as a surgeon.

The Rue du Gros Horloge with its gabled and beamed houses, leading out of the Vieux Marché, is Rouen's best known and most picturesque street.

The great clock, very colourful in red, blue and gold, looking down at you, is the city's most popular landmark. Notice the rat (or is it a mouse?) at the end of the hour hand. There is a clock face either side. Needless to say, neither of them work.

The clock was originally in the belfry on one side, built in 1389, but to make it more conspicuous the townspeople had it incorporated into the arch, built in 1525.

The Rue du Gros Horloge leads out about opposite Notre Dame, which is considered to be one of the finest Gothic cathedrals in France. Its exterior bristles with intricate carvings, although it is badly in need of the repairs which it is at present undergoing.

The cathedral's main features are its two towers and spire, all quite different, yet somehow in harmony. The tower on the left, that of St Romanus, is squarish and plain, while the one on the right, the Butter Tower, is flamboyant and intricately carved. This last-mentioned got its name because its construction was financed by the sale of indulgences, which allowed devout people to eat butter and drink milk during Lent. It was never completed and was crowned not with a spire, but with an octagon, inside which is a carillon of 55 bells. Between these two towers soars the delicate open-ironwork spire, which at 151 metres is the tallest in France.

Rouen cathedral was constructed mainly in the thirteenth century after a devastating fire in 1200 which destroyed most of the eleventh- and twelfth-century building. Parts of it, such as the library, the very fine carved stone staircase and the Butter Tower were added in the fifteenth century; the spire was added in the nineteenth. In the eleventh-century crypt are the tombs of Richard Lionheart, dukes of Normandy and Georges d'Amboise, the Cardinal Minister of Louis XII.

After the cathedral St Maclou and St Ouen are Rouen's two next monumental treasures. If you leave the cathedral by the north transept door, you will emerge into a narrow alleyway, the Cour des Libraires (Booksellers' Court), which winds down to the Rue de la République, then to the square in front of St Maclou.

St Maclou is a masterpiece of flamboyant Gothic and has a magnificent five-gabled portal and carved wooden doorway. Like the cathedral – though this time in wood – it has a fine carved staircase (1517) to one side of a rather beautiful organ loft. Its spire was added in 1868.

After St Maclou find, if you can, the St Maclou cloister, down the side-turning beside the cathedral. There is an old fountain in the courtyard. The frieze of skulls and bones round the wooden beams of the surrounding building refers to a plague. Places get adapted and used in Rouen (like the Renaissance Bourgthéroulde mansion, just off the Vieux Marché, which has become a bank): these cloisters, most appropriately, house an art school.

Then take the Rue Damiette, a quaint old street which will lead into the Rue des Boucheries St Ouen, and to St Ouen itself, an excellent example of later Gothic. This church is particularly renowned for its beautiful and harmonious interior, an effect created by slender delicate shafts and an absence of ornate decorations. Its organ is one of the finest in France. There is a magnificent rose window on the south transept side. The central tower over the transept (1490–1515) ends in an octagonal lantern, which is known as the ducal crown of Normandy.

Rouen has some good museums. The museum of Fine Arts has a splendid collection of local pottery and ceramics, and a very fine picture gallery, including early Flemish artists, Italians and seventeenth-, eighteenth- and nineteenth-century French painters, particularly those with Norman associations. There is also an important collection of Impressionists. The Musée le Secq specializes in wrought iron (third to nineteenth centuries), which is displayed in the church of St Laurent and the museum of jewels and religious treasures is in the old Visitandines Convent.

For trips round the port and to La Bouille you get tickets from Transport Joffet at the Gar Routière.

9. Eure

Eure, lying astride the Lower Seine, is Normandy's most wooded department. More than a fifth of its surface is covered in trees, forming shaded forests, so pleasant to walk in and explore.

Normans here live chiefly by agriculture, producing wheat, dairy products and cider. The towns are small. Most people live in sleepy villages, their houses grouped picturesquely round a tall, grey, steepled church. Eure's peaceful prosperity and easy access of Paris has attracted many Parisians to buy weekend homes here, or to commute daily to Paris.

There are a few châteaux – Beaumesnil, Acquigny, and Champs de Bataille spring to mind – but you will see more tall manor houses, their timber-framed storeys mounted on stone blocks and surrounded by massive farm buildings, which bear witness to the general well-being of this region.

The drive south from Rouen along the Seine to Vernon, which takes about three hours, is quite interesting, but not so good as the drive the other way. Moreover, this time the local bus rarely goes near the river, so, if you use public transport, the journey is quicker and better by train.

If driving, two places to visit en route are the Deux Amants hill, about $4\frac{1}{2}$ km. from Amfreville sous les Monts (D20), and castle Gaillard at Les Andelys.

Deux Amants hill is renowned for its magnificent views over the Seine and the legend of how it got its name.

This story was first told in the twelfth century by Marie de France, France's first woman writer. The king of the Pitrois had a beautiful daughter, named Caliste. Perhaps he needed a strong son-in-law to succeed him. More likely, he just didn't want his daughter to marry. At any rate, he forbade her to accept any man unless he could carry her at the run to the top of the hill. Raoul, her favourite, did his best to succeed, but alas, the strain was too great. When he at last reached the top, he dropped dead from exhaustion. The heart-broken Caliste died, too, almost immediately afterwards. So, the two ill-fated young lovers were buried where they fell. The exact place, I'm afraid, is not known, but their epitaph is romantically immortalized in the name of the hill.

One's first sight of Les Andelys is of its castle, looming white and gaunt, as if growing out of the chalky cliffside. You can take a car most of the way up to it, but the last bit, a fairly stiff climb, has to be done on foot.

Château Gaillard is one of Normandy's most attractive ruins, but is just to be looked at and scrambled over, although the guide there will try and charge you a franc if he can.

In its heyday it incorporated everything known to twelfth-century military architects, and Richard the Lionheart had picked up quite a bit of information from his campaigns in Palestine. He had every reason to be proud of his 'year-old daughter', although the story that it was actually built in a year is now disputed. There is evidence that it was built between 1195 and 1198.

After Richard's death, Philippe first took the fortresses at Lyons, Gournay, Conches and Verneuil before laying siege to Gaillard in August 1203. The castle, defended by Roger de Lasci, Constable of Chester, although short of food and munitions, withstood it until 6 March 1204. Even then, it was only taken by a ruse. A soldier, so the story goes, climbed in through the latrines and let down the drawbridge. After its capture, the other Norman fortresses capitulated, and Normandy became part of France.

It has held some distinguished prisoners, such as Marguerite of Burgundy, who was imprisoned there by King Louis x, along with her two sisters, in 1314. The king, wishing to be free to marry again, accused her of adultery. The unfortunate queen is supposed to have been strangled in her chamber with her own hair. The fortress changed hands many times during the Hundred Years' War. It was besieged for two years by Henri IV during the Wars of Religion. When it finally fell, he had it dismantled. Some of its stones were used in the construction of other buildings, one of which was the Convent of the Capucins at Andelys.

There is a magnificent view of the town, the leafy valley and curling Seine with its island and graceful new suspension bridge from the castle, although this is perhaps somewhat marred by the smoking factory chimneys of the new industrial Grand Andelys on the right. The Petit Andelys, nearest the river, most fortunately undamaged by the war, has an attractive square of old houses and plane trees with the sturdy twelfth-century church of St Sauveur to one side. Most of the Grand Andelys was destroyed in June 1940, but its sixteenth-century Notre Dame church, a mixture of Flamboyant Gothic and Renaissance, is still worth visiting. Nicolas Poussin (1594–1665), Normandy's most famous painter, was born at Villiers-sur-Andely, not far from here.

Vernon, situated either side of the Seine between the forests of Bizy and Vernon, is a pleasant relaxing town with a number of fine avenues and many of the amenities of a seaside resort. The best view of it is from its bridge – ruined piles of the old twelfth-century bridge, with the castle tower which was once joined to it, lie to one side.

Vernon, one of the gates to Normandy, was supposed to have been founded by Rollo, but old documents show that it had a charter in 750. Its position made it of strategic importance during the Middle Ages, when it became a favourite place to stay of both English and French kings. Louis IX (1214–1270), always known in French history as St Louis, because he was so pious, was a well-known visitor here, especially in hot weather.

Unfortunately, many of Vernon's old wooden houses in the centre were destroyed in the last war, so that there is not much old to see now, other than its twelfth-century collegiate church and a few old houses near by. The church has a beautiful nave and rose window (west front). But don't waste time looking for the six Louis XIII tapestries, as they were stolen at the end of 1972.

One of the loveliest places to visit in Eure is the beautiful beech and oak forest of Lyons, once a favourite hunting ground of the Dukes of Normandy, when it covered an area considerably larger than its present 26,500 acres. Experts from all over the world come to study its trees and the silviculture practised. Some beeches and oaks grow to an enormous size in this chalky soil. One great beech, known as God's Beech, is 275 years old, and has a circumference of more than 14 feet. One great oak is 300 years old.

Winding roads lead down to the village of Lyons, lying in a deep valley in the heart of this forest. It is pretty, peaceful and old with its eighteenth-century market place and 15th-century church. As it has several hotels, you could choose few better inland places to stay for a few days.

Lyons is best approached from Andelys, passing Lisors, or from Fleury-sur-Andelle, or, if coming from Rouen, via Vascoeuil.

Evreux, situated around the many arms of the Iton river, is Eure's capital. To me it will always be a city of water. The first time I stayed there, my hotel window opened dangerously out over a narrow noisy stream. Then everywhere were little stone bridges and brooks. The cathedral and bishop's palace, a delightful ensemble enclosed within walls covered in foliage, added their greenery to the weedy water below. A pretty walk, the Promenade des Ramparts to the left of the cathedral, leads past a moat, beside which benches have been built into the Gallo-Roman ramparts. Within a few minutes one can escape the city's noise.

Evreux, as the centre of a rich agricultural region and with plenty of small industries, is cheerful, active and bustling. At present, it is difficult to drive through, but will be less so when the ring road planned to divert the N13 Paris–Deauville traffic from the centre is built.

It has plenty of history, being both a Gallic and Roman capital, and having had a more than fair share of sackings and burnings – Normans in the ninth century, English Henry I in 1119, French Philippe Auguste in 1193, French Jean the Good in 1356. A further French king, Charles V, laid siege to it in 1379. In 1940 the city blazed for nearly a week after German air raids. The raids of 1944 were even more catastrophic.

Because of the town's hectic past Notre Dame cathedral shows a mixture of styles, dating from the eleventh to the eighteenth centuries. You should enter it through the Flamboyant Gothic north door, with its richly designed stone lacework. The interior is high and white: the great arches of the nave being the only part remaining of the original church. Note especially the stained glass windows; those of the apse are considered to be one of the best examples of fourteenth-century glass. Note also the wood carving of the ambulatory chapel. The screen to the fourth chapel is particularly outstanding.

The bishop's palace, next door to the cathedral, now houses a museum, which has a good collection of Gallo-Roman and medieval remains.

The former abbey church of St Taurinus, the first bishop of Evreux in the fourth century, is worth looking at. It was built during the fourteenth and fifteenth centuries and among its treasures it boasts St Taurinus' shrine, a gift to hold St Taurinus' relic from the French king, St Louis, to the abbey in the thirteenth century. Ornately carved, a masterpiece of craftsmanship, and in the shape of a miniature chapel, this silver gilt reliquary was probably made locally. It was wisely hidden away during the Revolution.

Evreux, situated about halfway between Paris and the coast, makes a good stopping place and is also a good centre for further excursions.

Louviers, about 20 km. to the north is worth visiting, if only to see its church of Notre Dame, most fortunately undamaged by the surrounding bombing. In any case, its exterior, especially the south wall, is so exuberantly flamboyant and covered with so much ornamentation, that probably a few missing decorations would not be noticed. Many works of art decorate the walls of its elegant thirteenth-century nave.

To the west of Louviers lies the famous old abbey of Bec-Hellouin, which is still in use. Its fifteenth-century St Nicholas

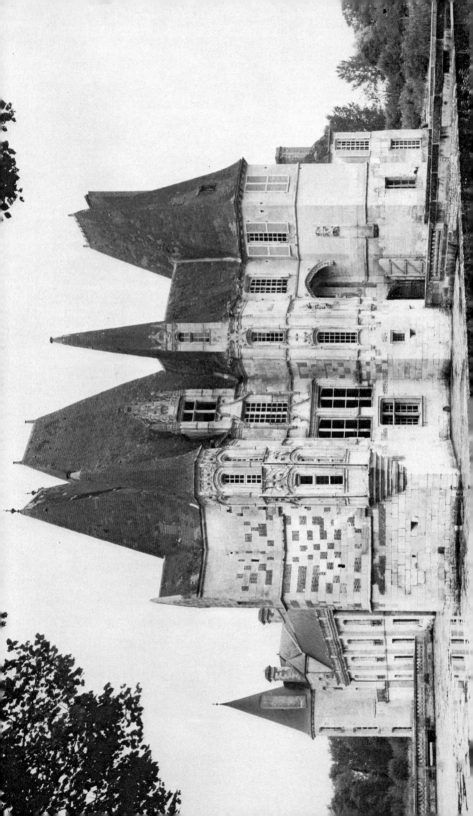

Tower, 45 metres high, a landmark for miles, is the chief reminder of the abbey's past.

In the Middle Ages Bec-Hellouin was a renowned religious and cultural centre. The abbey got its name from a knight called Herluin, who in 1034 exchanged his charger for a donkey and took a vow to devote his life to God. Within about ten years, many others had joined him here in the Bec valley.

Some quite illustrious people were attracted to stay there, such as Lanfranc in 1042, who later became the trusted friend and adviser of William the Conqueror and Archbishop of Canterbury, an office attained by another of Bec's abbots, Anselm, in 1093.

The first abbey, founded by Herluin, was at Bonneville Appetot, but was moved farther up the valley in 1060. It was fortified by Louis Harcourt, governor of Normandy in 1336, damaged by the English during the Hundred Years' War, and by the Protestants in the Wars of Religion. The monks were driven out during the Revolution and the great abbey church was demolished during the time of Napoleon.

Today, only the column foundations of the old abbey remain. The refectory, a majestically proportioned and vaulted hall constructed between 1742 and 1747, now houses the new abbey, which has been occupied by Benedictines since 1948.

Vernueil-sur-Avre, about 43 km. to the west of Evreux and a rather distinguished-looking little town, is descended from a fortifield city created in the twelfth century by Henry I when duke of Normandy. Along with Tillières and Nonnancourt it formed part of the Avre defence line against the French king's army.

Today, Vernueil's most attractive feature is the tower of Ste Magdalène's church, 56 metres high and rising in three tiers, crowned by an octagonal lantern. Massive yet delicately carved, it is more magnificent in some ways than the Butter Tower at Rouen. The church, a slightly older sixteenth-century Renaissance structure, suffered some war damage, and its interior, restored rather badly in the last century, is disappointing.

Notre Dame church, lying in a tangle of narrow streets, is difficult to see properly, but has an interior more attractive than the

23   *Château d'O, the entrance front*

reddish stone twelfth-century, but much restored, exterior. The many early sixteenth-century statues inside were mostly carved by local sculptors.

To the east of Notre Dame still stands the stout circular Tour Grise, built by Henri 1 to protect the town. The north side of Vernueil, near the Hotel de Ville and Rond-point de la Victoire has adapted the old to the new. A shaded park has been made on the hill, which must once have been part of the outer ramparts and which slopes down to the river, once a moat.

10. Orne

The Orne is predominantly a hilly country and especially so in the west, where the countryside is broken and wooded and the farm-land a patchwork of hedged enclosures. Its two highest points, the Signal d'Ecouves and Mont Avaloirs, both 417 metres, are also the highest in western France. Eastwards lie the flatter plains of Alençon and Argentan, where much wheat is grown.

Like Eure, Orne is chiefly a pastoral country, famed for its cattle and dairy produce. From the north-east, in the Auge region, comes Camembert cheese, perfected by Marie Harel at the beginning of the nineteenth century and named after the village where it was first made, near Vimoutiers. In the east is the Perche, the birth-place of a famous breed of draught horses, the Normandy Percheron.

Today, the chief area for horse-breeding lies between l'Aigle, an old industrial town, once renowned for its production of pins and needles, and Argentan.

Argentan to Alençon

Argentan lies on the plain between the Ecouves forest and the Gouffern woodland, which was where the final battle of Normandy took place in August 1944. The town was so badly damaged in the fighting that it has been almost completely rebuilt, so there is little interesting to see there now.

Even when I visited it, nearly 30 years later, the old church of St Germanus was still undergoing repairs and restoration and was closed to the public. Argentan was once famous for its lace. Although you can still see specimens in the Benedictine Abbey (1, Rue de l'Abbaye), it is no longer made.

However, Argentan is not far from two places of interest, Le Pin-au-Haras and the Château d'O.

The Pin stud, fortunately undamaged in the fighting, lies on the main road RN24*bis*, near Argentan. This fine building, lying at the end of the long Avenue Louis XIV and surrounded by 3,000 acres of woodland and pastures has a lordly and magnificent air as befits some of the aristocratic creatures bred there. You could call it the Horses' Versailles, as indeed it was designed by Jules Hardouin Mansart, the same architect who was responsible for Louis XIV's grand palace. The main courtyard, the Cour Colbert, is named after that king's minister, who laid the foundation of this and many other successful projects.

The main building, the château, built 1717–28, is the residence of the manager, while the 100 stallions – English thoroughbreds, French trotters, hacks, Anglo-Arabs, Norman cobs and Percherons, are kept in the stables in the wings. At one time, Le Pin was the principal nursery of horses for the army. It is now primarily a Stud Officers' Training School.

For anyone interested in horses, it is a great sight to see them all departing and returning from their daily exercise. The stud is open from 9 till noon and 2 to 6 every day. Entrance is free. A groom will show you round. There is an annual steeplechase on the second Sunday in October at Le Pin racecourse, and the annual meeting, including flat racing and steeplechasing, is on the first Sunday in August.

For anyone interested in horse riding, a very pleasant way to explore the woodlands and meadows of Orne is by horse. All-inclusive package holidays are available, excluding beginners – weekends, 250 frs: 3 or 4 days' riding 435 or 612 frs: a week, 965 frs. For details, apply to the Association Départementale de Tourisme Equestre et d'Equitation de Loisirs de l'Orne, 60 Grande Rue, 61–Alençon, France.

Château d'O, not far from Le Pin-au-Haras is famous for its

curious name and strange appearance, especially its fifteenth-century east side. Neither a house nor a castle, it is a mixture of narrow sloping roofs, steeples, turrets and gables. Château d'O, built out of plain rose brick, consists of three buildings surrounding three sides of a courtyard and overlooking a moat lake. The central part, with its tall windows, was added in the sixteenth century. Slim columns supporting its arcade are decorated with ermine carvings, the emblem of the house of O. The west side, rebuilt in the eighteenth century, is the living quarters.

Unfortunately, the château grounds are closed between 1 July and 10 September, and the castle is not open at all. So the visitor is only able to admire its grand and graceful structure, so attractively reflected in the water.

If you drive to Mortrée from here, then take the N158, you will arrive at the old cathedral town of Sées, the seat of Orne's bishopric, and not far from the source of the Orne river.

But Sées, in spite of its grand ecclesiastical past is now just a small town which has seen better days, with little streets leading to its cathedral. An air of seedy shabbiness hangs over it.

Sées, the Sagium of Roman times and a bishopric from the fourth century, was supposed to have been founded by a colony of Saxons. Its cathedral, St Latriun, was destroyed many times by the Northmen, and the present one, a good example of Norman Gothic, was built in the thirteenth and fourteenth centuries.

It is shaped like a vast Latin cross, 106 metres long. The decorations and stained glass windows are best over the chancels and transepts. Most of the stained glass windows tell stories, which are explained in notices below, a great help to sightseers. The high window glass disappeared in the Wars of Religion, in 1573.

Fortunately Our Lady of Sées, a white marble statue decorated with gold in the south transept, managed to escape all the pillages of the cathedral during the fourteenth century, in 1450, 1556, and especially in 1793. She has a most intriguing air of *songerie* (dreaminess) as she gazes down at her child, who holds an orange, the world, in one hand.

In spite of the town's past, its seminaries and monasteries and churches, there is very little to see in Sées, apart from its cathedral. True, there is a small museum near by in the square, but it is not a very important one. The old bishops' palace at the east end of the cathedral looked almost dilapidated behind its fine wrought-iron gates. In any case, it now houses offices.

The Château de Carrouges, one of Normandy's most famous castles, lies about 26 km. to the west of Sées. Unlike that of O it can be visited.

Huge, ornate, square and surrounded by a moat, it too is made of rose red brick. Carrouges' most famous features are its elegant, ornate, wrought-iron gates, made by Jean Goujon, at the end of the terrace at the entrance front. Inside, the house also has a very fine stairway. The state rooms are decorated in a mixture of Renaissance and classical styles, combining simplicity with splendour, and provide a rich background to the furniture. The portrait gallery is most interesting.

Carrouges was built between the thirteenth and seventeenth centuries, but mostly during the sixteenth and seventeenth in the reign of Henri IV, to replace a fortress built above the village at the top of a hill. The castle was owned by the Tillières family, a well-known Norman one, and Lords of Carrouges from the twelfth century.

If you have a car you should make the drive from Sées to Alençon through the forest of Ecouves, whose stretch of trees – oak, beech, pine and spruce – is reckoned to be one of the loveliest in France. Take the N808, then after 'Les Choux', at Carrefour de la Range, take the D226 on the left.

Although the area called Ecouves Forest is about 37,000 acres, much of it is scrub, moorland and pastures. The best bit, the real forest, only about 20,000 acres, which is state property, lies in the centre. Roads, tracks and lanes cut through it. Ecouves is renowned for its mushrooms, fishing, wild boar and deer hunting, reserved for members of the appropriate organizations, of course. Also, the variety of its insects, especially beetles. In summer walkers should beware of vipers.

Once hunted over by Norman nobles, Ecouves forest was appropriated to the French crown by Philippe Auguste in 1220. Some centuries later, Colbert, under Louis XIV, gave the use of part of the forest to glass-blowers, an industry which prospered there up to the end of the eighteenth century. In 1790, it became state property. The last war saw its greatest drama when it was the scene of the battle between the division commanded by the French general, LeClerc, and the entrenched Germans, who had taken refuge there.

A tank now stands at Croix de Médavy to commemorate this important battle and the men of the French 2nd Division, who cleared the forest of Germans on 12 and 13 August 1944. The viewpoint at this crossroads is marked by an old milestone, carved with old road names.

From here, you take the road towards Croix Madame, another viewpoint, and in the centre of the most attractive part of the forest. In fact, you should get out here and explore some of the walks on foot. That along the Sapie Pichon path is the best. If you drive down the D204 to the Vignage rocks crossroads, then bear right to the D26, you will eventually reach Alençon. The Vignage rocks are another and more attractive viewpoint over the forest. A walk to them takes about three-quarters of an hour, there and back.

Alençon, situated around the Sarthe and Riante rivers, and capital of the Orne Department, had the distinction of being the first town in France to be liberated by General Leclerc. The French 2nd Division entered it on 12 August, and on the 13th cut the Paris–Granville road at Ecouché. On the 19th the Poles (1st Canadian Army) and Americans cut off the German 7th Army retreat at Chambois, near Le Pin-au-Haras (a stele marks the place) and forced them to surrender. By 21 August the battle of Normandy was over.

Alençon fortunately escaped much damage and has retained her old monuments, houses and streets. Even so, I was not very impressed when I first saw the town. Like Sées, it appeared bitty, seedy and run-down. However, it is a town that grows on you, and I ended up by liking it, and would have liked to have spent longer exploring it.

Because of its position on so many roads, it is a town that visitors to France are likely to find themselves passing through on the way somewhere else. Anyone with time to spare would probably enjoy a few hours looking round.

The best place to start on a tour of Alençon is the Place Foch, because you can park your car there. Also, here stand the old palace of the dukes, the bridge, the Palace of Justice and Hôtel de Ville, all making an attractive ensemble and very photogenic, especially when seen from the little garden past the bridge.

Alençon on the border of Normandy, and once known as the city of the dukes, has had quite a long and bloodthirsty history. It was captured by William the Conqueror in 1048, but the oldest parts of the castle to be seen now are its fifteenth-century pepper-pot tower and fortified gateway. Today the castle houses a prison, and probably always will do, I was told. Between 1940 and 1944 many arrested French patriots were martyred within its grim walls by the Gestapo, either by execution on the spot or by dispatch to extermination camps.

The museum in the Town Hall opposite is chiefly one of paintings and would be of interest to anyone keen on French painters, such as Jouvenet, Rigaud, Chardin, Boudin, Courbet, and Géricault, but there are no Impressionists. It also holds a collection of lace, for which Alençon has long been well-known.

The bridge past the little garden leads to the Promenade des Rosaires, a park which contains a few animals – a donkey, goats, deer – which children might enjoy feeding. There are also some peacocks, those fine actors, who can usually be relied upon to put on a show and display their fine tails. Behind this is a pretty garden and aviary.

The Grande Rue, a mere rather narrow street, is Alençon's main thoroughfare and contains some quaint old houses. The interesting little well you will see (the Syndicat d'Initiative did not know the date) with steps inside a tower doesn't really belong there, but is a transplant from somewhere else 'because it fills the space rather nicely'.

The famous church of Notre Dame, fourteenth-century Flamboyant Gothic, seems to plunge straight down into the road, so that one has to walk backwards in the street opposite to see it properly. It is particularly renowned for its three-sided porch, very flamboyant and intricately carved. Christ stands in the centre, while John stands beneath him, his back turned unexpectedly to the street.

Inside, about the first thing you will notice is the sanctuary to Ste Thérèse, probably ablaze with candles. The stained glass windows above show her baptism in the church here with the words, *Sancta Thérèse ora pro nobis* below.

Ste Thérèse, whose full name was Marie Françoise Thérèse Martin, was born in Alençon in 1873, one of nine sisters. You can visit her home and see her birthroom, and there is a chapel dedicated to her in the Rue St Blaise, just off the Grande Rue.

Her father was a watchmaker and her mother a laceworker. Both were extremely pious and before they were married had both tried unsuccessfully to enter a religious establishment. Because of this it is not too surprising that Thérèse entered a convent when only 15.

She was, I suppose, a rather neurotic girl, who suffered badly from feelings of guilt, which she managed to hide under a pleasant and smiling exterior, doing good deeds, so that no one would have suspected her inner turmoil. She contracted tuberculosis and died painfully when only 24. It was the *Histoire d'une âme* ('History of a soul') – papers describing her feelings and experiences – which made her name. This work was first published in 1898, then after extensive revisions again in 1956. She was canonized in 1925 and in 1945 was named the second patroness of France after Ste Jeanne. Her feast day is October 3.

As well as being the birthplace of Ste Thérèse, Alençon is France's chief source of lace. You can visit the School of Lace in the Pont Neuf, a street just opposite the Syndicat d'Initiative in the Grande Rue. Ring the bell. The people here are usually glad to show visitors round.

However, you can no longer watch the laceworkers at work, as there are very few of them now. You can only see the famous collection. For 2.50 francs a voice in English will guide you round the rooms, although as the loudspeaker is in the first room, you have to listen rather hard when you enter the other two. Triumphant music accompanies these speeches.

It is a great pity that Alençon lace is likely to die out soon, because it is very lovely. But it is difficult now to find people willing to do this intricate and painstaking work. They can only work three hours a day at it. A small piece can take up to 68 hours to make. Only in Brussels and Alençon is lace still made by hand.

The collection is extremely rich, containing the beautiful Pointe d'Alençon veil worn by Marie Antoinette, while some of the lace is so delicate that it has to be looked at under a magnifying glass. Lace-making in Alençon is due to that indefatigable minister, Colbert, who, to help the town prosper, financed the making of lace here. In 1665, it was decreed that no more lace be imported into France from abroad.

In the showroom, you can buy pieces of exquisite lace – at a price! A tiny square costs about £13. A little cheaper are dolls with lace caps and cuffs, about £6. The hankies, trimmed with lace, come a little cheaper still, at about £3 each.

Alençon makes a good centre for excursions. Apart from the Ecouves forest to the north, it is within easy reach of the Perseigne forest to the south-east. To the west lie the Marcelles Alps, hardly mountains, but attractively steep, heather-covered hills enclosing the Sarthe valley. Farther west still lies Bagnoles-sur-Orne.

Bagnoles-sur-Orne

Bagnoles-sur-Orne, so picturesquely situated around a lake and surrounded by forest, must be the only spa in the world whose medicinal waters were discovered by a horse.

Exactly when it happened is somewhat obscure. But the story goes that a knight named Hugues de Tessé was too tender-hearted to put his faithful horse, Rapide, to death when he got old and senile. Instead, he bid him sadly goodbye, then let him loose in the Andaine forest.

Time passed. Then, one day, to his utter amazement, Rapide returned to his stable. But he was no longer a worn-out, old horse. He was a new, lively, rejuvenated Rapide. What had happened?

Tessé determined to solve the mystery and tracked his hoof marks, back through the forest. They led to a spring in which the horse had apparently bathed. Tessé bathed, too, and found to his delight that he also felt young again.

From that time onwards, Bagnoles was known as a place of healing and rejuvenation. One Capucin monk is even supposed to have become so randy that he made a 13ft leap from one rocky spur to another. This place is now known as the Capucin's leap.

Today, Bagnoles is a spa resort, chiefly for diseases of the circulation, gynaecological problems, and also for fractures from accidents. Its sulphuric salt waters are to be bathed in, not taken. Whether or not they do really possess all the curative powers claimed, I don't know, but it is such a pleasant, peaceful place, that a few days spent there would make anyone feel better.

Bagnoles used to be very popular with English and American visitors, but since the war few of them come here. This is rather remarkable as it is such a delightful place to stay and would make a pleasant break of a few days during a long journey through France. There are plenty of good hotels and restaurants.

A village of some sort or another has probably existed around the lakeside since early times. Its waters have long been used for bathing in, although the early baths here were very rough and ready. The place did not become really important until the nineteenth century, when a rich American, a Mr Gould, invested money in it. He built a casino and the large red-shuttered hotel beside the lake, which is now let out in apartments.

There are now two casinos, both overlooking the lake and open from the beginning of May to the end of September. The biggest casino, which includes a cinema and dance hall, was built by Mr Gould. The other one belongs to a family but has been recently bought by the town, which intends to improve it, so it should be open by 1974.

Apart from the casinos you can sit on one of the many seats

dotted around the lakeside, listen to the birds, or watch the swans glide over the water. Or, if you feel energetic, you can take out a white pedalo boat (a bit expensive though at three francs for a quarter of an hour). You can stroll round the town, which has some good shops, or explore one of the many forest walks.

The Hôtel des Thermes, on the edge of the town, can be reached from any of the hotels by a little bus which runs between Bagnoles station and Tessé church, every afternoon between 2 p.m. and 6.45. The Hôtel stands beside the road in a natural park, backed by rocks, gushing streams and forest paths. I met a woman who had been coming there for 22 years to bathe her legs, a treatment which she can get partly financed by the French equivalent of our National Health Scheme.

The best view of Bagnoles is to be had from the Roc au Chien. This rather blunt-faced dog is approached up the Sentier de l'Avenir and stone staircase, nearly opposite the Casino in the Avenue du Château. Turn left, and you eventually come to three posts. Not far down on the left fork is the left-hand path leading to this rocky projection. From it, you have a very clear view of the forest, Bagnoles, and the lake.

Bagnoles is an excellent centre for excursions. Near at hand is Tessé la Madeleine with its Château de la Roche Bagnoles, Renaissance in style, but built by a rich old lady about 1850, and now the Town Hall. If you buy an eight-franc book of tickets from the Syndicat d'Initiative, you can, amongst other things, attend concerts, visit exhibitions, the little cinema and take trips on the miniature railway. Further afield is the Zoological Park at St Symphorien des Monts (bus from Bagnoles every Tuesday), also the enchanted village at Bellefontaine, a park catering particularly for children. Both these two places are in Manche.

If you have no car or feel like a rest from driving, you can go on one of the many organized bus tours. There are two companies, Normandie Excursions and Les Circuits Bagnolais. You can visit Swiss Normandy, or even go as far as Mont St Michel. Prices range from 16 to 19 francs, which is reasonable considering the distance covered. However, these buses are small (they seat only about 22 people), comfortable and very popular, so that you need to book at least a day ahead.

Swiss Normandy

Swiss Normandy, shaped by the Orne cutting its way through the Armorican Massif, is one of the most attractive areas of Normandy, especially popular with walkers, anglers, canoeists and campers.

It is a region of deep gorges, high rocky cliffs, wooded valleys and occasional peaks from which to view the rolling countryside. Although it does not possess high mountains or lakes, you could call it a Switzerland in miniature.

Most of it lies in Calvados and its nearest large town is Falaise. However, I am putting it in at the end of the Orne chapter as it makes such a good trip from Bagnoles.

Ferté Macé, the first town you pass, is also a spa, and quite attractive with a large church. It is noted for its tripe cooked on skewers. Briouze, the next one, is famous for its cheese. After crossing the bridge at Forêt Auvray Pont, the road snakes down a wild, tree-covered valley, difficult to drive down quickly. It is very peaceful and hard to imagine swarming with soldiers as it was 30 years ago, when Montgomery's troops fought their way through this area.

Swiss Normandy's most famous viewpoint is the one from Roche d'Oëtre, which overlooks the deep valley of the Rouve through which this stream twists and turns between slopes massed with trees. Around another path near by is the Profil Humain, the outline of a rocky face with quite a sensitive nose. Although there is no charge for visiting the rocks, they form part of a café's grounds and you are supposed to buy some little souvenir there. These are quite nice – pottery, cheese, slippers, dolls, nuts, sweets, cards, etc.

Clécy, a large village, lying around a curve of the Orne, is the centre of Swiss Normandy and a place from which walkers start on their explorations. You can visit its folklore museum in a sixteenth-century manor house, climb to the top of the Sugar Loaf rock for a good view, or cross the bridge to Vey on the other side of the river. The Hostellerie du Moulin du Vey, situated so picturesquely beside the river, waterfalls and rocks, serves food and drinks, but would probably be expensive to stay at, also noisy because of the turning wheels and waterfalls. There is also a cider cellar at Clécy, which you can visit for a franc, including drinks of cider afterwards. You can also buy bottles of cider here and take a ride on the miniature railway through the Parc de Loisirs.

After Clécy, you can go on to Thury Harcourt, a pleasant tourist centre on the northern edge of Swiss Normandy, or return to Bagnoles via Condé sur Noireau, descending through forests past flint quarries to Pont Erambourg, and down the valley of the Vire to Flers. Flers, a rather grey nondescript town, boasts a fine sixteenth-century château, now a Town Hall and museum, partly surrounded by a moat and with a simple but attractive garden.

You could next visit Domfront, spread out along a rocky crest, once a strongly fortified border town. From the terrace of the public gardens made out of the old castle ruins is a splendid view of the river Varenne and the last wooded hills of lower Normandy.

11. Calvados

The Calvados, the department most visited by English tourists, is also the one which has played the most important part in our island history. Even its name, Calvados, is supposed to have come from a ship of the Spanish Armada, the *Salvador*, which after the defeat of 1588, while making for home, foundered on a reef near Arromanches.

Its highest part lies in the Swiss Normandy of the south-west; elsewhere it is low-lying, but varied, especially its coastline, with stretches of cliffs, reefs, and sands backed by dunes and marshes. The damp mild climate and rich soils of the hinterlands, the Pays d'Auge and Bessin, provide rolling hills of lush pastures and apple orchards. Most of the Campagne de Caen and Lieuvin is devoted to fields of wheat, sugar beet and apple orchards. Scattered among the cultivated fields between Caen and Falaise are stone quarries, the stone for which Caen has been famous for centuries. Later discoveries of iron ore led to the building of steelworks around Caen.

Falaise

Falaise, which has so many links with Britain, is still an attractive city in spite of the cruel destruction of the last war. Its rugged castle, birthplace of William the Conqueror, still stands on its high crag overlooking the town, set in the rocky Ante valley.

This stronghold, a tour of which takes about an hour, is reckoned to be one of the oldest in Normandy. Its history is long and exciting. It is sufficient to say here that it has endured many sieges, especially during the Hundred Years' War, and changed hands several times during the Wars of Religion. In 1589, after its thick walls had been bombarded and broken by Henri IV's artillery, it was dismantled and abandoned for about 200 years. However, it came back into use again in the eighteenth century, when the Town Hall was erected in its grounds, and in the nineteenth a college was built where the garrison barracks had stood.

Falaise castle came back properly into its own again during the Second World War when its Talbot Tower was used by the Germans as an observation post and the college assembly hall as a field bakery. During the furious battle that raged round it in mid-August 1944, machine-guns were fired through its windows at Montgomery's troops on the Caen road.

The castle and the town's monuments have now been restored from the débâcle that followed and are worth looking at, if only for their legends and their historical interest.

There is the Arlette fountain below the castle, and which once stood amongst old tanneries in a quaint area destroyed during the war. Today, two towers, a bas-relief and inscription mark the place where the 18-year-old Duke Robert was supposed to have first met the girl, Arlette.

However, as his castle window overlooked the stream, as she probably well knew, they had probably seen each other often before that fine spring evening in 1027, as told in the poem by Benoît de Sainte-Maure, Chronicler of the Duchy of Normandy, and written at the request of Henri II.

Duke Robert, younger son of Richard II, was returning home from the hunt when he saw this beautiful girl washing her linen in the stream. He didn't waste much time. Shortly afterwards, his chamberlain was sent to her father, Herbert, a well-to-do tanner, to demand that she be sent up to Robert at the castle the following nightfall.

It seems that the lovely Arlette was a girl of character. She would go, but on her own terms. All must see her. She would ride in on a fine horse, in her best clothes, accompanied by servants and in

24   *St Catherine's, Honfleur*

broad daylight. All turned out well. They were both young and attractive. But although it was a love match, Robert never married Arlette, and their son, William, born soon after, was a bastard.

Arlette lived in the castle where her son was born and most probably grew up. Before he was born, Arlette had her famous prophetic dream that from her womb there grew a tree skywards so broad that its foliage spread not only over Normandy, but also over the English kingdom as well.

The bronze statue of William the Conqueror in the Place Guillaume le Conquérant, erected in 1851, is considered to be one of the finest equestrian statues in France. Curiously enough, although practically every building in the square was bombed flat by the German *Luftwaffe* on the night of 17 August 1944, when Falaise was liberated by the Canadians, the statue was unharmed. It was as if it said, 'I, and I alone, can conquer England'.

Around its pedestal are the smaller statues of the first six dukes of Normandy, erected in 1875. Also of interest is the bronze memorial erected in 1931 in the Prix Chapel in the Talbot Tower. This bears the names of 315 prominent men who accompanied William at the Battle of Hastings in 1066. There were obviously many more, but these ones have been proved to have been there.

Falaise should be seen at night when floodlit. Every Saturday and Sunday night in June, every night in July, August, and September, pageants telling the legend of the Conqueror are held. Seats are provided for the show, and parking is free.

Lisieux

The best way to arrive at Lisieux is by train and on a summer evening when the buildings are floodlit. Then one has the ethereal and unexpected vision of its basilica on a hilltop. The contrast of a nearby skyscraper and prosaic station make it appear even more unreal, a flight of eastern fancy, a mirage rising above the treetops.

25 *Notre Dame de Grace, Honfleur*

The basilica is dedicated to Ste Thérèse and is an important centre of pilgrimage. From its grand formal garden in front there is a magnificent view over Lisieux and the surrounding countryside. Romano-Byzantine in style and with an immense rounded dome, it was started in 1923 and is still not finished. It was built to accommodate the large number of pilgrims coming to Lisieux.

Inside, it is spacious and massive, bigger than most cathedrals and ablaze with burning candles. In spite of its size, the large crypt can be jammed with people. As with Jeanne d'Arc, the worship of Ste Thérèse could be called a small industry. A shop sells candles, pictures, cards, mementoes, even on the basilica premises.

If you are interested in religion, or maybe, sociology, Lisieux is the town for you. Busloads of pilgrims come every day to visit the basilica, the Carmelite chapel and Ste Thérèse's home.

Thérèse lost her mother when she was four years old, and her father took his family of now only five daughters from Alençon to live at the house known as Les Buissonnets, on the outskirts of the then small, hilly town.

This sturdy bourgeois house, which lies up the slope of a winding path, now crowded with booths selling mementoes, has been turned into a museum. Thérèse lived there for about ten years. The heavy mahogany furniture, her toys, schoolbooks and bed have all been carefully preserved.

As early as the age of nine, she decided to enter the Carmelite order, and when she was 15 she approached her father to ask his permission. This episode is now represented by a tableau of statues in the garden behind the house.

Life in a Carmelite convent at that time was very severe, especially so to someone from a comfortable home. They rose at five in the morning in summer to the clatter of castanets. All private possessions were forbidden. Inmates slept on a board across two trestles with little to lie on or cover them. A notice on the cell wall read 'My daughter why are you here?', a constant reminder of their vows. Silence was observed as much as possible. If they spoke it was to make a confession of some sin. Food was frugal. Worst of all there was the cold. Even in the coldest weather, only one room was allowed to be heated to 50°F, so it is not too surprising that the delicate, consumptive Thérèse died at such an early age.

She wrote the *Histoire d'une âme* at the instigation of her sister, Pauline, then the Mother Superior (all her sisters seemed to have taken the veil). It was written between her many duties in snatched moments, which is probably why it sometimes appears incoherent.

Ste Thérèse defined her doctrine in the *Histoire d'une âme* as the 'Little Way', the way of spiritual childhood, trust and absolute surrender to Christ. It is artless and naïve, yet at the same time heroic. She seemed to have known that it would be important after her death.

Ste Thérèse's attraction for so many people must be her ordinariness. To the more educated and sophisticated she appears sentimental and sickly sweet, but her philosophy of the 'Little Way' of obedience and humility was, I suppose, in most people's power. She bridged the gap between the metaphysical arguments of the Roman Catholic church and everyday experience.

She died in obscurity as so many other nuns have done. After a death it was customary for an obituary notice to be sent round all the other convents. It is said that the Prioress at Carmel, then a Mère de Gonzague, felt that she had not always treated Thérèse properly, and so decided to print and distribute her *Histoire* instead of the usual obituary.

This was first read in convents, where it was lent to friends, until the circle gradually widened, extending to priests and missionaries all over the world. It became very popular. Then people who were sick invoked her help and claimed that they had been cured; others swore that her spirit had appeared to them. The legend grew, especially during the First World War, when the French army adopted her as their special protectress many preferring her femininity to the soldier, Jeanne d'Arc.

Lisieux, a very old town, existing in pre-Roman times, has long been a religious city. Its bishopric, suppressed in 1802, dates back to the sixth century. Thomas à Becket took refuge there for a time.

Some relics and his vestments are to be seen in St Jacques' church. St Peter's cathedral, twelfth to sixteenth century, which claims to be the oldest Gothic church in Normandy, had as one of its bishops Pierre Cauchon, who was responsible for Jeanne d'Arc's being handed over to the English.

Because of its position on an important road junction, Lisieux was a target for bombing in 1944, and has been rebuilt as a modern town with much wider streets. There are not many of its quaint old Norman houses left.

Both the basilica and St Peter's are worth visiting if you are passing this way. You should also get a cheap meal here. Some of the restaurant prices are very economical, ranging from nine francs upwards and of good value. Hotels, too, are reasonable and there are plenty of them. You should get in fairly easily, provided there isn't a big pilgrimage taking place.

Lisieux, chief town of the Pays d'Auge, is a centre for cheeses, such as Camembert, Pont l'Evêque and Livarot, also cider and calvados (cider spirit). There are many pleasant drives to be had around its lush wooded countryside, the best being to and along its famous coast, the Côte Fleurie. That this is and was a wealthy area can be seen by the number of châteaux and large old timbered manor farms.

Two popular drives are to Trouville along the Toques valley, and to Honfleur, at the start of the Côte Fleurie.

The Côte Fleurie to Caen

Honfleur has been hit not so much by bombs as by industrialization. Whichever way you enter it – car, bus or train – its approaches are grim. However, once past the ugliness and mess of the surroundings you round the buildings and quayside into the Vieux Port, and the aspect changes and you are in a truly delightful place.

Tall, narrow, rather sombre, slate-roofed houses, some half-timbered ones dating from the sixteenth and seventeenth centuries, cafés and restaurants, surround a harbour filled with a variety of

colourful sailing boats. The harbour was built from old fortifications and the harbourmaster's house you see at its entrance was
part of the drawbridge. Behind it was the governor's house.

Honfleur, which dates from the eleventh century, like so many
other Norman towns changed hands many times during the
Hundred Years' War and played a fairly hectic part in the Wars
of Religion. The St Leonard's quarter was badly damaged by
the Protestants in 1562. Henri iv besieged Honfleur twice, once
in 1590, then again in 1594.

The port and town had its heyday in the sixteenth and seventeenth centuries when trade with the American continent and
East Indies made it an important maritime and commercial town.
It was the home of many intrepid seafarers and explorers, the
best known of them being Samuel de Champlain (1567-1635). He
set sail from here in 1608 on a voyage which resulted in the
foundation of Quebec. Canada, which had been claimed for
France a century earlier by Jacques Cartier had been neglected
until Champlain's arrival. It rapidly became a predominantly
Norman colony.

Although Honfleur declined in importance as a port in the
nineteenth century, when it was supplanted by Le Havre, its
picturesqueness attracted writers, musicians and especially painters
to settle there. Many artists gathered around the local painter,
Eugène Louis Boudin at the Ferme St Siméon, about a kilometre
from the town, which became a centre for the Impressionists.
Monet, Sisley, Renoir, Pissarro, Cézanne all worked along this
stretch of the Normandy coast.

Because of this, Honfleur now boasts a very good painting
gallery, the Eugène Boudin museum, Rue Albert I°, which is
devoted chiefly to those artists who painted in this area.

The Vieux Honfleur museum, just off the old port, is also
worth seeing. Part of it is in the old church of St Etienne and part
in old houses in the Rue de la Prison. It is quite extensive, showing rooms of old furniture, even a shop, as well as clothes, weapons,
religious objects and Gallo-Roman remains.

However, no visitor to Honfleur should miss visiting the church of Ste Catherine, standing in a square opposite its tower in a most picturesque part of Honfleur. My immediate impression was of a Scandinavian stave church, because it was built out of wood, a rare phenomenon in a region so rich in good building stone.

The reason why is not known. Most likely, as it was built at the end of the Hundred Years' War, it was intended only as a temporary measure. Wood was easily obtainable, as were men who, although chiefly skilled at ship-building, could put it together and decorate it.

The result is unique. Inside are wooden pillars and walls beamed like the old manor houses in the Pays d'Auge, so that it resembles a hall rather than a church. It is spacious with two naves, while the vaulting above resembles ships' hulls turned upside down.

The bell tower, also of wood and about the same period, stands opposite the church. That it stands apart is probably due to the fact that the timbering would not withstand the weight and movement of the bells. It may also have been a safeguard against fire caused by lightning. Incidentally, the ticket for seeing the bell tower also includes a visit to the Eugène Boudin museum.

Honfleur is probably a place better to visit than to stay at for, although there are plenty of hotels and restaurants, they become very overcrowded in summer, and it has a poor beach. However, not too far away lie some of the best beaches in France.

The Côte Fleurie is a gentler coastline than that north of the Seine, and its low-lying hills sweep down almost to the sandy beaches. Behind the coast, crowded with hotels and houses, lies a pretty countryside of hedge-bound meadows, neat orchards, manor houses and stud farms.

At first, after Honfleur, is the Normandy Corniche, and a pleasant leafy road runs along hills above the sea, with a glimpse of blue through the trees. The road meets the coast again at Villenville. The corniche cliff ends at Trouville, where it is replaced by a splendid stretch of sand.

Trouville, lying at the foot of wooded hills to the north of the

Toques river, is this coast's most popular resort. It can claim two historical distinctions. One, it was the place where Henry v landed with his English army in 1417 to set out on the campaign that was to bring Normandy to the English crown. The second, and more useful, it was a favourite place of the Empress Eugénie. This is why so many of its older buildings date from the Third Empire, an architectural style which includes as many others as it can and was much liked by the newly-rich bourgeoisie.

Trouville, unlike Deauville on the opposite side of the Toques river, is geared as much to commerce as it is to holidays, and so is an all-the-year-round resort.

Deauville, internationally famous, luxurious, aristocratic, was founded by the Duc de Morny in 1866 and is built on a checkerboard plan with wide avenues. The Planches, a wooden plank promenade which runs the length of its beach (and Trouville's too), is famous for its promenade of fashionable women in smart clothes. Deauville's season starts in July and ends on the fourth Sunday in August with the Deauville Grand Prix horse race. Both Trouville and Deauville are expensive.

After Deauville, one resort comes after another, all rather alike, and overlooking vast stretches of sand. This stretch of coast, once a favourite place for the wealthy and cosmopolitan, its picturesqueness beloved by artists, is now attracting a different type of holidaymaker. Expensive hotels are being replaced by villas, rented apartments, camp sites and second homes.

The road leaves the coast after Villers-sur-Mer, renowned for its six-kilometre beach, and plunges through attractively wooded rolling countryside. At Houlgate, it returns to the sea. This is a particularly pleasant resort, combining the best of both beach and countryside.

Commercialized Dives, was where William the Conqueror set out for England. The port that he used and which was later used for shipping stone, silted up, and now only serves as an anchorage for yachts. If you visit its Gothic church, Our Lady of Dives, you will see a tablet over the door which lists names of William's chief companions.

Cabourg, facing Dives on the opposite side of the river, like Trouville became a seaside resort during the Third Empire. It is built in a fan shape, or half a cartwheel, and is leafy and green with shady avenues and villas surrounded by flowery gardens. No road runs beside the Promenade des Anglais, which borders its splendid four-kilometre beach. Fashionable and expensive, it boasts a casino and golf club.

After Franceville, the road follows the Orne estuary, first on the right side, passing Ranville, the first village in France to be liberated in June 1944, then crossing the river and canal over the Pegasus bridge to the left bank. This bridge was named after the exploit of the night 5–6 June, when it was taken by a British parachute brigade. Its possession played a vital part in the Normandy landings.

The rest of the journey to Caen is through an industrial belt even uglier than Honfleur's. This is made even worse by the fact that the previous part of the journey passed through such an attractive region.

Caen

The first Caen, which started on an island at the confluence of the rivers, Orne and Odon, became important in the eleventh century, especially when it was the favourite town of William the Conqueror.

Although not its capital, Caen is Normandy's most important city. It is progressive, well-planned, and predominantly a commercial city with some rather beautiful churches.

Caen has always played an important part in Norman history, but it was during the battle for it, lasting over two months in 1944, that it played its most dramatic and terrible rôle. Fires raged through it for 11 days, gutting its centre. Later, when the Germans retreated to new positions across the Orne, their shells added more to the debris. About two thirds of the city's buildings were totally destroyed.

The reconstruction of Caen was carried out quickly and carefully. Many narrow streets were replaced by broad thoroughfares; while those which had been attractive were restored and improved. It is a World War Two town, as its street names now show : Rue 6 Juin, Rue de la Libération, and the large flat cenotaph beside the Rue Equipes des Urgences to those shot and deported between 1940 and 1945, commemorate this dramatic episode.

Terrible though all this must have been, it has resulted in a pleasant, dignified and expanding city. Caen, with its separate residential and industrial zones, its much improved port, the creation of a new university and good communications, has attracted many major firms to settle there, thereby increasing its prosperity.

In spite of the destruction, its main sights are still the Abbaye aux Hommes and the Abbaye aux Dames.

When the ambitious William had consolidated his position as Duke of Normandy, he decided to marry his cousin, Mathilde of Flanders. However, she was less keen and stated that she would rather take the veil and enter a convent than marry a bastard. William, angered at being baulked, rode to Lille, where the Court of Flanders then was, seized Mathilde by her plaits and dragged her round the room, kicking her. Then he rode off. In spite of, or possibly because of, this rough wooing, Mathilde consented to marry him.

But they were related, and the Pope, objecting to their marriage, excommunicated them. This excommunication was later lifted in 1059 owing to the intercession of Lanfranc, William's friend and adviser. As a penance, William and Mathilde founded two abbeys at Caen, the Abbaye aux Hommes and the Abbaye aux Dames, and four hospitals.

The Abbaye aux Hommes is rather difficult to find because it is now joined up with the Town Hall and St Stephen's church. I had to walk round it before I could find a way in. There is a door near the Town Hall, but if this is closed, you should walk down the Rue Guillaume le Conquérant, past shops and houses, until you come to a square, where there is another entrance to it on the left-hand side. This integration with other buildings makes it difficult to see properly. I think the best view of it is probably from the Place Louis Guillouard.

Inside, the abbey is tall and cool with graceful sweeping lines, very superior architecturally and very beautiful. Because of extensive restoration it looks quite new, but the magnificent outlines still remain from the past. William the Conqueror's tomb before the high altar is marked by a stone bearing his epitaph. His remains are not in the church though, as they were thrown in the river during the Revolution.

The abbey buildings, reconstructed in the eighteenth century, and now housing the Town Hall, can be visited during the day (except Tuesday). There is some very fine woodwork to be seen there.

The Abbaye aux Dames in the Place Reine Mathilde beside a convent stands on a hill, and is some distance from Aux Hommes.

It is easier to see as a whole, but is somewhat squat and less attractive than Aux Hommes. This is not entirely its fault. The spires of the church were destroyed in the Hundred Years' War and were replaced by an ugly balustrade in the eighteenth century.

However, the inside at first appears more vivid than Aux Hommes. When you enter the red and blue mosaic windows have an almost dazzling effect, lighting up the church. When you walk towards them, then turn, the windows at the other end are of a subdued grey, black and buff mosaic. This contrast in colours helps to bring life to a rather dull interior.

Mathilde, like William, was buried in her church. You will see a dark slab covered by glass behind the altar. The chapel in the crypt, dedicated to St Nicholas, is worth seeing and is remarkably well preserved. Incidentally, people took shelter down here during the bombardment of the city.

Caen castle, also erected by William the Conqueror, profited in a way from the bombing, as it now stands boldly on the hill, as it once must have done, no longer hidden by buildings. From a distance, it looks more imposing than it is, as it is a mere shell consisting chiefly of ramparts. There are some very good views of the town from its battlements.

It boasts two museums, one of fine arts in a modern building, while the other shows the history of Normandy, and displays of pottery, clothes, kitchen utensils, etc; and also the Chapel of St George. This last is a very simply decorated memorial to those killed in action for Normandy during the centuries. There is also the tomb of an unknown victim of the bombardment in the city in 1944.

St Pierre's church, standing in a street of the same name, is near the castle and not far from the Syndicat d'Initiative. Less austere than the two abbeys, it owes its decorations to the rich merchants of Caen. The most elaborate are at the east end, built between 1518 and 1545, in Renaissance style. Behind the altar are five beautiful chapels. When you look upwards, the keystones of the first and second resemble stalactites hanging from a cave roof. St Pierre's famous fourteenth-century belfry, destroyed during the war, has been rebuilt.

Caen, because of its good position and communications, makes an excellent centre for tours and expeditions.

Near at hand is Fontaine-Henri, lying in an attractive wooded valley to the north-west. This château, built in the fifteenth and sixteenth centuries on the ruins of an old thirteenth-century fortress, is a good example of the Renaissance style. Its most unusual feature is its steeply sloping roof, set between towers and spires, which is even taller than the building below. Inside there are a remarkable François I staircase, sculptures and some interestingly furnished rooms.

Not too far away is the Swiss Normandy, the invasion beaches of the Côte Nacre and Bayeux.

Bayeux

Bayeux, capital of the Bessin country, is one of Normandy's oldest and luckiest towns.

It is old because it was the Gaullish capital of the Bajocasses, then a Roman town, and a bishopric from the end of the fourth century. It was captured by Rollo in 880, who married Popa, daughter of the town's governor. Their son was William Longsword. So Bayeux could be called the cradle of the Norman dynasty.

It was lucky because although it is only about 10 km. from the invasion beaches it was undamaged by the war. Bayeux, first town in France to be liberated, was taken on 7 June 1944 by the 50th Northumbrian Division almost without a scratch.

So Bayeux remains as it was, a medieval town, its narrow streets lined with picturesque old houses, stone bridges and all her chief treasures intact. These – the tapestry, the cathedral and museum – are grouped conveniently close together.

The famous Bayeux tapestry, showing William's invasion of England, is kept in the former bishops' palace. To see it costs 4.50 francs, plus one franc for the dark green tele-translation in English. Incidentally, when you put this long receiver to your ear stand close to the wall, otherwise the voice fades away.

The tapestry, or rather the 230-foot embroidery sewn in coloured thread, is kept in a glass case around the walls of a gallery. The tapestry claims to tell the whole story – from the Norman point of view, of course – of Harold's shipwreck, his promise to renounce the crown of England to William, his defection, and William's consequent rightful invasion of England.

The tapestry is in three sections, a top frieze, main story and bottom frieze, and gives some interesting detail about the armour and weapons of that period, also the people. The wicked Saxons all have long drooping moustaches while the Normans are clean shaven. The frieze above and below the story shows animals from Aesop's *Fables*, or little extras about the most important events; some are quite lewd if you know where to look.

Why it was made and who made it are not entirely certain. The legend that it was sewn by Mathilde is now generally discounted. Most probably it was made between 1070 and 1080 by order of Bishop Oddo, William's turbulent half-brother, to be hung round the nave of Bayeux Cathedral, a simple illustration to explain what had happened and why. Some historians believe that it was made at a school of needlework in Canterbury. A very good designer would have drawn it first, then highly-skilled women did the stitching.

When you leave the tapestry, keep your ticket, for it can also be used in the museum.

The cathedral, situated between the *tapisserie* and museum, has a fascinating and highly-decorated exterior in the Norman and Gothic styles. Inside it is lofty and the nave, although not uniform, is a harmonious blend of Romanesque and Gothic. It is best to get a good general view first from the door to get the feeling of its grandeur.

Bayeux Cathedral, built by Bishop Oddo, was dedicated on 14 July 1077 to Notre Dame, and consequently to God, by the Archbishop of Rouen, Lanfranc (Archbishop of Canterbury and Primate of England), and by Thomas of Bayeaux (Archbishop of York) in the presence of William of Normandy and a large crowd of people.

There is some rather fine stained glass behind the organ, and also an ornate black pulpit, which dates from 1786. The Renaissance stalls of the choir are rather lovely.

For interest, note the side altar by the doorway, where you can see the fresco showing the murder of Thomas à Becket at Canterbury Cathedral. To see the treasure, crypt and chapter house you have to apply to the sacristy in the north transept.

The Musée Gérard, which holds exhibitions of pictures, has a small art collection (tiny pictures by Thomas Regnault and water colours and caricatures by Septime Lepipre, which are quite interesting from a historical point of view), also pottery, clothes, dolls illustrating the court of Louis xiv and collections of lace and tapestry. The museum is well set out and interesting to wander round.

Although Bayeaux is a town that grows on you – even the peals of its tinny old bells – it is better for a short visit than a long stay. Three hours are sufficient to wander through its old streets and visit the tapestry, cathedral and museum. There are not many good hotels and restaurants, and it is not a good excursion centre. There are few bus trips: even Arromanches, which is only 10 km. away, is difficult to visit by local transport. Local people just do not go there, I was told. Anyone wanting to visit the Côte Nacre invasion beaches from Bayeux will have to go by car.

The Côte Nacre and Invasion Beaches

Over recent years this coastline, lying between the Vire and Orne rivers, has become increasingly popular with holidaymakers, especially campers. Bathing is good and the beaches are wide, flat and sandy, which is why it was chosen for the allied invasion of France. Most people staying in Normandy will want to visit it, along with the famous museum at Arromanches, especially those who took part in the last war.

The landing battle is too complicated to explain properly here but, as many books have been written on it, you would get more out of your visit if you read one before you came.

Very briefly, although a landing had been envisaged by the British since 1941, it was only after the entry of the Americans into the war that it could be considered seriously. The plan, COSSAC, got the stamp of approval after the Churchill–Roosevelt meetings in Washington and Quebec in 1943, and this Calvados coast, defended by the German Seventh Army, was considered the most suitable one to attack.

Surprise, the essence of attack, was difficult to ensure. The Germans well knew that an attack would come somewhere between the Belgian coast and the mouth of the Loire, and sometime in 1944. They also knew the best time of the year and the most suitable weather conditions. All they didn't know was exactly where it would be.

Allied propaganda did its best to make the Germans think that it would probably be in the Pas de Calais area, so that they would keep their main reserves in this region.

All preparations for OVERLORD, its later official name, had to be completed by 1 June, and the invasion was to be launched on the first suitable day thereafter, depending on a combination of meteorological factors. Eisenhower eventually chose 6 June, in spite of the uncertain weather conditions. It is interesting to note that if the invasion had not been launched on that day but had waited until the next suitable period, commencing on the 19th, it would have bumped into the worst storm in living memory.

At dawn on D-day, 6 June 1944, the British and Commonwealth ground forces established beach heads at areas known by the code names Sword, Juno and Gold, linking up with the airborne troops dropped to the east of Pegasus bridge. They obtained the critical foothold ashore with fewer casualties than expected. The Americans landing on the beaches with code names Omaha and Utah only linked up with their airborne troops' flank after the capture of Carentan on 12 June, and experienced more difficulty.

Intensive Allied air action prevented the German air force from interfering with the landings. Differences between the German commanders, von Rundstedt and Rommel, on the conduct of the campaign, also helped. Rommel won, but he had insufficient inland defences. Once his Atlantic wall was broken he could not collect enough troops together to endanger the bridgehead on the beach, and Allied bombing prevented reinforcements. Also the Germans, still believing that the main invasion was yet to come in the Pas de Calais, kept a large force there. The British and Canadians pressed on towards Caen, the hinge of the front. US troops in the Cotentin peninsula worked down towards them.

The Arromanches museum is the main place to visit along the invasion beaches and is quite fascinating. Here you can see a Royal Navy film of the actual landings, listen to a talk using lit-up models, a sort of *son et lumière*, and look at the collection of war paraphernalia, equipment and flags, etc., all well-labelled.

In the sea outside is the Mulberry Harbour which was towed across the Channel in 1944 to be used by the British troops, and which was in service up to the end of August 1944, when Cherbourg and Antwerp became partially available.

Probably the best place to start a drive along the invasion beaches is from Caen (bus companies also do a tour), perhaps making a diversion to Bayeux and finishing at Carentan, in the Cotentin.

From here, if you wish, you can drive to Barfleur, via the Utah beach, making a detour to the Saire valley, then drive across the Cotentin to Fermanville and take the picturesque corniche road to Cherbourg.

12. Manche

Manche is the French for 'channel' and this department takes its name from this stretch of sea. Manche's 200 miles of fine sandy beaches, especially those between Carteret and Mont St Michel, are becoming increasingly popular with holidaymakers, particularly campers.

Inland it is a department of small hills, cut by short streams, a region of apple orchards or pastures for cattle and horses. The Manche has the largest cattle population of any other: it even exceeds the human one. Cooperative processing and marketing is highly developed here, and the production of butter, cheese and milk powder are its chief industries.

It is a region of scattered farmsteads and hamlets, rather than villages, but there are many small market towns. The people, once very poor, developed many small industries, such as weaving and copperware, some of which still survive.

The Manche is made up of the Normandy Bocage, which has a landscape of woodlands and small meadows, bounded by tall hedges, and the Cotentin peninsula, which is more varied.

The Cotentin Peninsula

The Cotentin's rocky coastline is similar to that of Brittany and Cornwall. The peninsula is divided from the Bocage by low-lying marshland, grazed over by cattle, and from which peat is gathered. If the sea here rose by more than ten metres the Cotentin would again become the island it once was.

During the eleventh and twelfth centuries the Cotentin was the home of those Normans, such as the Hauteville brothers, who distinguished themselves by founding kingdoms in Sicily and southern Italy. Their armies were an outlet for the peninsula's teeming poverty-stricken population. This rough country has often played a part in wars and uprisings : the last one was in OVERLORD, when American troops landed either side of the Vire river to establish the Omaha and Utah beachheads. Their objective was to cut the Cotentin in two and seize Cherbourg, a much more formidable task than they had realised in this wooded, hedged country.

Cherbourg, lying at the mouth of the Divette river, overlooked by the steep Montagne du Roule, is both a naval base and an important transatlantic and ferry passenger port.

Spacious, sprawling and new, this city by the sea is chiefly a place to pass through. Its main function for holidaymakers being a point of departure for home, the coastal regions, or a journey through France, especially for those with cars. Cherbourg is not so good for the humble pedestrian, who will have to walk quite a distance from the railway station to the Gare Maritime, which, when boats are not in, resembles a stranded dead city, lying amidst quays, sheds and boats, only a distant cousin of the town behind.

Although Cherbourg was used as a port by Bronze Age traders, was a Roman station, and played quite an important part in the Hundred Years' War, it was developed later than other ports of similar size. This is because it was surrounded on three sides by rocks but the fourth side, the north one, was exposed to the sea, and installations set up there soon washed away. The large break-water there now was started during the time of Louis XVI, continued by Napoleon, but not finally completed until the Napoleon III era.

The Germans did as much damage to the harbour as they could before they evacuated Cherbourg in June 1944. But the Americans were so badly in need of a port – their own Mulberry Harbour had been wrecked during storms – that they managed to get it into order again by October, when it became the main port for supplies during the Ardennes offensive. The underwater pipeline, PLUTO, laid between the Isle of Wight and Cherbourg, supplied the Allies with petrol from 12 August 1944.

Many people are likely to find themselves in Cherbourg, probably with a few hours of waiting to fill. The town is quite pleasant, with some good food shops. The best place to make for fairly near at hand is the promenade to the left of the port. Here is a small garden, brooded over by a statue of Napoleon, overlooking a good sandy beach.

If you've more time to spare you can drive up to the Roule Fort, which was the chief pocket of German resistance in 1944. From the terrace there is a good view of the town and harbour. Here also is the War and Liberation museum, which uses maps to tell the story of the Allied landings in June 1944 through to the final German surrender in May 1945.

A nearby château worth visiting is the attractively situated sixteenth-century one at Nacqueville, about 9 km. from Cherbourg (N13 and D45), but not on Tuesdays. Or, only 5 km. away is the picturesque park, combining tropical plants and beech trees, surrounding Tourlaville château (N801, D63).

To the east of Cherbourg lie the lovely wooded Val de Saire (approximately a three-hour trip), a name which applies to the whole of this northeast peninsula, and the two small harbour resorts, Barfleur and St Vaast.

Barfleur, best seen at high tide, has a picturesque port now filled with pleasure craft. The view from the west end of its rugged old church towards the Gateville lighthouse is magnificent. This lighthouse, the tallest in France, is open to visitors. From its top there is a splendid panorama over the east coast of the Cotentin peninsula and the Saire river disappearing down into the sea. Although the sea here is shallow there are swift currents and it can be very rough. In fact, if it were not for the jetty to the north of the town, Barfleur would be swamped. Many ships have foundered, especially on the rocks on which the Gateville lighthouse now stands. The most famous of these was the *Blanche Nef*, which

was carrying William, only legitimate son of Henry I and heir to
the English throne, to England in 1120. That this should have
happened was also due to the intoxication of the pilot and crew.
The prince might have escaped in a small boat had he not insisted
on its turning back to rescue his natural sister, the Countess of
Mortagne. On arriving back at the sinking ship, his boat was at
once filled with a crowd of despairing wretches and they all sank
together.

Small but busy St Vaast-la-Hougue is of even greater interest
to English visitors. It was here that Edward III's army landed, an
expedition that was to end in the French defeat at Crécy. Later
landings here were those of Henry IV and Henry V. More important still, it was near here in 1692 that a combined English and
Dutch fleet frustrated the attempt of James II to regain his English
crown. They destroyed the French fleet, which intended to engage
the English one, while an army of French and Irish troops which
had gathered at La Hougue landed in England.

The fortifications you see there now were erected as a result of
this engagement – rather like locking the stable door once the
horse has gone. St Vaast today is first important as an oyster-
breeding centre then as a resort, as it has a good bathing beach
and fine sheet of water for sailing.

On the other side of Cherbourg (N12, D45) lies the bleak
granite spine, La Hague, which although flat has a sort of wild
grandeur. There are no trees to withstand the gales, but the short
turf is criss-crossed with stone walls to protect the sheep and divide
it into enclosures. On an island of low rocks stands a tall lighthouse
to warn shipping.

The Nez de Joubourg, a long rugged promontory encircled by
reefs, is one of the most spectacular sights of the coast, especially
when seen from the Nez de Voidries (approached from Goury,
D401, then D202 from Dammery).

From Beaumont (N801 from Dammery) to the seaside resort
Barneville-Carteret, is a picturesque drive. Although the road does
not hug the coast, the countryside is fairly low-lying and there are
good views of the sea and Channel Islands beyond.

The inland wooded country turns to plains, rather like a vast open park, where brindled cows and horses graze, especially around Ste Mère Eglise, Normandy's chief cattle market town.

The Bocage

Although Cherbourg is the largest town in the Manche, Saint-Lô is the departmental capital.

One's first sight of it is of its *Enclos*, the vast wall, partly rock, partly built, of the old town, with the tops of the houses and church peeping just above.

Known as Briovera in Roman times, it owes its present name to Landus, Bishop of Coutances, who died in 565. It was an important fortress town and also a centre of the weaving industry during the Middle Ages. In 1574 it embraced Calvinism, and was subsequently stormed by the Catholics. In 1796, Saint-Lô replaced Coutances as capital of the department. Alas, though, as a key-point of German resistance in the Second World War, it suffered such tremendous damage that earned itself the name, 'Capital of the Ruins'.

The construction of the new town began in 1948. In a way you could say that the bombing did some good in that it revealed and clarified the outline of its old ramparts. As with the castle at Caen, they are only a shell, but here they do enclose a small town, if a rebuilt one, behind them.

Numerous paths lead up this grand aspect of rocks, half-covered in foliage, into the new 'old' town. Wherever you come out, it is not likely to be far from the fourteenth- to fifteenth-century Notre Dame church, still undergoing repairs, and the symbol of the town that was. The extent of the damage done to it is shown by the photo in the church taken of its roofless nave, with the sturdy crucifix hanging dramatically above the rubble. Another picture on the wall shows the bombed houses surrounding the church.

The cenotaph in the Place Général de Gaulle, a half-ruined porch covered in leaves and dedicated to the victims of Nazi aggression, makes a strong contrast to the tall modernistic pillar, topped by a lion nearby. The walk round the Promenade des Ramparts, which begins near here, gives a good view of the town below the rocks. New houses, blocks of flats and the thin Vire river appear neat and well-planned, as is all the countryside around.

Saint-Lô, lying on main roads, makes a good centre for excursions. Nearby is the Vire valley, a quite pleasant 40 km. tour, during which you can visit the rebuilt Matignon castle, which possesses some interesting old tapestries and furniture, and also the magnificent Ham rocks.

To the west of Saint-Lô is the country town of Coutances, standing on a hill and crowned by one of the loveliest cathedrals in France.

Coutances, known as Cosedic by the Celts, had its name changed to Constantia by the Romans in honour of their Emperor. Coutances suffered badly during the Norman invasions, but later became one of their favourite towns. In 1066 one of its bishops, Geoffrey de Montbray, and several nobles from round about accompanied William on his Conquest of England. Geoffrey also started on the construction of the first part of the cathedral, the nave, while the sons Tancarville helped get the rest of it finished. However, after the destruction of the town by fire in 1218 a new cathedral, Gothic in style, was erected on the old Romanesque one, a difficult task involving considerable technical skill.

Most fortunately, Coutances Cathedral was spared by the bombing and only lost the spire above the central tower. As it stands at the highest point in the town and faces a large square, the Place du Parvis, rebuilt after the war, it is possible to get a good view of its twin west towers and the façade between.

Inside, you stand at the beginning of the nave to get a good general view of its beautiful upswept lines. There is little ornamentation to distract. The large lantern tower above the transept crossing is a masterpiece of construction, and the best example of its type in Normandy.

Coutances also boasts a very fine garden, once belonging to a private house. Terraces and steps descend the slopes, while trees form a leafy background to its lawns and flowerbeds. In summer this and the cathdral are floodlit and a *son et lumière* performance is held on Thursday, Saturday, Sunday and holidays.

The plain but majestic ruins of the Abbey of Hambye lie to the south east of Coutances. A guided tour round its church and buildings takes about an hour. It is closed on Tuesdays.

Granville, a somewhat grim but quaint town, situated on the coast at the mouth of the river Bisque, is in two parts; one is a fortified seaport, the other a bathing resort.

Its old town, the Haute Ville, built on a promontory, has a sort of austere attraction. Straight roads lead up between eighteenth-century houses to its robust granite Notre Dame. From the Place de l'Istre, an enormous square, you can see as far as Brittany on a clear day.

Granville should be of interest to the English as it was they who founded the town in 1439. Unable to capture Mont St Michel in the south, they decided to consolidate their position in this part of Normandy by building a strong defence on this rocky promontory stretching out to sea. Unfortunately the French captured it before it was finished, and found it very useful indeed themselves, as did the Germans in World War Two, when they converted it into a formidable strongpoint.

The new town, which grew round it below is popular in spite of its small beach, boasts a casino and golf course and is a centre for yachtsmen. From the harbour there are daily trips to the Islands of Chausey and the Channel Islands.

Avranches, standing on a hill above the Sées estuary, is most attractively situated. Moreover, it has the honour of having been the see of the Bishop St Aubert, who founded Mont St Michel Abbey across the bay. One night, the story goes, St Aubert had a strange dream in which the ghost of St Michael, the Archangel, appeared and commanded him to build an oratory on top of the mount.

Avranches was a bishops' see from 511 to 1790, when its cathdral seems to have collapsed, never alas to be rebuilt. But you can still see the paving stone, which was once in the cathedral, where Henry II kneeled to do public penance for the murder of Thomas à Becket.

Avranches also has the honour of being the place where on 1 August 1944, General Patton launched his famous counter-attack. His army smashed through the German lines, part going towards Brittany, and part towards Le Mans. A monument now marks the place where Patton stood before the start of this offensive. The square surrounding it, planted with trees from the U.S., is now regarded as American territory.

People interested in old manuscripts might like to see some in the Avranchin museum dating from the eighth to the fifteenth centuries, which have come from Mont St Michel Abbey. Those more interested in the bizarre might care to see St Aubert's skull in the St Gervais and St Protais Basilica. The dent in it is supposed to have been made by the imperious Archangel Michael when St Aubert at first ignored his instructions to build an oratory on the rock.

One of the main sights of Avranches is its botanical gardens, filled with exotic plants, once belonging to the former bishop's palace. From its terrace is a magnificent view across the bay of that strange conical shape, Mont St Michel, which looks at its most romantic by moonlight.

This town and abbey, ringed by ramparts, built on a rock, rising abruptly from a great stretch of treacherous silver sand, is the wonder of Normandy, and of France, too.

Centuries ago, the whole of the bay in which it stands was a vast forest, extending as far as the Channel Islands. Two rocky summits towered above this mass of trees. The one on which St Michel now stands was used first as a place of worship by the Druids and dedicated to the sun. This was later replaced by a Roman temple to Jove. Eventually, Christian hermits took possession of the rocks and built chapels on both of them.

Then came the great tides of the early eighth century, which cut the Channel Islands off from the mainland, turning the rocks into islands. These became places of refuge for people flying from the pillaging, burning Vikings. A little town grew round the monks' colony on St Michel's mount.

After St Aubert had built his oratory there it became so important a place of pilgrimage that in 966, Richard Duke of Normandy had the oratory replaced by a Benedictine abbey.

It grew rich, receiving generous endowments from Normandy, Brittany and England – the priory of St Michael's Mount in Cornwall was given to Mont St Michel by Edward the Confessor – and it became a celebrated place of learning. When it was burned down in 1203, the French king, Philippe Auguste, compensated the monks by providing for the construction of La Merveille, the superb Gothic structure that can be seen there today.

La Merveille had varying fortunes, being used as a fortress as well as an abbey during the Hundred Years' War. Its greatest period was during the time of Louis XIV when it was enlarged and made more beautiful. But its decline had already set in before the French Revolution, when the monks were obliged to leave. For a brief period, it was known as the Mount of Liberty. In 1811 Napoleon had it made into a prison, which it remained until 1863. It was not until 1966, its millenary year, that Benedictine monks held services in the great church again.

The first time, I saw Mont St Michel was on a wet day, when its abbey and church poked out of the misty rain like an enchanted castle. As its island was then almost surrounded by sea, I had to cross to the town below from the shore by a long strip of land, a natural drawbridge.

Buildings climbed the steep rock in terraces above high walls up to St Michel, glittering with wet, a shining tribute to the skill and love of those long ago monks. Each granite block, brought from Brittany or the Chausey Islands, had had to be hauled up to the site, no mean feat for that period.

The name Merveille really refers to the superb Gothic fortress abbey on the north side of the mount, the buildings of which are fit for kings, and indeed many were entertained here. The cloisters are particularly beautiful and should not be missed.

I felt like a real medieval pilgrim as I passed through the old archway, then up a steep slope past shops stacked with souvenirs, for this quaint old town now exists entirely on tourists and pilgrims. It was a long trek before I finally arrived at the twisting stone stairway of 90 steps leading up to the church.

There was a wonderful view of the surrounding flat land from the terrace outside, making the hard climb worthwhile. On one side, where the river runs into the sea, is the boundary line of the province, putting Mont St Michel just in Normandy. On the other side is Brittany.

APPENDIX

How to Get to Brittany and Normandy

1. *BRITTANY*

    Sea/rail, without a car

    Up to now, Brittany has been quite difficult to get to without a car because of its lack of large passenger ports, while the ports such as Cherbourg and Le Havre, in Normandy, do not link up easily by rail with resorts in Brittany. St Malo can only be reached from England by changing at the Channel Islands. However, now that the Plymouth/Roscoff line has opened. this should make things easier, especially for people holidaying in the west of Brittany.

    Sea/rail with a car

        Southampton – Cherbourg
        Southampton – Le Havre
        Weymouth – St Malo, via Channel Islands
        Plymouth – Roscoff

    Air

        Heathrow, London – Dinard, La Baule, Nantes, Quimper,
                            Rennes
        Plymouth – Morlaix

2. *NORMANDY*

    Sea/rail, with or without a car
        Newhaven – Dieppe
        Southampton – Le Havre

Southampton – Cherbourg
Weymouth – Cherbourg

Air

Heathrow, London – Deauville,
Gatwick, London – Le Havre,
Gatwick, London – Rouen

TRANSPORT

You really need a car in Normandy and Brittany, unless you have a lot of time and patience. Normandy is better linked by train than Brittany, where the service is probably about the worst in France. Buses in both provinces can be fun to travel on, and they are certainly a very relaxed way of getting around: also you do meet ordinary people. Bus timetables are displayed at the Gare Routiére, which is usually close to the railway station. Sometimes you have to buy your ticket beforehand, perhaps in a café near the stop (*Auto Arrêt*). Stopping places are not always very well-marked, so it is a good idea to check the exact place and time of the bus with local people. Bus times are casual, probably due to the fact that so many of the drivers act as 'postmen', delivering parcels as well as people at stops. On the other hand trains are very punctual.

ACCOMMODATION

Hotel prices are very variable in France, depending on where they are and who uses them. Those used by tourists are usually the most expensive. Charges are lower away from big highways. Before booking at a hotel, ascertain what the price will be (you can check this with the price which should be written up in the room itself). If *'service compris'*, the tip will be included in the price, otherwise there might be a supplement of $12\frac{1}{2}$ to 15% on the bill. Most hotel rooms in Normandy and Brittany are clean and have comfortable beds. Some seem to economize on lighting arrangements. Also on soap! — very few hotels provide soap. French plumbing sometimes make strange noises. At one hotel I stayed in, I spent about half an hour searching my room for a cat (although I couldn't imagine how it got in), until I realised that the mews were caused by pipes. Bolsters are sometimes kept in the wardrobe.

PLACES TO STAY AT

The Syndicat d'Initiative (which you should always call at when visiting a new place in order to get maps and information) will give a list of recommended hotels and restaurants. They will phone up and book for you if you wish (you will be charged for the call). Their offices usually close about 6.30 p.m. If you are booking on your own during the season (July/August) or during a weekend in summer, you shouldn't leave looking for accommodation much after six. If you are planning to make a long stay in one place, write and ask the local Syndicat d'Initiative to send you a list of recommended hotels.

You can rent a villa or flat in Normandy and Brittany. Make enquiries about this at the French Tourist Office, 178 Piccadilly, London W.1., or write to the Syndicat d'Initiative of the area of your choice (address can be had from the French Tourist Office).

Camping is one of the cheapest ways of holidaying in Normandy and Brittany, where there are some splendid camp sites. There are four categories, which are graded according to the facilities provided. You do not have to book in advance (except for some of the de luxe sites). You just drive in, as for a hotel, and ask if there is space for you. The International Membership card of the Camping Club of Great Britain entitles you to stay at any of the official camp sites throughout France. It is often possible to hire tents if you don't want to travel with heavy gear. A useful address is The Touring Club of France, 178 Piccadilly, London W.1. for further information about this. Michelin produces a guide: 'Camping and Caravanning in France'. There is also the FFCC Guide Official Camping Caravanning.

RESTAURANTS

As with hotels it pays to shop around as prices are very variable. Menu prices are pinned up on restaurant doors. *'Service compris'* means tip and service included, otherwise there will be approxi-

mately 12% extra on the bill. Bread is always provided free at
meals, and water too (ask for a *carafe d'eau*). Sometimes wine is,
but this doesn't often happen, and the wine would probably be
rather a rough one. Railway stations often supply good, reasonably-priced meals. You are unlikely to get a proper meal anywhere under a £1 in France. But a meal at about £1.50 is a great
deal better value than its counterpart in England would be.

SHOPPING

In my view the small shop, usually run by Madame and family, is
cheaper than the large supermarkets. Markets are better value
still. You can find out when and where they are held at the local
Syndicat d'Initiative.

GASTRONOMY

NORMANDY

Rich cream predominates in Norman cooking. Most famous
cheeses are, Pont l'Evêque, Livarot, Camembert (Auge region is
best), Suisses and Demi Sel from Bray.

Rouen is famous for its duck (especially pâtés) and sugar apples;
Caen for tripe and caramels; Ferté Macé for tripe; Mont St Michel
for omelettes; Dieppe for sole; Vire for chitterling; Avranches for
white pudding; Honfleur for shrimps and cockles; Villenville for
mussels; St Vaast for oysters; La Hague for lobsters.

Normandy, a great cattle country, is also renowned for its meat,
especially Cotentin lamb.

Cider is drunk everywhere and with most foods. The Auge
Valley cider is reckoned the best. Calvados (which takes 12 to 15
years to mature) a cider spirit, is drunk in the middle of a meal –
the '*Trou* (hole) *Normand*' – and also at the end with black coffee.
There is also Poiré (perry alcohol), and Bénédictine (produced at
Fécamp).

BRITTANY

Brittany, surrounded by water, is a paradise for fish-eaters, especially those of shellfish – crabs, lobsters, oysters, cockles, mussels, etc. Lobster Armorocaine, which is lobster served grilled with cream and a special sauce, is one of Brittany's most famous dishes. Salmon and trout are popular dishes in the Black Mountain and Monts d'Arrée area. Highly-flavoured mutton from sheep pastured in the Prés Salés, salty fields round Mont St Michel, is another favourite. Crêpes (pancakes) – savoury or sweet – are served with ham, cheese and jam, also cider. There are many crêperies in Brittany. Vegetables and fruit are plentiful – I have never eaten better tomatoes and apples than in Brittany. Nantes is famous for cakes, biscuits and sweets.

The best cider comes from the Fouesnant area, but it is not as good as that produced in Normandy. Brittany only produces wine in the Rhuys peninsula, and it is of poor quality. Muscadet, grown round Nantes, is the standard drink. Popular wines drunk in Brittany are Gros Plant and Côtes de Layon, which both come from the Loire region and go well with shellfish.

UNUSUAL HOLIDAYS IN BRITTANY AND NORMANDY
Sleep in a castle :
    Write to the French Tourist Office in London to enquire about staying in château - hotels.

Attend a Bagpipe Festival in Brest in August :
    Write to the Syndicat d'Initiative de Brest,
    Pavillon du Tourisme, Place la Liberté, Brest.

Go on a golfing holiday :
    Write to Fédération Française de Golf, 11 Rue de Bassane,
    75 Paris 16.

A lorry drivers' holiday :
    You can eat and sleep cheaply at a Relais des Routiers. Get addresses of Les Routiers from Hachette (Booksellers), 4 Regent Place, London W1.

Ride a horse in Normandy:
  Write to the Association de Tourisme Equestre, 60 Grande Rue,
  61 Alençon.

Go on a caravan holiday in Normandy or Brittany :
  Write to Cheval Voyages, 4 Rue de l'Echelle, 75 Paris 1.

A cooking course at Dieppe :
  Write to Syndicat d'Initiative, Boulevard Général de Gaulle,
  76 Dieppe.

Attend a French summer school:
  Write to Cours Universitaire d'Eté, Faculté des Lettres,
  35 Rennes-Ville Jean.

For information about Son et Lumière and Pardons, apply to the
French Tourist Office in London, who have special lists printed.

BOOKS ABOUT BRITTANY AND NORMANDY

BRITTANY

NOVELS

Balzac, *Les Chouans*
Victor Hugo, *Quatre Vingt Treize*
Pierre Loti, *Pêcheur d'Islande (An Iceland Fisherman)*
Julien Gracq, *Un Beau Ténébreux (The Dark Stranger)*

NON-FICTION

Peter Anson, *Mariners of Brittany*, Dent, 1931
Anatole Le Braz, *The Land of Pardons*, Methuen, 1906
Glyn Daniel, *The Hungry Archaeologist in France*, Faber & Faber, 1963
Glyn Daniel, *Megaliths in History*, Faber & Faber, 1973
Henry Myhill, *Brittany*, Faber & Faber, 1969
Nora K. Chadwicke, *Early Brittany*, University of Wales Press, 1969

NORMANDY

Sir Frank Stenton, *The Bayeux Tapestry*, Phaidon Press, 1957
David C. Douglas, *William The Conqueror*, Eyre & Spottiswoode, 1964
Charles Homer Haskins, *Normans in European History*, Constable, 1914
Viscount Montgomery, *Normandy to the Baltic*, Hutchinson, 1946
Dwight D. Eisenhower, *Crusade in Europe*, Heinemann, 1948
Mrs Robert Henrey, *Madeleine, Young Wife*, Dent, 1960
Anthony Glyn, *The Seine*, Weidenfeld & Nicolson, 1966
William Gaunt, *The Impressionists*, Thames & Hudson, 1970

Index